PRAISE FOR CAMERON JOHNSTON

T0062557

Cameron Johnston

THE LAST SHIELD

ANGRY
ROBOT

ANGRY ROBOT
An imprint of Watkins Media Ltd

Unit 11, Shepperton House
89 Shepperton Road
London N1 3DF
UK

angryrobotbooks.com
twitter.com/angryrobotbooks
I'm too old for this shit

An Angry Robot paperback original, 2024

Cover illustration by Steve Stone
Cover design by Sarah O'Flaherty
Edited by Eleanor Teasdale and Paul Simpson
Set in Meridien

ISBN 978 1 91599 803 3
Ebook ISBN 978 1 91599 804 0

Printed and bound in the United Kingdom by CPI Group (UK) Ltd, Croydon CR0 4YY.

9 8 7 6 5 4 3 2 1

MIX
Paper | Supporting
responsible forestry
FSC
www.fsc.org   FSC® C171272

This book is dedicated to my home, Scotland, in whose misty glens and ancient places I find a constant source of inspiration. I could do with a little less rain though...

PROLOGUE

The howling of a nearby wolf pack roused the campsite sometime before the dawn, and when the chorus showed no sign of ceasing, seven solemn druids and their entourage grudgingly rose from their furs. The four men and three women comprising the party of wise ones were stark naked save for an abundance of whorling black and blue tattoos that covered their bodies.

While their servants huddled around the fire for safety, eyeing the darkness between the trees, the druids felt no fear. They entered the nearby circle of standing stones and looked up at the sea of stars. Their mystically opened minds, aided by a supper of sacred mushrooms and mead flavoured with heather and thyme, swam among the omens and portents the gods secretly scribed across the night sky. They drank in the moonlight and added their own primal howls to those of the wolves until darkness began to retreat before the fiery glory of the sun.

In the half-light, they checked the shadows cast by the circle of standing stones: only one stone before sunrise, not enough time to resume their slumber. They still had a fair distance to go to reach the Sunweald Palace, so the grand druid, Balfor – a balding, reed-thin greybeard with majestic bushy eyebrows – ordered them and their sleepy servants to rise and get moving lest they feel the sturdiness of his greenwood staff.

The druids pulled on long woollen tunics that hung past their knees, donned elaborate horned headdresses and buckled on leather belts festooned with beaten copper and bronze tokens denoting their sacred status, each token representing a different god that had appeared in their visions. Next, they hung bearskin cloaks around their shoulders to grant them strength and stamina, and secured them in place with gleaming bronze pins. Lastly, they donned all-important charms and relics around their necks and wrists: some were made of elaborately carved scrimshaw bearing blessings and symbols of power, others were of teeth and feathers from those beasts held sacred by their ancestral clan's tutelary deity, and the most personal and potent of all were the finger bones of those druids who had come before.

The grand druid groaned as he bent over to pick up his staff. "The joys of age," he muttered to the others before leading their prayers to the gods and spirits of the forest that provided for and protected them. Once done with the rituals, they picked readily available bog-myrtle leaves and crushed them in their hands, wiping the juice over every exposed bit of skin. The scent was a mix of sage and lavender, and, while pleasing to the druids' noses, was loathed by the little biting flies that swarmed during high summer.

They resumed their barefoot march through the Havenswood, heading for the Sunweald Palace and the summer solstice celebrations. Ten servants and musicians with wicker baskets strapped to their backs trailed after them, utterly silent as they transported all the tools, oils and instruments the wise ones required for the sacred rites. The great drums were borne on the back of a burly but musically gifted young mute, bent over like a turtle under the weight of all that horn, bone and stretched hide.

Beheld only by the eyes of druids, curious but shy nature spirits observed the party as they walked the same ancient paths trodden by their ancestors. Balfor wondered if the sacred mushrooms were more potent this year, as the bright and bold colours of the forest ebbed and flowed around their party.

Or perhaps the otherworld had drawn closer to the world of mortals this year – if so, that was a portent of great change to come.

The rich, fragrant soil was evidence of a good summer, and the grass and moss felt soft and lush between their toes. As the druids passed through the woods, they communed with nature and did not stop to eat or drink or even talk until the moon once more graced the sky with her presence. As the sun prepared to slumber, they happened upon a group of travellers camped in a glade of wildflowers by the side of the trail. A stream of fresh, cool water trickled over rocks, inviting them in to soothe tired feet. A brace of rabbits were roasting on sticks over a small fire, their meat charred and almost ready for eating.

Two rough-looking but smiling men – local hunters, judging from their poorly tanned leather tunics and the crude torc tattoos around their necks – leant against a boulder beside the crackling fire. Next to them sat a somewhat plump woman in a fine but plain linen dress and a strange, white-painted wooden mask. Her husband or companion had braided shoulder-length hair, and his chin was clean shaven – not often seen outside the larger cities. He was born far from this place, judging from the lack of any visible tattoos. A long knife was sheathed at his left hip, and a small but solid bronze buckler, a shield the size of his head, was looped around the wooden sheath in the style of Sunweald's vaunted Shields – the realm's elite warriors, who guarded the royal family and its current regent. The shaven man was in high spirits, laughing and joking with the others while he turned the cooking rabbits.

Such a small group hardly seemed like a threat to their much larger party, Balfor thought, and none in Sunweald would ever risk the wrath of the gods by harming a druid. The breeze carried mouthwatering scents of cooking towards the druids, and with it came a strangely comforting scent besides the usual woodsmoke and roasting meat, which he could not quite place. It nagged at him as they drew closer to the travellers' fire and company. Rosemary? Lavender? Not quite. Some herb his long-deceased mother had used in her cooking, perhaps?

The shaven man noticed their approach and unhurriedly finished attending to the meat before he rose to greet them, his arms flung wide in welcome. "This is a most blessed encounter," he said, his smile crooked but his dark eyes filled with warmth. His voice bore hints of a worn-down old accent from the foreign lands of the Ves. "You are all most welcome to share our fire and our food. We have already eaten; these are but leftovers destined to stretch our bellies."

"The blessings of land, sea and sky be upon you," the grand druid replied. "Your hospitality is most welcome." He eyed the woman's strange mask, and his curiosity did not go unnoticed.

"A roundhouse fire," the man replied, nonplussed. "The thatch went up, and her entire family was lost to the flames. All who see her ask about the mask, but there is nothing to fear. She was long in healing, and though the wounds have healed, the scars remain. Come, come, good people. Sit at our fire and rest your weary feet. You must have travelled a long way to reach the festival at the palace."

The druids all knelt on the grass and removed their headdresses, not sorry to be rid of the weight of bone and antlers that strained their neck muscles. Balfor warmed his old hands by the fire while the acolytes and musicians silently unpacked furs and supplies. The scent of cooking and those unusual herbs was beguiling, and he and his companions could not help but breathe it all in.

The woman of the travelling group remained silent behind her mask as she cut off slices of herb-encrusted rabbit and served them on broad dock leaves to the druids and their entourage, none of whom needed encouragement to begin feasting. The grand druid and his second, Nyfain, refused the gift, having vowed to eat no meat until the evening of the ritual.

The shaved traveller crouched by the fire and tossed a few more sticks onto the glowing embers. "Would you honour us with a tale?" he asked. "The renowned wisdom of the druids is not oft encountered by humble people like us." He sat back and began oiling an extraordinarily fine bow crafted of yew to protect it against the rain. He was, it seemed, a man of wealth, and such people always had their eccentricities.

The grand druid preened a little. Pride was something to be watched carefully lest it consume you, but everything could be enjoyed in moderation. "Have you heard the tale of Assa's Sin?"

The man frowned and looked to the woman. Behind the mask, her eyes crinkled in a smile, and she nodded back. "We have some experience there," he replied. "But I have never heard it from a master of lore such as yourself. We would be most honoured to learn from your wisdom."

The grand druid launched into the ancient tale of Assa's Sin, of the immortal guardian who burned away his honour by shedding the blood of the Queen of Summer for a purse of bronze and silver and a herd of cattle. Of her divine lifeforce, the gods could only preserve a part, leaving weary mortals with a legacy of barren ice and snow for that dead part of the year.

As the sun sank and the darkness deepened, Balfor noticed his entourage dropping off to sleep while the travellers listened, rapt by his storytelling. Only he and his second remained awake to...

His eyes flew wide. Those herbs. He had indeed smelled them before! On his travels far to the east, past the lands of the Ves. They were used to ward off attacks by night terrors, and lulled the mind into a deep and dreamless sleep. He lurched to his feet and lifted his staff. "What is this treachery?"

Nyfain rose with him, her brows lowered in puzzlement. The shaven man grabbed her and pressed his knife to her throat, hard enough to draw blood. "Best be very still," he said.

The traveller woman chuckled behind her mask. "Maddox here is intimately familiar with Assa's Sin. In fact, killing for coin is his profession. As for you..." she waved to the woods across the trail, and a dozen armed men emerged from the undergrowth, draped in the russet-and-green wool and crude furs of forest brigands. "I must advise you that you are well and truly fucked. You will not be attending any summer solstice rites at the palace this year."

She nodded, and two men grabbed the grand druid from behind. He yelped and struggled, managing to clout one of them on the knee with his staff. "Finish these useless old moss-lickers," she demanded.

Balfor watched the man named Maddox slit Nyfain's throat and drop her twitching corpse to the earth. Then wicked knives dug deep into his chest. Spikes of hot pain stole his breath, and hot wetness gushed down his tunic as the brigands tore the weapons free.

The grand druid fell to his knees, gasping, heart racing erratically, the taste of blood and vomit in his mouth. His killers looked down on him, laughing. He spat blood on their deerskin shoes. "May the gods curse you," he muttered.

The woman yanked his head back by the hair and stared down into his eyes. "The insipid gods of Sunweald are not my gods," she hissed. "They have no hold over me." Her knife thrust into his breast and his body convulsed. He flopped to the dirt, muscles refusing to obey. He could feel his life draining into the soil and the chill of death seeping into his old bones as his ancestors called to him.

"Pack the headdresses and belts for our own little celebration at the palace," Maddox ordered his men. He turned to the woman and grinned his crooked smile. "Let us feast, Imperatrix. Killing sure gives me a powerful appetite."

The woman called Imperatrix snorted and thumbed the wax seal open on one of the druids' jars of sacred mead. "You lie so well, Maddox. Nothing to fear in me... hah. One of your better jokes."

Sunweald's grand druid died mouthing his curses.

CHAPTER 1

It was a hot and sticky summer's morning in the palace, and the breeze through the window of the regent's tower did nothing to cool its occupants down, especially if one wore the stiff green-and-brown padded tunic embroidered with silver and gold that was used only for feast days, festivals and diplomatic events. Exceedingly bored and standing guard inside the study beside the closed-and-barred door, Shield Briar watched a tiny spider crawl across the roof beam and drop onto her head. She swatted it out of her freshly cropped red hair and suppressed a sigh as more strands of grey than she liked came away with it. It was also the most action she'd seen in seasons.

As the regent's quill scratched across goatskin parchment, her fingernails tapped the pommel of the trusty old bronze sword sheathed at her left hip, belted above the studded leather kilt that hung to her knees. Looped onto the scabbard was a golden-hued buckler decorated with a spiralling pattern of oak leaves: the traditional 'weapon' of her station. The common warriors of Sunweald's warbands usually armed themselves with spears and wicker-and-wood shields that could protect the whole torso, but unlike those larger shields, a buckler could defend inside the narrow tunnels of the palace without issue, and due to being made of solid bronze, it also served as a deadly close-combat weapon in its own right. She hadn't bothered to buff out the teeth marks left on the reinforced centre by the last assassin she'd beaten to death with it. There had been more of their sort of honourless scum in the early days of her career, back when the regent's rule had been on swampy ground. Briar had enjoyed that blood-pounding action far more than the endless waiting around of guard duty while the Lord Regent sat at the desk writing his letters, waging an unwinnable war on the scrollwork of ruling a nation.

She had encountered three types of assassin back in those days, and her preferred prey was the first lot: the common dull-witted brigands found lurking in wretched taverns and gambling dens all across the land. The service of their strong arms and weak minds could be bought with no more than a few goats and a jug of ale, or perhaps even so low a payment as a pretty smile and a promise. They were straightforward, and even when employed in numbers she found them easily detected and dealt with using simple countermeasures – a shield rammed into the face or a blade stuck between the ribs usually did the trick. It was always a rewarding day ending those miserable ticks that leeched a half-life off the hard toil of their betters.

Yes, she thought, being locked away in the regent's tower, just standing there, was a far less satisfying way to spend a bright and breezy summer's morning. With the shutters and drapes drawn back, sunlight streamed in the large windows, illuminating the motes of dust in the air and warming the regent's yappy wheaten dog, sprawled across a bearskin rug. He had been the runt of the litter, small and weak when all his brothers and sister were fine hunting dogs, but the beast had been cunning enough to prey on his master's affections. Briar scowled at the lazy little stinker, entirely envious of his morning nap. He cracked an eyelid and grinned in that particularly smug way animals do when they know they are winning at the game of life. She stuck her tongue out at him and he huffed, closed his eye and broke wind in her direction.

Behind the dog, light glinted off the regent's clock: intricate gold cogs, gemstones, silvery moon-metal mechanisms endlessly ticking and turning wyrm-bone dials inside a flawless tall amethyst case. On the left side, its etchings depicted Assa's Sin, and on the other the endless chase of sun and moon and the cycle of summer and winter. This artefact of the ancients was worth an entire town or three, and it baffled her that so much effort, artistry and expense had gone into telling the time when any fool could just go outside and squint up at the sun, or look to the stone circles to see what stone the sun's shadow had moved round to. Venerated lore masters from all over Wrendal, the cities of the Ves and even further all came to the Sunweald Palace just to see the pointless thing. She grudgingly conceded that it might serve some small use when black rain clouds hid the sun, or during the night, but who needed to tell the time with such precision then?

She scratched at the stiff collar of her formal tunic and plucked at the long, too-tight sleeves that fully covered the thorny briar tattoos that spiralled from shoulder to wrist on both her arms. The expense and expanse of all that elaborately embroidered silver-and-gold foliage irked her – give her comfort over fanciness any day. Plain dyed lambswool was luxury enough for her. Usually, it all ended up bloodstained anyway, but the regent had insisted on something to show her status at important events, and this was the least painful option. She was the eighty-eighth commander in a long line of devoted, deadly warriors, and the shield-shaped gold brooch of Commander of Shields pinned to her chest, crafted by the hands of the twelfth commander himself, was the only jewellery she cared a whit about. Her formal clothing reduced her effectiveness in guarding the regent's life, and she did not like that one bit.

Her mind turned away from her current discomfort and towards the second and far more expensive type of assassin she had encountered: the hawk-eyed archers who could put an arrow in a man's heart from a hundred paces, the poisoners and the elaborate trap-makers sawing through bridge supports and slicking stone steps with grease. They were coldly calculating and patient, and that made them deadly. Unfortunately for them, Briar was ruthless, stubborn as a stone, and she would have made for a superb assassin and a far richer woman had she not been cursed with a measure of loyalty and morality. She had been the commander of Sunweald's Shields for ten years and had never lost a regent yet – for which, in her informed opinion, said high-and-mighty regent had not shown adequate gratitude.

As if sensing her thoughts, Lord Regent Alaric Summerson chose that moment to look up from his monstrous writing desk of black oak with all its drawers and hidden compartments. He peered over the mountains of official scrolls requiring his personal mark, and the hills of cheaper reusable slate tablets of day-to-day business that surrounded him like a prison. The man was of an age with Briar, but relentless duty had worn him down, and the stress had gifted his face additional years. Crow's feet crowded his ice-blue eyes, and grey now streaked his short beard and the shoulder-length walnut locks that fell to the elaborate geometric torc tattoo marching along his collarbones. Still, he had kept his kind eyes and heart over the years, and in a ruler that was no mean feat.

Their eyes met. "See something you like?" he said, a smile creasing his lips. His attention dipped back to the vexing report she'd brought him, detailing the smuggling activity across Sunweald's borders between the Holy Wrendal Empire in the west and the Federated Principalities of Ves on the east.

Briar shrugged. "Something I like? Not even remotely." The shrug felt oddly light for a moment, before she realised that it was the day of the summer solstice, and she was wearing a stiff-collared dress uniform, green and brown, instead of her armoured shirt of bronze scales.

Alaric glanced up, their eyes meeting again for a lingering moment before each tore their gaze away like they had been burned. The smile crumbled, and she watched a scowl grow as he digested the rest of the report: over the last few years a group of devious brigands calling themselves the Wildwood Reivers had been raiding Wrendal holy sites and tombs, stealing dangerous arcane artefacts to sell to the Ves. Somehow, they had managed to escape every attempt to catch them.

Sunweald had been driven into a tricky political situation as its spies and warriors failed to thwart the illicit trade, and political tensions were now rising to a fever pitch between those two far greater foreign powers on either side of the realm's borders. The red-handed reivers did more than just rob Wrendal holy sites; they slaughtered every priest and young acolyte they came across before smuggling their loot through Sunweald and into the lands of the Ves, whose petty city-state princes were more than happy to purchase such rare and powerful items with no questions asked – and that bloody trade was increasing.

The Wrendal priesthood claimed all arcane artefacts were holy items directly touched by their gods, and this thievery was desecration to them, a blasphemy perpetrated on the entire Wrendal faith. The Ves, meanwhile, scoffed at Wrendal superstition and were more than happy to use the artefacts as status symbols and terrifying weapons. Only the buffering influence of the small but most ancient realm of Sunweald had thus far kept the two nations from all-out war. Their continued failure to catch the smugglers despite all oaths offered to the Holy Wrendal Empire had gifted Alaric and Briar many nights of headache and hangover. Oaths were every bit as holy to the people of Sunweald as anything the Wrendals worshipped. Honour was life. To break it was to invite darkness in to corrupt your soul and ask for the gods to curse you with all manner of misfortune.

As the sanctified cattle horns of the palace temple sounded out mid-morning, light rippled through the bafflingly expensive clock in the study, and it added bell chimes to the booming call of the horns. The notes were clean and pure, and the drifting purple streams of light the amethyst cast into the air faded with the last of the chimes. Briar had admired its prettiness at first, but its chiming every stone of every day had caused her to evolve one hundred and three elaborate fantasies of what 'accident' might befall it.

Alaric cleared his throat. "I see that Exalted Carmanilla is late." His lips thinned. "Again." He tutted and resumed his reading and his plotting.

It was another half a stone before the third type of assassin appeared at the door to the regent's study. Shield Hardgrim, Briar's second-in-command, knocked on the door to announce that Exalted Carmanilla, ambassador of the Holy Wrendal Empire, was outside and requesting admittance.

"I will inform the Lord Regent that the Exalted is here," Briar said through the closed door. She turned and gave Alaric the nod.

He took his time filing away all worrying reports of smuggling into the secret drawer in his desk, then rearranged the parchments and scrolls on top so those he wanted his visitor to notice and report back on were in easy view. Those he truly wanted her to report on were half tucked away further back, where only some of the text and part of the vital names were visible – those reports she would have to work hard at piecing together, and in their difficulty she would be thoroughly misled as to their importance to Sunweald, for what came easily was not always believed.

He kept the Exalted waiting outside in the corridor for a good quarter stone, with only the most uncomfortable seat in the palace and two stoic guards keeping the priestess company. It took him just a short while to sort out the desk, and the rest was spent admiring the view from his window – the regent was of the conviction that tardiness was never to be rewarded.

The regent's tower had the only large window in the entire palace, being in a position lofty enough for its builders to not even consider defence. The regent liked to boast that the view it offered was the best in all Sunweald, overlooking the verdant forest and chain of small glimmering lochs and rivers that stretched all the way to the mountains and the border with the Ves. Summer was in full flow, and beyond the outer walls the palace gardens were bright and beautiful. Striped tents and garlanded poles had been erected, and raised wooden platforms prepared for musicians and performers. The ancient mound of the honoured ancestors and the mossy stone circle atop it were being set up for the summer solstice rituals by the local druids who shepherded the living from womb unto tomb. The carved stone slab at the centre was in the midst of being cleansed with oil and incense, ready for the golden sickle and silver basins set out to collect the blood of the sacrificial bull. Once the grand druid and his elders arrived, the rituals would begin.

Briar joined the regent at the window but kept her eyes on the door and her back to the gorgeous view. She blocked out the sunlight, and the dog woke from his snooze to growl at her. She growled right back.

"Hush, Brutus," Alaric commanded. The dog blinked lazily, huffed and laid his head back down again.

"Do you want this Carmanilla to have an accident?" Briar said. "It would be a terrible shame if the proud Exalted fell off the battlements into the moat." She mimicked downing a skin of wine. "You know how these drunkards are..."

He glanced back, and his lips quirked into a smile. "Do not tempt me, woman. Alas, I have not the cause; she has not tried to have me killed even once. Not yet, anyway."

Briar's hand caressed the pommel of her sword. "I would humbly suggest that contact with fifteen thugs for hire, a poisoner, a metalworker and a jeweller amounts to some sort of plan in the offing." Exalted Carmanilla was a plotter and a planner, the most dangerous type of assassin and the hardest to counter, since they tended to be people of power and influence who hired disposable, deniable pawns to do their dirty work. They had deeper pockets and even fewer scruples than common brigands.

The regent shrugged, sighed and grudgingly nodded at the door.

Briar barely got the heavy door unbarred before Exalted Carmanilla flounced in, long braided honey-blonde hair and formal white robes swishing, that hair held back by a twisted circlet of masterfully worked red gold. Elegant, long-nailed fingers that hadn't seen a day of manual labour clenched into fists around thin rings of gold. The priestess seemed to be one of those women who only found beauty in jewellery, incapable of appreciating nature or understanding the sublime joy of wielding and caring for a well-crafted blade. Her eyes sizzled with barely concealed anger, and those pouting, puckered lips were painted red like a slapped arse. "Lord Regent Summerson!" she declared, offering a bow of respect so short it bordered on insult. "Why have I been kept waiting?"

Briar glanced to Shields Hardgrim and Iden, who guarded the outer doorway. The men were well built and imposing in their bronze-scale shirts cinched at the waist with embossed leather belts, armguards and helmets, but the effect was somewhat spoiled by their gaping mouths and admiring gazes. She rolled her eyes before shutting the door again. The Wrendal priestess was beautiful and blatantly knew it, but her beauty was a meticulously crafted artifice of plucked brows, face powders and immensely skilled servants who could probably make a donkey look like a clan chief's battle steed. The woman was a spindly deer when compared to Briar's she-bear stature, but the Shield couldn't spare too much pity for the woman's slim misfortune. She only wondered how it would feel to have hair that long instead of her own short and practical cut.

"Do forgive me, Exalted," Alaric replied. "It appears that I was so caught up in my correspondence that our meeting slipped my mind entirely." He waved a hand at the desk heaving with parchments. "I am sure you understand how it is."

His casual indifference took the fire right out of the woman's belly. "Ah, yes, well..." she said, apparently unused to a man's utter lack of interest. Her gaze fastened on the carefully organised disorder atop the regent's desk, scanning it from left to right. "It is... a great responsibility that we bear."

Alaric smiled, his pleasure lighting up the room. "That is very true. I knew one as dedicated as yourself would feel the same as I. Come, let us admire the view – it is the finest in all Sunweald. I find it helps to soothe the nerves of a long day. Nourishment for the soul, as you wise Wrendals might say." He stepped aside and waved her towards the window.

The Exalted's haughty nose lifted into the air, and she swept past Briar as if the Shield did not exist. Her eyes fixed on the magnificent amethyst clock, powered by magic, by what she considered the very breath of her gods. She loosed a small sigh of reverential appreciation. Then she caught sight of the regent's dog. For his part, Brutus unleashed an almighty gust of eggy flatulence in her direction; for once, Briar considered the horrible old beast a comrade-in-arms.

Carmanilla's nose wrinkled in distaste, then, much like a bear drawn to the scent of honey, her gaze darted to the regent's correspondence. She slowly made her way past his desk on her way to the window. Wrendal priests were renowned for their recall, which Briar put down to having to learn all those rambling oral tales and the tedious scriptures their ancestors had carved into baked-clay tablets. She was sure that Exalted Carmanilla was memorising all visible fragments of those reports. Later on, the woman would hopefully come to discover that, quite legitimately, three of the Ves principalities were trying to pay Alaric an enormous amount of copper and herds of cattle in exchange for establishing permanent trade embassies in the Sunweald palace, this realm's seat of power. After generations of refusing both sides in order to keep the delicate balance of peace and power, Lord Regent Alaric's half-written greedy reply suggested he would gladly accept their offer. The *proud and enlightened* Holy Wrendal Empire would scramble to match or exceed any offer from the *decadent* Ves. At least, that was the plan.

What none of the foreigners knew was that when the Royal Heir came of age in two years, he had every intention of moving his rule from the ancient seat of Sunweald Palace to the royal citadel at Drew Nemeton. The new site boasted a rich and exciting city that provided all manner of entertainments for a young, vibrant and altogether boneheaded boy-king. Alaric was selling them a pig in a poke for wagons of their riches. The princes and the priests would likely be furious with the regent, but in two years it wouldn't have been his decision to move... and they would still have their embassies, albeit rendered newly useless... so they could not object overmuch. They would get exactly what they asked for, and Sunweald would get the wealth to improve roads, dig wells and build libraries and hospitals.

Briar kept a careful watch as the two nobles made small talk about their peoples and places. She tensed as Carmanilla rested a hand on the regent's shoulder. At the first sign of her working her magic, Briar's blade would be in the bitch's throat before she could blink. You could never tell with these dangerous Exalted. Instead, the Wrendal priestess laughed, throwing her head back in mirth, one hand resting far too comfortably on Alaric's shoulder. For his part, the regent flushed, seeming to lap up her attention.

Eventually, Carmanilla stepped back. She smoothed out her robes, eyes modestly downcast. "As for my reason for requesting this meeting" – she lifted her eyes and gazed at him most earnestly, a faint blush creeping across her cheeks – "over the last two years I have spent working as an ambassador in Sunweald, I have come to greatly admire your diligence, your compassion and your keen mind. I understand that you have taken no lover these last fifteen years since you were widowed, and I was wondering if you had any desire at all to wed again? For my part, I have developed a most powerful affection for you."

Carmanilla appeared so earnest in opening her heart to him that Briar almost snapped her twig of a neck there and then.

How dare she covet what was not hers? Briar took a deep breath and fought down the impulse to murder the conniving creature. She had to give it to the Wrendal, the woman was a master manipulator and thought fast on her feet. It was undoubtedly not what she had originally come into the room for, but after seeing the parchments on the regent's desk her plans had changed. Assassins and spies of her sort had to be adaptable. It would be such a shame to see all that fine acting come to nothing.

Alaric's jaw dropped, his mouth half forming words before discarding them and struggling to choose others more appropriate.

Carmanilla's hand returned to the regent's shoulder as she moved in close, lightly pressing her breasts against his arm as she looked up into his eyes, expectant.

Briar watched the Exalted's hands closely, searching for any hint of reaching for a blade, or the dark discolouration that working magic caused in the veins of the wrist and hands, neck and face.

Alaric cleared his throat and backed away from her, slightly unsteady and clearly flustered. "I... This is most unexpected. I had no idea you felt like this."

The Exalted advanced on him like the vanguard of an army, intent on capturing her target.

Shield Briar decided it was time to intervene. She slammed her fist into the door, then turned to face it. "What is it?" she demanded. "The Lord Regent is in a meeting!"

From outside, Shield Hardgrim took his cue: "An urgent missive from His Highness, the Royal Heir."

Briar turned to face Alaric, who nodded and made a near-grovelling apology to Exalted Carmanilla as his Shield opened the door. From beneath his helmet, Hardgrim's cold eyes flicked between the attractive woman and the regent, and the grizzled man bore a knowing smile. Briar scowled and snatched the sealed scroll from Hardgrim's calloused hand.

With one last lingering touch, the Wrendal priestess prised herself off her prey and swished away, hips swaying as enticingly as she could manage. Hardgrim's lecherous eyes watched her go. He smoothed out his moustache and licked his lips. The youngest son of a rich and powerful clan, he was arrogant and had been raised getting whatever he wanted. The second man, Iden, glanced at his superior and sighed. Of all Hardgrim's recent promotions to Shield – his so-called Youngbloods – Briar had the highest hopes for this one.

Briar elbowed Hardgrim in the ribs, hard. "Eyes down. That one is a viper."

"But what a way to go," her second-in-command replied, sighing.

She mightily resisted the urge to punch him in the throat. If only Hardgrim's uncle hadn't once saved Alaric's life in battle and called in that old blood debt to obtain a position of responsibility in the Shields for his odious nephew... In all fairness, she'd also have taken any opportunity to foist the pig on to somebody else far away, so she could not fault the man in that. Alaric's rule as regent was a careful balancing act of pitting clan chiefs and other nobles against each other, and he couldn't afford to offend Hardgrim's powerful kin. The man was good at the job and the tedious scrollwork that came with it, but in Briar's informed opinion he was seriously lacking in character – just not enough to give her a solid excuse to dismiss him from his post and mire him and his kin in dishonour.

She slammed the door and tossed the unread scroll into a basket by the wall. It was blank anyway, just a ruse for whenever the regent needed an excuse to cut a meeting short. Alaric was back working at his desk now, quill scratching across parchment, the Exalted's advances already consigned to the rubbish heap at the back of his mind.

Briar paced the room, studying every inch of the area Carmanilla had trodden. It took her a second sweep of the room to spot the little gift their visitor had left for them, right beside the desk. She got down on her knees to examine a speck of gold half the size of a grain of wheat, wedged between two floorboards. She used the point of her knife to scrape it out of the dust, then held it up to her eye. Minuscule geometric lines almost too small for the eye to see had been etched onto it: a temporary arcane device that must have taken an eagle-eyed crafter many painstaking days of effort to make with tiny jeweller's tools. She moved over to the window of the tower and flicked it outside.

"Listening artefact," she said. Just because they were not priests or sorcerers did not mean they were unfamiliar with works of sorcery. "Let her listen to the worms and the bugs."

Alaric nodded, unsurprised. "I have no intention of wedding the likes of her," he said from inside his prison of correspondence. He lifted a tablet of slate from the pile and frowned at the badly scribed complaint from a group of merchants moaning about the sorry state of the roads. His stylus scratched across the stone, marking it for the attention of a minor functionary, to be replied to with promises of good news for their wagons soon. The slate was set atop a second pile rapidly growing precarious.

"I never asked about any wedding," she replied.

He snorted and switched back to more important foreign correspondence, dipping his quill thrice into the clamshell of ink and letting the excess drip off. "You were thinking it, though."

"She's a pretty little thing to dip your own quill into," Briar added speculatively. She couldn't keep the hard edge from her voice.

"You can have her for yourself if you like," Alaric replied, not even looking up. "I dare say she'd find you as much use as she would me."

Briar nodded her agreement, relieved at his indifference. "Were I otherwise inclined, I'd be tempted to take her for a tumble in the blankets."

The regent's quill poked a hole in the parchment that had been a reply to one of the most powerful priests in the Holy Wrendal Empire. Completely ruined. "Please, do not force me to imagine that too hard," he pleaded.

Briar loosed a throaty chuckle.

He set down his quill, carefully moved the clamshell of ink out of the way and mopped up a splodge of ink. "Many men do spend a lot of time and energy on their lusts," he admitted. "But even we base creatures desire to be loved for ourselves rather than used for accruing money and influence. It is a dalliance I cannot afford."

Shield Briar's mirth faded. His situation was indeed precarious. She knew the political turmoil any offspring of regent and Wrendal priestess would cause in Sunweald. Indeed, any female offspring at all would prove catastrophic. Alaric and Kester belonged to the line bearing the strongest royal blood, but they were both male, and the clans of Sunweald already frowned upon a man sitting on the Oaken Throne. The blood of the mother was always certain... the father's bloodline not so much. Alaric's sister had ruled the realm wisely and well, and Kester was but a babe when the plague took his parents. Briar dared not imagine Kester's fate should Alaric ever have a daughter, especially one with Wrendal backing.

Alaric smiled sadly as he resumed the endless work of a role that he had never sought.

Fifteen years of restraint was no laughing matter, and in the ten since Briar had been guarding his life, he had allowed no one but his dogs to crawl into his blankets. She pondered the future he spoke of for a moment, imagining assassins targeting Kester and competing claims for the throne being pushed forward by power-hungry clans of Sunweald blessed with women of lesser but more certain royal lineage. The blood feuds and ensuing slaughter would be a nightmare beyond Alaric's control, and realms had fallen for less than the perceived legitimacy of their rulers. The clan chiefs had possessed enormous respect for Alaric's sister, Kester's mother, and their conviction of her virtue had been one of the main reasons Alaric was able to become regent until her son came of age to wed his blood to one of their own daughters. Briar said nothing, and instead resumed her position by the door, back straight, hands clasped behind her as the regent immersed himself in his work.

The temple horns sounded midday, immediately followed by annoying chimes from the accursed clock in the corner. After no sign of movement, Briar had to go over and physically manhandle the regent out of his chair, a scroll still clutched in his ink-stained hands. He squawked an objection, but she ignored him and prised the scroll from his grasping fingers. "It's time to wash and get dressed. You don't want to be late for the ritual."

He grumbled but did as he was told, reluctantly taking himself off to the adjoining bedroom to scrub the dark stains from his hands and nails then put on the formal wear his scrupulous Shields had tested for contact poisons before setting out for him.

He came back out in embossed leather shoes, a long forest-green woollen coat worked with silver snakes intertwining down the lapels and the obligatory brown-and-gold oak-and-acorn emblem of Sunweald embroidered over his heart. A royal-purple half cloak was hung over one shoulder and pinned to the coat with a cluster of emeralds. Around his neck a heavy torc of twisted gold wire was placed, and on his brow no elaborate royal crown but a simple gold circlet, as befitting a regent, wrapped in the traditional ivy, meadowsweet and oak leaf held sacred by their ancestors.

He opened his arms wide and turned a full circle. "Well?"

She approached, circling him, adjusting the cloak and smoothing out creases. Brutus woke up and padded over to join her. He sniffed the coat and boots, then huffed and turned his back on his master. Ever a critic, that one.

"Tremendously expensive and extremely garish," she said, "but you wear it well, Lord Regent."

"Oh, now it's 'Lord Regent' in private?" he muttered. "I suppose it is time to get into character... but this outfit really is awful. You know how these court engagements are. You have to keep up with fashions and look rich and powerful, or the venomous snakes think you are losing your touch. I cannot show any hint of weakness, or you will have to deal with yet more assassins."

"I hear those killers still willing to even consider talking about it have raised their prices enormously over the last few years," Briar answered. "I can't think why..." She finished her adjustments and stepped back, offering an appreciative nod.

Her expression became hard and serious. "Are you ready, my Lord?"

After a deep breath, he nodded. "As I ever will be. Proceed, my Shield."

Shield Briar opened the door and strode through, hand on the hilt of her blade. Shields Hardgrim and Iden stepped aside, allowing them to pass into the outer chamber of the regent's accommodation. Two other Shields came to attention, only one dressed in a similarly garish formal uniform embroidered with silver-and-gold foliage. Shield Cathbad joined their escort, the older man's scarred visage and thick arms making for a daunting sight even without his armour. Hardgrim, Iden and the younger man, a new Shield called Ruith, stayed behind to secure the area and stop the damned dog from wandering off and making trouble.

They left the regent's tower with every expectation of enduring yet another uneventful solstice festival followed by a feast shared with tedious company. At least the major festivals were only twice a year, Briar thought, and the food was always exceptional.

CHAPTER 2

The summer solstice was the holiest day in the Sunweald year, symbolising the triumph of life over cold death, and the gods had gifted them a gloriously bright day to celebrate it. Shields Briar and Cathbad escorted the regent down the stairs of his tower, through corridors and then down the central spiral staircase that was the only way up or down from the ground floor of the palace. It made for a secure choke point, though to Briar's knowledge none had ever assaulted the inner palace directly.

They turned into the oldest part of the palace, where the walls were shored up with heavy support beams and covered in wooden scaffolding. Mouldering wood, crumbling steps and broken floor tiles were in the process of being ripped out to make way for the new. The roofing in many parts was rotten and leaking, and as a result the upper floors of the East Wing were in a deadly state.

"Making a right mess of this place," Cathbad complained as they passed the entrance, which was boarded up and closed off entirely due to unstable stonework that had come within a whisker of cracking a scribe's skull. The small but highly skilled army of officials that kept the wheels of government turning had been displaced to the spacious new citadel at Drew Nemeton, while carpenters and masons worked to make the Sunweald Palace safe. It would take years and would prove a great drain on the realm's purse.

"Better that than it comes down on our heads," Briar said.

"Though your skull is so thick you may not have to worry overmuch."

Cathbad rolled his eyes and ran a finger across a wall, scowling at the layer of stone dust that covered everything. He coughed. "Can't you feel it in your lungs?" He cleared his throat and coughed a few more times. "When you get to my age, you can feel these things affect you more."

"All *I* feel is irritation and a sudden desire for silence," Briar replied, eyeing him askance. Always coughing, that one, claiming dust and flowers and whatnot were trying to murder him.

"I was cursed at birth by gods of earth and air," he muttered as they passed by the doorless arch that led into the small temple. He glared at the dozens of altars dedicated to the gods of Sunweald, probably wondering which of the bastards had taken against him.

The party emerged from a small ivy-wreathed side gate leading into the grounds. The ground floor of the entire palace had originally been a cave burrowed deep into a huge outcrop of rock, and the other rooms were carved out of it, making the lower level immensely strong and durable. Many of the inner walls and the upper levels had subsequently been built and improved by generations of mere mortals, and they demanded constant repairs, which had been sorely neglected due to years of extensive construction at Drew Nemeton.

They made their way along gravelled paths into the gardens, where minor nobles in their rich tunics supervised small children more interested in playing with one another than gawping at the regent of the realm. Rose, yarrow, cornflower and geranium bloomed in the flowerbeds, and the scent of lavender and honeysuckle filled the air. The palace gardens were extensive and designed to lift the mood and nourish the soul, much needed to counteract the depressingly staid affairs of government. Vibrant blue-and-orange butterflies fluttered to and fro, much admired by the guests and much chased by the children. Honeybees buzzed from flower to flower, those messengers to the gods toiling away without rest – Alaric bowed his head to the bees, lest on this sacred day they carried unfavourable words back to their divine masters or his own ancestors resident in the otherworld.

Many of the realm's rich and powerful had gathered in the grounds to celebrate, drink and gossip. An austere pack of white-robed priests from the Holy Wrendal Empire kept their distance and exchanged glares with flamboyant ambassadors of the Federated Principalities of Ves in their multicoloured velvets and lace and fanciful hats, their teeth studded with gold and gemstones. The standoff would continue until both sides were a few cups into the bountiful supply of sacred mead and wine. Sunweald Palace staff and Shields had already placed bets on who would try to dance with the other side first. Briar's sizable bet was on Carmanilla: that one would try to seduce anything to advance her goals.

The festivals were Shield Briar's nightmare, and she kept one hand close to her sword at all times. Not only were the guards outside the palace disallowed armour on festival days, but there were far too many people packed into the gardens and not nearly enough trusted eyes on them. It was vanishingly unlikely that any of the foreign dignitaries or local nobles would try anything in public themselves, but every one of them arrived with a minimum of five servants in their entourage. Then there was the army of hired staff to consider: the painted actors, jugglers, dancers, firebreathers and musicians, soothsayers and mystics, herbalists, cooks and kitchen staff brought in from elsewhere to facilitate such a large event. It was impossible to do everything herself, and she could not inspect everybody as thoroughly as she would have liked. As for the druids, they were above mundane mortal concerns and controls and as bafflingly mysterious as ever – and it was not wise to meddle in their affairs.

Briar and Cathbad exchanged a glance, wordlessly sharing their concerns. He nodded and scanned the crowd.

A series of long tables and benches had been set out on the grass, all decorated with ivy and spaces laid out for the feasting. Five hogs and ten sheep were roasting over fire pits, the scent making her mouth water. Their skins were crisping up nicely, and she vowed to descend upon them like a ravenous horde when they were ready.

Cathbad's gaze was caught by the mousy middle-aged maid, Aisling, who had returned from visiting family this very morning. She raised an eyebrow at him, and he grinned back. He had only two teeth missing and thought himself quite the catch. The maid rolled her eyes and turned her back on him as the procession passed by.

"Even the servants have better taste than to dally with the likes of you," Briar said.

"Maybe so," he replied, "but I grow on you like mould. Leastways, that's what you told me a few weeks back. Just a matter of time before that one falls for my charms."

Briar sighed heavily and scanned the crowds. The boy who would be high king was already the centre of the party. Briar could just barely see his chubby cheeks and ridiculous, oiled beechnut-brown hair bobbing in the middle of the swarming sycophants and swine aping his style, or lack thereof. Lately he had taken to donning the garish garb of the Ves – thankfully without one of their ridiculous hats – and wore not even a nod to the traditional green-and-brown woollens of Sunweald. Two years until his sixteenth name day, and the heir to the Oaken Throne was already drunk and surrounded by a gaggle of hopeful older women with flowers in their hair and ambition blooming in their hearts. He only had two sober women beside him, a pair of harried-looking veteran Shields called Sleen and Barik, who cast despairing glares in their commander's direction. Both women looked every bit as uncomfortable in their formal uniforms as Briar felt, but the boy responded better to women in positions of authority than he did men, so they had been all out of luck.

The Lord Regent's expression was set in stone, and just as neutral. He could not afford to condemn the boy with the rest of the nobility watching and weighing up their political positions: the crown rule of Sunweald was far from absolute, and much power was in the hands of noble clans arranged into political camps that had to be carefully shepherded along sensible paths. Mostly, it was like herding cats. Alaric strode over to the Royal Heir, and the swarm of scavengers parted before him.

"Uncle!" Kester Summerson cried, sloshing towards the regent with a mug of hideously expensive imported red wine in his hand and the cuff of his coat already stained purple.

Alaric offered a short bow and a carefully crafted smile hinting at amusement. "Your Highness," he said, eyeing the wine. "The day is still young, so I hope you will leave enough room in your belly to enjoy the feast later. I have sourced some truly exquisite wines to pair with each dish."

Kester's eyes lit up, and he nodded vigorously, oiled curls dancing. "And people say you are a dour old stick in the mud." He looked at the crowd of dignitaries, searching, as they suddenly found their attention drawn absolutely anywhere else. "Somebody said that, anyway... I am sure..."

Alaric's smile seemed nailed to his face, and Briar could tell he was itching to grab the entitled brat by the ear and drag him out of the nest of vipers that surrounded him. "What is being served later will delight your senses," he said. "It would be a shame if any of these... fine people... were to waste your tongue on something merely adequate." He nodded and departed for the mound of the ancestors. Briar and the Shields surrounding him shouldered aside any drunken idiots who dared to get too close.

"He is becoming a drunkard and a pampered fop," Alaric growled to her under his breath. "The boy needs to be tasked with some real work. No more of these indulgences can be allowed lest they become habits. A king cannot afford such weaknesses."

She had to admit putting the boy to some hard physical labour would be for the best. "He should redouble his training to become a warrior," she advised. "His current teachers of spear and sword and fist have been far too soft on him. I'll do it myself."

Alaric winced and glanced to his right. "Perhaps Cathbad..."

Her scathing response was silenced by a procession of clan chiefs and minor nobles, master crafters and renowned silver-tongued bards, all eager to clasp hands and exchange greetings. The price of power was that everybody wanted a hunk of the loaf. Even the decent women and men among them had personal priorities to push. Alaric knew them all by sight and asked after their fourth daughters and distant relations by name and discussed their current deeds. Briar admired his thoroughness, and his ability to deal with them without bloodshed, because she was most certainly not cut out for the job of ruling. Lucky, really, given she was the eldest daughter of a sheep-farmer-turned-warrior serving Drew Nemeton's council of elders. She had started her career first by protecting the sheep from hungry wolves, bears, and greedy men, and then by helping him patrol around the local villages, collecting rents and rooting out brigands. It hadn't been long before she'd moved on to scouting for warbands tasked with exterminating the larger groups who had been reiving villages, and her effectiveness in that role was how she came to the attention of the Shields. Simpler times.

The regent's progress to the ancient mound slowed to a crawl as he exchanged the same old meaningless pleasantries with the same old faces, some who were friendly and some who would be happy to cut his throat if they thought they could get away with it – one or two of the latter type felt Shield Briar's gaze fall upon them and started sweating. Accidents could happen in the palace, with its crumbling steps and ancient corridors, not to mention the maze of cellars and caves hidden away beneath centuries-old floorboards and cracked flagstones. Indeed, several accidents had happened over the years – and, amazingly enough, mostly to those bastards plotting to remove the regent and install themselves as Kester's guardian.

An eerie, undulating noise droned out across the land. The sound of the carnyx was heard for leagues all around and compelled every face to look towards the mound of the ancestors. Seven painted druids in long bearskin cloaks and horned headdresses stood among the towering ancient stones, their plaited beards and long hair adorned with carved bone beads. Each blew into a sinuous bronze horn fully the length of a tall man, the open mouths of the instruments worked into the maws of snarling beasts.

A slow drumbeat joined in, booming out across the palace grounds: powerful, primal. Briar sniffed, unimpressed. The musical skill of this batch of druids and their musicians was sorely lacking; last year the music had been otherworldly. It had brought her out in goose bumps and sent a superstitious shiver up her spine as if the gods were close enough to touch. This lot, well… she reckoned she could do just as well herself, given a stone or two of practice.

The horns droned on, summoning the sacrifices to the sacred mound, the pitch rising and falling. The call of the carnyx was said to awaken the ancestors interred within the bones of the earth, and on the day of the solstice their spirits would walk among their descendants, bestowing blessings. Briar was not sure she believed in everything the druids said, but over her years patrolling the ancient caves and passages below the palace, among the tombs of Shields who had died in service, she had seen more strange things than she could explain away.

The sea of people opened to form a corridor between the regent and the mound. A young man and woman went first, a thin rope in their hands braided around the neck of a sacred white bull destined to have its throat slit in the centre of the stones at the top. The great beast went willingly to its death, glassy-eyed and pacified by potions and prayers.

Briar rested one hand on the hilt of her sword and followed after, with Cathbad bringing up the rear. Her eyes flicked from side to side in case anybody brandished anything more dangerous than a cup of mead. Shields Sleen and Barik herded the Royal Heir into the human corridor behind them.

The beat of the drums increased its pace as the royal party reached the foot of the mound and began to ascend the spiralling path to the peak. Kester was out of breath in less than a hundred heartbeats and grumbled all the way. He might not have liked his part in the event, but even he dared not ruin the solstice ritual. The blood of high queens and kings was a necessary part of the rites: the people of Sunweald shed blood, sweat and tears in service to the land, and twice a year their rulers did the same. They would shed royal blood to nourish the spirit of the land that she may recognise them, bestow her favour and sustain their people. The gods were present in this sacred place, at this blessed time. Watching. Judging.

Halfway up, Alaric and Kester paused to lay small offerings before two wickerwork shrines bearing the leathery, bog-preserved corpses of the mother and father of the Summerson bloodline: High Queen Kennocha and King Wynne Wyrmslayer, a thousand years dead and each wrapped in fine white shawls so only their dark and shrunken faces were revealed. Even to the long memories of the druids, the truth of those dark times they lived in had been lost to the mists of time. All any knew were the legends of the clans fleeing before hordes of monsters that were led by the last living great wyrm of old. Once they had paid their respects to the ancestors, the procession continued up the hill.

They reached the top of the mound and passed between eight posts of oak wrapped all around with ivy, oak leaves and mistletoe. The bull was tied to the slaughter stone, and then the young man and woman that had led it up rejoined the masses waiting below.

The eerie call of the carnyx died away with a lingering wail, and the seven druids set their instruments down on the grass, instead taking up bowls of fragrant oils and brushes of sage leaves to anoint the chosen of the gods. The half-masked drummer with braided hair behind them struggled to keep a fast-but-steady beat on the stretched skins.

The Shields knelt on the earth behind their charges as the Lord Regent and Royal Heir stepped forward three paces and sank to their own knees to receive the blessings of the wise ones. The pounding of the drums sped up, and Briar's heartbeat raced to match it, expectation building with the beat.

The grand druid, leading the ritual, stepped forward. Like his fellow druids, he wore an antlered headdress masking his face, though its skull was carved all over with intricate whorls and jagged lines that caught the eye and mesmerised it. Instead of a bearskin cloak, his was of crow feathers sewn into a pelt of soft human skin taken from a willing sacrifice: a most potent magic linking him to the otherworld. He dipped his bunch of sage into the bowl of oil and flicked it twice, scattering it onto Alaric's left shoulder, then his right. The regent bowed his head, and the druid held the brush aloft, letting the light of the solstice sun illuminate and empower the golden droplets.

The grand druid's arms rose skyward to beckon down the sun. His cloak flapped open to reveal crude deerskin shoes with the hairs still on. Briar's eyes widened in shock. Her breath caught in her throat – the wise ones were always barefoot for their rituals, each man and woman connected to the living earth beneath them. This man's shoes were worn and muddy and spotted with day-old blood splatter. With the regent's head bowed before him, the grand druid let go of the sage brush and grabbed hold of the antlers of his headdress, with all its sharp tines. The drums boomed like thunder as an antler came free in the false druid's hand.

"Shields up!" Briar yelled, surging to her feet. "Assassins!" She drew and threw her belt knife, praying to all the gods her aim was true. Her knife was for eating, not weighted for throwing, but what choice did she have?

The druid swung the antler down, deadly tines aimed at the regent's neck.

Briar's gods-blessed knife pierced hilt-deep into the man's shoulder, and his makeshift weapon dropped to the grass.

Alaric flopped back, shocked. The assassin hissed in pain, his other hand going for the ceremonial silver sickle hooked into his belt.

Briar drew her sword and buckler and slammed into him, shoulder set.

The man stumbled and fell, and she went with him. He landed on his back, and the reinforced metal edge of Briar's buckler hammered down into his neck. Throat and cartilage crunched inwards. She hammered the shield down a second time and then rolled to her feet.

Her heart racing, she assessed the threat: the supposed grand druid was down, crow-feather cloak covered in blood and face purpling as he pawed at his crushed throat and struggled to breathe through swelling tissue.

Cathbad was on the other side of the regent. He bled from a gash on his cheek, trapped in a desperate defensive battle with two more assassins, buckler and blade fending off their curved silver sickles.

Sleen fell to her knees at Kester's feet, taken by surprise, dying, throat cut and blood spurting. Nothing could be done to save her.

Barik had put one assassin down, the man's knee shattered with splintered bone jutting from the flesh, but she faced three more trying to murder the Royal Heir. Kester was curled up on the grass, screaming in terror, utterly useless.

Alaric scrambled to his feet, looking around wildly, the fallen antler wielded in his hands.

Distantly, Briar noted the drumming cease and people in the palace gardens shouting in horror. Help would come, but too late.

Cathbad faced two. Barik three. Briar moved to protect the regent. One of the assassins went for Cathbad, who blocked with his buckler and cut the fingers from the man's knife hand.

The man shrieked and staggered back, staring at his ragged stumps. His other hand cut into Cathbad from the side before he could re-establish his guard, sickle slicing through uniform and into the belly beneath – sickles were meant to cut crops, but they reaped lives easily enough, and though silver was too soft a metal for battle, it could still kill.

Briar was on the assassins a heartbeat too late, her bronze sword punching into the unwounded man's back, through his lung and out the front. She wrenched the sword free, shoved the dying man aside and charged the fingerless bastard. A buckler to the face broke the assassin's nose and snapped his head back, exposing the throat for a vicious cut that ended his life and left Briar's face dripping with his lifeblood.

She looked to Cathbad, but Alaric was already there, desperately trying to staunch the blood gushing from the Shield's wound. "Go," he commanded.

Barik still stood over Kester. The boy cowered and sobbed while she fought for him. Her shield arm was badly cut and her garish uniform rent and bloodied as she desperately fought to keep all three assassins at bay, a whirlwind of precise cuts and feints. She was good, great even, but nobody was skilled enough to fight three while immobile in order to protect a brat of a boy. Like many female Shields, she relied on swiftness and skill to counter her male opponents' greater strength, so if the boy had fled, she would have stood a chance of warding them off in time for Briar to reach her.

One of the assassins attacked Barik from the front while the other two moved round to flank her. She faced the one dead ahead and blocked his sickle with her buckler. The silver implement bent, rendered useless. Her sword plunged into his chest even as the sickles on either side cut in and disembowelled her. Her backswing, before she fell, cut a furrow up another attacker's chest and sliced through his jaw. Shattered teeth and spittle flew as her killer gurgled a scream.

Kester pissed himself in terror as his dying Shield collapsed atop him, covering him in blood and guts.

Briar's rage ran cold, not hot. Her eyes took in the enemy positions, and she quickly weighed up her actions before attacking. The one on the left was slower, weaker.

She went for him, cutting for his face. He jerked back and, in his haste, forgot there was a boy and a corpse at his feet. He flailed and fell, the sickle slipping from his grasp, his horned headdress knocked askew. For the moment he was out of the fight, so she went for the second false druid.

He too was armed with a short silver sickle meant for cutting herbs, but Briar had a bronze sword built for battle. Her downswing sheared through the raised silver tool and crunched into the skull behind. The sword grated on his spine, stuck fast.

Briar abandoned the weapon and turned back as the tripped and prone assassin tore his askew headdress off to reveal a scarred, weather-beaten bearded face. He gawped up as Briar's boot descended towards his face.

"Son of a sow," he said.

Poor last words, she thought, as her heel slammed down again and again until he lay still. She scanned the area. The grand druid was still where she'd left him, face like a rotten plum, still struggling for breath. The man Barik had put down was on the ground, clutching a leg that would likely need to be sawn off. Something else niggled at her, something she'd forgotten...

The musicians! Shit!

Most had dropped their instruments and fled. She scanned the mound and spotted the drummer with the braided hair and half mask, his chin clean-shaven. He stood beside one of the great standing stones, a bow in his hands, a quiver at his hip and dark eyes fastened on the regent.

The man nocked an arrow to the string of his fine yew bow with practised ease. His mask exposed a crooked grin as he drew back the string and took aim.

She ran for the regent as fast as she ever had in her youth, sprinting across the sacred earth with dread in her heart. He was still kneeling on the ground, tending to Cathbad's wound and entirely unaware of his peril.

The archer let out his breath and loosed. The arrow flew true.

Briar leapt in front of the regent, buckler intercepting the shot. The point screeched off the metal and buried itself in the grass to the side.

The archer blinked in surprise, having seriously underestimated the speed and dexterity she was famed for.

"Stay behind me," she ordered the ruler of Sunweald.

"I can't!" he growled, hands still clamped to Cathbad's horrid wound.

The archer spat, and then tried again. She shifted to block it, the arrow tinging off her buckler and into the grassy mound. A third she swatted from the air. Then he drew two and set both to string. He smirked and loosed both at once.

She blocked the one aimed for the regent's chest, but the other punched into her left leg, just above the knee. It was painless while her blood was up, but that wouldn't last. The archer cursed and had to fetch more arrows from his quiver. She glanced at the arrow embedded in her flesh, dismissed it for now and used the temporary reprieve to grab a dead assassin and hold him up as an extra shield. An arrow hit the corpse with a meaty *thunk*.

The archer darted right, trying to open up a better line of shot as he drew another arrow from his quiver. Briar turned with him, and while Alaric was no hardened warrior, he knew when to keep his head down and let his Shields do what they did best. The shouting from below was increasing in volume. All they had to do was wait for more Shields to arrive from the palace, and the archer knew it. Time was on their side, and between corpse and buckler they had enough cover that he would be forced to close in if he wanted to try to finish this quickly. She grinned, daring him to try.

The assassin sighed heavily. He shrugged, admitting defeat, then smiled crookedly and lifted two fingers to his forehead in salute. The man turned, ripped off his mask and fled down the other side of the mound, away from the angry mob charging up it.

"Gods, Briar..." Alaric said, staring at the arrow jutting from her leg.

"Check on the boy," she hissed as the pain began to build. "I'll see to Cathbad."

She had served with the veteran Shield for eight good years. He stared up at her, his face twisted into a rictus of agony, body twisting this way and that and fingers digging into the earth. His skin was deathly pale, and a pool of blood spread from a deep and ragged wound. The sour stink of shit and bile was on him from ruptured guts. He would not survive, and he knew it.

"End it," he said, handing her his own knife. "Make it quick."

She grimaced and looked at the sun, then the sacred mound he lay dying upon. "All of you gods, spirits and ancestors had better be watching this. Cathbad has sacrificed his life for Sunweald. Honour him in the otherworld as I do in this one."

The knife went in, quick and painless, slicking across the artery in his neck. He didn't even feel the cut. Twenty heartbeats later, Cathbad was gone, his pain and his duty ended. She limped over to check on Alaric and the boy, and found the regent slapping some sense into the cowardly little shit.

Alaric thrust Barik's knife into Kester's hand. "Your Shield dies in agony. It is your responsibility to end her torment."

Oh, ancestors, Briar thought, seeing Barik's chest still rising and falling. She'd been disembowelled but still lingered on, half conscious. Briar fought back the urge to vomit; the inferno of pain building in her knee helped focus her.

The Royal Heir trembled uncontrollably. He was drenched in his own piss and puke. "I... I can't..." he sobbed.

"I'll do it," Briar gasped, almost falling as the pain in her leg spiked.

Alaric's eyes turned on her, red and full of empathy but coldly determined. "No. He will be high king. He must live up to his responsibilities. She fought to protect you, Kester. She dies for you. You will do this, wretch of a boy." He clamped his hand around the boy's hand and hilt and guided it, setting the point over Barik's heart.

"Do it," he commanded. "She saved your life. You owe it to her to end her pain."

Tears were a river down Kester's gory cheeks. "I can't!"

"DO IT!" Alaric commanded, as Barik went rigid, writhing in agony.

Kester sobbed as his hand pushed the blade into her heart, guided by his uncle. They drew the blade out, and Kester dropped it like it was on fire, staring at his bloodied fingers.

Barik shuddered, and her chest fell with a soft wheeze. It did not rise again.

"This is what it means to be a ruler," Alaric said. "This is the grave responsibility you owe to those who serve you."

Briar stumbled, her entire leg burning now. She felt increasingly faint and overwhelmingly nauseous. Then her vision began to blur. She squinted at the arrow in her leg and the angry red veins now webbing out from the wound. "Oh," she said. "A poisoned arrow. Fucking fantastic."

She toppled into the arms of the Lord Regent, and into darkness.

CHAPTER 3

Briar woke screaming and strapped to a bed, her leg a mass of raw nerves. She passed out immediately, then later spent an age fading in and out of consciousness as she drifted on an endless sea of agony. Blurry faces and ice-cold hands on her burning skin. Pain, thirst, fear. The acid sear of bile in her mouth. More screaming. She was dying. It was too much, and in a moment of complete, awful awareness, she demanded the bone saw to hack off her accursed leg. She screamed that she'd do it herself if she had to and struggled against the straps holding her down – then begged for an end to her life when she was denied. Somebody took knives to her leg and peeled her open like rotten fruit. The all-consuming agony punched her back down to gods-blessed nothingness.

Time passed. Days. Weeks, maybe. Her waking moments were struggles to choke down salty, lukewarm broth, most of which she threw right back up when the waves of agony struck. Then came the bundles of herbs washed down with a bitter-tasting liquid administered by druids and servants that served to dull the pain. A little.

In one of her more lucid moments, after taking copious medication, she felt somebody place a soothing, cold cloth on her burning brow. She opened gummy eyes to see a mousy middle-aged woman in a clean white apron sitting by her bedside. It took her a moment to dredge up a name: Aisling, one of the palace servants. A sinister shadow surrounded the woman, a black mist with burning eyes and malevolent intent. It opened a fiery maw and laughed at Briar as she screamed on her bed, thrashing. Alaric was there in a moment, his face pale and drawn. The shadow reached a clawed hand towards his throat, and she fought to drag the regent aside. A claw touched his cheek, and Alaric's face rotted off to reveal the grinning skull beneath.

"Sleep," the skull said, pouring the contents of a small wax-sealed jar into her mouth. The thick, bitter medicine slid down her throat, and all consciousness fled.

Briar was woken from the throes of twisted nightmares by the queerest feeling that something warm and comforting had pressed against her forehead. Then the stench hit her: a mix of rot and rancid sweat. She was in bed but no longer strapped down. Her lower body was cold and numb and unresponsive, like she was already half dead. She'd been dressed in a white linen nightdress, but it was now drenched and yellowing, and the damp blanket that covered her clung to her skin like a death shroud. She forced open an eyelid the weight of a horse and found herself staring up at the ceiling beams of the Lord Regent's own bedroom. Wickerwork talismans and druidic healing charms hung from ceiling joists.

She tilted her head to one side and blinked bleary eyes to see washed bandages hanging on a screen. Alaric's beloved musical instruments had been shoved into the corner to make way for a table bearing an army of medicine pots and ointments. His cherry-wood lyre and flutes were some of the few things he truly loved, and in another life, he might have become a famous bard. As it was, he lacked the time to play for pleasure, never mind perfecting the craft. A blurry figure was seated beside the screen. Was he here with her? She forced her eyes to focus and felt a dull stab of surprise that it was Exalted Carmanilla asleep in the chair. The woman's long honeyed hair hung limp and greasy, her robe grimy and heavily creased, eyes puffy from exhaustion. Black veins crawled up her neck – signs of recently used sorcery!

Briar struggled to sit up, fumbling for a knife at her hip that she didn't have.

"Shh," Alaric whispered from her other side, his voice strained as he stroked her cheek. "Let her rest."

Briar turned her head the other way, every movement a leaden ordeal. Her voice emerged as a croak, from a throat dry as a desert.

He turned to the chest next to his bed, picked up a blue-glazed jug and poured spring water into a cup, then carefully pressed it to her lips.

The sips of cool liquid refreshed her throat like it was the blessed drink of the gods he held in his hand.

"Wrendal sorcery," Briar rasped, glancing at the foreign priestess sleeping in his bedroom.

"Yes," he replied. "They are not all bad, you know; even the druids admit that. A good thing she was here too, otherwise" – he swallowed – "I'd have lost you. And that... I could not... could not..." He shuddered and looked away for a moment, wiping an eyelash from his eye. "She knew something of how to treat poisons."

The battle on the mound came rushing back to her, as did her horrendous losses. Barik, Sleen and Cathbad were dead. She closed her suddenly wet eyes for a moment, shuddering, heart aching. Then she forced them back open and looked down at her left leg, noting the bloodstains on the sheet. "How bad is it?" she rasped. "The leg, did you take it off?"

He lifted the cup for another few sips. "No," he said. "But it's not good. Do you... need to see it?"

"Always better to know than not," she said, dread swelling in her belly as he set down the cup and gingerly peeled back the sweat-sodden sheet and the sticky bandage covering the wound.

With the dressing gone, the stench from the wound intensified. Her stomach lurched, and the dread changed to a horribly informed certainty she should be dead. The leg was as bad as she had ever seen on a still-living body. The arrow had been removed, but the wound had not closed up and was now a weeping pit, the edges an angry red, and oozing green pus told a tale of infection. Blood and yellow fluids caked the skin and had soaked right through the bandage. By all rights, she should be insensible, writhing in pain and burning up with infection and fever. She tried to move her leg, and it didn't so much as twitch.

Her panic must have shown on her face. "It's only a temporary paralysis," Alaric said, his face grim. "Carmanilla has numbed your senses from the waist down, as best I understand it. The pain would be immense without her expertise. We'd have taken the leg if it would have done any good. The librarian identified the poison as red-scale viper venom, and it was already running rampant through your veins. We have dealt with that poison, but I am afraid damage was done. Infection took root in the flesh around the wound."

Briar swallowed, and bile seared the back of her throat. "Will I ever walk again?"

He paused a moment too long. "I hope so."

"Shit, shit, shit," she croaked, her throat red-raw and fingernails gouging holes into the blankets. "If I ever find that archer, I will skin him alive. I'll be slow about it, and I will enjoy every moment. How long have I been out?"

"Five days," Alaric said. "The Exalted has not left your side."

Briar grimaced. "Out of the goodness of her heart, I suppose."

He sighed and checked to make sure the topic of their conversation was still sleeping. "I expect she'll want some concession or other, but I am more than willing to grant it for the boon she has provided us." He smiled at Briar, and in that smile was an entire world of exhausted relief. "Let's replace your bandage." He carefully wiped the crusted blood and slime off her leg and placed a mossy mass of healing herbs into her gaping wound, then wrapped it all up tight inside a new bandage.

A crushing weariness descended on her as he worked like he was her servant and not her master and the ruler of an entire nation. "I'm glad your face didn't rot off," she said in a cracked voice, recalling the strange visions.

He glanced at her, worried. "I too, am happy to report my face is still intact."

"I'm unclothed and in your bedroom," she mumbled, with the ghost of a smile. "You sly old dog. You've finally managed to get me into your bed. What will people say?"

For once, he didn't return her attempt at humour. "Do not worry about our reputations: if any gossipmongers fucking dare to disparage you, I will fling them from my tower window. You will rest here, and I will be right next door if you need anything at all. Anything."

"Who were those assassins?" she asked, struggling to stay conscious, eyelids dipping and rising only to close further.

"Shield Hardgrim is investigating that," Alaric said. "You left two alive. One can no longer talk, but the man with the broken knee that Barik put down has been squealing all he knows. They ambushed the druids the day before the solstice and took their places. Two hired servants and a wine-seller also made a run for it when your archer made his escape, all heading east towards the lands of the Ves. The country is in an uproar, and the populace are out for blood. Those bastards committed the ancient taboo of murdering holy druids, and every town and village between here and the border has warbands out seeking their heads."

She groaned, exhaustion taking her despite her best efforts.

"Thank you for saving my life," he said.

She grunted. "It's my job."

"I have to know," he continued. "How did you realise they were assassins before they struck?"

"Shoes," she slurred. "Druids… don't wear bloody shoes… ritual…" And then sleep's black tendrils pulled her down, down, down…

When Briar next woke, she knew she still lived. She knew that for a certainty because nothing dead could possibly feel so much pain. She was once again securely strapped into the bed. Knives and medical tools jutted from a copper bowl of boiling water placed above a brazier, mixed with healing herbs: dill, lady's mantle and rosemary, from the smell. A grey-beard druid draped in charms and animal teeth retrieved a hot bronze needle from the bowl and stabbed it into her thigh. Pus squirted, and the druid tutted. Briar's yell wheezed into the air, her voice long since broken by the screams. She thrashed against her bonds.

Carmanilla appeared beside the man. "We cannot give her more potions to kill the pain," the priestess said, "otherwise we risk stopping her heart. We have done this many times in the temples of Wrendal, and this is the only way to save the limb." The druid nodded his agreement.

The regent loomed over Briar's sickbed, his brow furrowed and his eyes dark. "Proceed, venerable druid." He grabbed her hands, pressed her back down on to the bed and held her there.

The druid brandished a flint blade the size of his thumb and got to work. He cut slits around the wound and peeled back flaps of skin to expose the infection beneath, then he began to scrape away the stinking, dying flesh. She wheezed her pain and whispered bloody threats to no avail. The gods and spirits did not bless her with unconsciousness for a horrifically long time.

In the catacombs beneath the palace, a masked figure paced to and fro, her fists trembling with fury as she regarded the three men in the candlelit cavern with her. The shadows writhed around her as two of the men knelt on the cold wet stone, cringing. Those two bought traitors, Bevyn and Jund, were dressed in the homespun garb of the Sunweald Palace's lowest servants, but the other wore a blooded druid's robe, a fine bow stave leaning on his shoulder.

"You failed," she hissed to Maddox, the assassin who had missed his shot.

The archer shrugged. "That Shield was exceptionally fast."

"Briar, the Commander of Shields," she said. "That woman lies writhing in agony as your poison courses through her veins."

"Her fault she didn't die there and then," Maddox said, flashing his crooked grin. "Want us to try again? You are a sorcerer – could you not work your arts on her?"

The masked figure shook her head. "No, you are to take no actions until I order it. For now, we must lie low and wait. Many druids, and that accursed Wrendal priestess, walk the halls, wary and watching. Our time will come again once the palace's heightened security slackens off. I will get what I want, no matter the cost."

It was a slow and faltering climb back to awareness. Briar's left leg was still a fiery inferno, but the rotting stench of her dissolving flesh had disappeared from the room. Small mercies, she thought as she struggled up into a sitting position. Her mouth was a desert, and the sour taste of bile lurked at the back of her throat. It felt like she had been unconscious for many more days.

The window shutter was open, and a warm breeze freshened up the room, causing the dangling talismans and wishing ribbons to swish and sway. For some reason her toes felt wet. She was still in the regent's bedroom, now a fully kitted out medical room. Aisling was at the foot of her bed, dressed in a clean white apron and busy wiping Briar's feet with a damp cloth. The servant was thankfully unaccompanied by that unholy demon with the burning eyes Briar had hallucinated in her delirium as her life hovered between this and the otherworld. She recalled from her background checks that the woman had spent several years under service in a hospital near Drew Nemeton before joining the palace staff three and a half years ago, so she was at least competent.

"You are finally awake," the servant said, noticing Briar's eyes were open and watching her. She smiled reassuringly. "Truly, your recovery is a blessing from the spirits."

"It doesn't feel like it," Briar replied in a voice like gravel. "How long have I slept this time?" She smelled fresh baked bread, butter and cheese, and it caused her stomach to growl. The wooden serving tray on the corner table called to her, if only she could muster the strength to crawl out of bed to reach the food on it.

"Eleven days," Aisling said. "The Lord Regent has been pacing the halls in worry and will want me to bring word to him immediately."

Briar gritted her teeth to keep a scream in as she shifted and the blanket rubbed the padding over her leg. If this was the state of it after another eleven days of healing... "I will go to him myself," she gasped, trying to swing her legs out of bed despite the pain. By all the gods, she would damn well walk again.

She almost blacked out.

The servant caught her. "What are you doing, you idiot?" She pushed Briar back into bed with frightening ease. The warrior was as weak as a newborn kitten, and she found such feebleness beyond unsettling.

Aisling pulled a small jar of milky liquid from a pocket in her apron and moved to pull out the stopper. "Best you take this and go back to sleep."

"Enough," Briar said. "The last thing I want is sleep. I will be sure to tell you if I need it."

"At least take these herbs," Aisling said, holding out a pellet the size of a fingernail. "I'm told it will dull the pain."

Briar eyed it suspiciously. "What's in that?"

Aisling dropped it into her hand. "Nothing sacred or special: just dried willow bark, feverfew and a few other things, all wrapped in a boiled nettle leaf."

Briar grimaced as a new wave of pain rippled through her, thanks to her attempt to rise from her sickbed. She popped the pellet in her mouth and chewed. It was like eating salty wood. She choked it down. "Tastes funny."

"Hmm, now that I think about it," Aisling said, "a druid did say something about adding ground-up snails."

Briar gagged and reached to throttle her. The servant brushed her hand aside like she was a child.

Hardgrim sauntered into the bedroom to see what the noise was about, one hand on the hilt of the sword at his hip. The grizzled veteran scanned the room and then rested his gaze on his commander. "Fuck me," he said. "You're still alive, then? A damned shame, so it is: I've been doing a much better job while you've been in here napping."

Briar grunted. The man wasn't even pretending to be relieved. He had been coveting her position for years, as much for the prestige as for the increased daily pay. "Report," she barked. "And help me up." She had to get back to work, to ensure the regent and the palace were properly protected. Hardgrim was solid and dependable, but also hidebound and inflexible in his thinking. He was also an insufferable arse.

The man stiffened, grinding his teeth, but he nodded at the servant to wait outside. She gave him a disapproving scowl but made herself scarce. He barely had time to open his mouth before the regent stormed in from the study, Aisling dogging his heels.

Briar struggled to rise from bed but froze as the regent's furious gaze fell upon her. His jaw muscles clenched, lips thinning in disapproval.

"Hardgrim," he said to his stand-in commander. "Escort Aisling out and guard the door beyond my study." Then his attention turned to Briar. "As for you: you are going nowhere, woman. You are going to sit in bed and not do anything but eat and drink until I deem you well enough. That is an order."

She sagged back into his plump pillows. An order was an order, after all. Also a timely one, given all strength fled her as if from a leaky waterskin.

He approached the bed and held her hand, his smooth noble-soft skin pressing against her own calloused, scarred fingers. "How do you feel?"

"Like I almost died," she said. "And I have a most foul taste in my mouth."

"I came within a whisker of losing you," he said, glancing away and shuddering. The regent laid her hand down and moved over to his drinks cabinet. He pulled out his most expensive pot of metheglin, a sacred mead flavoured with the rarest herbs and spices. He poured a small measure into a silver cup and carried it over to her.

"This was brewed and blessed by the druids of the forest," he said. "The blend of honey and healing herbs is most beneficial. Many a headache of mine has been cured thanks to this."

She sipped at the concoction, and its sweetness chased away the rancid taste in her mouth. The alcohol went straight to her head, numbing some of the pain. Either that or the herbs were more potent than the regent suspected. Bless the druids and their debauched ways.

He retrieved the serving tray from the corner of the room and set it beside her on the bed, then tore off a hunk of bread and used a small silver knife to slather it with a generous portion of strong-smelling butter that was a darker shade of yellow than she was used to.

She nibbled on a corner of it, frowning at the pungent smoky cheesiness. "What is this? Sheep? Goat?"

"Two-hundred-year-old bog butter," he said proudly. "The druids swear by its healing properties."

She dropped the bread to the tray and spat out the rest. "I refuse to eat butter that's been sunk in a peat bog for centuries," she said.

"It's perfectly edible," he said, taking a bite for himself. "The cold waters and darkness preserve it forever. Come, take another bite – you must eat."

"Then bring me meat," she complained. "Not whatever pigswill this is."

He tried to argue with her, but she sighed, closed her eyes and let him rabbit on. Whatever distractions he thought to bring her could not stop her dwelling on the attack and what she should have done better.

"I will have missed the internment," she stated, thinking of the fallen: Cathbad, Sleen and Barik now resting within cold stone tombs in the darkness beneath the palace. Her chest hurt, and it was more than the effects of the poison. If only she had noticed sooner, moved faster...

"You have," he said, resting a hand on her shoulder. "Kester gave a fine eulogy."

She stared at him hard, saying nothing. Not needing to.

"It was beautiful," he hurriedly added. "Truly touching and heartfelt. The boy has never had anybody die for him before. It changes a man."

"The death of my Shields is not a teaching moment for a spoiled brat," she said, perhaps unwisely. But she was exhausted, in pain, and simply did not give a shit about giving offence. She wished for nothing more than to go back to the blessed nothingness of sleep, where everything made sense and nothing could hurt her.

"Of course it is, Shield," he snapped. "Kester will be high king of all the clans of Sunweald in only two years. In the future, many more people will die for him, and he will be the one ordering many of them to their deaths. He *must* be ready."

She was done, too tired to argue. "As you say, Lord Regent."

"I'm sorry," he said. "I have to find the gain in all things. It is how I survive."

The vicious pain in her leg began to dull to a throbbing ache. It seemed the druids' pellets worked at least a little, though they served to dull the senses too. She closed her eyes and felt exhaustion taking her. "I know," she replied, just before she went under again. Her brief bout of anger had taken the last dregs of energy she could muster. Instead of a dreamless rest, she descended into a twisted nightmare of the poison spreading to both legs...

When she woke again, she was entirely alone in the bedroom, which smelled faintly like vinegar and wet dog. The window was shuttered, but the thin, translucent slats of cattle horn that let light in and kept rain out were turning golden, and red rays of dawn light crept around the edges of the frame. Somebody had removed most of the druids' talismans and spells and suchlike from the room – a good sign that she had escaped the cold grasp of the otherworld, at least now. The pain had dwindled to a bone-deep ache with raw edges, but that she could deal with: Shields were no strangers to pain.

She couldn't feel her feet. Both of her legs were heavy and immobile. She panicked and, full of dread, lifted her head to look down at them. Fears of amputation or permanent paralysis rampaged through her imagination.

Brutus was sprawled atop the blankets, pinning her feet. The dog snorted and snored, his paws twitching in the air.

She growled, low and hard.

The regent's dog started and spun round to face her. Mournful eyes stared at the unwanted occupant in his soft bed. He gave a hopeful wag of his tail.

"Get!" she growled, painfully rolling her weakened body from side to side until he grudgingly leapt down. He glared up at her and then huffed, claws clacking away over the floorboards towards his spot by the window in the study.

With nobody left to stop her, she awkwardly shuffled into a sitting position, gritting her teeth against the pain. She debated pulling off the blankets and removing the bandages to get a good look at her leg, but she wasn't sure she could face that quite yet. More important to her was if she would ever walk again. She was a Shield of Sunweald. It wasn't just what she did, it was who she was. If she couldn't walk... The terror of being bed-bound and unable to fight nearly overwhelmed her. What would she do with her life? And what sorry sort of a life would it even be?

She took several deep breaths and then flexed her toes, experimentally moving both feet. So far, so good. Her right leg was just weak, and it bent and flexed as normal. Another deep breath, and then she tried to bend her left knee.

She clamped her jaw shut, stifling the cry of agony. Her eyes welled up, and she shook until the pain ebbed. That... had not been a good result.

A crow alighted on the window ledge and cocked its head at her, blackest of eyes sizing her up.

"I'm not carrion yet, you daft bird," she said.

It cawed as if laughing at her, and then took flight, leaving one of its feathers to drift to the floor. Like the bees, the crows of Sunweald were said to be servants of the otherworld, but instead of carrying news of import, they were charged with carrying the bewildered souls of slain warriors off the field of battle. To be a lonely spirit still walking the land of the living was not a fate any would wish for: to see what you once had, nevermore to touch and taste, would be utmost torment. The crows were worthy of respect for that comforting final service.

She marshalled her bravery and slid back the blankets to examine her legs. Her nightmares had lied: the right leg was entirely fine. The wound on the left was wrapped in bandages and the remnants of another herbal poultice. The blankets were crusted with a mix of dried blood and only a little yellowish fluid. The seepage from her wound smelled, but not of rot, thank the gods. She had to know if she could walk, so she pivoted and swung her legs over the side of the bed, groaning as she did so.

Would her leg bear the weight? Could she recover to fight again? She set her right foot on the cold floor and pressed down. All well and good, if unsteady. Then the left, shuddering and halting.

She stood. For about half a heartbeat, before her leg gave way. Her face slammed into the floorboards, barely felt as the leg screamed, raw and burning. This had not been one of her better plans.

The crow returned to watch her, just in case she'd changed her mind about dying.

CHAPTER 4

Interminable days of recovery oozed past, the boredom driving her mad. Hearth Mistress Morna had noted Briar's problem, and had taken time away from running the palace kitchens each day to teach her how to needle-bind yarn into garments. When not doing frustratingly gentle leg exercises to strengthen her muscles and avoid bedsores, Briar worked on her new craft. The true skill of it escaped the warrior as she wove her bone needle into loops of wool and pulled it through into stitches, but over the next four long, dreary months, she managed to produce serviceable mittens, a hat and two shawls. It kept her hands and mind busy.

After an unconscionably long time, the druids grudgingly stated that Briar could leave the bedroom without enforced supervision and servants watching her every moment. Conquering the ten shuffling steps to and from the latrine adjoining the bedroom, assisted by no more than a walking stick, had been one of her greatest and most difficult victories ever. She reckoned she could have endured some pain and been out of the room and moving about on her own much sooner, but after her previous misadventure the Lord Regent had commanded her to obey the advice of the gaggle of druids who trooped in and out of his bedroom and wait an extra few weeks – and now even that damned Aisling seemed to outrank her, for the moment. Alaric allowed the commander of his Shields many liberties not granted to others in Sunweald, most especially in private, but in this he had been deadly serious.

The Lord Regent would most definitely have her strapped to the bed and sedated again if the druids deemed it necessary for her health.

She had nodded and agreed and endured all the weird rituals and ways of the wise ones, blindly holding on to the hope that they could make it all go away. She had prayed with them, had carved a wooden likeness of her leg and burned it in sacred oils as an offering to the gods that they might recognise her wound and aid in its recovery, and even endured the druids' gory medicinal baths, soaking in hot water with blood, bones, fat and hearts from stout boar and mighty bears so that her weakened body might absorb their potency. She felt stronger as the weeks went by, due perhaps to their mystic arts, or perhaps just to her body naturally recovering from its trauma.

She had done away with the druids' bitter painkilling potions entirely, and only took the less effective herbal pellets when the pain grew too much to bear – and even that reliance was becoming less frequent.

Her own weakness had astonished her. She had gone from being at the peak of fitness for a woman of her age to struggling to walk a hundred paces without being out of breath and gasping in pain – and that with assistance from Aisling! The servant had established herself as a constant but grating necessity in her life, even to the extent of quietly sitting in the shadows for stones while Alaric and Briar talked, just in case her charge needed something. Briar resented having to rely on anybody for anything, but it was unavoidable if she wanted to build her body back up. There wasn't much she could do to hasten the recovery of her leg, but she had started lifting rocks to regain some strength in her upper body. As you got older, she bitterly mused, it wasn't so much that you fought any worse… it was that you hurt more afterwards and took longer to recover. Aches and strains that would once have vanished in days now lingered for weeks, months, even seasons.

Her left leg was not what it was, and it never would be, from what every wise one told her. But to her immense relief, it was slowly regaining some of its prior strength. She was now able to hobble short distances on her own, with a stick taking some of the weight, and she was starting to retrain that clumsy, disobedient leg to obey her commands. She had never worked so hard in her life – the fear of being bed-bound was immense. She had come to terms with nothing at all, instead stubbornly clinging to the past and hopes of a miracle as long as humanly possible. People were wrong all the time, she assured herself, even know-it-all druids and Wrendal sorcerer-priests.

She rose at the crow of dawn, determined to be up and out of the room before Aisling arrived to tend to her needs while spying on her. Today, the regent was closeted in council meetings elsewhere in the palace from dawn until dusk, affording her a rare chance to escape without him being there to order her back into bed. She had until now only roamed the nearby hall and rooms, but her plans today went further.

After months of rest and recovery, it was time to undertake a long-overdue task: to visit the tombs of the fallen Shields in the depths of the palace and pay her respects to Cathbad, Sleen and Barik. She had been their commander, and they had died on her watch. She had lingered in bed long enough.

She heaved her legs out of bed and dressed herself. She opened the chest beside the bed and looked long and hard at her standard Shield uniform of padded tunic and studded leather kilt before reluctantly setting it aside in favour of a light, loose smock. The poison that bastard archer had used meant her wound had not yet fully healed, and anything that rubbed her leg would be torture.

She prepared like she was embarking on a military operation, ransacking the regent's rooms for her key to the catacombs, waterskin, beeswax candles, a hunk of bread and cheese, painkilling pellets and spare bandages. She dropped them all into a satchel and tested her most vital equipment before heading out – in this case, trying and failing to bend or break the new walking stick Alaric had given her. The thing was as solid as a tree trunk. It had belonged to his formidable grandmother and had seemingly been crafted to withstand a bulk far in excess of Briar's. She could easily crack a man's skull with it, a comforting thing when she felt naked without sword and buckler. She didn't even have a belt knife, for a woman in her sickbed "does not need weapons when she has guards", apparently. Alaric, for all his intelligence, was a man, and could not understand why a woman might feel more comfortable having a blade close to hand.

She finished her packing and noticed that her stubbornly optimistic crow was back on the window ledge, this time with a shiny pin of carved antler clutched in its beak. A few of its curious kin accompanied it this time. It dropped the pin on the ledge and hopped back, head quirking this way and that. She scooped the pin into her belt pouch and fed the bird a morsel of her bread in recompense for her stubbornly surviving flesh. It had been a regular but undemanding visitor all throughout her recovery, and one of the few things she had to look forward to each day. At some point, the bird had figured out how to barter goods for food, meaning it was already as clever as Kester. She put out a handful of extra crumbs for its kin and wished them a good day. Crows had long memories for those who treated them well, and they bore grudges even longer.

She slung her bag across her chest and, leaning on her stick, set off on her trek. The journey from the bedroom to the study and then the door was uneventful, if prolonged.

Shields Iden and Ruith were stationed outside, in the hallway. Iden smiled and nodded at her, but Ruith frowned, his beeswaxed moustache quivering in annoyance. He blocked her path. "You are meant to be resting, Commander," he chided, his full lips pursed in disapproval. Another overly entitled wayward son of a noble clan Hardgrim had taken under his wing, one that hadn't yet had enough sense beaten into him.

The man had been promoting many more of their sort to bolster security during her convalescence, and she wasn't best pleased with most of his Youngbloods. As soon as she was well, there would be sweeping changes.

Briar silenced him with a withering glare. She was not about to be told what to do by a man not yet able to grow a fulsome beard. Apart from Iden, all of Hardgrim's Youngbloods thought more highly of themselves than their achievements deserved. "It is time I made my way to the tombs," she said.

Ruith froze, thinking furiously, possibly pitting his somewhat vague orders from the regent against his commander's wrath.

Iden put a hand on his shoulder. "Better let the commander past to pay her respects to the fallen."

Ruith cleared his throat and stepped aside, his back pressed to the wall. He pretended he didn't see her. She nodded approvingly at Iden. The young man rose in her estimations again as he steadfastly ignored her slow, laboured journey down the hallway.

Shield Gwilherm was in the chamber beyond, and he raised an eyebrow as she slowly exited the hallway and made her way towards the spiral staircase at the far end of the hall. His short hair was greying, and his scars told tales of a dozen brutal fights. "Commander," he said, with a nod. "What should I tell him when he asks awkward questions?"

"Just taking some early-morning exercise," she replied.

He pointedly looked at the doorways to the left and right of the chamber, leading down other corridors where a person might walk without obstacle. "Heading down the stairs?" he queried, brow furrowed. "Is that wise?"

She shrugged. "Probably not. I'm bound for the tombs."

Understanding dawned. Gwilherm nodded gravely. "Exercise. Understood. I will give you as much time as I can before they find out you are missing, and I'll make sure that Ruith and his lot keep their mouths shut. Gods, I loathe being on duty with those pompous pricks – why Hardgrim recruited and promoted them, I'll never know." He eyed the walking stick with distaste. "You take care, now."

She nodded in acceptance and resumed her trek, hobbling on, slowly mustering all of her willpower and courage to face a foe more dreadful and implacable than any she had ever before encountered. Finally, she stood at the top of the spiral staircase and stared down the bare stone steps. A daunting prospect for somebody with an aching leg liable to betray her at any opportunity. She gritted her teeth and began to work her way down, one step at a time, right hand using the wall to steady her descent. By the time she passed the ground floor and approached the entrance to the catacombs, she was drenched in sweat, and her left leg was trembling from the strain. Pain spiked through her thigh with every lurching step. Lying in her sickbed had robbed her body of strength and stamina, but she was determined to fight on and win it back. The relief when she made that final landing was as acute as surviving a life-or-death battle, except this one was against her own weakness. She had never feared any man or woman as much as those gods-damned steps.

She leant back against the wall, chest heaving and heart pounding at her ribs as she caught her breath. Her knee was a ball of fire, and she was forced to take another of the druids' painkilling pellets and wait for it to take the edge off. The chamber at the bottom of the stairs was dimly lit by a smoky cattle-fat lantern, its clay pot hanging from a hook next to the heavy oak door. The door hadn't been closed and locked by the last person to come through. She shook her head, tutting at the sloppiness of whichever Shields were on duty. She would uncover their names and chew them up and spit them out later.

The doorway was surrounded by seven niches, three to each side and one at the top, all containing the skull of a long-dead Shield whose spirit remained beyond death to guard the catacombs of Sunweald from evil spirits. The way ahead was a descent into Mother Earth that brought mortals into the bosom of ancient deities of the land, and it was devoid of all natural light. Briar did not require a lantern, not in this place where she knew every nook and cranny. She closed and secured the door behind her and moved on into the ancient tunnels, careful of her stick on the wet, slippery floor. The catacombs were far older than the generations of construction built atop it. Much of it had been carved from the bones of the earth by the ancestors, and the dressed stonework down here was cruder work than Sunweald's masons were now capable of. Indeed, the new palace at Drew Nemeton was a work of art in comparison, one far less cold and draughty and crumbling than Sunweald's current seat of power.

The tunnels were barely wide enough for two people to walk abreast, and in the oldest parts the ceilings were strangely high, probably carved to accommodate those fae creatures the Sleaghan Mhath, the elder race who had dwelled in Sunweald's forests before human histories began. The druids usually claimed that the catacombs marked a thin place betwixt earth and otherworld and that the site was meant for ritual use. Some also claimed there was an actual gateway into the otherworld to be found deeper in the darkness. It was an eerie place, right enough, but Briar held a different opinion than the druids: due to the narrow tunnels she had always assumed it was made for defence. A handful of warriors could hold off an entire army in this place.

Water dripped in the distance, but otherwise all was silent, just the way she liked it. Cooler air chilled her sweaty brow as she walked into the darkness, but though her eyes were blind, she knew the feel of every stone beneath her feet, recognised every doorway and branching passage from the feel of the air and the sound of her footfalls. The pathways and shallow, ancient steps were worn into hollows from the passage of countless feet. She took her time and eventually came to a Y-shaped intersection, where she listened to the voices coming from the right-hand branch. Up ahead, four Shields were talking, their voices muted. The glow of lanterns could be glimpsed through a peephole set into the foot-thick solid-bronze door that protected the Heart of Sunweald, a sizable cavern where the crown and the most important historical relics of the realm were stored, including the shrines and preserved remains of the Summerson ancestors. The Heart and all its mortal treasures were guarded day and night by vigilant Shields, but for all its importance, they were as nothing compared to the mystical Wyrm Vault embedded in the back wall of the cavern, so named due to the bones of those ancient and terrible beasts imprisoned inside the natural stone. The Vault was guarded by most potent druidic magic and contained no gold, jewellery or other merely mundane valuables – those were kept in a strongroom in the upper palace – but something far more dangerous: arcane artefacts. The Wrendal faithful were obsessed with worshipping such holy items, and the Ves were desperate to possess them as terrible weapons that conferred untold power and influence. To the rulers of Sunweald, these artefacts were only as holy or unholy as the people using them, and as such were not to be entrusted to any mortal hand. The Wyrm Vault had not been opened in nine years and, with the mercy of the gods, never would be again.

Briar took the left-bearing branch and trudged along a downward-sloping tunnel. Somebody had been here recently, judging from the lanterns lit along the path. She unhooked one from the wall and gave it a shake, listening to the semi-liquid cattle fat sloshing inside the pot. It would last a couple of stones, maybe less. Whoever it was did not know the catacombs and, taking into account the number of lanterns they had lit, most definitely feared its darkness. Briar rather liked the place: she felt at home in the peace and quiet and had enjoyed exploring on her few days off. So many of the deeper tunnels and chambers had never been mapped by others, or if they had been, then any record was forgotten in a dusty pile of scrolls somewhere, unseen in centuries. She found the thrill of discovery exhilarating and had hoped to venture even deeper in the coming years. She brought Alaric down here once, years ago now, and while he shared her interest in the history of the catacombs, he lacked the time to spend entire days on an expedition, or indeed time to indulge in any hobby whatsoever.

The catacombs were not as eternally peaceful as might be expected by surface-dwellers, for water constantly dripped from above to form spikes of stone, and the earth too moved, grumbling in its millennia of slumber, its skin cracking and splitting. The path leading to the Hall of Broken Shields was carpeted in its sheddings, a gravel that crunched underfoot. With so many staff and Shields being sent off to prepare Drew Nemeton, too few remained to sweep these rarely frequented tunnels of debris.

She limped onwards, listening intently. Her legs might have been weak, but her hearing was as strong as ever. The murmur of prayers reached her long before her own careful footfalls could alert whatever living soul had intruded in the Hall of Broken Shields. She kept a firm grip on the head of her walking stick.

Lit by two more lanterns, the path ahead was blocked by an entire wall of bronze bars, with only a narrow opening leading to the hallway beyond. They had once been a shining golden hue but were now green with verdigris and centuries of stony deposits that seeped down from the ceiling, almost as if the earth was slowly reabsorbing the space hacked out by human hands so very long ago. Assuming they were human hands, of course. In such a dark, silent place, the old tales seemed much more real than when she was walking free under the sun and sky.

Her attention was caught by a flickering light at the end of the long hallway beyond the bars of bronze. Light danced across the hundreds of upright tombs carved into the rock walls. Every single tomb was capped with a truthful likeness of the loyal Shield interred within: Ablar the Bold, whose ugliness was as legendary as his kindness, Elena Swiftkill, who slayed the seven Sacred Blades of Ethinil after fighting seven deadly duels in a row, Sersha Stormspear, Brigant the Breaker... and so many more whose stories were familiar friends.

Whoever had ventured into this hallowed place was located where the newly fallen had been interred. A slight, cloaked figure knelt at the foot of one of those tombs, a beeswax candle and holder on the floor beside them. A surge of anger had Briar clenching her jaw – whoever this was, they were no Shield and had no business here.

She stepped through the opening in the corroded bronze bars and had to grab on for dear life as her unruly left foot twisted beneath her. Her gasp of pain alerted the intruder, who shot to his feet and turned to face her.

The Royal Heir, Kester, gaped at her, a look of terror on his unexpectedly gaunt face. His previously curly locks had been cut short and severe, and his eyes were red and shadowed. His foot knocked over the candle and it rolled towards her, sputtering and flickering. He scrambled after it, hands flailing and missing.

Briar swallowed her pain and strode forward, leaning on her stick. "What are *you* doing here?" she demanded, drawing close.

Kester finally retrieved his candle, and he stood there like a frightened rabbit, his wide eyes searching the shadows for another exit. There were none from this place but the one behind her, so far as he could see. His fear flipped to haughty denial – he was about to be a king, after all, and was well used to getting what he wanted. "I can go wherever I like," he said in a quivering voice.

He was not yet grown to his full height, and for now Briar was taller. She reached out with her right hand and seized him by the clasp of his cloak. He yelped as she yanked him close to her face. "This is no place for queens, kings or regents, druids or soothsayers, nor little boys playing stupid games," she said coldly. "This is the Hall of Broken Shields, and it is our domain alone. Here, all you are is somebody that got Barik killed."

He struggled to say something, anything, in objection, but a look at her darkening expression caused all that to flee his head. Instead, he wriggled out of his cloak and slipped from her grasp like an oiled eel. She cursed, flung the cloak aside and made to give chase as he took to his heels.

Her knee gave way, pitching her to the stone with a cry of pain and frustration. The walking stick clattered down out of reach.

Kester glanced back. He slowed, then stopped his flight, chewing on his bottom lip. The boy returned, shamefaced and silent, to pick up her stick and hand it to her.

She spat in the face of the boy's pity, spurned his offer of a hand and clambered to her feet under her own power, savouring every gods-damned ache and pain. She was about to chew him up and spit him out when she spied exactly what he had been doing in this sacred place. At the end of the hall, the stone likenesses of Cathbad, Sleen and Barik serenely awaited their commander, and before each of their tombs he had placed ritual offerings of small cups of mead and posies of wildflowers tied with prayer ribbons. Abruptly, her ire drained away into a pit of loss and exhaustion.

Kester swallowed and sweated, looked at his feet and nervously waited for her to shout and chastise him.

"Why?" she asked.

He dredged his gaze up to meet her own, and she found his eyes churning with... shame. Yes, shame. "I... I should have fought," he said, hands curling up into trembling fists. "Instead I curled up into a ball and cried." His face contorted as he attempted to hold back the tears welling up. "It's all my fault," he sobbed, then laughed cruelly. "The coward king that cried.

The blood of queens, kings and great warriors flows through my veins, and yet I am useless. I have shamed my ancestors. I am even afraid of the dark!"

She looked at the boy, for a boy he still was. Not a king and not a warrior, just a youth trying to figure out his place in the world after making a terrible mistake, and yet one that was not his fault. He had all the luxuries the world had to offer, but no living parents to guide him through its perils and temptations. She sighed. "Help me down to my knees." She didn't bother with honorifics, not in this sacred place.

He blinked in surprise, but offered his arm, and she took it, awkwardly lowering herself to the cold stone floor in front of the three newest tombs. With the condition of her left leg, properly kneeling was out of the question, so she had to sit there with it sticking out straight and ungainly. Kester knelt beside her, his eyes expectant, pleading.

"Do Shields seem like cowards to you?" Briar said.

He gawped at her in disbelief. "No!"

"You think us fearless," she said, staring at the stone faces of her fallen Shields. "That is exactly what we want everybody to think. The truth is we are as scared as anybody else. The only difference is that we are accustomed to that fear, and we use it instead of letting it use us. You would be surprised at the terrible things you can get used to, with enough exposure."

He stared at her, a dozen fleeting expressions appearing and disappearing as he tried to make sense of her words.

"What do you imagine Barik felt as you cowered at her feet?" Briar continued, merciless.

All colour fled his face. He swallowed and wrapped his arms around his chest, staring at the floor.

"Answer me," she snapped.

"Disgust," he croaked.

"Wrong," she replied. "As if Barik had time for that nonsense. What else?"

"Fear," he added.

"Naturally," Briar continued.

His eyes lifted. "Why didn't she run?"

"It's not who we are," Briar said. "We protect Sunweald and its rulers – if we run, then what are we for? I imagine she mostly felt bloody furious. She might have survived that fight if she hadn't been hobbled."

His eyes moistened, overflowing with hurt.

"I am not your mother, here to coddle you," Briar said. "I say this as a cold, hard fact. She also might have died from her wounds afterwards. We'll never know."

"I killed her," he said, staring at his hand as if it was still drenched in his Shield's blood.

Briar nodded grimly. "It was a mercy killing. I also hastened Cathbad's end. Best they did not linger on to finally perish in excruciating agony when we could make their ends quick and painless. You would relieve a dying animal from its torment, would you not? It should be no different for us."

"What can I do?" he pleaded. "I... I... I don't know what to do!"

"Barik kept you alive," Briar said. "In that, she won. All you can do now is not be such a drunken little letch. You will be high king in a year and a half. What you can do now is do your fucking job. Imagine her spirit is watching you from the otherworld, and do not let her death be pointless."

He stared at her, about to say something heartfelt. But his wet eyes widened at the sight of something past her shoulder. "Assassin," he hissed.

Briar glanced up at the man in the doorway, night-dark cloth wrapped around his mouth and nose to disguise his features. Under that cloak, a cheap tunic and dirty shoes. He seemed surprised to see her accompanying the Royal Heir, but it wasn't enough to make him abandon his plans: he drew a pair of slim knives from his belt and cautiously advanced into the darkened Hall of Broken Shields. The bronze blades glinted blood-red in the candlelight.

"Get me up, and then stay behind me," Briar ordered Kester, cursing her lack of buckler and blade.

The boy stood and grabbed her arm, heaving her up on shaky feet. The assassin was halfway to them by the time Briar was ready to face him. For now, she leant on her walking stick with feigned nonchalance, but she was ready to whip the sturdy length of wood up at a moment's notice.

"What do you want here?" she demanded.

The man lingered in a black absence of light, saying nothing. A knife flashed through the air. Briar didn't move a step. She lifted her stick and swatted the blade aside. "Is that all you have?" she taunted. "What kind of idiot throws their weapons away?"

Another knife followed. Whoever he was, the assassin was no expert blade-thrower – the hilt bounced off the tomb beside her and clattered to the stone by her foot. "Kester, fetch me that knife," she demanded, eyes relentlessly scanning the hall. The boy hastily retrieved it and slapped the hilt into her palm. She hefted it and studied the darkness, waiting. If he was so willing to part with two blades then he probably had more, but her sturdy walking stick had a much greater reach if he was unwise enough to come close.

At the first hint of movement in the darkness, her hand and knife flicked out. The assassin grunted from an impact, but whether from blunt hilt or blade buried in flesh she couldn't tell. She was far more adept with a shepherd's sling and stones than throwing good knives away. "Hurry up and toss that weapon back again," she shouted. "Shall we make a game of this and see who throws better?"

The masked man rushed from the darkness, knife plunging for her heart. The heavy walking stick came up to crack into first his elbow and then his face. The knife fell from his spasming fingers, but the man crashed into her, and they went down hard with him on top. He was heavier and hadn't spent months bedridden. Fists hammered down on her face, and she was unable to fend them all off. She didn't even try: her strength was shit and her stamina abysmal – there was no possibility of overpowering or outlasting the man. The only way to win was to outfight him.

She tasted blood and spat it in his eyes. A moment of distraction was all she needed. Her good knee jerked up and caught him in the crotch. He cried out, half blind and gasping. She summoned her meagre reserves for a quick succession of strikes: a palm strike burst his nose, followed by a punch to the throat and a liver shot between the lower ribs on the right side. He groaned and sagged atop her, realising he had made a terrible mistake. She sank her teeth into his ear and rammed her knee up into his crotch again. He howled and tore himself free, leaving part of his ear behind. He rolled away, blood gushing down his face.

It was a clumsy reprieve from her savage assault, but one that still took him out of reach and away from an easy finish to the fight. Had Briar been fit and healthy, the bastard would have been dead a heartbeat later.

She spat his flesh out and chuckled, low and malevolent. "Come, let us play some more. Next time I'll rip your throat out with my teeth."

The assassin flinched and staggered two steps further back, one hand clamped to the side of his head, and the other cupping his brutalised balls. He yelped, stiffened and spun. Briar glimpsed a knife jutting from his shoulder. Kester stood behind him, staring at his own hand.

The assassin reached back over his shoulder and wrenched the weapon free.

"Move, boy!" A sudden terror lent her strength enough to grab her stick and fight to her feet.

The boy heeded her command and dived aside. A clumsy slash sailed through the space where his face had been.

She lurched towards the assassin, who quailed before her fury and limped for the exit, slow yet still too swift for her to catch. He retreated through the narrow opening in the bronze bars, moaning in pain, and extinguished the two lanterns in the tunnel beyond, plunging that area into total darkness. The only exit to this hall was a damned good place for an assassin to wait in ambush – assuming it was, in fact, the only exit.

"Nobody knows we are here," she said to Kester. "We are on our own."

"What shall we do?" he whispered, huddling close to a stone tomb behind her.

She flashed a bloodied smile and replied in a calm, low voice. "What you do, Kester, is you snuff out that candle. I'll show you a secret tunnel only two other people know about. Call it a reward for your bravery in sticking him with a knife. Not such a coward as you supposed, eh?"

He balked at the idea. "We'll be blind – I..."

"So what if you are afraid of the dark?" she said. "I promise you, boy, you should be far more afraid of me and that assassin out there than any evil spirit."

He shuddered and snuffed out the candle.

She grabbed his hand and led him to the side of a tomb. "This belongs to Quinn the Eel," she whispered, "a paranoid Shield who escaped death ninety-nine times, and then had his tomb built many years before he died in hopes of making it a nice round hundred." Her fingernails dragged across the old stone until they caught an almost-invisible crack. She gritted her teeth and pulled, fingers aching as the stone ground back to reveal a low chamber behind it. She guided Kester to crawl in, then followed and slid the stone back into place. Inside, there was no sign that any linen-wrapped corpse had ever been laid to rest under Quinn's shield of office.

"Where is his body?" Kester whispered, hands groping the way ahead.

"Where indeed..." she replied. "Maybe he succeeded in escaping death one last time. Now shush and get crawling, and if you break wind I swear I will bite a bloody big chunk out of your arse."

When the assassin got bored of waiting to ambush them and ventured back into the hall, he would be sorely puzzled and most disappointed to find his target long gone.

CHAPTER 5

Alaric Summerson was sat at his desk aggressively stamping his seal into beeswax on parchments with enough force to dent the wood beneath. Of the commander of his Shields there was no sign. She was not nearby, which meant she must have risen at the crow of dawn, avoided Aisling and, in her precarious condition, taken the spiral stairs down the tower.

"Went for a walk, did she...?" he growled, cursing the Shields for allowing her to wander off. He dreaded receiving a report of her broken body being found at the foot of stairs somewhere. He swept the sealed scrolls off his desk and into a basket to the side, uncaring of any damage he caused his missives to foreign princes and priests. His shaking hand hovered over the quill and ink, ready to write his next angry letter – but he'd already stabbed holes through three pieces of pristine parchment and thought better of it.

A knock at the door caused his head to jerk up and the quill to fall from his fingers.

Shield Ruith answered. An exchange of harsh words followed.

The regent shot to his feet. "Have they found her?"

"Bram the librarian is here," Ruith said, lip curled in disdain. "He demands to see you and is not taking no for an answer. Shall I ensure the scroll-worm does not dare to disturb you again?"

"Let the man in," Alaric snarled. "So, he demands an audience, does he? Well, we shall certainly give him one he won't soon forget. Let him in and then get out. No witnesses. I'm sure you understand what I mean, Ruith."

The young shield smirked and nodded. "So shall it be." He yanked the door wide, grabbed the librarian by the front of his tunic, hauled him in then stepped outside to keep out any further interruptions.

The lanky, balding librarian with watery eyes swallowed and bobbed his head in greeting. "Lord Regent," he said in a nasal, whining voice. "I have come about–"

"You *demand* an audience?" Alaric roared. "Exactly who do you think you are to demand anything from me? You are a nobody, while I am the Lord Regent!" His voice shook with rage. "You dare... you dare..." he slapped Bram hard enough to leave a red handprint on his cheek. Outside, Ruith chuckled at the smack of flesh and yelp of a man crashing to the floor.

The librarian was on his back, staring up at Alaric. He knelt down beside Bram and winced at the mark he'd left. "By the gods, man," he whispered, "what are you doing up here in the tower? My master of spies is my greatest secret, and you should never be seen in this study lest somebody suspect how important you are. I'm so terribly sorry for the violence shown to you."

"Please stop!" the librarian shouted, before lowering his voice. "Unavoidable, my Lord: your commander and the Royal Heir crawled out of the secret tunnel behind my fireplace a short while ago, covered in dust and sporting fresh bruises but otherwise intact. There has been another assassination attempt, I'm afraid. The Shields have been alerted, and you should get an official report shortly."

"What did you just say?" Alaric shouted, not even pretending this time. He stamped about the room, cursing and kicking anything within reach, thinking furiously. He knelt back down and spoke more quietly. "If anybody asks, say you found her at the bottom of some steps. An unfortunate accident to explain away the bruises. Let the healers have at her if necessary, but I want both of those troublemakers brought up to my study as soon as possible. Have Briar carried here if you must." He clapped a hand on his master of spies' shoulder. "I promise to make up for this indignity later on."

Bram nodded and carefully ripped the collar of his tunic. "Throw me out of the door, and I will make for you a most magnificent sprawl and crawl."

They did just that, and Ruith nodded approvingly as the lanky librarian fell on his face, drooling blood and spit. The Shield's foot up his backside got him crawling for the stairs and a swift exit.

"Imbecile!" Alaric said as he retreated to his desk. "Worms! He comes to me about a problem with worms eating his books and scrolls. Gods and spirits, if he was not the only one to know where everything is in that dusty old library, I would have him replaced for that instead of letting him off with a beating." He resumed his writing and found his hand smooth and the text free of tears and blots. They were safe: that was all he needed to know.

It was not long before a Shield arrived to give him the report, advising that a party had already gone in to scour the catacombs in search of the assassin. Briar and Kester were escorted into his study shortly after, both somewhat bedraggled and wearing dust-caked clothes. His commander sported a crusted lip and a remarkable array of bruises just beginning to bloom across her face, but at least somebody had given the cuts a proper clean. She was leaning heavily on his grandmother's walking stick with one hand while the Royal Heir supported her weight on the other, without either of them seeming to begrudge the aid. The regent found that most surprising.

With a face like thunder, he waved Ruith out. When the door was closed, they retreated to the bedroom, and he pulled the curtains closed over the doorway to ward off unpleasant draughts and eavesdroppers. "Dear gods and spirits," he said. "It is good to see you both alive." Then he glared at Briar. "Report."

She groaned as she sat down on the bed without asking permission, rubbing her aching, swollen knee. Kester stood there, sweating and wringing his hands, fearful of kindling his uncle's wrath as Briar told him about everything, including her woeful inability to beat a somewhat lacklustre assassin.

Alaric paced back and forth, chewing on stray wisps of his beard. "The main thing is that you escaped serious harm." He glanced at her bruised face, then to her knee, and his face darkened. "Kester, where were the Shields assigned to guard you?"

The boy swallowed. "Gave them the slip. I wanted to be alone."

The regent slapped a hand to his forehead and began massaging his temple. "As for you, Briar, what in the gods' names were you doing going down those stairs alone in your condition?" His hand dropped, and his eyes blazed with fury. "What if you fell?"

She shrugged. "Then it would be my mistake."

All anger drained from his expression until it became a calm-and-collected blank slate.

"I took it slow and steady," she swiftly added, knowing that when he went so calm, he was truly angry, truly dangerous. "I kept one hand on the wall all the way down. I have no desire to die just yet."

A measure of emotion returned to the regent's face as he frowned at her. "Now you've knackered that knee again. You'll be longer recovering now than if you had done as you were told in the first place and laid up a while longer."

She sighed. "Good thing I'm such a bull-headed and stubborn woman, or your nephew here would have had his throat slit from ear to ear."

Kester paled and clutched his neck. "Thank you for saving me. Again."

"You stuck a knife in the assassin," she replied. "We can call it even this time. I didn't think you had it in you. Neither did you, I wager. It seems we were both wrong."

"Who knew you were bound for the tombs?" Alaric asked his nephew.

The boy shrugged and shook his head mutely.

The regent sighed. "No doubt some miscreant has been spying on your movements. They must have seen you fleeing from your own Shields and followed you down there."

"The door to the catacombs was left open," Briar said, looking at Kester. "This genius didn't secure it behind him, and anybody could have come and gone that way."

Kester's brow furrowed. "But I was su–"

"Why were you in the tombs in the first place?" Alaric stormed over to his nephew and stared down at him. "Drinking? Fornicating with some disgusting overly ambitious harlot?"

The boy froze, wide-eyed and tongue-tied.

"He appeared to be paying his respects to the dead," Briar interjected grudgingly.

Alaric stared at him for a long moment. "Were you now." He pivoted to Briar. "Commander, what are your recommendations?"

"Double security at all vital areas," she said. "Have warriors sweep every inch of the palace and its grounds for intruders, especially the wing under repair. The catacombs too should be searched for traces, though anything could easily get lost in that maze of tunnels. The assassin has a freshly broken nose, a chunk of ear missing and a stab wound in the left shoulder, so all the male servants and guests should be inspected on the off chance they are stupid enough not to be long gone."

"I'll have it done," the regent replied. "Let us hope they have misstepped and left some sort of evidence behind."

Deep in the catacombs, the would-be assassin Bevyn groaned in pain and slumped down onto the remnants of an ancient altar, or at least he assumed that was what it was from the primitive carvings of bears and wolves all over it. A horned well-muscled man adored the centre – the Horned God, master of the hunt. The dim light of his candle hinted at shadowy animals on the walls and ceiling too. The stained bowl carved into the stone top might have once held sanctified spring water or holy oils. Maybe blood – hopefully animal and not human. Now it cupped his buttocks as he sat atop it, winding strips of cloth around his head and the wound in his shoulder. Being a practical sort of man who assumed druids and priests were all charlatans unless he could see their power with his own eyes, he didn't fear the wrath of distant gods or spirits more than his own employer's.

He'd thought he had the perfect chance to get rid of their little problem. He'd used the key he'd been given and followed Briar down into the catacombs. It had all been nice and quiet, like, and he'd figured it would be a great place to hide a body. He would have had her too if the boy hadn't been there mucking things up. His boss needed the royal coward alive, so he'd ignored the brat and got on with killing Briar. Who'd have ever expected that whiny little runt to stick him with a knife?

Bevyn looked up and swallowed. His masked employer was right there and busy pacing the chamber, ranting about his foolishness and waving a deadly knife about – a wyrm-bone-hilted arcane artefact that sparked and hissed and glowed orange like it had just been drawn from a fire.

"Come on, Imperatrix, how was I meant to know there'd be two of them in there?" he complained. "No idea how they upped and vanished into the air, either. Ain't nobody said old Briar could still fight. You claimed–"

Imperatrix spun to face him, the white-painted mask she wore seeming to snarl at him, the eyes behind it furious. "You were all told to lie low until the fuss caused by the solstice attack died down," she said, her voice distorted. "I ordered you to watch and await my next command. Now, did I tell you to try to kill anybody? Well? Did I?"

He cleared his throat. "Not exactly. But our target was alone, and I just–"

"And nothing," she growled, pointing the artefact at him, sparks leaping from the end towards his face. "I pay you to do exactly what *I* tell you to, not to enact whatever idiocy you want. I swear to the gods, if you have ruined this venture for us, I will rip out your organs one by one while you still live. Why did I ever think to trust you?"

Bevyn shuddered. "Ain't nobody more dedicated to this mission than me. Us deep-forest folk have no good farming land, no wealth and no opportunity to live free of Sunweald's control and taxes. I've watched my woman put three babes in the ground thanks to bad food and disease. We got nothin' but what we can take, and I mean to take all I can get."

Steps in the tunnel outside stilled them. The crunch of gravel was coming right for them. Bevyn cloaked his face and drew his knife as a dim light began to show from the entrance to the chamber. He swallowed, fearing an armed Shield had discovered them. He was right.

Hardgrim stepped into view, dressed in shining bronze scale. "I finally found you. The palace is in an uproar."

Bevyn lowered his knife and sighed in relief. "You scared the crap out of me. Imperatrix here was about ready to cut me up for dinner."

Hardgrim chuckled. "She's a bloodthirsty one, right enough." He clapped the assassin on the bloodied shoulder, making him hiss. "Return your key to the catacombs." The failed assassin handed it over, shamefaced. "Don't worry," Hardgrim added as he slipped it into his belt pouch. "I'll fix everything."

Bevyn didn't see it coming. He felt something punch him in the chest. A wave of weakness overcame him with shocking swiftness, and he slumped to the floor, puzzled and panting. He lay there confused and gasping for breath as his world darkened along with the front of his bloody tunic. He pawed at his chest, and his hand came away dripping red. "Oh," he said. "You absolute fucker." Then he said no more.

* * *

Hardgrim wiped his knife on the assassin's clothing. "Stupid prick has made everything so much harder for us. We couldn't have a wounded one-eared man roaming about to squeal on us when he got caught, especially not common-born scum like him. We'll need to delay the operation even further until security relaxes again."

Imperatrix sighed behind her mask. "How long? I need this task accomplished by winter. I have orders to fill, and Ves princelings eager to pay me fortunes for more artefacts. Uradech and his reivers grow ever more impatient for the fortune I promised them."

He shrugged. "It's complicated. Briar was well named – she's a real thorn in my side. After that first debacle of an assassination attempt, I'd wanted to wait for the right chance to try to dispose of her and Alaric. I wish she'd just succumbed to the poison and her wounds. That stink... It would have been understandable. Expected, even."

Imperatrix snorted. "Impossible. With the Wrendal priestess supervising Aisling as she saw to Briar's health day and night, I did not dare make any attempt. The risk of being exposed was much too great: you can be sure that cold fish of a Lord Regent would have summoned every druid, wise one and Wrendal priest that he could force to come in order to determine the exact cause of death of his precious commander. They would most certainly have uncovered that some among his people were working against him."

"Fair," Hardgrim admitted. "Just a shame is all I'm saying. I really thought that poisoned arrow would have done for the bitch."

"Get your house in order," she said. "Everything is arranged on my side, and the reivers are ready for the attack. I just need you to hold up your end of the bargain and open the doors when the time is right. This winter would be best. Can you do it?"

Hardgrim grimaced, reining in his temper and weighing up his options. Eventually, he nodded. "Late winter, when the snows are thick but soon to melt. I reckon it can be done, but with the increased security right now it won't be easy to get my people into position."

"See it done," she replied. "No excuses."

He sighed. "Aye. I'll go drag this corpse back and say I've caught the last assassin. In a few months, when all is nice and quiet, we'll arrange for Briar's disposal, and I'll have total control of the Shields. Then you can have everything I've promised you and more."

Hardgrim needed this to work. Their bargain would supply him with enough livestock and gold to live in the luxury he deserved. He again cursed his uncle for sending him off to this dreary place with only a sword and a pouch of silver to his name, forced to bow and scrape to that tedious wretch of a regent. Soon he would never need to serve another again. He imagined setting himself up as a mighty Lord of the Ves with a fine hill fort, herds, women and wine. I deserve the whole lot of it, he told himself.

Imperatrix paused, thinking. "You have been true to your word, helping me to smuggle artefacts across the borders over the last few years, and I will be true to mine. I trust your greed, and it is good business to keep your partners happy and invested. One way or another, all of our obstacles need to be dealt with before we can seize the entire contents of the Wyrm Vault."

CHAPTER 6

It was a long, slow road to recovery, but six months after her wounding, Briar was up and able to walk without relying on her stick. Only half a year... the realisation made her chuckle hollowly as she laid out the padded tunic and studded leather kilt of her Shield uniform on her bed, and then her sword and buckler.

Her breath misted the chill winter air as she checked her equipment. She'd spent all of summer and much of autumn sat at a window watching the days pass, with only the rare visitor, ungratefully received, for she'd been in no mood for pity or pleasantries. She didn't need condolences, just their understanding. Briar's grizzled old veterans, like Gwilherm, were the only exceptions, having known many wounded warriors in their time, often missing limbs. They kept her sane by keeping her abreast of local news and internal developments, sharing their troves of terrible jokes, and most of all by treating her no differently to usual – save when she chose to ask for a little assistance.

She had also endured Exalted Carmanilla's visits to check up on her, but it was obvious the ambassador was attempting to befriend her in order to exert even more influence over regent and realm. Briar was unfailingly polite to the ambassador: it was the least she could do after the woman had helped save her life. After a few visits, she even came to admire the priestess a little. She was just so good at what she did: beautiful, intelligent, ruthless, stubborn, charismatic, cold and cunning. The woman had even managed to place another of her magical listening devices in Briar's room without her noticing – if the Shield hadn't developed a healthy paranoia over the years, she'd never have thought to check for it. Alas, for all Carmanilla's efforts and expense, she might as well try to get blood from a stone. Not that the woman was going to give up any time soon. At least she brought more of those painkilling pellets with her on each visit. Briar was trying to wean herself off a reliance on them, but she still kept them in a jar by her bed just in case: nobody else was aware of the times her leg felt like the blood was boiling and the tendons taut and ready to snap. They couldn't see the fiery pain inside her, and that was the way she wanted it. The pain she could deal with, mostly, but the disability gnawed at her entire sense of self as a warrior.

Kester had also visited a few times, more out of duty than desire, she suspected. He was quiet and thoughtful, and had little to say. The bragging and bravado of previous days seemed to have been scoured away by the assassination attempts, but she doubted his change would last. Though, she had to admit, he had accounted well for himself in the Hall of Broken Shields, so perhaps the boy might surprise her.

The tedium of six months of inactivity without her work had been driving Briar mad with excruciating slowness. Once she was well enough and angry enough to reject Alaric's fussing, she'd hobbled off to heal up in her own far less luxurious chamber elsewhere in the palace. There, she began taking regular walks of increasing length without the use of a stick, and could lift stones to strengthen weakened muscles without well-meaning but infuriating supervision or restriction. A kindly serving lass called Enid would no longer be forced to smuggle her in greasy pies and other druid-banned foodstuffs past the annoyingly attentive Aisling. Unlike the obliging Enid, that snooty older servant had turned her nose up at a little bribery, something that would normally have elevated her in Briar's eyes but had instead only fostered resentment and

vows of future punishment once the commander was fit for
duty again.

The lack of purpose was killing her. Faced with Briar's
increasing ire, the regent had grudgingly relented and allowed
her to do some scrollwork and accounts while her leg healed.
It was the worst part of the job, but at least it was something.
Hardgrim and his new men had made a right mess of her
records, and she was only just starting to get to grips with his
misspending and skewed duty schedules. What she craved now
was getting back into her uniform and back on actual duty,
putting her hands to proper work. The regent and the Royal
Heir, who had uncharacteristically avoided trouble of late,
were due to leave the palace and make their ritual offerings at
the waterfall grove on the day of the winter solstice. She was
determined to go with them, even though she had barely set
a single foot outside these dark and gloomy palace halls in six
months. Finally, here was the day she got to escape her prison
of stone steps! Just the thought of a trip away from walls and
out under sun, sky and stars set her heart soaring. Trees! Oh,
how she missed walking through the forest with the scent of
wet foliage and a carpet of pine needles underfoot.

Briar rose at first light and began her morning exercise
routine. Her shoulder was starting to ache in the winter thanks
to an even older injury, and she paid particular attention to it as
she stretched stiff muscles and then carefully massaged her left
leg to prevent it seizing up later. She lifted stones in each hand
until she felt the burn, pleased at the ropes of firmer muscle
that had grown back all along her arms. Small steps towards
a full recovery. Then she sat and pushed her feet against the
wall, gently working the muscles to eliminate the remaining
tightness. Her left leg was, above the knee, still a pitted mass
of uneven scarring from the poison and surgical knife, but the
angry red had faded to a grumbling, blotchy pink. She could
walk just fine on the flat now, but a small set of low stances
and lunges with her sword was all she could manage without

the risk of overtaxing it. Still, a few months ago she couldn't even do one. She ignored everything the druids told her and was determined that sooner or later she would be back to how she was.

She took out a chew stick and cleaned her teeth with the frayed silver-birch twig end, then scrubbed them with a small cloth rolled in a mix of ground sage and sea salt, said to ward off the tooth-worms that ate holes in root and gum. A servant brought up a bucket of fresh well water, and Briar used a rag to scrub the sweat from her face, neck, pits and bits with pine-scented soap. The icy water burned against her skin and chased away the last of her grogginess. She cracked the frozen window shutter and tipped the grey water out into the snow, then brushed the build-up off the sill for the birds to land on. She broke off a few crumbs of bread and left them there for the crows. It seemed that they had accepted her as one of their own: a woman who had trodden the dark path of death to the very threshold of the otherworld before turning back to the land of the living. She also had plenty of food, which might have had some bearing on the matter. But who was she to deny the quiet fellowship of the carriers of lost souls?

A breeze brought the cold air inside, and goose bumps rose along her arms. She shivered, hastily pulled on her tunic and buckled on the kilt. It hung loosely on her thinner frame. Toned muscles had wasted away in her sickbed, and at her age it would take months of hard work and exercise to rebuild them back to the peak of fitness. She slid her feet into lamb's-wool socks, fastened on leather boots padded with straw and then wound winter leg wrappings up and round her calves and pinned them in place before she opened up the chest at the foot of her bed. The shining bronze scales of her armoured shirt clinked as she ran her hand over them. She had polished it regularly but hadn't worn it since the assassination attempt. She hadn't deserved to wear it. Now she felt ready. She shrugged the leather-and-scale shirt over the padded tunic and tightened the straps, fastened on bronze armguards then buckled on her sword and belt knife. Last, she slipped on the woollen hat she'd made herself, then the helmet over it, and tightened the chin strap. By the gods, she thought, all this felt heavier than she remembered. Yet another unwelcome reminder of weakness that needled her confidence.

She had not worn any of it since the summer solstice – the last time she had actually felt useful. Saving Kester beneath the palace didn't count, what with it being more an accident than anything else. And she hadn't even managed to kill the damned assassin: that glory had gone to Shield Hardgrim, who'd lapped up the regent's praise like a starving puppy, as if he hadn't just finished off the job she'd started – the assassin had limped away with half an ear, a broken nose, black and blue balls and a stab wound, for spirits' sake! On top of that, Hardgrim had identified the man as a common drudge taken into service just before the summer solstice, charged with mucking out and scrubbing the latrines of the palace. It was a task nobody else wanted, the man had a good reputation from his work in a local sub-chief's household, and he'd had been sly enough to escape further scrutiny. Hardgrim had taken the precaution of releasing all servants taken in around the same time – the palace would lack in staff until they could be replaced with more trustworthy people, but it had to be done.

Briar ground her teeth. Oh how that bastard enjoyed rubbing her face in the dirt, gloating that she'd missed the threat – as if there had been any way to know beforehand! He didn't say anything aloud, but his smug smile told the tale.

She scowled and shook off her anger, knowing she was just bitter because she *hadn't* been able to finish the job herself. Her attention turned to packing: she shoved extra clothing, rags, a wrap of salted beef, a few pouches of boiled honeysweets and some personal odds and ends into a waxed and waterproof linen sack, and then stuffed it into her leather travel satchel beside a spare waterskin. The last item was her best bronze knife, a gift from Alaric after ten years' loyal service, and once that was secured she stared hard at the spear propped in the corner of the room. Shields didn't carry longer weapons day to day, being elite warriors mostly working in the narrow confines of the palace, but all were well trained in their use. A spear was much more practical outdoors, and in her case, it would also serve as a makeshift walking stick without having to admit it to anybody, even herself.

Briar growled and grabbed the spear, banishing any further hint of doubt. This journey was only an overnight trip, and it was an easy walk to the waterfall grove. She slung her bag across her chest and fastened on a faded fern-green cloak of thick twilled wool that had served her well over the years. After a few moments' hesitation, she added a few of the painkilling pellets into her bag. Just in case somebody – anybody – needed them. Then she boldly marched out on a mission to prove herself capable. "Good riddance," she said to the room she had seen entirely too much of over the last few months.

At the outer gate of the palace waited six more Shields dressed for war, and twenty spearmen of the regent's warband – mostly very distant kin – dressed in thick woollens and hard-boiled leather. Beside them waited a pack of local nobles and their servants, the latter weighed down with wicker travel packs padded with sheepskin. A small, horse-drawn open carriage had already been decorated with holly and ivy, the red berries like blood against the ankle-deep snow. There were no seats, the occupants meant to stand on display, to be seen by their people. Two dun mares had been harnessed to the carriage, and the Lord Regent and Royal Heir, in fine winter furs, were standing behind the driver, waiting for the last of the preparations and late arrivals.

Hardgrim stood guard behind them, wearing a matching set of torc and armbands formed of twisted gold wire that seemed far beyond his means. He had assumed Briar's place as Commander of Shields until she was fully fit and able to resume her duties, and she was looking forward to the day she could stamp the prick back into his place. He was amusing himself by throwing pebbles at the squawking palace crows.

"Briar?" Alaric said, eyebrows rising as he noted her weapons and travel clothing. His mouth opened to demand what she thought she was up to, but it was entirely self-evident, and he quickly changed his words. "I specifically exempted you from my service today."

She nodded. "Indeed, which is why I have agreed to be one of Kester's Shields on this very short journey along mostly flat trails."

Kester swallowed and looked only at the path ahead. She could tell from Alaric's expression that he knew only too well she'd been the one doing the telling, and him the agreeing.

The regent glared at his nephew. Then he looked at Acting Commander Hardgrim beside him, who stood stiff and unimpressed. Alaric swallowed any harsh words and visibly shook as he resisted the impulse to order Briar to climb aboard the carriage. She, and he, and even Hardgrim, knew that to do otherwise while surrounded by warriors and watching nobles would be noted as the regent blatantly undermining the Royal Heir while also insulting the Acting Commander of Shields, given there was not space for another body on the carriage and he'd have to get off and walk.

Alaric gritted his teeth. "Do not push yourself too hard," he said.

She pressed her fist to her heart in salute. "Understood, Lord Regent."

Kester glanced at her and exhaled all the tension he had been holding. She winked back, and his face reddened.

Gwilherm sidled up and nudged her with his elbow. "You're a stubborn old nag, eh. Didn't think to see you up and trotting off down the trail to the waterfall grove so soon."

She snorted. "Even with a knackered leg, I can still kick your sorry arse up and down this path."

"Of that I have no doubt," he said, grinning. He stuck to her side as half the warband set off ahead and the carriage lurched into motion behind them, wheels churning up the snow. The Shields formed up on all sides of the carriage, with Gwilherm and Briar in the rear, then the party of nobles, followed by the other half of the warband marching up the trail behind them.

Briar turned to look at the palace, glad to see the back of it. Exalted Carmanilla was watching them leave from a window on the third floor, disapproval at their heathen religious practices writ all over her face. Briar gave the woman a cheery wave, and the ambassador's frown deepened.

The tramp of boots on fresh snow was a most pleasing sound as they crossed the bridge over the stream that flowed past the walls, carrying away the palace's sewage, and entered the countryside. As they walked, her leg muscles began to tighten. She reminded herself that it was only an easy half-day's march to get there, one night spent encamped at the grove and then the return journey. She could do this, she reassured herself. Gods and spirits, she thought, it felt so good to be doing something useful. She wasn't up on the carriage in the commander's place of honour, but as much as Hardgrim irritated her, he did know his job, and the man's eyes constantly scanned the farmhouses and fields for potential threats.

They passed through dozens of farmsteads and scattered hamlets of thatched roundhouses on the outskirts of the Sunweald Palace, the humble places that kept the palace and all its important occupants fed and supplied. Alaric knew how much these farming folk were owed, and his determination to give something back and not be a swamp leech sticking to their backs was one of the reasons Briar had served him all these years. The locals had all turned out in their best tunics and woollen cloaks to watch the procession and cheer them onwards, looking well fed after the winter slaughter of livestock. The outsides of the smoky roundhouses were decorated with green pine branches, ribbon and elaborate webs of dyed yarn. Noisy children pushed and shoved to get the best view of their rulers. Alaric gave them all jolly waves, looking very fine indeed atop his carriage.

Briar noted one little girl with her leg all splinted up. She looked dejected and was struggling to see through the press of bodies. The Shield couldn't help but sympathise. She pulled a pouch of boiled honeysweets from her satchel and tossed them to the girl.

"Remember to share!" she said as the girl's face lit up with a wide grin on realising the treasure she had in her hands. There was not much chance otherwise – her older brothers and sisters descended on her like a pack of starving wolves. Honey was expensive, and these people were poor but proudly making a living off the land, or by working in the nearby tin mines. That child's brothers and sisters were still scrawny enough to squeeze into the narrow mines and hack away at the rock with antler picks, seeking out precious ore. It was backbreaking work, and they too deserved a little joy in these dark winter nights.

The party left the hamlets behind and approached the edge of the forest. They exchanged greetings with a group of charcoal makers huddled for warmth beside a steaming mound of turf that covered a pit of smouldering wood. Days of constant tending to the fire to keep the temperatures just right had left them frozen as well as sooty and seared, and had parched their throats. Alaric tossed them a skin of expensive Ves wine as he passed, bathing in their enthusiastic acclaim.

The farmland and flat pasture gradually gave way to rocks and hillocks, and soon they passed on into the Havenswood proper, a silent forest of stark oaks, silver birch, rowan, alder and snow-capped evergreens. The oldest maps in the library named this place the Coille Samhraidh in the elder tongue: the Summer Forest, the haven where Alaric and Kester's ancestors had once led the ragged clans of Sunweald in search of refuge.

The quiet of a winter forest was a balm to Briar's ears after so long spent inside the palace. A picturesque brook gurgled right alongside the trail, icicles hung from rocks and low branches glittering in shafts of sunlight that broke through the tree canopy. She took deep breaths of crisp, pine-scented air and sighed in pleasure. "I have missed this, Gwilherm. How have things been without me?"

He shrugged, bronze scales clinking. "A lot of shuffling of posts and responsibilities. Most of our best have been off on deep forest patrols or securing Drew Nemeton, leaving Hardgrim's Youngbloods to strut about the palace like they own the place instead of merely being the castoff younger kin of corrupt nobles. Some of us crusty old veterans were left behind too. I guess somebody had to see the job done right." He grinned. "Been a mite more relaxed, though, what with you laid up in your blankets."

Briar grunted. "I bet you have all become sloppy. Too much drinking, gossiping and playing knucklebones, I'd wager."

He gasped in mock-shock. "Knucklebones? Me? Who has been spreading such scandalous rumours? Now, if you want the real goings-on…" As they walked he gleefully filled her in on recent events, the minor mistakes and merits of the other Shields that nobody else would have thought worth note. It served as a good distraction from the fatigue building in her left leg.

A stone later, they left that part of the Havenswood, and the trail curved around the foot of a hill. The way ahead climbed slightly before it descended back towards the waterfall grove. She had managed walking on the flat trail, though feeling far more drained and uncomfortable than she'd expected, but the ascent proved hard work. By the time they reached the top of the trail she was panting and sweating, and she found herself leaning on her spear more than she'd wanted. Gwilherm said nothing of her slowing down, though he'd have had to be blind not to notice.

The regent stopped the carriage at the top of the rise to admire the view over the valley ahead. He leant close to his nephew and began pointing out the great oaks and many standing stones of the sacred place ahead. Kester nodded along as his uncle enthusiastically related the most ancient tales of warring clans of giants turned to wood and stone by each other's deadly spells, and those more modern stories of mere mortals cursed by the gods of earth and water for misdeeds, or of wise druids turning monsters to strangely shaped boulders and thick-trunked trees. The regent knew the stories as well as many druids did, and the darker ones better than most – the benefits of a misspent youth, he'd claimed to Briar, who remained dubious that the man had ever boasted a wild side. Likely he'd just read them in one of those dusty scrolls clustered on the shelves of the library.

"These hills, they are hollow," Alaric said, "and home to the fae." They looked out over the craggy valley that appeared as if it had been scooped right out of the mountains by a true giant of the dawn age. Jagged, strangely shaped rock pillars rose towards the sky. Icicles twinkled in the light of the sinking sun, and the dark rocks were limned with pure white hoarfrost. Breathtaking and magical. "We come here every three years for the rites," he added, "but I have witnessed the Sleaghan Mhath dance only twice since I was a boy your age." The local nobles fell into deep discussion over the matter, some boasting of seeing similar scenes and others scoffing and falling only slightly short of accusing their fellows of spouting falsehoods.

Briar's tired eyes drifted away from them and lingered on a boulder lying by the side of the trail. If she squinted hard enough, the stone bore a vague likeness to a giant's head, complete with beard of moss. She wondered if this really was the remains of one of those ancient giants the legends told of, or a just a natural rock whose likeness had given rise to those tales in the first place. Only the gods and spirits could possibly know the truth of such things. She sat on the boulder to rest, not afraid of old stories or supernatural curses. "I feel old and slow," she admitted to Gwilherm. "I was a fool to think myself ready."

His eyebrows climbed. "Briar pushing herself too hard? I am shocked." The mirth faded. "We are all fools at times, Commander. I can't say if you will fully recover or not, but you do have my respect for not giving up."

She scowled at her leg. "I'm good at not giving up. I don't know how to. That might be the very problem I'm having with this accursed wound. I fear I expected too much too quickly from it." She moved off to one side and chewed on one of her herbal pellets while she massaged the muscles. After a short break, the stiffness and pain began easing off. She caught Alaric studying her from the corner of his eye as he pointed out more sights to Kester, as if the boy had never seen anything like them before...

Ah. That considerate bastard.

She shot the regent a stern glare and then readied herself to resume the march. He looked away and finished his conversation with Kester, then signalled the party to continue to the grove. The carriage lurched back into motion but moved downhill at a more sedate pace as the Lord Regent admired the woods and the beauty of so many streams gushing from the rocks to form fetching little waterfalls of white water. Bone wind chimes rattled and moaned in a slight breeze, gifting the woods an eerie air. Small carved wood and bone sculptures hung from branches all along the path to the sacred site, along with clootie ribbons bearing the wishes of many who visited this place. A line of painted standing stones flanked the final part of the trail. Many of the ancient, mossy stones had been carved with spiralling designs and rings around smooth cup marks carefully ground into the hard rock, and their corners bore notched lines that said something in a language lost to all but the druids.

Despite the slower pace, the ache spread from the muscles of Briar's left leg into her back and bones. She was exhausted by the time the forest thinned out and they arrived at their destination. Her sense of achievement was cut short as she stood at the top of the stone-cut steps leading down into the valley, and she cursed herself for forgetting their very existence. Previously, such steps had been barely worth noticing. She gritted her teeth and took them slow and steady, her knee burning with the effort.

The valley opened out into a sacred grove protected from the weather on three sides by ice-wreathed white cliffs. A mighty waterfall called the White Mare's Tail gushed down the south-western face from a notch in the skyline and plunged into a deep black pool whose centre was said to have no bottom. Her soul soared at the majestic sight, but her body had more mundane needs and yearned to find a seat – she'd have broken out into a run to find one if she'd been able.

Robed figures with painted skin rose from benches and chairs to greet them, hands raised in welcome.

CHAPTER 7

The druids were dressed in all their ritual finery of belted robes and wolfskin cloaks, charms and animal teeth, golden torcs and exquisite wooden bangles. Briar was not the only one who seemed relieved they had forgone the masked-and-horned headdresses for owl-feather caps that revealed many familiar faces, and cheeks and foreheads painted with blue whorls and geometric designs that bewitched the gaze of simple fighting folk. Their lips had been stained berry-red, and their smiles were wide and genuine. Briar still studied their feet and didn't relax until she had determined there was not a bloodstained shoe or boot among them. These druids were barefoot in the snow, seeming not to feel a cold that would blacken and bite the toes of others.

The party rushed over to warm their own hands and feet by roaring campfires. A huge central bone fire had been prepared to be lit as a centrepiece for the rituals and feasting, and the upright log in the centre was already topped with the horned skull of a great ox. A stag and two boars hung from the branches of an oak tree, their throats slit and the blood draining into bronze bowls. Butchers had gutted the beasts and were preparing the meat for stews and roasting. Winter vegetables and dried herbs were already stewing in an enormous steaming cauldron, but as famished as the travellers were, the feast would not begin until the sun went down. Briar squinted up at the notch in the cliffs where the white waterfall gushed, swollen with meltwater. A little while yet until the sun sank into those plunging waters.

The air slowly filled with mouthwatering scents as meat was salted and basted in honey, then arranged on slates laid atop embers raked out into cooking pits. Druids in training ladled generous portions of sacred mead from a bubbling cauldron into birch-bark cups they handed out to the nobles and then the warriors. Seemingly unaffected by the cold, three maiden druids in thin, clinging dresses sat around the unlit central bone fire and played their flutes to an audience of rapt warriors. Another danced and sang with a voice smooth as butter, her body flowing in perfect time with the lilting tune escaping her painted lips. A trio of muscular young men with oiled chests leapt and spun in the air, their expert acrobatics and superb showmanship delighting their audience.

Briar ditched her satchel, and while others sat on benches and tree stumps near the fire, she chose to sit on a vacant high-backed chair further away that offered support for her aching back. Her hands were warmed around her cup while she waited for her leg to stop aching. The fragrance rising from the hot mead tickled her nostrils with a hint of warming spice. She took a sip and savoured the heat flowing down her gullet.

Alaric was greeted by the senior druids, but when they turned to exchange words with Kester, the regent caught her eye. His brow furrowed, and he mouthed, "Are you well?"

She nodded and lifted her cup in salute. His look of relief was a sight for sore eyes. Were it up to him, he would have been right here fussing over her, but his duty came first. Always. His diligence was one of his best attributes, and after ten years of serving him, it was something she wholeheartedly understood.

She didn't get Alaric paying her a visit, but she did get Hardgrim. His pride in the post of Commander of Shields shone from his smile and with every swaggering step. She noted his expensive new white fur cloak and embroidered rabbit-skin gloves, judging him for his vanity. "Hardgrim," she said, nodding.

He stood beside her, sipping at his own cup. Not one for small talk, he got right to his point. "How is your leg?"

"I'll survive," she replied.

He grunted. "Surviving is not enough. With a leg like that, can you properly protect the regent? If he marches off to war, can you march beside him over land and forest, bog and mountain?"

She ground her teeth. "Never fear; it is improving swiftly. I could still take you apart in a fair fight."

He sneered at that idea. "It brings me no pleasure to bring this topic up."

It took all her willpower to stifle her snort of derision.

He continued: "We do not see eye to eye on many matters, but let us put any personal contest between you and I aside. I only ask you to consider your heroic actions during the summer solstice attack: as you are now, could you do the same again? Could you run and dive in front of that arrow to save the Lord Regent's life?"

She had no biting retort to offer. The bastard was right.

"If you were asked to weigh up the abilities of another warrior as afflicted as yourself," he added, "would you ever allow that woman to be the Shield of your regent?"

She took a gulp of mead and felt it warm its way down into her belly, to war with the icy dread forming in her guts.

Her torment was cut short as the sinking sun finally topped the waterfall gushing down the cliff. The white waters burned red and gold, chasing away the gloom. A soft mist began rising from the hills, shrouding their valley from the outside world. Gasps rippled through the sacred grove as the music of the flutes echoed weirdly through the valley. Their tune was taken up and transformed into something otherworldly by dozens more flutes played atop the craggy hills, twisting and turning in an elaborate dance around and within the merely human music. The ethereal, unseen flutes drew out a sense of mournful loss within every human heart, and then their tone changed to bursting joy. All emotion was skilfully herded along to accompany the rise and fall of their exquisite music. This was no mere melody; this was a magic living within blood and bone and spirit.

Hardgrim gawped, his twisting of the knife in her warrior's heart forgotten.

Briar's pain vanished as the fae music thrummed through her body like an eldritch heartbeat. "The fabled Sleaghan Mhath," she said, as glimmering golden figures tattooed with moonlight began to dance through the mists, every one of them slender as a maiden yet standing head and shoulders above the tallest man Briar had ever seen. They were stark naked save for loins clad in leaves and vines, and it was impossible to tell their gender, but all had skin akin to golden bark and large acorn-green eyes slitted like a cat's. As a group, they swirled widdershins in a ritual dance around the ancient standing stones that topped the hill, reversing the path taken by the sun, before breaking off into smaller spinning groups who turned to face one another.

They bowed, and then the silvery tattoos drained into their hands to form spears of glittering moonlight. They shrieked like owls and charged each other, weapons raised. Spears cut and thrust through the mist in what would have been deadly combat, save none ever found purchase in fae flesh. Any notion that these tall-and-slender figures were as fragile as they looked was firmly disabused as combat raged – their bodies were as strong and pliable as greenwood saplings. Fierce fae weapons struck sparks, the glowing fragments swirling up into the night sky to join the stars. A green glow formed in the sky to the north, shifting and dancing in time to the battling fae.

The druids were the first to rouse themselves from the enchantment. "A blessed night!" one cried. "The Good Spears have left their hills to join our celebration. Let our rituals begin!" The druids got to work on their sacrifices, gutting goats atop altar stones and divining the future from the way their innards fell out. Other wise ones cast painted stones or carved bones for similar purposes, and they argued constantly among themselves in a strange sing-song language only those of their kind learnt.

As for Alaric, he poured mead into a silver cup, divested himself of his guards and climbed halfway up the hill. He held up the cup and waited. Briar watched intently, grinding her teeth at how unprotected he was. The druids' assurance of his safety didn't count for much with her. One of the shining Sleaghan Mhath peeled away from their dance and descended to meet him. The golden figure and the Lord Regent nodded to each other. The fae creature took the cup in its long-fingered hand, studied the mead and then downed it in one long swallow. It crushed the cup into a shapeless mass in its hand and laughed, the savage joy infectious. It rejoined the dancing battle on the hill above, and Alaric returned to his own people.

The eldritch music began to rise and quicken, anticipation of the climax flowing across hill and valley like a vitalizing fog. It heightened the emotions of all who heard its call and urged them to rise and join the dance. Briar's foot started tapping, and she found herself forced to her feet, swirling around the fires, filled with the endless energy of a long-gone youth. The bronze scales of her armour flashed and flickered red, gold and green. The druids disrobed and coiled together with the nobles, warriors and servants of the warband. The Shields attempted to hold themselves back from the worst of it, their duty rising above such earthly desires, though in some cases Briar and Hardgrim's fists had to remind them of that.

Kester's eyes were glazed over, his mind and heart fully succumbed to the beguiling song floating down from the sacred hills above the grove. Briar had to prevent him from scrambling up the hill to dance and drink with the fae – legend had it some took a fancy to mortals and kept them in their golden halls for a hundred years and a day before growing bored. Those poor bewildered souls were released back into a land that had entirely forgotten them, and she wasn't having that happen to the Royal Heir. Instead, the boy drank and ate, sang and danced – and eventually he dared far too much. His questing hand climbed Briar's thigh, only to be met with a bruising punch to the face that sent the boy face-down in the dirt and knocked some sense back into him. Alaric nodded to her as he swirled past, his eyes crinkling in vicious appreciation of her swift but restrained rebuke.

The night vanished in a blur of food and fucking, dance and drink. But not for Briar and Alaric, who did their duty and watched over their charges, allowing themselves only a modest indulgence in food and dance, and barely any alcohol at all. It wouldn't have taken much more to ignite the fires of their lust.

Sunrise brought the strangest of all hangovers with it. Instead of a pounding head, crushing weariness, queasy guts and loose bowels, Briar seemed to be full of vigour. Truly it was a miracle after so much mead and mayhem and not a scrap of sleep. She had stayed awake while most of the mortals fell to drink and exhaustion, and even the otherworldly golden fae figures tired of music and dance and slipped back into their hollow hills. The remnants of their magic scattered as the sun rose, and Briar's aches and pains and problems returned as the temperature dipped.

A burning copper sun peered above hills now seeming silent and empty. Her muscles began to stiffen up, returning all the overstrained punishment from the day before. Legend had it that the Sleaghan Mhath's gifts were ephemeral things, leaving her wondering if she had seen their dance at all or if the druids had just slipped some vision-inducing herbs into the mead.

Kester was face-down and snoring, and of all in the grove, only Briar and the other Shields remained awake to greet the rising sun. The common warriors and the nobles lay sprawled all across the grove, and even Alaric was asleep in his furs. She pulled over a wooden barrel and sat on it, massaging her cramping leg as she chewed over what Hardgrim had said to her last night. The man was not even trying to hide his agenda. Worse, he was also right. The rest of her body had regained much of its strength, if not its stamina, but after half a year had passed, her wounded leg was not up to the ability required by an elite Shield charged with guarding the regent's life.

The sacred grove was silent save for snoring and the sounds of wind and water. It calmed her nerves after such a hectic night. The air was crisp, carrying the scents of wood smoke and pine. Her duties had kept her inside the palace for years, and while the carefully maintained gardens were nice enough, Briar craved the wild places of her youth. She found herself missing the days when she wandered the woods and hills with her father and his warriors, camping under the stars and having nothing to do with politics and scrollwork. Places like this grove called to her on some instinctive, primal level, and she wondered if in another life she might have become a druid. She eyed the pile of naked, sweaty bodies still unconscious due to overindulgence and thought, perhaps not. She liked to be in control too much to let go of herself like that.

The pool beneath the waterfall called to her, and she knew that it was time for her sacrifice. She stripped off her armour and clothes while carefully avoiding all sight of her leg, with its loathsome puckered scar. She retrieved the exquisite bronze knife from her satchel. It was a masterwork, and she reluctantly ran calloused fingers over the carved oak handle and inlaid golden pins one last time. Then she pulled out a small wood-and-cloth effigy of a man, complete with crooked grin and little wooden bow. Thorns had been driven through the cloth and into the wood of the hands, legs and groin. Naked in the winter chill, Briar limped through the packed snow and across the frozen earth towards the plunge pool. Those awake averted their eyes, not because of her nakedness but because a sacrifice to the gods was such a deeply personal matter. Woe betide the fool who angers those who reside in this sacred place.

Briar stepped into the black waters and hissed at the burning cold lapping her ankles. A momentary fear of kelpies stole upon her – those furious water horses that pulled unwary swimmers under. She reassured herself that there would be none in a place so sacred to the gods and waded deeper, her jaw clamped shut to avoid gasping as the icy water swallowed her waist. The chill stabbed into her left leg like a dagger to the bone. The stones underfoot were slick and treacherous, and she went as deep as she dared. The black waters leeched away all heat, leaving her numb and tingling.

The silence deepened, as if the trees and stones and waters of the grove were watching and judging. She lifted her knife high and pointed it at her breast, golden bronze catching the ruddy first light creeping over the sacred hills. "Great gods and spirits of this sacred place," she said. "I offer you this knife, the most valuable and meaningful object that I own. I ask for your blessing in health, and recovery from the wound taken in service to this land and its people." It was a beautiful object, but it was Alaric's sincere thanks and respect it represented that made this knife so special to her, and that made it a worthy sacrifice.

She ducked under the water and hammered the knife point-first into the stone bed. The gleaming bronze blade bent back on itself, forever ruined. Her stomach clenched with revulsion at what she had just done, but there was little point in a ritual without actual sacrifice. She lifted the twisted ruin of her weapon sunwards once more to catch the sunlight, and then lowered her hands and let the water take it. Black waters swallowed the offering. A barren sense of loss followed. If the gods and spirits of this sacred place acknowledged her sacrifice, she had no way to know. No mortal could restore her leg, so she had no option but to hope she had done enough to earn their blessing.

Then, with shaking hands, she gripped the effigy, which bore all her burning hatred for the archer who had inflicted the dreadful poisoned wound upon her. She'd had enemies before but had not thought she could ever hate with such ferocity. It was as deep and all-consuming as the darkest pit in the earth. The knife bore her heartfelt wish for healing, and this handmade effigy bore her darkest curse of painful death.

"I curse the craven archer who attempted to murder Alaric Summerson and inflicted this terrible wound upon me," she growled. "I was faithful in my service to this land, and I ask you to return his dreadful gift threefold. Let him suffer thrice the pain I have endured." She plunged the effigy under the water and let it go. As cloth and wood rotted, hopefully so would the bastard's body. It was an old magic, practised by many without the talents and learning of the druids, but failing a knife in her hand and the opportunity to thrust it into the archer's flesh, she had no recourse but to put her faith in the gods. As the waters swallowed her curse, she felt the burning hatred dampen to embers of resentment. What could be done had been done, and there was nothing more to do now but get on with living.

She limped back to her pile of clothing, pulled on her tunic, kilt and armour and tossed a few sticks on the embers of the nearest fire, then sat savouring the warmth returning to her body while the others slowly roused.

Most of the druids were wasted, sprawled about in heaps of semi-naked flesh, snoring and speaking nonsense in their sleep. A few of their number tiptoed between the post-orgasmic drunken heaps like thieves, stealing delirious mutterings that could later be proclaimed omens and portents.

Alaric rolled from his blankets and groaned as he heaved himself to his feet. One hand clutched the small of his back and he winced, stretching until his back popped. He relieved himself against a rock. When he was finished, the regent spotted Briar and came at her like a hunting hound.

She tossed him a waterskin, and he took a deep swig, swilling the liquid around his mouth. He spat it out and then stood beside her in a comfortable silence, taking in the golden beauty of the sun only just rising over the hills. A morning mist curled around the standing stones and flowed down into the valley. Shafts of sunlight pierced through those shifting mists, only to be gone again a moment later. A faint rainbow formed atop the waterfall, where the hissing water kissed the sun – a sure sign of the tempestuous love between the gods of fire and water.

He looked around at his slumbering warband and the few watchful Shields going about their business. "How I crave such peace and quiet, and wish we could do this more often."

"We?" Briar queried.

He flushed. "You know exactly what I mean. Just the two of us. No warriors, no servants and certainly no ambassadors."

She did. Only too well. Their accursed duty...

He cleared his throat. "Anyway. How are you feeling?"

She glared at him. "I'm fine. Stop asking."

He held his hands up in surrender. "I will take your word for it." For a while, they spoke of nothing of import, just the scenery and what they recalled of the mayhem of celebration, and of course the fae figures dancing on the hillside. They laughed and plotted the embarrassments and emotional blackmail they would inflict on the Royal Heir after his many drunken antics. The boy lay face down on his blankets, his cheek swollen and his naked arse painted bright red. They doubted he would remember any of what had transpired.

When the others began stirring, Alaric's face fell back into a diplomatic blank slate. Their rare moment of peace and tranquility was over. It was time to get back to the palace, and to work.

CHAPTER 8

Most of the party were still stuffed to the gills from the previous night's feast, and the fae magic might be handy for curing hangovers but it did nothing for over-full bellies or the aftereffects of rich food. They forced themselves to nibble on a little meat, bread and leftovers to keep them going on the day ahead and packed some away for later. Within a stone, they had broken camp and hitched the horses to the carriage, ready to set off. The most senior of the druids bade Alaric and Kester kneel, and with her liver-spotted and shaking hands she set woven crowns of holly, oak twigs and dried flowers around their brows. A trio of young women dipped bundles of sage into a bowl and anointed the rulers with holy oil and secret words before wishing them good fortune on the return journey.

Briar smirked at the scions of Sunweald as they scratched at the crowns pricking their skin. Tradition dictated they could only take them off after they'd paraded through the countryside and returned to the palace; to do otherwise was to invite winter to linger on long past its welcome. There were many old traditions that those bearing Summerson blood had to follow, and though not many knew why such things were now done, all from the lowliest beggar to the wisest of druids knew that not doing them would invite bad luck and the ire of the spirits. The Summerson line were powerful and privileged, but for the most part they bore that responsibility well. She reckoned even that wastrel Kester was gradually coming round to the role he'd been born into.

As the front of the party set off on the trail, Briar took a deep and shuddering breath and stretched her leg a few times. Her thigh felt solid as a boiled ham thanks to yesterday's exertion, and it took a while to ease off.

Gwilherm sidled up to her, eyeing her stretches. "You ready for this, lass?" he said. "Want me to carry you? It'd be easy; you're not as fat as you used to be."

Briar scowled and set off, ignoring him entirely. Gwilherm hurried after her, making his apologies as he marched by her side. She gripped her spear tightly in her left hand, hoping to take as much strain as she could off her sore leg as she ascended the steps to the top of the valley. His incessant chattering proved impervious to her vague nods and grunts of agreement. The man could not take the hints that she did not wish to talk. She needed all her breath for the climb. The ache in her knee built with every step uphill. She gritted her teeth, choked down her gasps of pain and walked on without voicing any complaint. She *would* make it back. She was a Shield, a veteran warrior who had survived a dozen battles, and she refused to let one little poisoned arrow dictate the rest of her life. She would do her job. Briar forced one foot in front of the other and turned all her attention to the surroundings, searching for any sign of threat.

Standing atop the decorated carriage, lurching along the trail at a sedate pace, Kester and his uncle had nothing to do but wear their winter crowns and be symbols to the inhabitants of the hamlets and farms they passed through – visible signs to those they ruled that the gods had blessed them for another year, and that summer would return.

The boy groaned and rubbed a bruised cheek. "Why am I hurting? Did I fall last night?"

Alaric glanced at him. "In future, you should learn to drink in moderation instead of re-enacting last night's foolishness. You got off surprisingly lightly. Had it been left up to me..."

The Royal Heir's eyes widened. "Wait, did somebody hit me?" He gasped. "Who would dare to… to…?" His eyes widened still further as the residue of memory congealed like grease on a half-eaten dinner. He turned round to face Briar as she trudged behind the carriage. His face snapped forward again after they momentarily locked gazes and her eyes darkened.

Kester stared at the offending hand he dimly recalled putting on her thigh, and all blood drained from his face. "Oh gods. Oh spirits… I'm dead. Dead!" He grabbed his uncle's arm. "You have to protect me."

Alaric chuckled. "You had best make amends once we return. And quickly. Although, were it me, I would be equally concerned about why my arse was painted red and my legs all scraped by branches."

Kester's swift investigation resulted in a thoroughly horrified boy. "What did I do last night?"

Alaric shuddered and shook his head. "I dare not speak of it. Some things a man should not see." He turned away, lips twisting in what Kester took to be a scowl.

By the time Briar reached the edge of Havenswood, it had become blatantly apparent there was no sudden and miraculous cure coming her way. Shadowy hope in the mercy of the gods could not hold up in the glaring light shed by her physical fatigue, her failure. She stubbornly soldiered on, trying to keep up with the others, drenched in sweat, her breathing laboured and each step a red-hot spike driven into her heel and up through the bone of her thigh. Her knee trembled due to the punishing pace, but she leant heavily on her spear and forced the accursed thing back into compliance. One step at a time, one step closer to home…

Halfway along a narrow passage through a rocky outcrop that led deeper into the forest, the trail became more uneven. Gnarled roots jutted from the earth, and leaf mould and a layer of pine needles hid ankle-snapping holes. They slowed and chose their footing more carefully, Shields guiding the horse and carriage by hand.

Briar heaved a sigh of relief as they slowed, grateful for the chance to rest her leg a little and regain its strength. The fiery pain in her knee began to ebb. The crack of a snapping branch off to the right set her eyes scouring the tree line for any attackers. In that moment, she stepped on a branch, and it rolled out from beneath her. Her leg gave out and pitched her onto the frozen earth, twisted beneath her. It was gone: a dead weight through which a river of fire flowed. Tortured muscles twitched and trembled, clenched solid as the stone beneath her fingers.

Pain filled her with nausea, and bile surged up her throat. She leant over and threw up, dimly aware that the Lord Regent of Sunweald had called for his carriage to come to a halt beside her. Shields swarmed up the rocky outcrops on either side of the trail, wary and keeping watch.

"Keep moving," she gasped between retches.

Alaric paused, one foot hovering between carriage and ground. "Briar, I–"

"That's an order," she growled. "It's not safe here. Keep moving. I will catch up on my own."

"She is right, Lord Regent," Hardgrim said, scanning the surroundings and the many hollows that could easily conceal a dozen archers. "This is the perfect place for an ambush. Your safety must always be our priority."

Alaric gazed at her, worry writ large all over his face.

She glared back, her pride needled by his concern. "Go!" she demanded, and mouthed "please" to follow it.

He swallowed and nodded, then waved the party onwards. "You have until the dawn," he told her as the carriage lurched back into motion. He did not order anybody to stay behind with her. He knew better than that. She was not good at asking for help and would rather crawl back on her own than be carried or coddled like a helpless babe.

Once the others were out of sight, she screamed in rage and pounded the nearest tree with her fists, denting the bark and skinning her knuckles. All that anger and frustration was pounded into the wood, and the stinging pain felt good. For a fleeting moment she had felt back in control of her life. The rage vanished as quickly as it had erupted, leaving a desert of emptiness in its wake. She slid down the trunk until she was sat with her back to it, massaging her leg with bloodied hands and waiting for her breath to come easier. The winter air quickly chilled her sweat-drenched skin, but did little to cool the raw fire running through her leg.

She fumbled one of the herbal pellets into her mouth and choked it down, waiting for it to take effect before she tried to move again. She loathed having to rely on such things to see her through, but felt she had no other choice. For somebody who had taken such pride in her physical prowess, it was galling to realise that those days were now firmly in the past. Until now, old age and illness had been things that happened to somebody else, but her body had betrayed her, and she could not ignore the wear and tear in her back and joints. She should have still had years of marching and fighting before her, but now travelling long distances quickly on foot was impossible, and she would never be the deer-footed and viper-swift warrior she used to be. She was no Shield, and not a warrior anywhere near worthy of the position. Maybe her leg had improved, but it was not enough to carry out a Shield's duties every day without fail. She had to accept that – failure in her duty could not be tolerated.

Which left her what in life?

She had been so certain about everything for most of her years, from the simple job of hunting brigands and thieves with her father outside Drew Nemeton to becoming a Shield tasked with guarding the Heart and the Wyrm Vault inside the Sunweald Palace, and then the vital task of protecting the Lord Regent himself. All of her energy and skill had gone into those roles, leaving her with nothing to fall back on once they were gone.

She had a lot to ponder later, but she was a warrior, and she stamped that down deep inside to focus on the pressing issue of getting home. When the pain ebbed, she retrieved her spear and used it to lever herself up and take a few exploratory steps. Agony from ankle to hip with every step, but she could endure. Because she had to.

She hobbled onwards, one more small step homeward bound, her rage at the assassin built with the pain. She distracted herself by devising a hundred ways to kill that smirking archer. Anger carried her onward, raging at the unfairness of it all. But burning rage cannot last forever without consuming its owner. It eventually ebbed away into a winter-chilled abyss of weariness. Finally, all she was left with was bitter acceptance.

She concentrated on taking one step at a time, both hands wrapped around the stout spear to take as much weight off her leg as she could. She should never have come, she admitted. Pride and arrogance had led her thoughts astray. She had blindly assumed that this journey to the grove and back would be bearable, assumed that her damned leg would hold out. Assumed... every bit as hot-headed as a young warrior who had just been blooded and gleefully flung herself back into battle, thinking herself immortal. She'd seen so many of their ilk dead on the grass and had thought herself immune to making the same mistake. Arrogant and delusional.

It was a gruelling journey home, her slow progress seeing her through dusk and sunset and well into the darkling stones of night with only the moon to light her path. The forest sounds of unseen movement through foliage and hair-raising cries of distant beasts gave her some small worry, but she dared any wolf to try to take her. A twig snapped off to the side, and she levelled her spear at it, scanning the darkness for any hint of attack. The moment passed without event, and she warily continued on. The forest trail eventually gave way to muddy tracks passing through pasture and farmland, and then on to the slumbering hamlets. Snowflakes drifted down from the sky, beautiful in the moonlight, but entirely unappreciated as she tripped over her own feet and fell, gasping as she landed atop her bad leg. She cursed, spent far too long getting back to her feet and shuffled on.

She fell and rose a dozen times before she stopped counting, trudging through snow and ice, dragging her leg behind her. "It doesn't matter how often you fall. What matters is how often you get back up." It was a nice folk saying, but scant comfort to a half-frozen woman with bruised-and-bloodied knees and hands, and a split lip. She hurt all over in a dozen ways, and she was completely and utterly spent. She chewed another herbal pellet and somehow managed to get back to her feet one more time.

At the first sight of the towers of Sunweald Palace peeking above the trees, she sobbed with relief. Her wet eyes were drawn to the regent's tower, where a flicker of candlelight shone in the window of his study. That man was still awake at this time of night? Of course he was. She wiped her eyes and shuddered. Shield Briar straightened up and took a step forward. "Almost there," she growled. "Almost there..." She shuffled on into the gardens with dreams of warm blankets and a soft bed seeing her through the last and most arduous part of her trek.

The East Wing came into view, with thick wooden beams shoring up the upper floors of those ancient walls and supporting the sagging roofing against winter storms. The regent's tower overlooked the part of the gardens she entered, and even in her frozen exhaustion she swore she could feel Alaric's burning gaze settle upon her.

The side door swung open. Kester stood waiting for her, a blanket draped over one arm and a steaming cup of warmed mead in the other hand. Her spear dropped to the snow. He didn't offer to help her, didn't say anything at all. He just flung the blanket around her shoulders and pressed the cup into her shaking hand while he slipped his shoulders under the other to take her weight. The warmed mead tingled its way down her throat. She didn't have the energy to object as he helped her indoors. Everything went cloudy, and she remembered nothing past setting that first foot back into the palace, for which she would be eternally thankful.

As the Royal Heir helped Briar inside, a shadow slipped out of the bushes in the garden and startled some slumbering crows. Shield Gwilherm brushed snow off the shoulder of his cloak, sniffed and wiped at his numbed nose, then drew his sword and waved it towards the tower, reflecting moonlight. In the regent's study, the candlelight snuffed out.

"Next time, I wager she'll just get on the damned carriage," Gwilherm grumbled to the complaining crows. "Traipsing about woods at night, at my age, trying not to be seen and putting my foot in a puddle – if I've got the frostbite, I swear I'll claim a bar of silver off him for each toe that drops off."

Gwilherm looked back the way they had come, the drifting snow already masking most of the drag marks and uneven footprints of Briar's harsh journey, the spatters of blood and vomit. He sighed and shook his head. "Reckon I'd have just sat down and frozen to death were it me. Bloody stupid, stubborn woman…" The crows eyed him funnily, and he sniffed at them too. "Back to sleep, you feathered rats. There'll be no carrion for you lot this night."

It had been a brutally hard task to watch and do nothing. During all those stones of shadowing her he'd been itching to leap out and lend a hand, but Alaric had forbidden all intervention until she had no choice but to accept his help. Every time she'd fallen he'd thought she was finally done, but the stubborn old mare had climbed back up and continued on.

Nobody should have had to go through that torture, but then Briar wasn't one to accept help from anybody. Or she hadn't been. Now… well, he wasn't sure she had any choice.

He shook his head, refusing to think about what she was going to do now. He certainly wasn't about to suffer that conversation with her. Let her beloved regent weather that particular storm.

Gwilherm picked up her discarded spear and hurried off in search of his blankets, wishing they contained a woman to keep his bed and his heart warm. Alas, his wife now dwelled in the otherworld, and no other would ever compare. She'd ruined him for others in every way that was important, and it was a blessing from the gods he'd met her at all. Ah well, he thought, a sour old goat like him would just have to make do with the plate of beef and jug of expensive wine the regent had promised to set aside for him in the kitchens.

CHAPTER 9

The shattered and scattered parts of Briar's consciousness slowly congealed. She gradually became aware of her body, a heavy lump that refused to obey her commands. The ache in her muscles ebbed and flowed, coming back stronger and fiercer each time it battered her against the rocky shore of wakefulness. Eventually, voices filtered into her dark world. Alaric. Aisling. With heroic effort, she cracked her eyelids open and immediately regretted it.

She was back in her old sickbed in the regent's chambers, staring up at a ceiling she had come to loathe and without any memory of how she'd got there. A fire crackled and spat, warming the room. Waning winter light shone through the horn window slats – she'd slept right through the day and into the edge of dusk.

The maid, Aisling, stood over her with a bowl of salted porridge, a spoon, and an imperious attitude. The Lord Regent was behind her, arms crossed. "Feed her if she can't eat it herself," he ordered. "And if not, then perhaps I will ask Exalted Carmanilla to attend to her."

Briar struggled to sit upright and winced as every part of her body cried out in pain. Her leg was hot and swollen, the muscles feeling like they were filled with spiky rocks. Aisling set down the bowl and fussed over her, intent on propping her up into a better sitting position. Briar warded her off with a clumsy, bruised hand. "I'm not an invalid – I have hands, and I can feed myself. I need none of your pitiable aid!" She grabbed the bowl and began shovelling the porridge into her mouth, barely tasting it as she choked it down just to prove a point.

"Leave us," the regent ordered, his voice hoarse.

The maid slunk off, and he stood there silently watching her eat, unimpressed. The silence stretched and deepened, roiling into some unsaid angry thing between them that neither wanted to face.

Alaric broke first. He scrubbed a hand through his hair and sighed. "You cannot go on like this. Look at what your stubborn pride has done to you. I will not let you destroy yourself."

Briar tried to rise from the bed, grimacing as she failed and slumped back. "In a few weeks I will be fitter. Then–"

"Enough," he interrupted. "That journey and the fall almost killed you. I spent the entirety of last night at the window of my study, staring out into the darkness, waiting and watching for any sign of you. And don't think I haven't noticed your reliance on those herbal pellets the druids made with Carmanilla."

She swallowed and held her tongue from replying with barbed lashings of her own. She'd never asked him to do that, and the thought of him up waiting and worrying was not pleasant. And of course he'd noticed her using remedies for her pain more than she probably should.

"Are you lying to me or to yourself?" he asked softly. "I want this no more than you."

Her hands clenched, breaking the scabs on her knuckles, earned from the stupidity of punching a tree.

Alaric glanced at the beads of oozing blood and then looked deep into her eyes. "I'm sorry." He took a deep shuddering breath, and then all concern vanished behind the mask of the regent. "Your assessment of this Shield's fitness for duty, Commander?"

Her stomach lurched. Whatever physical pain she felt, it was as nothing compared to the pain of her own words. Here, finally, she was forced to confront the fate she had struggled so hard to deny. She licked her dry, cracked lips. "Unfit," she whispered.

He nodded gravely. "What are the chances of a full recovery?"

She would not – could not – lie to him with half-truths and blind hope. "None," she said, the words bitter ashes on her tongue.

His mask almost cracked under the weight of his concern. Almost. "Can the Shield serve in some reduced capacity? Perhaps with a proper length of time dedicated to recovery?"

"The leg will not improve enough for active duty. She is" – Briar hesitated, disgusted by her own conclusions – "suitable only for scrollwork and light service." She carefully stretched her sore muscles, and felt them immediately threaten to cramp up.

"Your recommendation?" the regent asked.

"Pension her off," she replied, bile searing the back of her throat.

The regent nodded. "I will take your recommendation under advisement. I am sure there is something else she can do instead. Training new Shields in the arts of sword and spear and close combat. Quartermaster, perhaps..."

She shook her head. "I will not serve under Hardgrim to train his 'handpicked' warriors. You think I will look forward to the moment they discover they can run rings around me thanks to this leg? Piles of dreary scrollwork would leave me wanting to slit my own throat within a single season."

That left him rattled, the mask slipping and his voice cracking. "What else do you have?" he hissed. "Being a Shield is your whole life, and I refuse to let you eke out a meagre existence on handouts for past service. It is not like you've saved any of the wealth you've earned."

"True enough," she replied with a bitter chuckle. She'd imagined many more years left to start saving for her old age. In a moment, everything had changed. A line had been carved right through her life, separating the before times from everything after, and she'd only just noticed it – had been forced to notice it. "And yet, the anger and frustration would kill me as quickly as a poisoned arrow to the heart," she added, feeling like a hostage trapped inside her own body.

The emotionless mask of the regent shattered, showing the broken man beneath. "Shit," he said, collapsing onto the chair by the bed, his face buried in his hands. "May all gods and spirits curse that fucking archer!"

She squeezed his shoulder – a mighty effort all on its own. "Oh, I did that at the grove. The gods being kind, he will suffer something threefold worse."

He lowered his hands and locked gazes with her, the fires of determination burning behind them. "I *will* find something suitable for you. I promise you that. You are far too good a woman to waste away at the bottom of an ale cup." They'd both seen retired Shields and wounded warriors slip into a spiral of drink and druids' potions, bored and bitter and spending their waning days reliving old glories. Many had ended up taking their own lives or been thrown out by their kin, scraping a survival in the woods and wild places.

"Rip the bandage off," she said. "I may not know what I want for now, but all spirits as my witness, I will not endure anybody's pity. I plead with you to dismiss me from your service. Do it now."

He shot to his feet, shaking his head. "I refuse."

"You must," Briar said. "I am unworthy and incapable of the role. You asked for my assessment of the situation, and now you have it."

"You gave me your oath of service," he growled. "I do not release you from it."

"Do not make me oath-broken," she demanded. "I swore to guard the blood of Summer, but that is impossible now. Let another warrior serve you with honour."

He gritted his teeth, one eye ticing in anger. "I do not want another! I lov–"

Briar cut him off. "What we want is not what the gods have given us. All I can do is endanger you, in more ways than one."

Alaric swayed on his feet, stunned. Distressed.

She sighed and felt her own anger ebbing away. "Our roles are not to seek our own happiness. They never have been."

He paced back and forth, hands clenched into fists. "I refuse to accept this. Time. Aye... time is what you need to properly recover and reconsider. Then we will find you a position that is suitable."

"Alaric..."

He refused to even look at her as he paced closer and closer to the doorway. "There must be some role in the palace that would challenge you."

"Dismiss me," she said again, more forcefully. "Don't make me grow to hate you."

"You could train Kester!" he said, his eyes brightening. "Yes! Of all of us, he holds you in the highest esteem. You are a hero to him."

She chewed it over, a faint flicker of hope. The boy had managed to turn her previous contempt into a seed of respect, and he sorely needed the skills she could pass on... but no, she trained hardened warriors and didn't imagine she had the patience for snot-nosed whelps. "No," she stated. "Have Gwilherm do it. I am not up to the task."

He didn't seem to hear her, and instead wove unsteadily through the doorway and into the study beyond. "Just let me think," he mumbled. "I... I will find you something else. I have to."

"Alaric–"

"Rest and recover however you can," he said, and promptly fled, disappearing from view.

"Alaric!" she yelled, trying and failing to rise from the bed.

Instead, Aisling peered around the doorway, her eyes wide. "He's already gone. Can I get you anything? Food? A bed bath?" She ducked back just in time to avoid the bowl that came hurtling through the doorway.

Briar wasn't angry – not at Alaric, anyway. The man was neck-deep in denial, just as she had been until recently. If the long walk and longer crawl home had taught her anything, it was grim acceptance of her situation. She needed to deal with hard reality instead of flimsy dreams and impossible desires, and so did he. They had spent almost every day of the last ten years together and had never once grown bored of each other's company. She reckoned their relationship was better than most marriages. But it would all end in blood and fire if he tried to cram her into some tedious role just to keep her lingering around like a bad smell – he already had one bad-tempered pet stinking up the place, and Briar refused to become a second.

In that moment she made a plan. She would make the decision for him. She would leave the palace and head off to her second brother's farm, just south of Drew Nemeton. His girls must be almost fully grown by now, and she was long overdue a visit to the rest of her nearby clan. There, away from the constant reminders of what she couldn't do, she might have the chance to recuperate and attempt to discover what she could do with the rest of her life. She had to find her own way to feel useful again. As bitter as she was about the whole situation, she reminded herself that unlike Cathbad, Barik and Sleen, she was still alive and fighting. So, she couldn't run as far and swift as the wind, like she had before... but at least she still had the leg. She could still walk. It was not the end of all things, however much it felt like it.

She sighed. The only problem was Alaric would not allow it. That lonely and aging man needed her. She had been his trusted aide, confidante and crutch for ten years, and one of the very few ever to earn his absolute trust. If they were honest, both would reveal that they meant far more to each other than any duty demanded. Friends and bloodied warrior-kin certainly, but... Well, she refused to travel further down that trail of thought – oh, how she'd perfected *that* over the years. There was no future there. She chewed it over, dreading the thought of abandoning him and her duty, but loathing even more the idea of wandering these halls decrepit and useless. He had ordered her to 'rest and recover however you can', so she would not be oath-broken if she obeyed him in that. Her honour would remain intact if she left with the very real aim of recuperating. All she had to do was give him no chance to countermand that order – she wasn't entirely sure she would have the strength to leave him otherwise.

With a plan of attack in place, she lay back on the bed and finally felt at peace with herself. Now she just needed to figure out the logistics of it all. Her leg gave a twinge of warning and threatened to spasm with cramp. She scowled down at it. A week or two of recovery would see her back on her feet, and she would be well enough to walk on the flat a goodly distance, then ride or sit on a cart to get far away from this mouldering old palace. She would be gone, and Alaric would just need to deal with it.

"Aisling!"

"You called?" the maid said, poking her head through the doorway.

"I will be moving back to my own chambers," Briar replied. "Move my clothes and any needful things back in there. I will not disturb the Lord Regent's work and rest any further, and I also need a good dose of peace and quiet to recuperate."

The maid frowned, eyes narrowed. "I suppose that makes sense. As long as you can sit up on your own."

Briar tried, but her leg and lower back were locked solid. She groaned and settled back down. "Maybe tomorrow…"

Aisling rolled her eyes and shook her head. "It's your funeral once Himself finds out, but I'll make the arrangements."

* * *

In a secret chamber in the depths of the catacombs, Hardgrim, acting Commander of Shields, paced to and fro across the slick stone. His footsteps echoed weirdly down the twisting passageways, the only noise apart from a constant drip of water from stalactites. He cursed the fact he was reduced to skulking around in the shadows instead of sat on a throne while lesser men kissed his boots and begged for his favour. One day, he promised himself. One day soon.

His ears strained to catch any hint of footfalls approaching, and his eyes constantly searched the darkness beyond the light of his two lanterns – he liked to have two, just in case one went out and he got lost in the maze of tunnels. He was not used to being kept waiting, especially during these last two seasons when he had been Commander of Shields and guardian of the palace in all but name.

He paced forward and back, forward and back, forward and– "Shit!" he cried, discovering Imperatrix's mask right in front of him. He had to force his hand away from the sword at his hip.

Behind the snarling white mask, the woman's eyes crinkled in amusement. "Best keep your wits about you," she said. "The tunnels under the palace can be dangerous, or so I hear." His lanterns flickered and dimmed, shadows crowding around them, while black veins of sorcery crawled up her throat. "Down here in the dark," she added, "who knows what could happen to an unwary man…"

The light died, plunging him into utter darkness. The only noise was the drip of water and his own increasingly rasping breath. Orange light bloomed in the dark, and he found her knife at his throat. The artefact crackled and spat with eldritch energies, sparks sizzling painfully against his skin. He dared not move, or breathe.

"Take care, Hardgrim," she advised. "There can be no mistakes this time."

She withdrew the knife and slid it into the silvery moon-metal sheath at her belt. The black veins ceased crawling up her throat and reluctantly retreated towards her heart. Hardgrim swallowed, encouraged by the sight of that eerie weapon rendered harmless. He rubbed his neck, feeling the needle points of pain where tiny burn blisters would soon be rising. "Do you always have to sneak about like a rat?"

"Rats are safest lurking in the shadows," she replied. "But I prefer to think of myself as a venomous snake. I did not spend years growing my personal power and my organisation just to lose everything in a single careless moment. For years, we have been stealing minor holy artefacts from those pompous priests in Wrendal and smuggling them over for auction in the Ves principalities. The contents of this palace's Wyrm Vault will make those seem like children's toys. Are you ready?"

He grinned, his annoyance washed away by naked greed. "My Youngbloods are trained and ready, handpicked and loyal only to me. The perfect lure is in place. In twenty days, word will come down from the village of Blaen Mhòr that the Wildwood Reivers have been discovered wintering nearby with their latest haul of stolen artefacts, and that they are readying to depart for the Ves border. Given the rising political tensions, most of the remaining Shields and warband loyal to regent and realm will be sent off in a hurry to deal with the problem. Blaen Mhòr is two or three days' journey either way in winter, so we should comfortably have four days at an absolute minimum."

"I mislike the word 'should'," she replied, "but it is what it is. With some small measure of luck, we should have the Vault open within two days and be away enjoying our riches and glory before the Shields even realise they have been duped."

"Are you sure you can open the Vault?" Hardgrim asked. "I have searched this cavern myself and found no openings. Nobody even knows where the door might be. I have no idea what's really in there."

She scrutinised him, eyes glittering behind her mask. "You think those deranged nature-worshipping druids and holy

Wrendal priests are the only ones with powerful magic? I've been studying this palace for years, and with your recent rise to power, the closer access you've arranged for me has borne ripe fruit. I now know how to open the arcane locks on that door – or, rather, the way to find out. It will be a painful process, but not for us."

He had the unsettling suspicion she was grinning most foully behind the mask.

"As for what is in there," she added, "who keeps such a place guarded at all times if there is nothing of greater value than musty old historical relics stored within? Sunweald is an ancient realm, older than the Holy Wrendal Empire and the Federated Principalities of Ves. Older even than the kingdoms and cities that coalesced into those great powers. I have heard tales and seen fragments of crumbling scrolls that hint at the horrors contained deep inside its Wyrm Vault. Weapons beyond anything you can imagine." She fingered the hilt of her knife. "Have you ever been to the Charred Waste?"

His brow furrowed. "Along the border with Wrendal? I've ridden that far on a patrol, but there is nothing of note anywhere near that barren plain of scorched boulders and bubbling bogs."

She picked at a hangnail, examining the bead of blood she drew. "The Charred Waste was once an expanse of fertile farmland, forest and rolling meadow, if the tallies of grain and cattle are to be believed. Those records, carved into clay tablets, are now scarce, as you can imagine. It was once a mighty realm ruled by the enlightened city of Hisparren, the beating heart of a growing empire five hundred years ago."

Hardgrim's eyebrows climbed. "What happened to them? To change farm and forest into a charred waste they must have truly angered the gods."

"Worse," she replied. "They angered Sunweald. They invaded this realm with a great army. Tales passed down to me say the noble Hisparrens were provoked to do so by Sunweald raids, but in any case, the entire realm of Hisparren abruptly disappeared from history. Those of us who practise the arcane arts can feel the traces of terrible magic left in that charred and broken land." She shuddered.

Hardgrim whistled. "Ah, my dear Imperatrix, your words make my greedy little heart swell. That sort of power will fetch us a pretty hoard of coin and a massive herd of cattle."

She stared at him for a long moment. "Indeed it will. Assuming all our problems are dealt with appropriately." She rolled her eyes. "Coin and cattle – is that truly all you dream of?"

"Wine and women, too," he said after a moment's thought. "As for our problems, all is well in hand. My men know their plan. They will round up all those you have asked for and sweep through the palace to eliminate everybody else."

"What of Briar?" Imperatrix asked.

He snorted. "That tired old thing? She wasn't on your list of required bodies, was she? She'll die the day you give the order."

"Do not underestimate her," Imperatrix replied. "She's a stubborn survivor. Nobody rises to the position of Commander of Shields without talent." Her eyes fastened on Hardgrim, weighing him up.

He scowled and stroked the hilt of the sword at his hip. "She's just a decrepit old sow," he retorted. "She'll be murdered in her sleep like any other old whore."

Imperatrix's knife slid a fingerbreadth free of its sheath without her laying a finger on it. It hissed and sparked as she drew it to examine the glowing edge, seeming to divine meaning from the pattern of sparks. "Someday a woman is going to kill you over that tongue of yours."

He snorted. "Not likely. I like my women soft and compliant. Besides, you haven't had to work directly under crusty old Briar for the last few years – if you had, you'd know my anger is well deserved. She will die as easily as all the rest, that I swear. How much fight can one broken old woman have left in her?"

CHAPTER 10

Twenty days after she came home crawling through the dirt on bloodied hands and knees, Briar was back on her feet, rested and more than ready to turn her back on the palace. Her leg was still stiff and aching, but that was her new normal, and she hadn't exactly been a spry little lamb even before the wound, if truth be told. It was midmorning on an overcast day, and the light shone wan though the narrow window of her chamber. She had refused to see Alaric since their last disagreement and thought it for the best, lest her resolve to leave waver.

She scanned her room, taking in all the details of the place she had lived in for ten whole years. Now that she really looked at it, it was deeply disappointing, and would have been hardly different if she had just moved in yesterday. Usually, she barely noticed any of it: to her it was just a place to sleep, and she spent more time in the regent's study anyway, but this would be the last day she spent in the palace, and she couldn't help but feel a little regretful to be leaving with so little to show she had ever existed. Her eyes took in the flaking yellow paint on the stone walls, the old bed frame carved all over with oak leaves and acorns, the wonky table and the creaky chair worn down to fit her rear perfectly. Only the weapon rack in the corner was dust-free and well-maintained, the spear, sword and buckler cared for as well as any child. Her helmet, scale shirt and armguards hung on wooden pegs, the bronze polished and presentable, if scratched and scarred by battle and training. Beside these she placed the fine walking stick that had once belonged to Alaric's grandmother – the plain stick she'd spent time carving from a fallen branch over the last week was crude, but it also carried far less emotional baggage.

The bed was a mess of embroidered blankets and furs from beasts she had hunted herself, but she couldn't be bothered to tidy them up, nice and ready for a new owner to take her place. She couldn't abide making everything pretty for Hardgrim. Shelves recessed into the wall held souvenirs taken from battles over the years: a broken sword from the raid on the Blackwood Brigands; a silver disc with a stylised horse on one side and a log boat on the other, rescued from the purse of a pair of notorious murderers and thieves called the Snakeling Brothers, who had once haunted the forest trails, picking off travellers. She picked up a bronze mace taken from a Ves marauder and smiled at the comforting weight in her hand. She had wrenched it from the fist of the would-be chieftain who had thought Sunwealders all soft-bellied farmers and lazy shepherds. The big ox's skull had been crushed with this very mace after she'd bashed his teeth to splinters with her shield. Good times, she thought, running a finger down the dented metal.

She sighed and replaced the weapon on the wall. She would need nothing more than a belt knife on her brother's farm, and anything else would serve as an unpleasant reminder of what she had lost. Best to clear the plate of old food and dine on fresher fare. She owned no jewellery or gems, and wore no gold or silver trinkets, but what little wealth she did have now hung on her belt, inside her coin purse. Soon all of this would belong to Hardgrim, and she had no doubt her second would be in a hurry to move out of his more cramped accommodation and into the commander's official chambers. He loved all the trappings of power and the sense of importance it gave him, but she wouldn't miss any of it: her satisfaction came from the job and the duty, not any personal gains her service bought. It had made her feel useful to help create something good for the realm, and even as a child she had liked to make useful things. The other side of that impulse was that she now had precious little left outside that duty.

Ripped out of maudlin introspection by the sound of booted feet and the clink of armour in the hallway outside her rooms, she stuck her head out of the doorway and watched warriors tearing past her. "Gwilherm?" she said. "What's happening?"

The veteran Shield's grey-shot beard jutted from underneath a polished bronze helmet. He too was geared up for battle, dressed in his helmet, scale, studded kilt and warm woollen cloak, with a sword at his hip and clutching a shield and spear. A travel pack was slung across his shoulder. He grinned, exposing stained yellow teeth. "Word's come down from Blaen Mhòr – they've discovered the winter camp of the Wildwood Reivers. At the regent's command, Hardgrim has put together a warband to root them out." He stood straighter and jutted his chin out. "Most of us veterans are going this time, to make sure it's done right. And me, I'm in charge! This is my chance to prove myself worthy of being Hardgrim's second, and I'll make sure they don't slip away this time. We'll be coming back with the heads of those artefact-stealing bastards."

"Well, shit on a stick," Briar said, itching to pull on her own gear and strap on a sword. She glanced back at the scale shirt hanging on her weapon rack.

Gwilherm noticed her hand dropping to her belt, to where a sword should have been sheathed. "We are to set off immediately," he said. "One of our spies spotted the reivers hollowing out log boats to carry their loot downriver, and I mean to catch them before they are finished. It'll be a hard two and a half days' march to Blaen Mhòr, but if we want to catch them before they strike camp we need to leave now. The snows are melting, and the swollen rivers will ward off any rapacious kelpies in the area and carry those boats right over the Ves border if we don't catch them now."

Briar grimaced. "It sticks in my craw that I won't be going with you. How I would love to be there to see an end to those scum."

He grinned. "Just for you, I'll be extra brutal about it."

She clapped a hand on his shoulder. "See that you do, my friend. Take care out there. We've had a right good run, you and I."

His grin faltered, and his gaze bored into her, forcing her to look away. "You won't be here when I get back, will you?" he asked. "I'm no druid, but I can sense which way the wind is blowing."

She smiled sadly. "No. I aim to retire to my brother's farm, up near Drew Nemeton. but don't you go spilling that knowledge. I need to get out of here for a time and try to work out what to do with myself."

"Might do you some good at that," he admitted. "As our leader you were a hard-nosed hound, ferreting out all our mistakes and tearing the arse out of us for the least of them, but I'll still miss you. Hardgrim and his Youngbloods just don't have the same dedication." His fist thumped to his chest in salute. "Commander." Somehow, he managed to fill that last word with depths of feeling she hadn't known he possessed.

Her throat and chest felt suddenly tight. "Good luck, Shield. You will serve the realm well. I suppose that's my last act as your commander. You'll be serving under Hardgrim in truth now."

His face twisted as if he'd bitten into rotten meat. He slipped off his helmet and rested it in the crook of his arm, then stepped in close and hooked his other arm around her waist. She froze as he planted a kiss on her cheek and slipped away before she could object. "Fare you well, Briar," he cried, beating a hasty retreat before she could brain him with something.

"Your breath stinks like a hog in heat," she yelled after him.

"Aye, well, yours is still worse!" he fired back, then turned the corner and was out of sight. "I'll visit you sometime."

She stared at the empty corridor for a long moment, fighting the impulse to ride out to battle beside her Shields one last time. It ebbed, as she knew it would in the face of all practicality. A sea of loss surged in to replace it. She felt hollow, a shell of a person.

Briar cupped her hands around her mouth and breathed out, sniffed and winced. Gwilherm hadn't been lying. Fearing tooth-worms, she carefully cleaned her teeth with salt crystals and sage, and felt fresher for it. She donned the thick, padded tunic that went underneath her armour – it was badly stained but would serve to keep out winter's chill. Spare socks, wraps and woollen kilts were shoved into her satchel beside the small bag of soap, chew sticks, latrine rags and bone comb. Then she added a wooden bowl, spoon, eating knife and horn cup, sparkstone and flint for fire and tinder fungus to kindle the spark, and all the other little bits and pieces she would need on her journey. On top, she squeezed in pouches of dried meat and some boiled honeysweets to keep her going if the weather turned. She looked long and hard at the jar of herbal pellets by the side of her bed, and grudgingly left them untouched – she would just have to be more careful with her body.

Her travel blanket and warm fur were rolled up and secured with a leather thong, and her belt knife was sharpened and sheathed. After a moment's thought, she wrapped a shepherd's sling around her wrist, tied off the cords and added a few rounded river stones to her coin purse in case she encountered any rabbits on her travels. The sling was only braided cord with a woven cradle for the stones, but as simple a weapon as it was, it could easily crack a skull at a goodly distance.

Her last act as Commander of Shields was to unfasten the gold brooch of her status. She turned it over in her hands, caressing the shield-shaped bit of metal that was as much a part of her as her own heart. Best to cut it out in one go. She summoned all her resolve and set it down on the shelf. It took an enormous act of willpower to prise her fingers from her old life – it felt like ripping off a limb and leaving it for the wolves. Hardgrim would no longer merely be acting in the role; Commander Hardgrim was now an unpleasant reality. She'd rather be cursed than hand it over in person, though.

And that was that. It was time to leave the palace behind and head off to make a new life for herself. Whatever it may be. The only problem was that she had intended on obtaining a ride on the back of today's firewood cart, coming up from the nearby hamlets, but with the Shields and warband forming up in the palace grounds, that part of the plan would have to be delayed. Tomorrow would bring the fish trader down the river with seafood to supplement the palace's supply of dried meats, winter vegetables and grains – she would just have to find her way onto his boat heading onwards to Drew Nemeton, stinking as it would be. All of which left her at a loose end for the rest of the day. Just enough time to pay her last respects to the fallen Shields.

She left some crumbs of bread for the friendly crows on her window ledge and walked from her room, her rough walking stick clacking across the stone. She took her time, easing herself down the stairs and resting between floors to stave off potential leg cramps. When the pain spiked, the only thing that helped was to mutter curses down upon the head of the smirking archer who had caused it. Due to his arrow, she had been forced to look at the world through new eyes, ones that noted every handhold, and every step and incline that would pain her leg, calculating how many steps were too many to handle. The palace was not built to accommodate people with disabilities – nowhere was, she had learnt – and facing all those steps made her consider, for the first time in her life, how people with one leg or one arm managed to cope at all in daily life. Not to mention those old warriors who had back and head injuries or had been blinded. There was nobody in the palace able to teach her how to manage her disability better, as all wounded veterans had been paid a small pension and entrusted to their families to look after them. Yes, it could have been far worse, she mused: at least she could still walk a good distance on the flat before her leg gave out.

At the ground floor she made her way down the hall and into the kitchens. Bunches of dried herbs and haunches of meat hung from the ceiling beams, and a big tub of fresh and frothy ale brewing in the corner gifted the room a nutty aroma. A small army of harried servants were hauling sides of salted beef and mutton and lengths of pork and beef sausage up through the trapdoor that led to the cool room, ready to be cut up into portions. The menial drudges hauled and hurried to and fro while their superiors portioned and packed the sacks of supplies for the warband about to embark on an extermination of the Wildwood Reivers: strips of smoked venison, fresh-baked sweet bannock breads, nuts, extra waterskins and whatever else they could rustle up for a group constantly on the move.

The regent's dog, Brutus, sat at attention beneath a hanging haunch of beef, ever hopeful for somebody to drop something he could steal and scoff down. The kitchen was his favourite place in the entire palace, for obvious reasons. His second preferred napping spot was the old disused armoury several floors directly up. It was a wretched place, and Briar could only assume he liked the peace and quiet and the cooking smells that drifted up the chimney.

A reed-thin white-haired woman with flour-dusted skirts and shrewd, dark eyes spotted her lurking and nodded to her. "Hello, Briar," she said, finishing off tying up a leather sack of oatmeal to sit beside a slab of butter wrapped in cabbage leaves. The warband shouldn't be gone long enough to need extra supplies for cooking, but many a journey had been delayed by bad wounds or weather, and any snowbound traveller would be glad of fresh and buttery oatcakes baked on hot stones, huddled around a campfire.

Briar inclined her head. "Hearth Mistress Morna," she replied. "As always, it is good to see you." Other than the regent and the Commander of Shields, the hearth mistress held the most respected role in the entire palace. Nobody with any sense would dare anger the woman who fed them so well, not unless they loved unsalted porridge and soup that was more like water.

Morna glanced at Briar, and then at a wicker basket in the corner of the room. "I'm busy," she said. "I've set your goods aside for you, so help yourself." Then she got on with her work and ignored Briar's existence.

Briar took no umbrage; it was just the way of the hearth mistress. She explored the food supplies she'd bribed her to set aside for the journey and noted Morna had slipped in a wineskin, the red stain around the stopper giving away that it wasn't well water. Expensive and unasked for, but very much appreciated. As she packed away the supplies, Brutus sidled over, wet nose snuffling at her satchel.

"Back, back, you terrible beast," she said, shooing him away. He woofed and huffed and settled back down, eyes wide and pleading. "You can get more food if you earn it," she added. He looked mortally offended, as if he might perish right there on the spot from the mere suggestion of work.

Briar rolled her eyes, hefted her sack and turned to Morna, who was busy cutting up a length of blood sausage on the table. "Please take care of this place while I am away."

A titbit of sausage dropped to the floor, and a wheaten blur snatched it up and wolfed it down. Brutus stood at attention, fixated on what was occurring above him, tail wagging hopefully.

The hearth mistress waggled a finger at Briar. "Don't you worry your pretty little head about Himself and his. I'll look after them." She turned her shrewd eyes on Brutus and stared him down. The dog whined and slunk off, tail down and defeated. For now. He knew he'd had as much of a treat as he'd be allowed for one day. "Now be off with you, Briar, before somebody notices his wine pitcher has gone empty."

Briar smiled her thanks. "Fare you well, Hearth Mistress, and thank you for all you have done for me over the years."

Morna waved a dismissive hand. "Pshaw! 'Twas just doing my job. Good health to you, lass."

Supplies in hand, Briar left the kitchens behind and slowly, carefully descended to the door of the catacombs. She drew out her key and unlocked the door, marvelling as always at the ingenuity of the druids and master bronze workers who had built such intricate mechanisms. Their arcane secrets were beyond her ken, which was just the way they wanted it. She grabbed a lantern from the wall and ventured into the darkness, locking it behind her again. The air was cool and comforting, and the tunnels silent as the grave. When she reached the Hall of Broken Shields, her hand tightened on her walking stick. She took her time exploring every nook and cranny, ready to crack the skull of any assassin who dared to raise their head. This time she was alone, the only living soul in the long tomb.

There, among the carved likenesses of her past brothers and sisters in service, the enormity of what she was about to do hit her like a fist to the face – after today, she could never claim to be a Shield, and she would never lie to rest among them. She swallowed and walked the hall, committing to memory the cold, hard faces belonging to women and men harder still than any stone. They had died for honour and duty, each and every one. She sighed and shook her head, moving past the tombs of the long-dead and towards those she had known in life. She stopped at the tombs of Barik, Sleen and Cathbad, and the empty space where her own tomb should have one day rested.

For a moment, just a single one, she wished that arrow had killed her outright instead of merely destroying her entire life and purpose. That arrow had wrought terrible change, but she was not about to succumb to dark despair just yet. Barik, Sleen and Cathbad would never forgive her if she travelled to meet them in the otherworld without making a fight of it. Shields endured. Shields never gave up. Shields protected. She eased herself down onto the cold stone, set her back to Cathbad's tomb and took the wineskin from her belt.

She poured a little of the ruinously expensive imported wine onto his tomb as an offering, hoping that somewhere in the otherworld his spirit appreciated it. "It wasn't the dust and flowers and coughing that killed you in the end, Cathbad." She could almost hear his voice in her head, objecting. That one would complain and argue until the cows came home. "Though I imagine wherever you are now you'll be claiming that bronze comes from the bones of the earth too. I will accede that it counts." She took a gulp of wine. It was ridiculously good and strong as anything, bursting with ripe berry flavour. Alaric did like his wine, one of the very few vices he allowed himself.

She found it easier to talk to the dead than to the living. Shields, especially women warriors, were not exactly known for displaying their vulnerabilities to all and sundry, but the spirits of the dead saw right through her mask of coping. They already knew all her weaknesses, and they would not judge her for them. She began to talk, and soon the fear and torment flowed out of her like a river. Stones passed down there in the darkness, all that anger and frustration pouring out of her – far more than even she knew she had kept dammed up inside. At some point she found her eyes damp, her nose running and the wineskin emptied.

Her abrupt laughter surprised her, black mirth bubbling up from some deep, dark well. "What a sorry state to fall into," she murmured, scrubbing a hand across her face. "I am still a Shield. Now and always, in heart if not in body."

The alcohol had warmed her belly and fogged her fears, but the sober part of her pointed out it was unwise to attempt the stairs while she was unsteady on her feet. She laughed again at the absurdity of her life: wounded and weak and leaving behind the stubborn man she loved with all her heart.

She set the lantern up out of reach of any flailing arms or feet. Nightmares were all too common these days. She put down her furs, unrolled her blankets and made a nest out of her bags and supplies right there among the tombs. She laid down to rest for a short while among her fallen sisters and brothers, appreciating the peace and the quiet company. Barring some kind of disaster, tomorrow she would be leaving the palace and her duty behind, but on this final day she was still a Shield.

CHAPTER 11

The slaughter was to begin in the heart of darkness, six stones after nightfall. Most of the palace residents were deep in slumber, safely curled up under blankets and thick furs to keep out the winter chill. With the main warband out hunting the Wildwood Reivers, only a few Shields were left behind to guard the walls, but the defences were stout and the trained warriors skilled enough to see off anything short of a small army – and even then they would simply retreat into the palace proper, bar the doors and force any attackers foolish enough to attempt a winter siege to suffer out in the open while they waited in the warmth.

Outside, Hardgrim stalked the walls that surrounded the palace, his breath fogging in the moonlight. Sword and buckler were at his hip, ready for use, and his belt knife was recently sharpened. This starry night held a sparkling clarity that only winter nights could offer. The air was deathly still, as if the earth and heavens held their breath.

He approached the outer gatehouse, where Ruith, Ahern and Keelin were on duty, taking turns to warm themselves around a brazier when not keeping watch over the moonlit farmland and forest. Ruith and Keelin were huddled by the fire, shrouded in thick fur cloaks and gloves. Hardgrim nodded to Ruith, and the younger man smiled back.

"Commander?" Ahern said, frowning. The heavy-set man approached him. "What brings you to the walls this night? We are not so undermanned that we need you to keep watch with us. Or could you not sleep with the warband out on a raid without you there to lead it? Trust in Gwilherm: he will prove himself a worthy second with this opportunity you have given him."

Hardgrim sighed. "I still worry all is not going to plan. There was just so much here to organise. Damn all scrollwork!" He clapped a hand on the man's shoulder and steered him to face the lands beyond the walls of the palace. "Tell me, what do you see?" The surrounding gardens were barren and white, studded with slumbering beehives made from baked clay and straw, and beyond those the forest stood dark and silent. A few flickering lights in the distance marked the fires of scattered farmsteads.

Shield Ahern's reply was a desperate bubbling and brief hiss as Hardgrim's knife punctured his neck and sawed outwards through throat and vocal cords in a messy spray of blood. Ahern had been a decent enough man, Hardgrim thought, but unambitious and fatally overburdened with honour and loyalty to regent and realm. He could not be bought or swayed. What a waste.

Hardgrim eased the jerking body down to the stonework to minimise the noise, then went to help Ruith. Shield Keelin was struggling in his grip, her voice muffled by the glove clamped over her mouth and nose. Hardgrim secured the Shield's arms, allowing for Ruith's knife to find its way up through the bronze scales in her armour and plunge in and out until the woman stilled.

Hardgrim and Ruith dragged both corpses to one side, out of view of the palace windows. They scraped snow and ice off the walls and dumped them into the brazier, causing a signal plume of smoke and steam to rise into the night air. They hurried to unbar the main gate, heaving the thick oak beam from its stone settings. Twenty hard-faced men and women in thick leather and furs sauntered through: the Wildwood Reivers, led by a black-bearded and scar-faced warrior called

Uradech, their self-styled chief. Beside him walked a smirking cleanshaven failure of an archer Hardgrim knew only too well. The outer palace was theirs now.

"What a lovely night for a spot of murder," the assassin Maddox said, keeping his voice low. "Imperatrix will fly into a rage if this doesn't go smoothly."

Hardgrim scowled at the archer. "If your arrows had flown true at the summer rites then we'd already have everything we want. With that ignorant brat Kester on the Oaken Throne, I would have been free to let Imperatrix do whatever she liked without more bloodshed."

Maddox shrugged. "My aim was perfect. That woman got in the way, repeatedly. Hardly my fault we ran out of time – she was accursedly good at her job. Blame your own hirelings, who gave themselves away to the Shields before their deed was done. I was only ever meant to be the backup."

Before Hardgrim could punch the arrogant pig in the mouth, Uradech interrupted their feud, the older man's voice like gravel. "Enough flapping your jaws. We are here to kill and become wealthy men. Show us inside."

Hardgrim shrugged and escorted the men to the heavy oak door leading to the inner palace. They didn't have long to wait before somebody unbarred it from the inside and the way to the inner palace yawned open. Shadows deepened as the masked form of Imperatrix stepped into the courtyard with a lit candlestick in her hand, flames dancing madly in the breeze. The former Shields Phelan and Owyn were with her, and they offered Hardgrim a nod of acknowledgement, their knives dripping blood in the moonlight. Six other armed men lurked in the shadows behind them, dressed as the lowly servants they had pretended to be for months. Six traitors and Hardgrim's eight Youngblood former Shields had achieved what entire warbands never had: the conquest of Sunweald.

"Uradech, Maddox," Imperatrix said, "it is time." She stepped aside and waved her people through into the Sunweald Palace.

"I need Alaric or Kester taken alive to gain timely access to the Vault. Bring me both if you can manage it, but if not, I would prefer the boy intact. He should prove far more malleable. Kill the slumbering guards and capture the senior household staff – I may need some leverage to force those two noble pricks to reveal all their family secrets."

Hardgrim grinned. "You heard her, lads. Kill the remaining loyal Shields in their sleep, dispose of all lowly servants and then drag the rest of those pompous pricks to the Great Hall. You are all castoffs of this realm's so-called noble clans, and tonight we take what should have been ours by right. Tonight, it is we who rule. Fuck Sunweald – follow me and we will all be living like clan chiefs soon."

Maddox rolled his eyes at the impassioned speech. "Don't get overexcited, lads," he said as he followed his men into the guts of the palace. "Best be quick and quiet as you go about your work."

Hardgrim led the way into the dark and slumbering palace. He retrieved a stash of candles and lanterns he'd left out earlier, lit them from Imperatrix's flame and handed them out. They split the armed host in two, and he sent one lot to work their way down the nearby hallways. Here on the lower levels, where the servants lived, most rooms were communal, and many made do with thick drapes instead of solid doors. The men slaughtered their way through the rooms while their occupants slept, thinking themselves safe and secure. Knives and clubs rose and fell, callously ending the lives of cooks, kitchen aides, gardeners, messenger boys, cleaners and washerwomen. A shame, Hardgrim thought, but their total force of thirty-five men was too few to occupy the entire palace while guarding all its current inhabitants, even if eight of his men were competent former Shields. If a single moment of negligence or bad luck allowed word to escape these walls... No, it was certainly not worth the risk. Most of the servants had to die. Hardgrim shook his head and left them to their grisly work. He made for the Shield barracks, stopped outside the door and nodded to Maddox.

The archer got his men in position either side of the doorway, clubs and knives poised for action.

Hardgrim took a deep breath, opened the reinforced door and entered. Only two men currently occupied the long room designed for dozens, but Trahern and Sloane were veterans who had been handpicked and trained by Briar; they instantly woke from their slumber and reached for their blades.

"Commander?" Trahern said, his good eye squinting up into the light of the candle. The older man had a puckered scar running the length of his other cheek and over a milky eye.

"Need you both on the walls," Hardgrim said.

The two men shot to their feet and grabbed swords and bucklers.

"Calm yourselves," Hardgrim said softly. "Keelin and Ahern ate something they shouldn't have is all. They're too busy shitting themselves to keep a proper watch."

Sloane chuckled and sauntered towards the door. "I said to them, I did, that frozen trout would get its revenge on 'em."

Trahern stiffened, his good eye fixed on Hardgrim's boots and the bloody footprints he'd left on the way in. It seemed Briar's story from the summer solstice had made an impact on the man.

"Not again," Hardgrim growled as he flung himself at Trahern. He grabbed the man by the throat and squeezed to stop him screaming a warning. Hardgrim's men bludgeoned Sloane to death as he exited the room unawares, and they came pouring in to give their leader aid.

A club came down and brained Trahern, splattering Hardgrim with the Shield's blood and brains. Hardgrim glared at Maddox, who smirked at the work of his gory club. "You'll pay for that indignity," the commander whispered to the archer, wiping his face and hands on a crumpled blanket.

Maddox shrugged. "Sure. I'd happily pay to do it again, too." He slipped away into the corridor before Hardgrim could throttle another man.

They swept through the darkened hallways of the ground floor, killing most and capturing and gagging those of higher status before they knew what was happening to them. Then they dragged the survivors off, up towards the Great Hall on the second floor, where Imperatrix now kept court with Phelan and Owyn to guard her. Six men split away, four to block off the smaller exits and two to guard the central stairwell, while the rest ascended to raid the upper levels, where the most important officials of Sunweald slept in large and luxurious chambers.

Hardgrim sent a group of reivers led by Ruith off to the western side of the palace with the twins Newlyn and Nealon, among the most dependable of his former Shields, to act as his seconds. Their task was to drag Kester and Alaric from their warm beds, while Uradech and Maddox led another group in capturing people of lesser importance. Hardgrim himself had more pressing and personal plans to see to before he could turn his attention elsewhere.

First, he made sure the heavy oak-and-bronze door to the palace strongroom was locked. Other than the regent, only he had keys to the room that guarded the realm's riches in gems and precious metals, and soon he would also have that second set in his hands. He forbade the reivers from trying to break in, telling the superstitious fools that this was where the diseased, the plague-ridden and the cursed were confined and treated by druids – he wasn't about to let their grubby paws root through his property. Fortunately for him, Imperatrix had her mind set on more arcane matters and had shown little interest in obtaining the palace's mundane treasures – she had been happy to forgo any claim on those to secure Hardgrim's aid.

The brigands shied away from the strongroom door, clutched their crude folk-magic talismans and promised to pass on the warning to their fellows. With his treasure secured, Hardgrim moved on to something he had been looking forward to for a very long time. He took two men and made his way to crusty old Briar's chambers. It was his room by right, and on this night he would take ownership. He'd deserved to be promoted to Commander of Shields for years now, had even been acting as commander for two whole seasons, and that rat-faced regent had still not seen fit to give Hardgrim his dues. Well, he thought, Alaric Summerson would be paying for everything now.

He handed his candle off to one of the men and tested Briar's door. He grinned as he found it unbarred. The woman had become old and weak-minded, he thought, as he eased it open. The blankets and furs were a crumpled mess in the middle of the bed. He eased his sword from its scabbard and snuck in, lifting the bronze blade high. He savoured the moment it arced down. His glee lasted a single instant. The blade cut through heaped bedding and into the bed beneath. There was no body inside the blankets. Briar was missing.

Hardgrim flung open the window shutter to let in the moonlight, startling the crow that had been perched there. Before it could raise a ruckus, he swung his sword, cleaving the scavenger in two. As the little black corpse dropped to the ground below, its kin took up their angry screeching. How he hated those noisy, flying vermin that covered everything in bird shit.

He scanned the room for any sign of where its owner might have gone, but came up short. "Search every room," he said to the two with him. "If you find Briar, you save her for me." He snatched up the golden commander's brooch she'd carelessly left on the shelf and suppressed the urge to howl in victory. He searched the room and, as he was sure he would, found a ball of cord in a basket – old warriors always kept some nearby for repairs on the move. He cut off a length, fastened on the brooch, tied it off and looped it around his neck. He admired how right it looked against his armour. "Finally," he muttered. "This should have been adorning my chest long ago."

A woman's angry roar rent the silence. "Shit," he said as the clang and cursing of battle rang out, no doubt waking people from their sleep.

Newlyn and Nealon were busy breaking down Kester's door. He left them to it and followed the sounds of combat to the regent's study. Ruith lurched out of the open doorway, one hand clutching his bloodied face. More of his men charged in, shouldering open the door that the Shield inside was desperately trying to close. The clash of metal and thud of bodies hitting stone accompanied yelled warnings and shrill screams of wounded men.

Hardgrim's sword was in his hand as he reached Ruith. Blood trickled down the man's cheek from a small wound in his forehead. "Shield Brenna," Ruith explained. Hardgrim scowled and shoved past. The man had only been given one job here – to get her to open the door and then keep it open. Apparently, he couldn't even be trusted to get that right.

Hardgrim ran in to find Brenna in the doorway to the regent's bedchamber, blocking any from entering. The woman was built like a bull and was just as fearsome when enraged. She laid about her with sword and buckler, driving back five men, cutting the hand off one and breaking a short and stocky man's face with the boss of her bronze buckler. Her scale armour was drenched in blood from taking a club to the face, leaving her with a split lip and shattered jaw.

Some whispered warning from her ancestral spirits must have alerted her to new danger. Her buckler darted up to deflect Hardgrim's sword, and her foot lashed out, barely missing his knee, driving him back. She glared at him something fierce, outraged at his betrayal, but the shock of his appearance caused her to hesitate for a single moment. It was long enough for one of the men to get inside her guard and grab her sword arm and hang on for dear life. They swarmed over her and clubbed her to a messy death, with only one broken arm and numerous bruises among them to show for it. The man with the missing hand wailed piteously, staring at his spurting stump. Hardgrim slit his throat and let him drop, bubbling and jerking. Nobody here needed to listen to the screeching of a now-useless man.

"Quiet down!" Hardgrim demanded, stalking into the regent's bedchamber.

Alaric Summerson was awake and standing by his bed, blankets clutched in one hand to hide his nakedness. In his other, he wielded an exquisite bronze blade decorated with gold and amber. Hardgrim was grudgingly impressed that the man's hand didn't shake.

"Why have you done this?" the regent asked, shifting his stance with the intent of fighting Hardgrim. "The gods curse you as a betrayer and an oath-breaker."

Hardgrim snorted. "What neither the gods nor you have given me, I take with my own two hands." He sheathed his sword and took a club from one of his men, then advanced with the buckler in one hand and the weapon weaving dangerously out before him. "Be sensible and drop the pretty blade, *Lord Regent.*"

Alaric gritted his teeth. "Make me, wretch." He charged instead of backing away. A hand whipped up, and the blanket billowed out before him like a net, wrapping around Hardgrim and entangling his club and buckler. The regent's blade swung for the former Shield's throat.

Hardgrim lurched to the side, turning a killing blow into a gash on the chin. He snarled and tore himself free of the blanket, using his buckler to knock the regent's next strike aside. The club came round and smashed into the regent's ribs.

Alaric gasped in pain and fell to his knees, the sword dropping to the floor as he clutched his broken ribs.

Hardgrim's men grabbed hold of the regent and held him tight as their leader staunched the bleeding with a rag held to his chin. "A brave attempt," he said. "Now it's my turn. She wants you alive, but she didn't say you had to be intact." He grinned and kicked the regent in the face three times until he hung in his captor's hands, dazed and drooling blood. For good measure, and personal pleasure, Hardgrim kicked the regent twice in his broken ribs, savouring the shrieks of agony.

He grabbed Alaric's hair and yanked his face up, then spat on it. "Not so high and mighty now, are we, Lord Regent? You and yours are not our betters. You never were." He chuckled and waved for his men to drag him off. "Deliver him into Imperatrix's tender mercies."

The regent's sword he took for his own, admiring the mastery of its maker and the richness of its furnishings.

"Commander!" Ruith yelled from further up the hallway. "A little aid, if you please."

Hardgrim sprinted from the regent's study and immediately cursed at the tangle of struggling men outside Kester's rooms – the loyal Shield Afric had been brought down under the mass of bodies, but the older man had bought time for Kester to slip through the press. The boy wore only a long night tunic, and clutched a belt in his hands, complete with purse and small knife. His hands fumbled for the blade.

"We'll have none of that foolishness," Hardgrim said. "Come here, boy."

The half-naked boy paused and stared at him, hope blooming in his eyes. Then he spotted his uncle, dragged from his rooms all battered and bloody with the supposed Commander of his Shields doing nothing about it.

"Come here, Kester," Hardgrim demanded. "Before you get yourself hurt."

The Royal Heir swallowed. He glanced at all the armed men before turning and making a run for the stairs, bare feet slapping across the cold floor as he darted and dodged outstretched hands like he was more slippery eel than boy. Somebody grabbed a handful of his night tunic, but the fabric tore, and the boy managed to reach the stairwell and race down the steps.

"Catch the brat!" Hardgrim ordered Newlyn and Nealon – they took off after him, woollen winter cloaks flapping out behind them. Hardgrim had no doubt his trained Shields would be able to best a mere boy. If nothing else, the cold would slow him down eventually.

Hardgrim stalked the halls in a rage, battering down doors and hauling people from their beds. If they resisted capture, he beat them bloody and left them to be dragged off like sacks of meat. The casual brutality went some way towards restoring his mood. He had secured the regent, but the others had lost Kester, and Briar was not even here. They'd made a piss-poor job of it, but then he couldn't be everywhere.

Kester's heart hammered against his ribs as he sped down the spiral stairs at a dizzying pace. Bile seared the back of his throat. He had to run. Had to hide. The slimy head of his cowardice uncoiled inside his belly. He couldn't catch his breath. It was happening all over again.

He mistimed a step and slammed a shoulder into the wall, skinning it and leaving a bloody smear behind as he bounced off and teetered on the verge of falling down a hundred stone steps.

Kester managed to steady himself, narrowly avoiding plunging down headfirst. What would Briar tell him to do? he asked himself as he caught his breath. Run, get help and get to safety. He had to raise the alarm, get to the barracks and wake the Shields. His stomach lurched as he remembered that Hardgrim, Ruith, Newlyn and Nealon were among the attackers. They'd murdered Afric right in front of him. Probably Brenna too, if they'd got through her to his uncle. Unless... had she also been a party to their treachery?

"Come back to us, boy," Newlyn shouted from above, his feet on the steps and armour clinking.

"Did your nursemaid not warn you of the danger of running down stairs?" his brother, Nealon, added. "You wouldn't want to have your legs... broken."

Kester shuddered and forced himself to keep moving, to speed up until his feet drummed the stone. The ground floor came into sight. A haggard man he'd never seen before glanced up, dressed in grubby winter furs and a stained cloak. He lifted his axe, and a gap-toothed yellow grin slicked across his face. Kester abandoned any thought of getting help and kept going down. He tore open the purse attached to his belt, heedless of the silver coins and precious amber beads that spilled out. What he needed was the key to the catacombs he'd borrowed from an unwary Shield.

He raced down and down and then found himself at the locked door blocking his route to safety in the tunnels beyond. If he could get to the tombs, he reckoned he could hide himself away. His hand shook as he desperately tried to fit the key into the hole. He had to use two hands to steady it. Newlyn and Nealon were right behind him as he managed to unlock it and shove the heavy door open. He squeezed through the gap into darkness just as Newlyn and Nealon emerged from the stairwell.

"You little–" Newlyn growled, charging towards him like an angry bear.

Kester slammed the door shut and locked it, flinching back as it shuddered in its frame from the heavy impact.

"Do not dare move from that spot," they said from the other side of the door.

The door between them gave Kester a measure of bravado. "The gods curse you as oath-breakers," he yelled. "The spirits of your ancestors will spit in your face when you meet them in the otherworld – and that will come sooner than you think!" He wrapped his belt around his waist and felt for the knife, only to find the blade must have fallen from the sheath on his flight down the stairs.

Something heavy slammed into the door. One of his pursuers mumbled something about a key, and Kester's courage deserted him. Before they could unlock the door and grab hold of him, he turned and ran blindly into the all-consuming darkness. He kept his hands out in front of him and tried to find his way by memory, stumbling across the slick, winter-chilled floor that numbed his toes. Cold air wafted through his torn night tunic and across his buttocks. Every crunch of gravel sounded to his ears like a horn-call alerting all the world to his location.

He sped up, heedless of bruises and cuts. This time, he was far more afraid of what was coming behind him than anything else that might be in the dark tunnels of the catacombs.

CHAPTER 12

Briar snapped to awareness with a hand already wrapped around the hilt of her belt knife. Something was wrong. She could feel it in her bones. A deep-seated animal instinct had roused her from a fitful rest, and hot blood pumped through her veins, readying her body to fight and kill. The small flame of her lantern sputtered and swayed in a draft.

She held her breath, ears straining and eyes searching the shadows of the tombs for any sign of what had disturbed her slumber. A crunch of feet on stone sheddings from a nearby tunnel, followed by a distant echo of an angry man's shout. She grabbed hold of her walking stick and levered herself to her feet. She hid her lantern away behind a tomb and padded into the darkness, listening intently as she headed for the entrance to the Hall of Broken Shields.

The sounds were hurrying closer through the darkness, and whoever they belonged to did not have anything to light their way. Briar hid in the shadows and eased her knife from its sheath. She was taking no chances. She readied herself to strike, but the sight of a familiar young face stayed her hand.

"Kester?" she said, stepping out from the shadows and into the well-lit doorway of the sacred Hall.

The boy startled, and squinted into the lantern light.

"Where is your Shield?" she asked, peering behind him. "Do you not remember what happened last time you…?" Her question crumbled at the realisation the boy was half-clothed, barefoot, bloodied and trembling in terror.

His lip quivered. "Briar!" He ran to her, sobbing into her breast, and began babbling about an attack: Alaric taken, Shields murdered, and of Hardgrim's treachery.

For all that Kester seemed to have turned over a new leaf, she still harboured many reservations about him, but even at his worst, he would never have lied about something like this. She cursed, and her stomach dropped into a black pit upon realising that this enemy had invaded the palace the very evening after the warband had taken the bulk of its veteran defenders out on a raid. It was no coincidence most of the older warriors were away, and she had no trouble believing that Hardgrim was behind it all.

"Where are you, boy?" a voice called. "If you come out now we won't hurt you more than we have to."

"The brat is not hidden among the treasures of the Heart," a second added. "So he must be cowering behind these tombs."

Kester shuddered. "Newlyn and Nealon," he whispered. "Hardgrim sent them after me."

There was no time to affect an escape. "Go to the tomb of Cathbad," Briar said. "I need you to take hold of the lantern there and stand in the centre of the hall, right where they can see you." He'd fought an assassin for her once, and she prayed he had the balls to hold strong this time too – if she had to stand and protect a mewling heap of cowardice, they were both dead. "I promise they will never reach you – but try to look pathetic and terrified, so they do not suspect my presence. Do you have a weapon?"

He swallowed and shook his head. "I will have no problem looking scared."

She handed over her own belt knife, favouring the reach of her stout walking stick in the wide area of the Hall. "That is your last resort. Hide it away, and if one of them gets past me, you bury it in his gut and run like the wind."

Kester swallowed and did as he was told, while Briar leant her stick against the right-hand wall and uncoiled the cord of her shepherd's sling from around her wrist. She pulled two smooth river stones from her coin purse and slipped one into the sling's woven cradle.

She waited and watched, listening as heavier footfalls approached the Hall of Broken Shields. Somebody was about to be in a whole world of pain. The noblest warriors of Sunweald's clans valued their decorated swords and spears above bows, and outright sneered at the humble shepherd's weapon made from a length of simple woven cord. As a child, she'd killed hungry wolves with sling and stone, and this two-legged prey would be a far easier target for a diligent shepherd such as she.

"There's the little shit," Newlyn said, breath misting the chill underground air. The warrior stood right outside the doorway, fully lit by the twin lanterns that flanked it. He was staring at Kester, and any night vision he might have had was ruined by the light. A perfect target – and while he wore a scale shirt and armguards, he wasn't wearing a helmet, praise the gods! Briar shook her head, disgusted at the lack of training from one of Hardgrim's handpicked Youngbloods. What kind of idiots went into a fight without having prepared when they had plenty of time to do so?

She spun the sling, swinging it up and over two times to build up force before releasing it. The stone struck Newlyn's eye with an audible crack even as she slipped a second stone into the cradle and spun it up. He reeled back, face burst, cheekbone crushed. The next stone shattered teeth and jaw and put the man on the ground. His brother stepped forward into the light, hunting for the attacker. Nealon couldn't see Briar, but he could see Kestor, and capturing the boy became the furthest thing from his mind: he drew his sword and raised his buckler to guard his face from stones. Then he roared and charged.

Briar dropped her sling and swept up her walking stick, swinging from the darkness. She struck Nealon's ankle as the man charged ahead like a maddened bull. He sensed her presence a moment too late and hadn't a hope of keeping his balance. He fell flat on his face, but immediately rolled to the side, suffering a second strike to his elbow rather than his throat. His shield hand flopped, numb and useless, but he rose to his knees, sword lashing out at his attacker.

She batted the blade aside with her stick, reversed the stroke and cracked him on the chin, snapping his head back. "You are about to die, oath-breaker," she said, as he shook his head and tried to struggle to his feet – as if she would let him.

He was on his knees, and she had the reach. He hadn't a chance of recovering enough to make a fight of it and his brother was still down, clutching his shattered face. With her leg she couldn't run far or fast, but her upper body and hips worked just fine. Brutal blows rained down on Nealon, Briar's outrage at the betrayal of his sacred duty granting her furious strength. His armour and the padding beneath blunted many of her blows, but his elbows, legs and head were all vulnerable. She took out some of her frustration on his flesh, beating him until he was blackened and bloody and broken.

Nealon lay mewling and motionless at her feet. "Mercy," he hissed, a bloody froth dripping from his mashed lips.

"Mercy? For a traitor?" she asked. "You should know better than to ask that of me. The best you can expect is a quick death. You will answer me, or you will writhe in indescribable agony before the end. How many of you are there?"

He chuckled. "Too many. You are fucked. You are all fucked."

Briar smiled, cold and hard. "Kester, bring me that lantern. Nealon's brother is about to become a living pyre. It will be an excruciating death."

"No!" the former Shield gasped as the Royal Heir approached, lantern in hand. He grimaced as his broken body tried and failed to rise. "Please…"

She jabbed the tip of her walking stick into his groin and then shoved, putting all her weight behind it. He shrieked and writhed, the movement causing every broken bone in his body to grind together, resulting in waves of absolute agony.

"Answer me, or I will make you watch as your brother burns alive," she said. "I'll start with his feet, and I'll make it last. How many are you?"

"Thirty-five warriors and one sorcerer," Nealon hissed. "That is all. I swear."

She grunted, believing him. "What is your purpose here?"

"Imperatrix–" As the word left his mouth his eyes flew wide, and the insides of his eyes burst, red flooding across the whites.

Briar and Kester jerked back as the man shook and screamed. His skin sizzled and crisped. A gout of fire erupted from his throat and eye sockets, briefly lighting up the Hall before it died off into greasy curls of smoke that filled the air with the stench of burnt meat.

Briar and Kester stared at the corpse. "By the gods," Kester said, "what was that?"

"Blackest magic," Briar hissed. "A killing curse, designed to burn him from the inside out if he tried to reveal the sorcerer's vile secrets to an enemy. I have heard tales of such corrupt magic, but I thought it mostly a myth. Oath-broken indeed."

"What about Newlyn?" he asked.

She grunted as she bent over to pick up the discarded sword, sheath and buckler and attach them to her own belt. Then she took Nealon's belt knife and swapped it with Kester to have her own trusted blade back where it belonged. She leant on her stick and clacked over to Newlyn, who lay on his back, barely conscious and half drowned in his own blood from his shattered jaw. The man wouldn't be able to talk, and she had no more use for him. She slid the point of the sword between the armoured scales of his shirt and nestled it between his ribs, then shoved it through leather and cloth and into his heart. The man stilled after a few moments.

"His sword is now yours," she said to Kester. "Use it better than this disloyal waste of skin. Put on that tunic and kilt before you freeze to death down here."

"Do you feel... anything?" he asked. "You just killed two men."

She looked at the body sprawled by her feet. "They were no men. And it was one – their sorcerer killed the other. Not that it matters, so long as they are dead. All I feel is disgust that their tainted blood stains the floor of this sacred place."

Kester nodded, then disrobed Newlyn's body and pulled on the dead man's clothing. He fastened the boots and wrapped the cloak around himself, savouring the warmth. All of it fitted him poorly, but it was better than frostbitten toes and fingers, or other bits.

"Not the armour," she said as he reached for the scale shirt. "It is much too large and heavy for you, and it will hinder more than it helps."

He sighed and, unbidden, put in the effort of dragging the traitors' corpses out into the tunnel beyond the Hall of Broken Shields, unceremoniously dumping them into a heap.

Briar nodded her gratitude and found her opinion of Kester had improved slightly. "We are safe for the moment. Tell me everything, and leave not a single detail out of your tale."

Once he was done relating all he knew in a much calmer fashion, he added, "I don't know who that Imperatrix person is, though." He glanced around, worried about sorcerous fires. "Or what else they can do."

"Two down and another thirty-three warriors to go, if Nealon was to be believed," Briar said. "Mighty odds to face."

"But you are Briar," he countered. "You are the Commander of Shields and the best warrior in all Sunweald. You can save us. Can't you?"

His eyes were so full of hope. She hated to disappoint him, but she was also not about to lie over something so deadly serious. She slowly looked over her left leg. "I'm not what I was. Even without this wound they are far too many for any one Shield to fight head on. We don't even know why they are here – this could be a prelude to invasion by the Ves or the Wrendals, and more might be on the way. My primary duty is to keep you alive. Once the future ruler of Sunweald is safe I can act to get your uncle out of this mess." Assuming he was still alive.

Kester shivered, then nodded in understanding. "What can I do to help?" He drew his sword and held it in a shaking hand. "I can fight. I've been trained by the best."

"Practice is no match for life-and-death experience," she replied. The boy's strength and skill were still poor, despite a newfound enthusiasm for his training. "I don't doubt your stout heart, Kester, but you are not ready for this." She paused, weighing up the risk of putting him in some small amount of danger versus the risk of them blundering about the palace without a plan. She grimaced, then tapped her wounded leg. "If you want to be a warrior under my command then I will give you a vital task. I cannot run all over the palace gathering the information we need to make a survivable plan, so I need you to be my legs for a while. I require your good eyes and ears."

He frowned and reluctantly eased his sword back into its sheath.

"The twins mentioned they had been in the Heart, looking for you," she said. "They came to no harm, which indicates the traitors are likely in control of that cavern as well as the ground-floor stairwell. Hardgrim is pond slime but, as loathe as I am to admit it, he is not a complete fool. He would not try to capture you and the regent without securing the routes in and out behind him. They will already have the inner gate and side doors under heavy guard, especially with you on the run. What I need you to do is crawl into Quinn the Eel's tomb and use the secret tunnels to spy on them. With luck, you can discover if their reported numbers are true, if Alaric is alive and what their ultimate goal is. Only then can we act. Can you do that for me?"

Kester gulped and looked at the lantern in his hand. "I assume taking a lantern is out of the question. Perhaps a candle?"

She shook her head. "Darkness is your friend now, Kester. Hold her close to your heart, and wrap her around you like a silent shroud. If they see even a glimmer of light through a crack in the stonework, you will die. Keep to the tunnels, and keep your eyes and ears open."

"Crawling about filthy tunnels in the dark is not what I had in mind when I said I wanted to be a warrior," he mumbled, eyeing the lantern mournfully.

"The wise warrior strikes when and where the enemy least expects it," she replied. "The most important thing I can teach you is this: stay alive. Glory doesn't keep you warm at night. Glory does not regrow severed limbs and heal broken bones. Seeking glory only gets those around you killed, and even if you survived to bask in it, I promise you would come to regret that sacrifice. My own glory comes from keeping those I care about alive."

She unwrapped the warm cloak from his chilled body. "Best take this off so it doesn't get snagged and choke you. Now, be off with you – stay quiet and stay safe."

Kester stared up at her with wide, worshipful eyes. His fist thumped his chest. "Yes, Commander. I am honoured to be your eyes and ears." He squeezed into the tomb and tunnel, leaving Briar as the last living thing in that hall of the dead.

Briar watched the boy leave and then returned to the bodies. Now that she had a sword and shield, she felt ready for a fight, but she pondered donning the armour as well. It smelled like burnt meat and bastard's blood, but being without armour felt like going naked into battle. She fought her instincts – stealth and speed and cunning would be her greatest assets if she was so heavily outnumbered. What she did instead was strip off Nealon's sooty scale shirt and studded kilt and secrete them inside Cathbad's tomb, in case she needed them later. That curmudgeon would have been more than happy to help out however he could, and he wouldn't object to a little grave desecration between old friends.

She returned to the front of the Hall, dumped the contents of her coin purse on the floor and then searched for sling stones, packing good-sized rocks into her coin purse. Sooner or later, others would come searching for the boy, and she intended on being ready for them. Once that deed was done, she rested on a tomb in the darkness and waited, opening her mind and her ears for the merest hint of the enemy. All she could do was pray the boy had the favour of the gods and hope he didn't get himself into even more trouble.

CHAPTER 13

Rock dust trickled into Kester's hair as he squeezed through the tunnel in utter darkness. He seemed to recall Briar cursing this narrow section the last time they had been through here. He had often envied the broad shoulders and muscles of the Shields, but he certainly didn't now.

The stone was cold against his hands and knees as he crawled, slowly leeching away his body heat. Something brushed across his forehead, and he pawed at it, praying it was more dust and not spiders, all those spindly legs tickling his skin as they scurried over him. He shuddered and lifted his head, cracking it off the ceiling. More dust rained down on him, coating his face and irritating his nose. He resisted the urge to sneeze and kept on moving. A small stone clacked down behind him, raising sudden fears of a collapse. He'd found more than one tunnel branch blocked off by rockfalls the last time he had taken this route.

"You've been here before," he whispered. "You can do this. You are not a coward." His own voice gave him a measure of comfort in the silent darkness as the mountain of rock closed in around him. He took a deep breath and released it slowly. He told himself that he knew exactly where he was, and that after escaping the assassin, he and Briar had made their way up through the palace to the library without incident. In the months after, he had brought a lantern and candles and explored a good portion of these tunnels using maps sketched by Briar for Bram's personal records. He'd pilfered them and copied them before slipping the originals back into the librarian's desk, with none of the adults any the wiser.

The thrill of exploration had been immense, every moment filled with wondering if he'd stumble across hidden chambers, ancient forgotten temples and secret treasure hoards with magical weapons or even rings that granted wishes. Mostly, he'd used the tunnels to evade his guards whenever he wanted to be somewhere they disapproved of. One of the tunnels even came out into his very own bedchamber – he'd been sure to push a heavy chest over that loose flagstone so he could sleep without fearing knives in the night. He'd never imagined those knives would march right through his front door.

The tunnels were filled with strange noises. Half-heard voices, eerie echoes and… breathing, for want of a better word. The current of air came and went, warm and cold, like the earth itself was breathing. At first, he had balked at exploring further than a hundred heartbeats from his chamber, fearing the darkness and the possibilities of lurking monsters or rock falls. But the lure of mystery had got the better of him, praise the gods!

"I'm no coward," he whispered again as he crawled up into the narrower walls of the palace near the Great Hall, where the likes of Briar could never fit. Here, chinks of blessed lantern light showed through cracks in the old stonework, and in some places, voices carried through the stone. The terror of being buried alive with spiders and bugs crawling all over him receded as he climbed towards the light, only to be replaced by the fear of being discovered spying.

He stilled and held his breath as a voice approached, growing more distinct as he listened with his ear pressed to the wall.

"…dragged him off to the Great Hall…"

Harsh laughter.

"…Imperatrix wants the blood…"

Then a series of unintelligible words as they spoke over each other.

"...needs it for the Vault. Supposed to be a fortune hidden inside there..."

The voices carried on down the hallway and then faded.

Kester loosed the breath he had been holding, thinking furiously. Why did they need blood? Not for anything good. Whoever they were talking about had been taken to the Great Hall, and Kester could only imagine they meant his uncle. He thought for a moment, recalling his previous explorations. One route led right past the Great Hall. He took to crawling again, his knees and elbows and the heels of his hands starting to feel rubbed raw. Something crunched underneath his fingers, and he flinched at the tiny bones and fragments of rat skull stuck to his skin. He swallowed, brushed them off and ignored the stinging pain of a cut as he crawled for the Great Hall and the chinks of light in the darkness. Voices grew more distinct as he approached, so he moved forward, slow and safe and stealthy, to set his eye to a crack in the ancient stonework. He peered into the smoky interior of the Great Hall, where dozens of people in their nightwear had been bound together and armed men were watching them like hawks.

The Oaken Throne of Sunweald was a thick trunk of still-living oak that pushed up against the ceiling. Its blessed branches were evergreen, and they sprawled across the whole expanse of the Great Hall despite never having seen a speck of sunlight in their long life history. The tree's roots grew up through the bedrock and twisted around themselves to form a throne slightly too tall and too odd to be comfortable for most humans: the druids claimed it to be sized for the Sleaghan Mhath, but it was nothing a footrest and a good cushion for royal buttocks could not fix.

Kester squinted, his view heavily restricted. He could see a dozen or so guards and a worryingly small group of bound captives: the Ves and Wrendal ambassadors and their attendants, the hearth mistress and senior servants, librarian, stable master, master bronze smith and a gaggle of senior scribes. The heads of every druid living in the palace had been struck off and impaled on spears driven into the floor – a sacrilegious act that Kester could not have imagined before today. His stomach lurched as a bound and naked man, face down on the floor, stirred. Kester's battered and bruised uncle was turning his head to face the masked woman occupying his throne...

At the far end of the Great Hall, Imperatrix lounged on the mighty Oaken Throne of Sunweald, busy carving her name in Hisparren runes into the roots with the point of her knife artefact. The Ves ambassador was hauled towards her and forced to kneel at her feet. She blew charred wood dust off into his face and admired her handiwork for a moment before casting her gaze over the pompous dignitaries, nobles and officials all watching in stunned silence, bound and utterly helpless before her. She smiled, savouring her domination over every soul in the palace. Some were naked and shivering, and others clad only in thin nightdresses. She catalogued their usefulness and social status and weighed up any monetary or political worth. She could only take a few hostages with her once her work in the palace was done, and the rest would be disposed of. She felt a little sad that old Morna would not make the cut – the hearth mistress' cooking was delicious.

The Hall's central fire pit crackled and snapped, spitting sparks to sear the bound captives kneeling on the floor beside a communal bucket for their piss. Imperatrix demanded more logs added, savouring the warmth and taking a small measure of satisfaction in the seared and reddened skin of those captives unfortunate enough to be too near the fire.

The exquisitely carved wooden wall panels were resplendent with hundreds of years of history: swords and spears of fabled warriors, banners seized from fallen foes of vanished realms and clans. Faded tapestries depicted battles with hordes of scaled beasts straight out of legend, and the harried flight of the ancients into the forests of the Havenswood aided by the gilt forms of the Sleaghan Mhath. Then followed the depiction of a valiant and victorious last stand before the caves that wormed into the sacred hill at its centre, where the palace now stood. It meant nothing to Imperatrix, merely the cheap baubles of a degenerate bloodline of leeches.

Hardgrim stood at ease beside her, dressed in full armour, sipping at a goblet of a fine Ves red and sneering at the bound and beaten regent, face down on the floor. The former Shield's chin had finally stopped bleeding, but it would leave a nasty scar. The reiver chief Uradech lounged in the corner of the room, gnawing on a greasy chicken carcass.

The snarling mask of the imperious invader looked down on the foppish Ves ambassador who knelt at the root of her throne. His heavily embroidered nightdress hung off a bulging belly. He wisely held his tongue as she toyed with her knife, angry sparks from the artefact pitting his clothing with tiny burns. "You dare demand anything of me?" she said in a voice cold as winter ice. This man was the third son of a minor Ves princeling – an expendable spare – and his trappings of wealth were ill-fitting and had been handed to him on a silver platter without a day of work to his name. He was exactly the sort of man she loathed.

"All of you here," she said to the captives, "should know that your supposed grandness and noble blood means nothing. I am Imperatrix, and to me you are the same meat and blood and bone as the lowest village simpleton, and any one of your disgusting bodies will serve me as well as the next."

She booted the Ves ambassador in the face, splitting his lip and sending him sprawling. Two tiny rubies – enough wealth to buy a good-sized village – clattered across the floor, dislodged from their settings in his teeth. He flailed back up to his knees, face reddening and full of outrage and bluster. Phelan stepped forward and slammed his bronze buckler into the man's face. Once. Twice. Thrice. The man sagged to the floor, and one of Imperatrix's men dragged the ambassador off, leaving a slug-slime trail of red across the floor of the Great Hall.

The other captives looked on sullenly. If they were surprised at her audacity in daring to anger the mighty Ves people then they didn't show it, which she found a tad disappointing. Perhaps, she mused, they felt a woman who had seized the palace was capable of anything. That fact she took a mighty pride in.

"Bring the priestess, and humble her before me," Imperatrix ordered. She turned her raptor gaze on the ambassador from the Holy Wrendal Empire as the woman was dragged forward and forced to her knees, her bound hands clenched into fists in her lap. All of her rings had been ripped from her fingers and the necklace torn from her neck – still pretty, despite the black veins of the sorcery sign that marred it. The bruising was just beginning to bloom across Exalted Carmanilla's cheek and throat, but she sat with her back straight and her chin lifted, eyes fixed not upon Imperatrix but on the arcane artefact in her hand. Disgust showed in the priestess' expression, intensifying with every twirl of that sacred knife in heathen hands.

"You killed one of my men, priestess," Imperatrix said. "Boiled his eyes and brain inside his own skull. I must say that I do admire your ferocity. Alas, an example must be made. Shave her head." She leant forward and watched with interest as Hardgrim licked his lips and stepped forward, knife in hand. He hacked chunks of honey-blonde hair free and dropped them in the priestess' lap, then held a golden braid aloft, laughing as he pressed it to his nose and inhaled deeply.

He leered at the priestess with a dark promise in his eyes. "The hearth mistress says that old Briar left the afternoon before I could deal with her. Perhaps I will take out all my frustrations on you."

Imperatrix scowled at him from behind her mask. "Enough of your perversions. She has killed one of mine, and now I shall take her hand off for it."

Carmanilla's face was as stone. Hardgrim's leer crumbled into a snarl. He turned away, an unvoiced objection showing in the clenching of his jaw muscles.

"Enough!" Alaric shouted from the cold floor. "The woman simply defended herself. If your men could not capture an unarmed woman without suffering casualties, that is only due to their ineptitude."

Imperatrix chuckled. "Ah, but a sorcerer is never unarmed, my dear regent." She slipped from the uncomfortable throne and seized the priestess's bound hands. "Now, shall I take the left or the right? I wonder which one you need more..."

Carmanilla said nothing, her face blank.

"What do you want from us?" Alaric said. "You have us at your mercy and have no need for more violence. I am sure Exalted Carmanilla will give you her oath not to fight against you if you leave her unharmed. Hurt me if you must, but please let the others go."

"Oh?" Imperatrix replied. "Is that so, *Exalted*? Will you give me an oath upon your gods that you will work no sorcery and do no harm on me and mine?"

Carmanilla tilted her head, studying her like one would a decomposing corpse, not quite sure what manner of creature it once was. "Absolutely not," she said. "You have no intention of leaving me unharmed whatever I do, and neither does that pigeon-pricked betrayer stood beside you."

Hardgrim snarled, but Imperatrix lifted a finger of warning, and he clamped his jaw shut, a vein throbbing on his forehead. "Very true," she admitted. "I had wanted to make you beg for mercy – but, oh well, I have been looking forward to this long enough." She cut, quick and precise, and Carmanilla's right hand tumbled to the floor, fingers twitching.

The Wrendal priestess moaned and shook but did not

scream. Her teeth sank into her bottom lip, drawing blood. The stump of her wrist sizzled and blackened, cauterised by the arcane artefact that had taken her hand.

Hardgrim scowled at the maimed limb, but then a thought seemed to strike him. He picked up the severed hand, and a sickening smile spread across his face as he played with the fingers and moved them to form an O shape.

Imperatrix sighed, dissatisfied with the woman's subdued reaction. "Take this wretch away." She snatched the severed hand from Hardgrim's perverse grasp, skewered it on the end of a bronze spit and set it on the edge of the fire pit. The skin quickly began to bubble and char.

Her men dragged the shivering priestess off and threw her against the wall, next to the librarian. She fell face down and did not rise. Bram whispered soothingly in her ear, but with his hands tied he could offer nothing more than words of solace.

Imperatrix surveyed the rest of the captives. "If you behave, then I may choose to ransom some of you," she said. "Take care not to anger me, and your life and freedom may be returned to you, for a price. As for you, Alaric Summerson, what I want from you is your blood."

"My blood?" he replied. "What possible use can that be to you? Take what gold and silver you can carry and let us live, before this ill-advised invasion is discovered by my warriors and they surround the palace. If you have any sense left, you will cut Hardgrim's throat before he betrays you as well."

That got a laugh from her. "You can hammer no wedge in hard enough to split us apart, O high and mighty Lord Regent. Our goals align far too well for that. Let us not bandy wasteful words," she said. "I know royal blood is the key to opening the Wyrm Vault. That fresh supply is the only reason I am keeping you alive for now. I have you at my tender mercy, and soon I will have Kester, too."

The regent's expression was carefully sculpted stone, but she knew that stoic demeanour would soon break under torture.

"I will get my hands on all the arcane artefacts hoarded away inside," she said. "This wretched realm wastes all that power, but I assure you, I will use those artefacts to their full potential."

"I had them destroyed years ago," he stated. "Flee while you still can."

Alaric's words washed over her without effect. "As if I would believe that nonsense. And as for your warriors: who do you imagine lured all those loyal to you away into the wilds chasing a false trail?"

The regent choked back an outburst and controlled his ire admirably. "You are the leader of the Wildwood Reivers?"

"Oh, yes," Imperatrix said, studying one of the faded, moth-eaten banners hanging from the far wall, this one with crossed spears over the wheel of the sun. "What a merry chase I have led you on over the last few years. And now I have taken the Sunweald Palace with only thirty-five men and lost only one to your vaunted Shields – and another due to that maimed bitch over there." She removed her mask and looked Alaric in the eye. "What a fool you have been."

Her laughter was cruel and mocking.

Kester's eyes widened, and he gasped. "Aisling!" The woman that had been his maid, living in his house, washing his clothes and tucking him into bed at night. The treacherous killer right in front of him had kissed him on the forehead and wished him sweet dreams every night for years!

Bile bubbled up to sear his throat. He shuddered and, in his turmoil, accidentally nudged the wall with an elbow. His blood ran cold as a fragment of crumbling oak panelling clattered down on the other side.

Aisling, or Imperatrix – he hadn't quite wrapped his head around it all yet – ceased laughing. She glanced over at the wall as his heart began pounding. He held his breath, and his brow beaded with sweat. Finally, she looked away again, and he slowly exhaled. He swallowed his fears and concentrated on gathering more information: Briar would need to know every word.

"Who would have expected a simple maid living in your very own palace to be the head of an entire group of brigands?" she said to Alaric. "I was a serpent lurking in your midst."

She laughed and plucked the seared and smoking hand from the fire pit. She locked gazes with the horrified Wrendal ambassador. "In ancient lore it is said that if you devour the flesh of a sorcerer then you take in a measure of her power."

Kester couldn't look away. Oh no, he thought. No, no, no, you are not going to–

She was.

Imperatrix began gnawing on the blackened fingers, sharp white teeth nipping off the tender human flesh. Some of the captives vomited. Even some of her own reivers, all hard and brutal men who wouldn't balk at rape and slaughter, paled.

Kester gagged at the sight of her eating Carmanilla's flesh. He'd kissed that hand! He clamped a filthy palm to his mouth and managed to keep his jaw clamped shut at the cost of choking the burning bile back down. He didn't dare make another noise.

"Hmph," Imperatrix said. "Just another folktale, it seems. Or perhaps I need to eat the heart fresh from the cutting." She tossed the gnawed hand back into the fire, wiped her mouth and then trailed greasy nails over her fresh carvings into the Oaken Throne and padded over to the regent, looking down her nose at him. "I will take everything from you, Alaric, as you once did to me and mine." She knelt down beside him and began to whisper in his ear as the blood drained from his face...

She rose, chuckling. "Come the dawn," she stated, "one way or another, you will help me open the Wyrm Vault. It is entirely up to you how much it will hurt."

Kester eased his hand from over his mouth. His stomach churned, and his heart thudded in his ears, so loud it was a wonder it couldn't be heard by those on the other side of the wall: his gasp and sudden movement had almost cost him his life. Despite his growing horror, the need to know urged him to take a bigger risk. He couldn't hear a damned thing more, so he'd have to get closer. Briar and his uncle were relying on him. The entire realm was. The tunnel did pass through to the other side of the Great Hall, but it narrowed alarmingly, and he was loath to try it in case he got stuck. It wasn't like he could cry out for help... There, the walls were thin, and the ancient oak panelling riven with cracks. That side of the hall was badly in need of attention from the masons and carpenters, but it also afforded him a much closer vantage from which he might see and hear what was being whispered.

He silently crept closer to Aisling, squeezing through spaces that adults never could, ears straining. He paused and peered out through a mousehole in the crumbling wood panelling where the Wrendal ambassador had been flung.

He froze. The librarian, Bram, met his gaze, and the man's eyes widened ever so slightly. The man leant in close to Carmanilla, and whatever he said made the moaning priestess crack an eyelid to stare at the crack in the wall that separated them.

Kester made a snap decision, probably unwisely. He took his belt knife and carefully manoeuvred it through the crumbling gap. She rolled towards him, grimacing, and the fingers of her remaining hand closed around the hilt and drew the slim blade through the crack.

Beyond the priestess, Aisling rose from the bloodied regent and reclined into the Oaken Throne that was his birthright. Kester had missed his chance to eavesdrop on what had been said. All he could do now was head back to report to Briar.

CHAPTER 14

A faint scuff of leather on stone roused Briar from her meditation. Holding her breath, she listened intently. Another scuff, closer. She rose and padded forward, tracking the source of those almost imperceptible noises. It was a relief to find they came not from the tunnel outside the Hall but from inside the nearby wall, and the sounds were heading towards the tomb of Quinn the Eel. Only a handful of lore-masters had even heard rumours of the tunnels' existence, and even fewer knew the truth of it. She hoped it was Kester returning, but Briar had not saved the regent's life multiple times by making assumptions.

She stretched her neck and limbs to ready herself for action, then set the lantern two paces in front of the door, ready to dazzle whoever opened it. She drew her knife and held it in a hammer grip, ready to plunge down through their neck. The fingers of her other hand dangled over the entrance like a spider ready to strike. The door slid back, and somebody stuck their head out, hair brushing her fingertips. She grabbed hold and yanked the face up, exposing their throat to her descending blade. A boyish yelp of surprise caused the knife to halt its deadly descent. She let go of his hair, slid the knife back into its sheath and offered Kester her hand.

"You are a sight for sore eyes," she said.

The shivering boy who issued forth from the tomb was a ghost, his hair and newly ragged clothes caked in white dust and debris. She brushed the worst of it off him and then wrapped him up in the warm cloak he'd been forced to leave behind. He huddled into it, moaning with relief as sensation seeped back into his half-frozen fingers.

"What have you learnt?" she asked. "Leave no detail out."

There was a pause as he nervously rubbed his throat. "Thank the gods for lanterns," he said hoarsely, sliding the stone door back into place. "I've had quite enough of crawling about like a worm in the darkness." He shuddered and said no more about his ordeal.

He coughed, and she offered him her waterskin. The boy gulped at it gratefully and cleared his throat. "It sounds like they have secured the entire palace. Thirty-five reivers and traitors were mentioned. Apparently two died in the taking, and you killed Newlyn and Nealon, so that's thirty-one left. And then there is Aisling..."

Briar frowned. "That vexing maid? What has she to do with this?"

"Aisling is the sorcerer called Imperatrix," he replied. "She's the leader of that whole group of villains."

Briar stared at him in stunned silence. Then she cursed, and her fingers curled into trembling claws, wishing nothing more than to gouge that bitch's eyes out with her nails. She shook and snarled and looked around for something or somebody to smash into tiny bits.

"She sprawls on the throne in the Great Hall," he added. "They have Uncle tied up on the floor, and she, ah... cut off Exalted Carmanilla's hand." He shivered as he told her every last detail of what he saw and heard while spying. "Then she said something about needing Uncle's blood to open the Wyrm Vault. Mine, too. I... I... What do we do?"

"We get you out of here," Briar replied, knuckles white around the hilt of her sword. "Then I go and save Alaric and rip the guts out of any of those cannibals that get in my way. If they intend to keep our people for ransom, then we will have a chance to free them before further harm can be done to them."

"I'm no coward. Let me fight," he pleaded. "This is my home

too. Those are my people and what's left of my family. I can't just run away and leave them to die."

Briar paced back and forth, thinking furiously. Then she spun and clapped him on the shoulder. "Very well. You will fight. But with speed rather than sword and muscle. My order for you is to ride swift as the wind to Blaen Mhòr – you must find Gwilherm and bring the loyal Shields and the rest of the warband to our aid with their greatest speed. The treacherous vermin that infest our home cannot be allowed to kill our people and steal the contents of the Vault."

He nodded grimly. "What exactly is in there that is so important?" he asked. "I've been inside the Heart of course, but Alaric has never once let me into the Wyrm Vault itself."

Briar paused, frowning as unpleasant memories rose. "Actually, you have been there, but it was just after the plague took many of our people, including your parents. You were a babe sleeping in the crook of Alaric's arm at the time. Only we three were present, and a good thing, too. It's the only time in living memory that damned Vault has been open, and it needs to stay closed. It stores terrible weapons, Kester. Abominations made by the ancients that should never, ever be used again."

He nodded, only faintly saddened by thoughts of parents he had never known. "How do we get out of here?" he asked. "They will be guarding all the exits. Do we fight our way out?"

She shook her head. "That would be folly. I wager I could get you out of the palace in one piece, but a pack of them would certainly give chase and run us down. I certainly don't relish the idea of fighting them out in the open with this accursed leg of mine. I'm sorry to tell you that any plans you might harbour of me accompanying you should be dropped headfirst down the latrine. I can get you out, but then you are on your own."

He swallowed and shivered, but nodded in acceptance of the mission.

"Good lad," she said. "Help me stuff the bodies of Nealon and Newlyn into one of the tombs – if the enemy can't find them, they won't know I killed them and raise the alarm before we are ready. Hopefully, they will think the search for you continues."

She took the feet and Kester the arms, and they dumped them into the nearest of the old tombs along with their broken teeth and any other signs of battle. "Sorry," she whispered to the crumbled bones of Ablar the Bold. "Needs must. Duty wins over desecration, I'm afraid, but I'm sure you understand that." She slid the stone lid of the tomb back in place, dusted off her hands and turned to Kester. "Come, follow me into the tunnels. There is a place I need to show you."

He looked mournfully at the lantern. She shook her head. The boy sighed heavily and removed his nice warm cloak again, while she grabbed her knapsack and wrapped it up into a bundle with the cloak. Briar laid her walking stick down with just as much regret, but there was no easy way to take that through the narrow passages – her sword and buckler would be more than enough trouble, and those she could strap to her belt and twist behind her out of the way. Together, they headed back into the darkness, shoving the bundled clothes and supplies up before them.

A good while of careful crawling later, they emerged unseen into a large guest room up on the third floor of the palace's disused East Wing. Once, it had housed priests, chiefs and kings from far-flung lands, but now it was a crumbling ruin ready to be ripped out and replaced as soon as time and funds allowed. Moonlight streamed through broken shutters and sections of outer wall under repair. The wind whistled and howled through the gaps like the cries of the dead, but at least the roof here was still mostly watertight. Briar peered out of the open door into the empty hallway beyond, noting the uneven and treacherous old flooring the workers had been tearing up, leaving gaping holes revealing the floor below, where piles of new timber and stone floor tiles waited to trip the unwary. This part of the East Wing was unreachable from the central stairs, and nobody would be likely to mount an expedition to explore this death trap of a place. She closed the door, grunting as she forced warped wood deeper into the stone frame.

She piled stones up behind the door, wiped her hands on her tunic and turned back to Kester, who was looking around the ramshackle room in puzzlement.

He scratched his grimy chin, dust sticking to the first hint of fuzz. "I thought we were going to find a way for me to escape, not climb higher."

She pointed at the far wall.

He followed her finger and stared in horror at the latrine, little more than a stone hole topped by a wooden plank. "Are you serious?" he said. "When you said my plan had gone down the latrine…"

Briar absently massaged her leg as she limped over to the latrine, aching from the exertion. She nodded at the long-uncleaned hole before them, caked in frozen brown slime and lumpy green fungus. "Why not? You are skinny enough to squeeze through there. It won't be fragrant, but given there is no longer any easy way to get up here, I suppose we can't blame the serving staff for not having cleaned up after the carpenters and masons who used it last."

He edged closer, lifted the wooden seat and peered down the glistening stone chute. He gagged as the stench hit him like a club. "I'm the Royal Heir," he protested. "I can't crawl down a tunnel caked in shit."

She smiled at him. "You won't have to crawl at all. You'll slide right on out of the stonework like a sloppy shit and plop down into a pile of fluffy white fresh snow."

He stared at her, one hand over his mouth to stifle his urge to vomit. "You cannot be serious."

"Do you have a better idea?" she asked. "Any kind of plan that has more chance of getting you out alive? I can't hide you away, safe and secure, while I head out there myself: I have no hope of reaching Gwilherm before my leg gives out. You want to be a warrior under my command? Well, this is your chance. Despite what the bards and boasters tell you, not every battle sees you covered in glory – mostly, you just end up covered in blood and shit and tears. The best you can hope for is that it all belongs to some other poor bastard."

The boy looked from the grimy latrine to her grave expression and then back again. He sighed heavily. "Do I have to?"

She nodded. "You do if you want to live. Dawn cannot be far off, so be quick about it." She pulled an unlit lantern off the wall and found a good dose of fat still in the pot. "Off with your clothes, and let's grease you up. It'll lubricate your descent, stop any chafing from your long-distance run, and probably help keep you warm in the chill winter air. Once you are outside of the palace, I'll dump your bundle of clothes and boots out of the window, along with my knapsack, which has some food, a flint and tinder and a waterskin. Grab them and sprint for the woods like all our lives depend upon you. Because they do."

"What if they have guards set?" he asked.

"They might have archers guarding the main gates," she admitted. "But your exit through the outer wall should go unnoticed. If any do spot you, don't run in a straight line – snake from side to side to throw off their aim."

He reddened as she stripped him and liberally slathered cattle fat all over his naked torso, working her way down from shoulders to waist. "Stop!" he squeaked, swatting her hand away from his nether regions. "I'll do those bits."

"Nothing I haven't seen before," she said, slapping more onto his legs. "Most recently at the waterfall grove…"

His face burned. "Sorry again. So sorry." He hurried the process, swiftly greasing up his groin and arse while he eyed the filth-crusted hole of the latrine with a newfound yearning, eager to escape his abject mortification. Kester took a deep breath and peered down into the dank and reeking black depths. He froze, unable to force himself to dive into the disgusting mess. "What if I get stuck?"

She gave him a hand, shoving his head down with one hand and planting her other on his slimy arse, nails digging in hard to help him topple forward.

He yelped in surprise as he plunged headfirst into the latrine, greased-up hands scrabbling for purchase on frozen filth and fungus. "This is revenge for putting my hand on your thigh, isn't it?"

"Let's call it even," she said, giving him one final shove. "Don't you go screaming, now." He went in and began to pick up speed, sliding down into the depths of the walls with only a muffled moan of fear.

Briar grabbed his bundle of cloak, kilt, belt, sword and knife, boots and foot wraps and limped to the window, just in time to see a slimy green-and-brown shape plop out of the stonework and drop to a patch of yellow snow beside the half-frozen stream that trickled past the palace walls. She'd lied about him landing in a pile of fluffy white fresh snow, but she hoped Kester was too dazed to realise it. She tossed out the bundle, then watched and waited, holding her breath as the naked boy scrambled to pick it up and make a barefoot run for the tree line, head bowed against the frigid wind. He followed the route of the stream rather than leaving a trail across pristine snow for all to see, and she couldn't help but be impressed at the boy's common sense. The darkness between the boughs of birch and pine embraced him, and the Royal Heir was gone with no shout of alarm raised from the walls. After a while, she exhaled, and the tension slowly left her shoulders. "Good luck, my boy," she whispered. "May all our gods and the spirits of Shields long past watch over you."

Even in winter, she could not help but feel that the boy was far safer out in the wilds on his own than he was trapped in the palace with people who wanted to shed his blood. He was certainly resourceful enough to have given his guards the slip on numerous occasions, and the last two seasons had wrought a powerful change upon his nature. He had learnt some harsh lessons and grown up because of it. She prayed it would be enough to see him through to Gwilherm and safety.

With the Royal Heir far away from the reach of traitors and killers – and her own aid – she banished all thought of him from her mind. His quest was now his own, and hers was just beginning.

It had been her sacred duty to guard the palace and its people, and she had failed miserably. She made no allowance for illness and injury and didn't have it in her to blame anybody but herself. Herself and Hardgrim. Her Second Shield had always been an ambitious swine, she had known that all too well, but despite his personal failings and grumblings, he'd been driven by that ambition to prove himself an efficient second, and he'd seen her commands carried out with the precision she demanded of her people. Low as her opinion of his personality was, even she had never dreamed him so corrupt and crooked-souled as to break every oath he had pledged in service to kin and clan, regent and realm. He had spat in the eyes of the gods and his own ancestors, and he cared not a bit. And this maid, Aisling, was behind it all! The sorcerer had played a long and cunning game, infiltrating the heart of the realm and laying low, gathering information and making allies until she was ready to make a play for the contents of the Wyrm Vault. The abilities of this 'Imperatrix' were an unknown threat, but one that had to be dealt with eventually. Briar reckoned a shield to the face and a sword in the guts would serve, if she could get close enough to the slimy worm.

Briar felt sick at the thought of all the treacherous scum daring to stain her halls with their presence. She'd no doubt they would be laughing and drinking to their victory right now, but soon she would be washing those halls with their blood. She would rescue her people, and she would take back the palace. The vermin that infested it needed to be rooted out, and she reckoned she was just the woman for the job.

She was meant to guard the inhabitants of the palace, but now her only chance was to reverse that sacred duty and use her knowledge of the terrain to slaughter those who sought to hold it against the will of all that was sacred.

Thirty-one of the enemy remained, and her with a bad leg. It was an impossible task save for two things: the first was that the palace was large and they would be forced to split up to guard all the ways in and out, and the second was that this was her home. Nobody knew its secrets and its security problems as well as her, not even that sneaky little mole of a librarian, Bram, who served as the regent's master of spies.

"I can do this," she said. She had to: she was the last loyal Shield in the palace. She cracked her neck, stretched her legs and flexed her calloused hands to warm up the muscles. Oathbreakers and invaders had to be purged from these hallowed halls, and she had been held back from doing her duty far too long.

It was time to cut and kill and crack some skulls.

CHAPTER 15

She decided to take an arrow out of the quiver of old foes: those notorious murderers and thieves, the Snakeling Brothers. The cunning siblings had managed to evade town patrols and pursuers for years. They had kept moving and never struck the same place twice, slithering their way out of every trap and ambush laid by town councils, the household warriors of clan chiefs and even small warbands. The bards claimed they had made dark bargains with the worst of the fae, twisted monsters that dwelled in the dark places of the forest, below the earth, trading them human blood and bodies in exchange for preternatural senses.

Utter horseshit, Briar thought. They were just a pair of sneaky pricks who scouted the terrain before they struck and always had an escape route or two prepared in case the gods were against them one day and their luck turned sour. While pursuing warriors blundered about, falling into streams and bogs, at the first sniff of trouble they'd take off like hares running before hounds. So she hadn't bothered to raise a warband to catch them. She'd noted that the men would need to eat and drink and obtain supplies somewhere, so she'd studied a map of their prior targets and spent a few weeks posing as a lone trader – driving a horse and cart full of salted meat and cheeses through the villages lining the West Road – and she'd let them come for her. Gwilherm had done the same on the East Road, but the gods had been on her side. The Snakeling Brothers had taken the bait, but instead of laying hands on a salty farmer's wife, they'd found themselves trying to kiss an angry badger. She'd slit them open from groin to throat. A messy end, but not undeserved.

The lesson she'd learnt from them was to keep moving. Strike where they least expect it. Make sure you know your escape route. Get out before they corner you. Wise words for any outnumbered warrior to live by – *live* being the most important point – and she'd kept a coin from their purse to remind her of those days.

Her primary goal now was to rescue Alaric and the rest of the ranking people Kester had said were confined in the Great Hall, to get them out to safety or, if that proved impossible, holed up behind oak and stone to await the return of Gwilherm and the warband. Her secondary goals were to free the servants and to prevent the enemy from opening the Wyrm Vault. No normal invader would have a hope of breaching its arcane protections, but this Imperatrix was a sorcerer herself, and only the gods knew what she was capable of.

The enemy didn't know the tunnels existed, so she would use those to crawl up to the ground floor, free any confined servants and instruct them to make their way to safety. In the uproar she would return to the tunnels and make her way to the Great Hall to free Alaric.

She made the decision and proceeded quickly, taking only her sword, buckler, belt knife, sling and stones. Much as she wished to go back and retrieve armour and walking stick, stealth was her best defence for now.

She crawled up through the dark tunnels, a tight squeeze for an adult. She prayed to the gods that if she saved straining her leg by taking the passage slow and steady, it would hold up for those life-and-death moments that were surely coming. She hoped her body was strong enough to see her duty done.

Briar spent a stone crawling through the tunnels, listening and peering through cracks to learn the timings and routes of guard patrols. She could say many things about Hardgrim, but she loathingly admitted the man had planned his treachery well. He had clearly learnt a lot in his last six months of acting as commander. Nobody could have foreseen that she'd not be in her bed. She'd be dead by now if his trap had been sprung one night earlier.

Knowledge was indeed a form of power – Bram's words came back to her once again. She mused that over the years she had learnt to pay heed to his words as much as to her own heart. The regent's master of spies had a way of insinuating himself into places he wasn't wanted.

"Knowledge is power, you ox-headed farm girl," he had once decreed in a drunken rant only a month after she was promoted into the Shields. She was the new blood in the palace, with a country accent and the manners to match, and the librarian, as she knew him then, was an obnoxious know-it-all with a powerful need to share it after swilling four cups of strong dark ale. At the time, she'd had no idea he was such an important man, but then nobody did unless they had to. A much younger and much cockier Briar had pressed the tip of her sword into the librarian's groin and made a very good point about her own musings on the nature of power. He had nursed that grudge and counterattacked the next time she was out leading a raid by neglecting to provide additional information pertaining to her mission to exterminate a squalid camp of reivers looting a trio of poverty-stricken villages on the edge of a swamp.

Her warband had spent ten days wading through that reeking swamp, suffering the attentions of leeches and saw-toothed cleg flies instead of trotting along a perfectly dry goat trail they only discovered on the way home. On her return to the palace, a gift from the librarian awaited her: that sneaky cur had marked up the goat trail on a map and left it laid out on her blankets, ready for her return. Muddy, stinking and covered head to toe in itchy, weeping red welts, she had stared seething at that detailed map for an absurdly long time, cursing the fact he'd had it the whole time without giving away even the slightest smirk of foreknowing. That was the sort of masterfully executed petty vengeance that you had no choice but to respect. A point well made, and the prideful young Briar didn't even have to admit she had been wrong. After that, she never forgot the importance of knowledge, and it was one of the main reasons she rose to the rank of Commander of Shields.

When the time between reiver patrols was right, Briar emerged into a storeroom on the ground floor, near the servants' quarters. She made an undignified exit, worming her way out of a too-small hole in the wall onto a sawdust floor speckled with mouse droppings, which was only a little cleaner and more fragrant than herself after a spot of murder. She replaced the stone slab, and if she didn't already know the tunnel was there, she'd have been none the wiser that there was any way in or out other than the main doorway. A good thing, too. She crept past piled brooms, baskets of clean toilet rags, a straw-packed crate of clay pots containing lantern oil, and leather sacks full of other needful supplies. Much like the rest of the palace, those sacks had seen better days, the corners of the hide having been gnawed away by the mice whose droppings she'd crawled across.

She set her eyes to the crack in the door and peered out into the dim hall beyond, lit only by a single oil lantern at the far wall where it intersected the main hallway. No guards: a puzzling but good start in her quest to free the servants from captivity. From here she could obtain swift access to the inner gate and the central stairwell, or retreat back into the tunnels if she encountered resistance she could not handle.

She took a deep and steadying breath as she willed her mind to become stone so that she might endure the fear and fury that was to come. The mantle of the warrior settled around her, and her heart hardened against the horrors she was about to face. She pushed open the door to the hallway, wincing at the creak of old wood, slipped out and closed it behind her. Her heart was hammering as she drew her sword and limped up the silent hallway to the nearest door, this one leading to the rooms of the children who worked as messengers and apprentices. A serpent of black dread uncoiled in her belly at the sight of a splintered door hanging off its hinges – somebody had taken an axe to it.

She peered through to find the room beyond it thick with silence. Moonlight filtering through two thumbnail-wide airholes in the wall afforded her a view of shadowy, motionless grey shapes. The walls bore decorative images of animals: wolves and bears and boars chasing a horde of children and then, as the drawings circled the room, those same children riding fierce horses, dragons and giant ducks to chase the animals right back to the start. Briar remembered the half-mad artist who had painted it in bright colours to amuse the children. Those walls were now stained with blood, the splatters, smears and streaks telling a darker tale. The cloying scent of blood assailed her, and she thought it a mercy not to have better light. She further fortified her nerves and stomach before venturing in.

The room was large and packed with straw pallets that slept four children top to tail – had slept... Wicker baskets for their personal belongings had been opened and carelessly rooted through. The woven-reed floor mats squelched, sticky underfoot, and the beds were drenched and dripping. Some of the youngest had been murdered in their beds, huddled beneath the safety of their blankets. The older ones had overturned their beds to form a crude barricade. There lay Cordelia and Gitta, Cara and Gwenith, Moryn and Oscka, all as kindly, well-spoken and hardworking as any mother could wish. A brave but hopeless fight, and yet still they stood, defiant to the last. Briar's heart swelled with a pride savaged by pain, and tears rolled down her cheeks. Losing a warrior in the heat of battle was one thing, but this... she wiped away her tears and swallowed her pain. This called for wrath.

There hadn't been much in the way of easily carried riches to be gained by keeping these people of humble means alive – at best only a few sheep and goats paid in ransom. Many of the palace servants were foundlings and orphans with no material wealth, so it seemed the invaders had disposed of this little problem. Youngsters she couldn't even identify lay where they had fallen, mercilessly cut and bludgeoned beyond any need to check for breath and pulse. The enemy had not spared a single innocent young soul. Rage erupted inside her, its burning need for vengeance welcomed, so long as she was its master, not its slave.

Briar left that tomb of a room and hastily worked her way up the hallway, checking the rooms on either side in the vain hope that somebody, anybody, had been spared, or that even one servant had managed to hide themselves away. Unwed men resided on the left and women on the right, but she found all brutally slain. There would be no freeing prisoners to cause a distraction that would allow her to rescue Alaric from the Great Hall.

She moved on.

The gardeners who maintained the grounds and herb beds had been stirring in their beds. Some had been able to rise and make a fight of it, bearing defensive wounds to the hands and arms. She checked the rooms belonging to the more senior cleaning and serving staff, who still lay in their blankets as if sleeping, save for the mess where their heads had been. Their skulls had been shattered in as savage an attack as Briar had ever seen. The young kitchen lass called Enid, who had smuggled ale and pies to Briar during her long convalescence, lay sprawled in the far corner atop a broken chair. The girl had managed to drag herself from her blankets before they decorated the freshly painted yellow walls with her brains. Briar shuddered and navigated the mess to rearrange Enid's corpse in a more dignified manner and cover her body with a blanket. She owed the girl more, but could only do that much.

Briar stood in the corner of the room, gripping her sword so tightly she feared the hilt might snap in two. She did not pray to the gods. There was no need – the wicked souls she would send into the otherworld would tell the tales of Briar's bloody vengeance for her. The need to kill seared through her veins. How dare they? How fucking *dare* they? Those monsters' heads would adorn wooden stakes before the dawn! She shuddered and bit her lip, using the pain to centre her. It took all she had to hold herself back from going on a bloody rampage. She took a deep breath and tried to calm herself. To stop herself doing something foolish. She needed to think, to come up with a new plan.

Which was, of course, the very moment that an unkempt older man in shaggy furs chose to saunter into the room and begin looting the corpses. Somehow he didn't see or sense the malevolence burning at the back of the room. The looter pulled copper rings from fingers and tore strung-bead necklaces from dead throats, chuckling all the while.

She could stand no more. Vengeance was a churning black beast inside her belly, and it demanded to be fed. Briar swept forward and lifted her shield high. "Die," she said simply.

The man gaped up at her. "Wha–?"

Her buckler punched down. The reinforced bronze boss at the centre shattered his jaw and cheekbone and pulped his nose. He fell back, choking on razor shards of his own teeth. Aye, she thought, the sword would have been far too quick an end for the likes of him. She wanted to hang the blackhearted bastard from the rafters and savour his screams whilst she skinned him alive, but tonight she could afford neither delay nor noise.

The shield rose and fell, its reinforced edge pulping his throat. Silencing him for all time. She glared down at him in satisfaction as he flopped and flailed like a dying fish. Finally, he fell still, leaving her with an emptiness no amount of bloodshed could fill. Not that she wouldn't try.

She needed to manufacture disturbances to draw the guards away from the Great Hall, so she decided to get creative. Briar took her knife and cut to the bone all the way around the bastard's neck, then stepped on the spine and wrenched to and fro until the head came loose. She grabbed a broken chair leg near Enid and rammed one end into the bottom of skull, then buried the other end upright in the vermin's arse, his severed head standing as a grisly warning to any more looters. One more disposed of and thirty to go.

She wiped her boots on his furs to avoid leaving a bloody trail that led right back to her, and then made her way down the darkened hallway, pausing every six steps to listen for approaching footsteps. Nothing. Her luck was holding. She reached the junction of servants' quarters and main hallway and peered round the corner. Twenty paces to her left was the inner gate of the palace, and to her right, past the kitchens, was the central staircase. Lanterns were lit, and the murmur of at least three male voices came from the entrance chamber. She felt she could take them, but not without a hue and cry echoing down the hallways. It was not yet time to reveal her presence.

She kept her sword and shield ready and crept down the path to the right, heading for the kitchens. If she knew anything at all about brigands, they would already be neck-deep into the barrels of ale and jars of mead and wine. A weakness that could be exploited: drunk men were overconfident, clumsy and easy to kill. She froze as an idea gifted from the very gods shone into her mind: she recalled that the druids had asked Hearth Mistress Morna to keep a few special herbs and medicinal powders in sealed jars inside a wooden chest in the cool room below the kitchen, where they wouldn't soon spoil. Some of those, tipped into jars of ale, might gift a good number of the invading scum with the messy and agonising deaths they deserved.

She slowed at the sound of breaking pots ahead. A man yelped and cursed, his pain accompanied by a familiar growl.

She peered through the doorway to see a reiver in sweat-stained tunic and worn boots, with his back to her. His savaged hand dripped red to the kitchen floor, where blackened sausages lay in a pool of pottery shards and congealing grease. Alaric's dishevelled dog, Brutus, faced the bastard down, baring bloody teeth and growling as he stood guard over a sobbing cook curled up on the floor. The woman's bloodied nightdress was torn; she was barefoot, and her face was all blackened and bruised.

The man cursed and aimed a kick at the small dog. Brutus ducked and then went for the ankle, snarling and snapping, driving the bastard back. "Dare bite me, ya mangy runt of a rat," he said, reaching for the club he'd left on the nearest kitchen table. "I'll rip your paws off and feed you to your cocksucking master."

Rage took Briar. Only she was allowed to talk to Alaric's horrible dog like that. She charged, leg protesting. Her sword chopped between neck and shoulder. Hammered bronze bit through cloth, skin and cartilage to half sever the head in a single blow. The buckler hammered into his skull from the other side before he could do more than loose a bubbling gasp of surprise. The reiver slumped to the floor, dying quick and quiet. She stabbed him a few times more, just to be sure. "Twenty-nine to go," she murmured.

Briar lifted her head and locked gazes with Brutus. The dog had ceased his growling but now looked terrified standing there, tail down and trembling.

Briar used the reiver's tunic to wipe the blood off her hands and then looked pointedly at a haunch of beef hanging from the rafter. "Such a shame it fell down in the fight." She cut the cord and let it drop to the floor. Brutus looked from the meat to her and back again but made no move to take his prize.

She sighed. "Don't go thinking I'll make a habit of this, but…" She reached over and ruffled the wiry hair on his head. "Good boy!"

Brutus's deep-brown eyes stared at her in shock and horror. She turned her back on him and saw to the cook on the floor, ignoring the immediate sounds of slobbery chewing that followed. When a human's attention was elsewhere, dogs needed no encouragement where food was involved.

She helped the sobbing woman to sit up. "Selma, are you hurt? Did he...?"

Selma shook her head, then scrubbed a sleeve across her face, wiping away snot and tears. She winced as she did so, working her jaw to check nothing was broken. "You are a sight for sore eyes, Commander. Please, do me a kindness and help me up."

Once up on unsteady feet, the cook marched over to the dead man. "Filth," she said, savagely kicking him in the head. "Ecksa claimed he was so big and strong..." A kick breaking his teeth. "So brave, to beat an unarmed woman..." She spat on him and kicked his broken face three more times for good measure. "Wish it'd not been so quick. The craven creature should've been roasted alive over hot coals."

"I would have been more than happy to oblige if there weren't a lot more of them out there," Briar replied. "How is it you are still alive? I've been to the servants' quarters..."

Selma shuddered and looked at her feet. "The rats wanted a woman to pour their damned ale and dole out hot food. And... other things. I was... I was just the closest drudge at hand. That's the only reason they didn't..." She choked back a retch. "They murdered everybody right in front of me. This blood..." she waved at the blood-spattered nightdress she wore and began sobbing once more. "None of it's mine."

Briar plucked a kitchen knife from the table and pressed it into Selma's hand. "Do not let yourself be caught again. Kill them if you can – or yourself if you must."

Selma sniffed and stared at the knife clutched in her shaking hand. "What do we do now?"

"Now you help me poison the bastards," Briar replied. "Fetch the druids' medicinal-herb supply from the cool room, and I'll get the ale ready."

The cook's gaze snapped up from the knife, and a cruel grin split her bruised lips. "Aye, that's a right good idea. Hope the bastards shit their stomachs right out their arses." Her hands stopped shaking, and she reluctantly let go of the knife, hiding it away in the folds of her dress.

While Selma climbed through the trapdoor and sought out the small wax-sealed pots of herbs and powders from the chest down in the cool room, Briar opened up the lid of the big brewing tub in the corner of the room and cracked the lids of the five barrels beside it that had already been filled with previous batches. Selma climbed up out of the trapdoor with an armful of jars and wraps of waxed cloth and set it all down on the table. "Hope you know what all this is, because the hearth mistress never let any of us cooks touch it. I know what mushrooms are bad, but as for the rest…" She shrugged.

"As well she shouldn't," Briar said. "It's all deadly if you take enough. I'm led to believe the druids use some of these poisons in small doses to treat various ailments, but I must confess that I too lack the medicinal knowledge to use it safely." She picked up a random jar, pressed her thumbnail into the wax and cracked it open, then tipped a bit of it into each barrel and the big brewing tub. "But we are not here to heal. Grab yourself something and tip it all in."

"Good point, that," Selma said. She picked up a waxed wrap of cloth, untied the cord and opened it out to reveal dried seeds of some sort. She shrugged again and distributed it evenly, then reached for the next. Soon the entire supply had been emptied into the ale.

Briar gave the mixtures a stir with the handle of the reiver's club, careful not to get any on her hands, then resealed the barrels and replaced the lid of the brewing tub. She nodded towards the corpse. "Drop that waste of meat in the cool room and cover it with sacks. That might buy us a little more time." While Selma disposed of the filth, Briar spread sawdust over the floor to disguise the worst of the bloodshed. Nobody would look askance at a little spillage on a kitchen floor, but a big pool of fresh blood was another matter. Brutus eyed her activities with interest, but for now his haunch of meat was more interesting than whatever else she was dropping on the floor.

"Tell me," Briar said to the cook, "these reivers had you bringing them food and drink – that was first thing in the morning? What time is it now?"

Selma reluctantly nodded. "It's around noon."

Briar hummed in thought. "The men guarding the inner gate are probably getting hungry and thirsty about now and wouldn't look twice if you brought them a jug of ale."

Selma swallowed and shifted her feet. "I don't much like where this is going," she said. "You can't mean for me to go back out there to face those monsters?"

"Oh, but I do," Briar said. "I would go myself if they were not expecting you and only you. There are twenty-nine of the vermin left, and I mean to whittle down their numbers however I can. I can't fight them all."

"But–"

"If you want to live," Briar said, "you will do exactly what I say."

Selma broke out in a cold sweat. "I…" She abruptly doubled over and began sobbing and retching. "I… can't fight them… Please… No…"

Briar laid a hand on her shoulder. "Still your tears, woman. I know you, and I know you are a stout Sunweald woman who can face those murderers without melting into a puddle of slime. You are no warrior, so I won't force you into fighting with a weapon in your hand. Your weapon of vengeance will be poisoned ale. You will give them the food and drink and then you will get out of there."

"Vengeance?" Selma stifled her sobs. She closed her eyes and took a deep, shuddering breath. "Will these herbs really kill the bastards?"

Briar nodded. "Oh yes. Even a pinch of a druid's medicine is potent stuff."

"Promise me it will hurt."

The Shield returned a cold, conflicted smile. "After my own experience with poison, I can say with some authority they will wish they were dead a good while before their souls depart their ravaged bodies."

Selma shuddered, then gave a terse nod. "Gods and ancestors be with me; I'll do it. I have to try to soothe the murdered souls of my friends."

CHAPTER 16

The heavy jug of tainted ale sloshed from side to side, held in Selma's sweaty and shaking hands. In the crook of her arm, she carried a basket of smoked fennel sausage, the heavy seasoning deemed ideal by Briar for hiding the taste of poisonous herbs and powders. Selma clutched the jug tighter, lest she drop it and the reivers take it out on her hide – and they would; of that she had no doubt. She forced her reluctant legs forward, one small step at a time, down the hallway to face the bastards that had murdered her friends.

She glanced back towards the kitchen, seeking a measure of reassurance that the sole loyal Shield remaining in the palace would come to her rescue if things went sour. Briar's stony expression stared back at her, and a firm, irritated wave urged her onward to victory or death. Little reassurance from the seasoned warrior. The cook took a deep, shuddering breath and then stepped into the main entrance chamber of the palace.

The four unkempt men guarding the inner gate looked up from their game of knucklebones and turned towards her, weapons rising. None of them had properly bathed in weeks, their ripeness lingering in the air like a sticky miasma.

"Ach, it just be that saggy drudge," said the man Selma knew to be called Milgen. He lowered his bronze-banded club and glowered at her. An older man with an eye patch and two fingers missing from his left hand, he was the chief of their wretched little pack of Wildwood Reivers, and the one Selma was most wary of. His weapon was well maintained, and his clothes and furs were old but well cared for. He was probably also the father of the others, given their crude, inbred resemblance.

Selma was too scared to take umbrage. She thrust the ale and basket out in front of her like a shield. "Ecksa said to bring you food and drink." They stared at her for a long moment, while sweat beaded her brow. Had they seen right through her ruse? Were they about to rape and murder her?

They came for her like a pack of hungry wolves, stripping her arms bare of food and drink. Grimy hands stuffed slices of spiced sausage into their mouths, yellow teeth ripping and tearing at the fatty meat. Hairy lips smacked, and tongues sucked the grease off fingers. Sighs of satisfaction filled the silences between wet open-mouthed chewing.

Selma started to back away into the hall, taking her chance while the bastards were busy gorging themselves. One of the reivers peered down into the jug. "Huh. What's these green things floating in the ale?"

"You stop right there, drudge," Milgen said, grabbing her arm. He cleared his throat and spat a glob of phlegm onto the floor right by her foot.

Selma froze, every muscle seized solid with absolute terror. Her back and armpits slicked with cold sweat. She wanted to run, to hide away in a dark corner, to cry out to every god she could think of.

"Innit rosemary?" another replied. "I hear these noble shits put all sort o' expensive herbs in their drink. Didn't you claim you'd stolen a cart of their booze before, Milgen? Sure that's what you said."

Their leader's single bloodshot eye pierced into her, flaying her lies open for all to see. She shuddered in his grip. "Eck-Ecksa said... he said to bring you the regent's very own brew," she blurted out, sweat stinging her eyes. "He said to come back and bring the rest to 'Her Upstairs'." She prayed they couldn't sense the inept lies on her tongue.

Milgen's eye narrowed. He chewed on his lower lip, staring into her eyes. Then his gaze slowly dipped past her breasts and into the ale jug that had been thrust before him for inspection. He sniffed at it once, twice and a third time for good measure. "Rosemary... Aye, that's what it'll be. Those rich pricks throw herbs and spices about like it were dust in a drought."

He licked a hot streak up Selma's cheek and then let go of her arm, but she remained still and sweating, her throat dry, eyes watering.

Milgen took a long draught from the jug. His eye immediately widened, and he spun to face Selma again. His grabbed hold of her arm once again, and she fought the urge to piss herself.

"Gods above and below, lass, that's a heady brew, right enough. Look at me, old Milgen drinking like a clan chief! He laughed and let go of her arm, his hairy hand painfully squeezing a breast instead. "Best be about your work, drudge. You keep Herself waiting and she'll cut your teats off to make bags out of them."

He laughed at her as she bobbed her head and made a run for it, the men's mocking laughter dogging her heels all the way back to the kitchen. Shame and shock overwhelmed her, and she collapsed into Briar's arms, sobbing and gasping for breath, caught in the throes of panic. Her ribs ached, squeezing her lungs and heart in a fist of terror.

"Look at me," Briar said. "Look me in the eyes. Breathe with me. In. Out. In. Out. You did well. You did all that I asked of you, and those vicious rats will die a more horrible death than you can imagine. Your friends have been avenged."

Briar let the cook clutch on to her and sob for a few precious moments, all too aware that the men might start screaming and vomiting blood at any moment. The woman was a dripping mess of shredded nerves, and even if they'd had the time, there was no point in contemplating asking her to re-enact her ruse and carry poisoned ale to more of the men guarding the walls and the stairs. Selma was no warrior, and Briar could not treat her like one. She'd almost certainly give the game away and get herself killed. Briar remembered the messy, retching aftermath of her own first battle only too well, and she imagined this sobbing cook would be utterly useless for a good few stones, if not days. It was hard to be a killer, however righteous the act was.

"Let's get you to safety," she said, steering the cook back out of the kitchen and down the hallway of the servants' quarters. Selma clung to Briar like a babe to its mother, sobbing softly into her breast. Briar paused and looked back. "Come, Brutus." The dog dutifully trotted after her, a haunch of meat almost the size of his entire body gripped in his teeth. She praised the gods that at least it kept the smelly beast from yapping and alerting more brigands.

Briar ignored the spreading wet patch on her chest and quietly hummed a tune used to quieten small children. She didn't ask what happened to Selma – the last thing the woman needed right now was a reminder of the horrors she alone had survived. That sort of guilt was an insidious worm that could eat away at even the most stable of minds.

Briar led them into the storeroom and firmly closed the door. Selma sniffed and scrubbed the tears from her eyes as Briar removed a stone from the wall to reveal the dark crawl space behind it. Brutus paused in his gnawing to sniff at the air flowing from the darkness – Briar assumed he was pondering what new trouble he could get up to. Selma stared at the secret tunnel, puzzled to find it located in a place she had been a thousand times.

"This ancient palace is riddled with secret tunnels," Briar explained. "But you had best never mention that fact ever again. If I ever hear even a whisper..."

Selma swallowed and nodded.

"Good. Now, we had best get the both of you away from here before those bastards start screaming and shitting out their internal organs. Get in that tunnel and get crawling. I am not here to be your nursemaid, so you will have to see to your own safety. I have a bloody task to do this day, and I will not have you or anybody else put that in jeopardy."

Selma got down onto her belly and crawled in without complaint. "Better blindness and honest rats than slaving for those human vermin," she said.

Briar smiled at her disappearing heels. "Oh, I don't know. I certainly appreciated you giving them one last meal." She grabbed Brutus's haunch of meat and pulled it and its growling canine attachment towards the hole, giving him a boot on the rump to encourage him to follow Selma in.

Briar went in after them and replaced the stone, plunging them into darkness. "Now crawl," she whispered. "Straight ahead, until you feel a breeze and the tunnel splits in two. Stay silent." They advanced on their hands and knees, shepherding a snuffling, wet-nosed dog between them.

"We're here," Selma whispered. "What now?"

"You go right and follow the tunnel sloping up to the next floor. Keep going straight until you see light coming through cracks in the wall. The wind will be howling all around you. There on your left you will find a low square stone with some druidic script lines carved into the back of it. That's your door into a secure room where they cannot reach you. Stay there until this is all over." She passed the haunch of gnawed beef forward, swatting Brutus's questing wet nose away. "Lure this scraggly piece of trouble in with you and keep him quiet. Go."

A man's scream echoed weirdly through the tunnel, then another voice joined it, full of agony. The screaming intensified into a chorus of terror that was music to Briar's ears. She chuckled, low and hard. "And so your vengeance begins. Twenty-five left."

Selma didn't reply. She shuddered and got moving, and soon Briar could not even hear the scuffs and scrapes, or the dog's panting.

Briar banished all thoughts of cook and canine to the back of her mind and went left. She picked up the pace, crawling as close to the Great Hall as she could manage with the nearby tunnels narrowing. She was too bulky to take the route Kester had traversed, but she could get near enough to emerge in the library. Then she would assess the situation and come up with a plan to spirit Alaric away to safety.

Hardgrim came down the stairs at a run with his sword in his hand and his Youngblood Cardew at his back – he wasn't about to trust his life to one of Imperatrix's assassins or her stinking hirelings. He wouldn't trust these dim-witted brigands to wipe their own arses and wash their hands before a meal. His Youngbloods had all been tried and tested and could be relied upon to stick to the long plan that was just coming to fruition, the plan that would see them bathing in riches before the season was out.

The weather-scoured reiver with pockmarked cheeks guarding the stairs started and half raised his hammer before stopping himself. He sagged in relief, as if he'd expected to fight a monster of the otherworld for his life.

"What is this unearthly din about?" Hardgrim demanded. "We could hear it all the way up in the Great Hall."

The man shook his head. He waved him onwards down the hallway to the inner gate and visibly choked back the urge to vomit.

Hardgrim scowled at the man. Only one guard present when there should be two... "Where is your friend?"

"Ecksa?" the reiver said. He shrugged and held a hand to his mouth to stifle another retch. "Not seen him in a while..."

Hardgrim cursed and took to his heels. He just had to follow the hair-raising screams shrieking out from the inner gate room. He paused outside the entrance chamber. The reek of shit and vomit and fresh blood assailed his nose, so thick he could taste it. He exchanged worried glances with Cardew.

The four men set to guard the inner gate were on the floor, writhing in a puddle of effluence, their faces purple and swollen like plums. Each breath between the screams wheezed between lips like bloated slugs. One vomited up blood and orange chunks of his own stomach, forcing Hardgrim to take a step back.

Two of the other reivers were there too, keeping their distance. "We have been cursed," one moaned.

Hardgrim's eyes rested on the jug of ale and basket of meats. He pulled on a glove and picked up the jug, sniffing and wrinkling his nose. "Poisoned, more than likely. Which one of you is Ecksa?"

The two unaffected men looked at him blankly. "He's on the stairs, ain't he? We were out patrolling the courtyard. 'Ere, how do we cure Milgen and the boys?"

The men on the floor all began spewing up quivering chunks of their own insides and torrents of black and reeking blood.

Hardgrim shook his head. "They are done for." He stepped forward and stabbed each of the writhing men in the heart. He felt relief as peace and quiet descended. "Ah, now that is better. Clean up this shithole. The both of you will now guard this place with your lives – and don't eat or drink anything you didn't bring with you." Without waiting for an answer, he turned on his heel and made his way to the kitchen, ducking his head through the doorway. His gaze swept the room and found nothing amiss.

He returned to the central stairwell.

"Has anybody passed by you?" Hardgrim demanded. "Up or down? The Royal Heir, perhaps?"

"Not a soul," the man replied. "Not seen the boy-king up here since those two men of yours gave chase."

"Not even this Ecksa?"

The man shook his head again. "Last I seen of him he was off to slap that saggy drudge for being tardy with our food."

Hardgrim grabbed him by the throat and stared at him hard enough to raise a sweat on his forehead. "What drudge would that be? Are you saying you kept one of the servants alive and put her to work?"

The man swallowed. "Some dim-witted cook is all. Didn't keep her alive to laze about. We didn't know where all the good stuff was kept, now, did we?"

Hardgrim let go. "Four dead and another man missing," he said. "Some menial drudge of a servant… Oh, she knew where the food was alright, and more besides, it seems." He grimaced and gazed down the steps, beginning to worry that Newlyn and Nealon hadn't returned with that royal brat in tow. "Shit. Cardew – pull men down from the upper floors and sweep every room on this floor. Check every basket and cupboard, every bed and every nook and cranny of this whole floor, until you find that wretched servant and cut her throat."

The people of this dreary palace all seemed born to plague him, Hardgrim thought, massaging his temples. If it wasn't staid old Briar with all her rules and duties it was that weakling of a Royal Heir, still missing in the catacombs, or some stupid little drudge wreaking a terrible vengeance. If these Wildwood Reivers of Imperatrix's had half the balls of that accursed cook, then he wouldn't be half so worried. He couldn't seem to relax. A niggling worry that he couldn't quite pin down was starting to burrow deeper into the back of his mind.

CHAPTER 17

While Bram was held hostage elsewhere, the fire in his beloved library had been left to die out, and the fragile scrolls and tablets were now at the mercy of harsh winter temperatures. Briar gave her thanks for that neglect as she slid back the heavy stone behind the hearth and crawled through cold ashes into the library. The door to the hallway beyond was shut – another bit of luck. She groaned and cursed her cramping leg as she used a chair to help push herself upright. Her front was now grey from head to toe, but there was little point trying to find water to clean herself up when the blood of her enemies would cover her soon enough. Killing was such a messy, sticky business.

Somebody had put up a fight here. Scrolls lay scattered all over the room, and a whole section of wooden shelving had been toppled and trampled to splinters. Priceless illustrated goatskin parchments lay crumpled on the floor, bearing muddy boot prints and spots of blood. Ancient baked-clay tablets with incised scripts from a time before the ancestors of Sunweald fled into this forest realm were lying in pieces. She winced at the sight, fearing Bram's wail when he discovered the desecration. Alaric's master of spies was every bit the librarian he masqueraded as, and losing such knowledge would wound him to his very core – if he still lived. But if anybody could survive, then it would be him. She spared the time to scoop up most of the ancient shards and store them away in a box before somebody thoughtlessly trampled them into dust – probably her, if she was being honest. There were few things she truly feared in life, but a librarian's wrath would be right up there with bards on her list of things to avoid. Entire realms had fallen because a foolish queen or king had angered the masters of words and lore.

Briar crept to the door, breath held, ears straining. She need not have bothered – angry voices rang out clear as war horns as men raced past the library, armour jangling and leather creaking. The bastards charged from the Great Hall and headed down the stairwell. Somebody had roused the guard and sent them off hunting the poisoner they assumed was hidden away down below, preparing to strike again. Many young warriors thought deceiving the enemy was beneath them, but many veteran warriors were of the opinion that a little misleading that helped keep them alive was preferrable to the often brief honour of an entirely fair fight. That level of honour was best reserved for duels, not a bloody battle against an enemy who would wipe their shitty arses on honour if they had any use for it at all.

As Briar waited for the flurry of activity outside to die down, she stretched muscles aching from her being hunched over in the tunnels and crawling on hands and knees. She was, she had to admit, getting too old for such sneaky nonsense. In addition to the serious leg wound and a shoulder starting to ache in the cold, she found herself valuing thick socks, comfy beds and nearby latrines more than ever before. It was a sad fact of life that the more knowledge and skill you acquired, the less you were able to use it. Whatever the druids and wise ones claimed, she could only view it as a sadistic trick of the gods upon all living creatures.

The sounds faded as the enemy went down the stairs, intent on rooting out their poisonous prey. Briar finally cracked open the door and peered up and down the hallway. To the left, some of the lanterns were gone, taken by the invaders. To the right was a darkened and entirely empty hallway leading to the servants' entrance at the rear of the Great Hall, behind the throne. Her ruse had worked, and at least some of the guards had been lured downstairs.

She slipped out of the room and made her way down the hall. To her right, the door to a storeroom opened. She silently cursed and spun, sword lashing out. A greasy pockmarked face caused a spark of recognition, and she managed to stop her blade cutting through the man's throat. Jund, a palace labourer who had been in the position for two years, stood sweating in the doorway, not even daring to swallow lest the blade nick his skin. He opened his mouth to speak, and Briar pressed the blade harder into his neck for a moment. "Be quiet as the tomb," she whispered as she pushed him back into the room, "unless you wish to bring the enemy down on our heads."

He nodded, and she withdrew the blade. He sagged in relief and rubbed his throat as she examined him. Unlike Selma, the lucky man had been spared the attention of the reivers. "What are you doing lurking about here?" she said. "You idiot – this place is filled with murderers."

"I... uh..." he said, face reddening. "I was hiding I was. Heard them go past and thought... well... maybes now might be a good chance to escape."

A clatter of stone on stone further down the hallway drew Briar's attention away from him, but the palace was old and crumbling, and it seemed nothing more. Jund seized the opportunity to draw his belt knife and lunge for her belly. It was an action she had entirely expected, given his hale and healthy status and location right outside the Great Hall, where the leader of the Wildwood Reivers held court, but she'd still had to give the man a slim chance to prove he wasn't one of the traitors.

She batted the blade aside with her shield and stabbed him in the throat to prevent any screams. "Twenty-four," she muttered as he fell back into the storeroom, gurgling pink froth. She dispatched the traitor, wiped her sword clean on his tunic and then returned to the hallway and closed the door behind her. She didn't bother to disguise her presence by going to the effort of hiding this corpse – the enemy would know she was here soon enough once she charged into the Great Hall.

She crept towards the arch leading into the back of the great chamber. It had been left unguarded; any men that might have been posted here had been reassigned to the hunt for the poisoner on the floor below. She prepared herself to face the worst: Alaric might already be dead. The pang of fear melted before her fury. If the scum had already slain him, then not even the gods and spirits themselves would dare try to thwart her vengeance – every one of those blackhearted traitors and reivers would follow him into the otherworld, suffering her red curse. No tomb for their bones but the rotten midden pit she would toss them into.

From here on, speed would prove safer than stealth. She clutched her sword in her right hand and readied her buckler in her left, then took a deep breath and peered through the archway into the hall beyond. The thick trunk of the Oaken Throne blocked sight of any who might sit upon it and thwarted any attack by intruders such as herself. To the left, two burly axemen in dirty furs. To the right, one reiver with a broken arm in a sling and the oath-broken Shields Kendhal and Cardew in shining scale shirts and studded kilts, who seemed to be left in command, judging from their angry cursing at three reivers. She glared at the oak-leaf-decorated bronze bucklers hanging on the former Shields' hips, a token of honour they no longer deserved. From her current location, she could see only some of the captives, the horrifically few survivors, bound face down on the floor. Every one of them had been beaten, bloodied and broken until they had no fight left in them. She couldn't see any sign of Alaric, nor Aisling or Imperatrix or whatever else the gut-worm called herself these days, but she did note Carmanilla and Bram, still sprawled right where Kester said they were. The one-handed priestess was pale and sweating profusely, not well at all, and her scalp was all scrapes and ragged clumps of hair.

Briar ducked back out of sight and swiftly came up with a plan. She faced tall odds, but it was nothing a hard woman couldn't handle. If the sorcerer was on the throne, she had to die first – a wise warrior never gave their kind time to work vile magic. The two treacherous former Shields would need to be taken down immediately after, before the armoured men could react and mount a proper defence. Fights could devolve into messy and chaotic brawls even among the best-trained warriors, and if they could hold her for even a few moments then all of her hard-won martial prowess wouldn't matter. It was an annoying truth for warrior women that many men were bigger and stronger, and she was still far from the peak of possible fitness. She had once relied upon her skill and swiftness to overwhelm the crude strength of men, but her leg reduced her mobility, and if those scum were able to bring their numbers to bear, she stood no chance at all.

She would grit her teeth against the pain and use the benefits of speed and surprise to cut down the oath-breakers before turning her blade on the two axemen. They used unwieldy tools unsuitable for war, but a solid hit would kill her as well as the finest spear or sword ever made. Then the broken-armed reiver would swiftly follow his murderous friends into the darkest depths of the otherworld. She prayed that her wounded leg would hold steady under the strain.

She took a deep and calming breath, wiped sweaty palms on her tunic and then silently slipped into the rear of the Great Hall. She went right round the back of the trunk of the Oaken Throne, heading towards the former Shields. Her eyes flicked towards the throne. Empty. No time to ponder. Kendhal and Cardew filled her sight, still arguing with the two reivers across the hall. Her leg burned as she broke into a charge.

Alerted by sudden movement, Kendhal glanced towards the throne, eyes widening. His hand fumbled at his belt to draw his own sword. Much too slow. She'd trained the fool better than that. Her blade clove his face in two, with his only half freed from its scabbard. Hot blood spattered her hand. She wrenched the weapon free of Kendhal's skull and swung for Cardew.

He lurched back, his cheek sliced open. She advanced and thrust at his eyes. His sword and buckler came up to block it. His view was blocked by his own defence and he couldn't see her buckler swing round until too late. It cracked into his right wrist. He howled as bone snapped and his weapon dropped to the floor.

She gave Cardew no time to recover. Cut. Slash. Shield-bash. Her left leg screamed at her as it trembled under the strain. He staggered, guard broken. The rim of her shield cracked into his temple. He dropped to one knee, dazed.

Before she could finish off her prey, the broken-armed reiver got in her way. He drew a knife and slashed at her. She parried the clumsy blow and punched her shield into his face. He lurched back, nose and teeth broken. She turned to face the two axemen, who had broken from their state of shock and hefted their weapons.

The two axemen closed their gaping mouths and lumbered towards her. She swung her sword menacingly and circled the corpse of Kendhal to put one reiver in the way of the other, and then she backed away towards the wall. One of the things she taught newly appointed Shields was an acute awareness of terrain and the tactics to exploit them – too many hotheaded fools thought fighting was only about charging straight towards the enemy and swinging your weapon as hard as you could. The axeman in the rear slipped on pooling blood and went down, leaving his friend to face an angry veteran Shield alone. The fool lifted his axe above his head and swung it like he was chopping wood, or a terrified peasant. Axes were great weapons – assuming you hit your target. She slid a handspan to the right, and his axe thunked uselessly into the floor.

He looked into her eyes, befuddled, as she buried her sword between his ribs.

The other axeman scrambled back to his feet and lifted his weapon. Before he could strike, Briar moved in close, blocked the axe with her buckler and rammed her sword up through his exposed belly and into his heart. She ripped it free in a welter of gore and shoved the dying man aside.

Only Cardew and the broken-armed reiver remained. The reiver was kneeling on the floor, hands bloody, one of them clamped around his ruined jaw in a futile attempt to keep the shattered remnants together. He was no threat, but the former Shield rose behind him, broken wrist held across his chest and a sword clutched awkwardly in his left hand. Cardew assessed the sudden slaughter and his angry commander advancing on them both. The blood drained from his face as the odds of his survival came up short.

The captives began to stir, some rising to their knees and warily lifting heads to see what was occurring. "Briar!" Bram cried. "You have come to rescue us!" Carmanilla glanced at the fresh corpse of one of her torturers on the floor and then grinned at the sight of Briar with a bloodied sword and shield. Beside her, the hearth mistress struggled against her bonds, gnawing leather cords with her remaining teeth.

Cardew had always been a sly one. Briar cursed as he turned and sprinted for the hallway leading to the central staircase and reinforcements instead of putting up a fight. He skirted the huddle of captives in the centre of the Great Hall, but his escape route took him past the far wall, where Carmanilla and Bram lay.

Kester's little knife appeared in the Wrendal priestess' hand and promptly buried itself in Cardew's thigh. He stumbled and fell, cursing her.

The hearth mistress kicked out her bound legs, and her foot sent the oath-broken Shield's weapon skittering across the floor.

Carmanilla's remaining hand let go of the knife to wrap around his ankle. "Die for me, heretic," she hissed. Black veins crawled up her throat. Cardew convulsed, blood and steam spraying from his ears, eyes and nose. The priestess slumped back, panting.

Briar stared at the steaming corpse for a moment, then nodded her regards to the priestess. She limped over to the broken-armed reiver and put him out of his misery before making her rounds of the other fallen, stabbing them all again just in case. She'd seen more than one evil-hearted brigand lurch back into motion with one last gasp of breath to take an honourable but unwary warrior's life. "Nineteen left," she muttered.

Her bloody work done, Briar now had time to properly survey the captives. It was a delight to her eyes to see so many she knew still alive. Her eyes sought out any sign of Alaric's greying hair and kind eyes. Nothing. "Where is the regent?" she demanded.

"Taken underground to the Heart by their leader," Bram said. "A woman called Imperatrix, who—"

"Aisling," Briar interrupted. "I know who the accursed traitor is and what she has done."

"And Kester?" he asked, brow furrowed with worry.

"Safer than any of us," she replied.

He nodded and did not enquire further. Her word was good enough for him.

With Briar's battle blood subsiding, the ache in her leg was blooming into a fiery pain that had engulfed her knee and was swiftly spreading up to her hip. The damned thing did not like to move fast. She limped over to Bram and sawed through the leather cords that bound his wrists and feet. He groaned as he stretched sore limbs, then hissed in pain and clutched a side full of broken ribs. He shook off the pain and took a knife from one of the reivers to work on freeing the others.

Briar regarded the black veins marring Exalted Carmanilla's

neck. Her lips twisted sourly like she'd bitten into a rotten fruit as she offered the priestess assistance.

"Most kind to offer me a hand," Carmanilla said as she was hauled up onto shaky feet.

Briar blinked at her. "Was that a joke?"

The Wrendal priestess offered a wan smile. "Humour is the last refuge of the damned and the dying. This Aisling of yours is a sorcerer of great power," she advised. "Do not think she is some rural hedge witch with mere scraps of true knowledge and ineffective charms. She is deadly, and I can sense the taint of bargains with dark denizens of the otherworld upon her soul."

Briar grunted her appreciation. "Get that stump attended to and it won't be the last I'll see of you, more's the pity. Good work, by the way."

She turned to Bram. "Head to the East Wing, third floor, through the tunnels."

"The tunnels?" he queried, frowning.

"What use are secrets if we are all dead?" she said. "The old chief's guest room is barricaded and defensible. Selma the cook and the regent's dog await you there. The way through the library is clear for now."

He nodded, wincing. It seemed he didn't approve of his secret spy tunnels becoming common knowledge, but he didn't have any kind of rebuttal.

"Bram will see you all to a safe place," she told the others as they rose to their feet, rubbing the feeling back into feet and hands. "He is now in charge. Do exactly what he says if you want to live."

"The librarian?" Morna asked, confused. "He's... Well... Are you sure he can be relied upon? Can you not lead us?"

This was no time for ruses. "He's the regent's master of spies," Briar said. "If you all want to live through this, obey him as you would the regent. I have more important tasks than coddling the lot of you."

The survivors stared at Bram in shock and disbelief. He sighed and shrugged off the mien of mild-mannered librarian. "Those of you who can still fight at all, grab yourself a weapon. The rest who can walk unaided, help the worst of our wounded into the library, where we will enter the palace's secret tunnel system. Keep your mouths shut about this forever more," he warned. "Or I'll have you all killed."

The palace's stable master, hearth mistress and head scribe picked up weapons and followed Briar's instructions as she shepherded the rest of the sorry group out of the Great Hall. They were not warriors and were barely standing. Most of them bore wounds needing sutured and bound, and all suffered from broken ribs, fingers or worse. The reivers had kept them alive but had ensured they would be in no state to fight back.

Briar went first, ears and eyes open as she crept from the Great Hall. An eerie, inhuman howling echoed up the stairwell to set the hair on the back of her arms standing. She swallowed and put it down to a trick of the wind rather than a tortured spirit's wrathful curse. There had been a river of innocent blood shed in the last day, and all knew shades could rise from such events to plague the living. There was no fighting such things with bronze and muscle, so all she could do was hope their wrath was focused on their murderers.

Briar kept watch as the survivors shuffled into the library, leaving a trail of bloody boot prints behind them. Bram came last, carrying a bucket of piss from the Great Hall. He slopped it down the hallway to wash away all trace of their passing and then hurried into the room. Briar closed the door behind them and stood guard while Bram directed the others to haul the hearthstone back and reveal the tunnel beyond.

"Where will you go now?" he asked. "And how can we help?" He caught sight of the broken shards of his ancient tablets and wobbled on his feet, hissing in pain and loss.

In their battered state, the survivors would have an ordeal reaching the guest rooms on the third floor at a snail's pace.

"You all stay safe and stay out of my way," Briar said. "Let me do my job without having to deal with more hostages. I will bring Alaric back or I will die trying."

Bram nodded. "Follow me," he told the group. "Each of you, keep track of the person in front by touch. Stay quiet unless you want them to take our heads." He grimaced as he got to his knees and crawled in. They followed him with excoriating slowness, stifling groans and yelps of pain. Briar stood, grinding her teeth at the delay, every muscle but one itching to charge onwards and race to save the regent.

Finally, it was her turn. She went to sheath her sword but found it scraping the poplar interior of her scabbard. She held the blade up to her eye. The bronze had acquired a chip and a slight bend from hitting some bastard's bones, but it was an easy fix. She took hold of the tip and hilt and pressed the middle against her thigh until it straightened out.

With that done, she sheathed the sword and crawled into the tunnel, then sealed it behind her, plunging them all into total darkness. The survivors crawled upwards while she steadied her nerves against the eerie howling twisting through the tunnels, and made her way down towards the catacombs.

CHAPTER 18

A reiver lurched out of one of the servants' bedchambers and retched in the hallway. Hardgrim rolled his eyes at the wet splattering, shoved the man aside and entered the room, squinting into the flickering lantern light. His eyebrows climbed at the sight of a man's severed head impaled on a stick, one driven right through the arse of his own corpse.

Ruith entered behind him and whistled at the mess. "Well, now. You don't see that sort of thing every day. Somebody sure is raging at us."

Hardgrim snorted. "These Wildwood Reivers..." He shook his head. "Happy enough to massacre sleeping wenches and children, but the sight of one of their own being mutilated entirely unmans them. Still, what kind of sneaky poisoner also makes this sort of grim spectacle?"

Ruith shrugged, then picked at the angry, seeping red wound on his forehead. "Does this look infected?" At Hardgrim's nod, he muttered vile curses upon Shield Brenna's soul.

More reivers crowded around, peering into the room. Hardgrim noted the man he'd questioned at the stairwell. "You, there! Is this your missing Ecksa?"

The man shuddered. "Nay. That be Uncle Saddis. Ecksa is still missing."

Hardgrim exchanged glances with Ruith. "Split them into pairs, and have them search every single room on this floor of the palace. Examine every possible nook and cranny somebody could hide in. Find me this missing Ecksa, and bring me the poisonous cook." After a moment's thought, he added, "Send Iden and two more men back down into the catacombs. I would have expected Newlyn and Nealon to have returned some time ago with that brat of a Royal Heir trussed up like a hog ready for the roast. Something smells wrong about all of this."

Ruith chewed on his lower lip. "Briar?"

Hardgrim winced. "I hope not. After some – heh – pointed inquiries of our captives, I was told she had already left the palace before we struck." He nodded towards the severed head on a stick. "She is easily capable of such malice, but this atrocity is not really her style. That woman lacks the imagination for such a thing."

"But have you ever seen her truly angry?" Ruith asked.

Hardgrim swallowed and forced his hand to stop creeping towards the hilt of his sword. "If she is loose within these halls…"

An eerie wail echoed through the hallways, seeming to come from all around. It stilled all chatter and set the reivers to muttering prayers and clutching myriad talismans and sacred symbols hanging around their necks.

"The spirits of the slain," a reiver cried. He clutched some folk charm of stone, bone and crow's feather and spun in place, searching the shadows for any sign of eldritch shapes and burning eyes. "We are cursed!"

Before he could panic the rest of the superstitious dull-witted peasants, their chief, Uradech, appeared behind him. The big man spun him around and buried a fist in his belly. The panicked reiver dropped to his knees, gasping for breath.

"You are cursed with stupidity," Uradech said. "It's just the wind, you lack-witted little prick. Are the fearsome Wildwood Reivers a bunch of weeping farm boys still suckling at your mother's teats, or are you hard men who can be relied upon to get a job done right? Think of the fortune in gems, bronze, silver and livestock each of you are due, and get moving. Find us his killer."

Uradech nodded at Hardgrim, rested his sword on his shoulder and left with Ruith to oversee the search.

Playing on their greed had got them moving well enough, the former Shield thought as they shuffled off in pairs to begin the search under their chief's command. Wailing wind or angry spirits, he wanted to get the job done and get out of this blood-soaked palace before the warband loyal to regent and realm returned – that was his real worry.

As Hardgrim waited for good news from the search party, he looked closer at the horrific scene in front of him, crouching down and using a lantern to get a better look at the wounds. The man's jaw and teeth were shattered. A brutal blow, but not the killing one. His throat was also a mangled, bruised mess around the wound, and the swelling would have cut off his air. He looked to the torso, studying the careful cuts used to behead the corpse and facilitate this macabre display. It was skilled work, but might as easily have been done by a cook as by a trained warrior. The face, though... That smashing damage... He tried to imagine the club that might have inflicted such a pattern of wounds. There were purpled lines on the throat, of a very particular width that led his eyes towards the bronze buckler hanging at his own hip. He set the rim of his shield to the bruises on the man's throat, and then the reinforced centre boss to his broken face. A perfect match.

He rocked back on his heels. "Gods and spirits," he whispered. "Say it is not so."

Ruith returned a little while later, his face grave. "We found Ecksa's corpse in the kitchen's cool room, covered up by a pile of sacks. A single cut between neck and shoulder and a blow to the skull. There is no sign at all of this cook they said is running free. Either she is a vengeful spirit, or she has already escaped." He eyed Hardgrim, whose buckler still rested on what was left of the corpse's pulped throat. "A Shield? Is it her?"

Hardgrim stood, grimacing. "Who else could it be? Find her

quickly. I want her hands and feet broken, and her forced to crawl across the floor to beg my forgiveness."

Ruith eyed the corpse. "But why all of this? Why not dump the corpse in the cool room beside Ecksa instead of going to the trouble of impaling his skull through his arse? Unless it's a—"

"Distraction," Hardgrim supplied, his eyes widening. He shot to his feet and took to his heels, heading for the stairs, Ruith at his back. "Shit, shit, shit, shit," he muttered as he pounded past the surprised guard and took the steps up two at a time, spiralling round and round until he was feeling dizzied. The stench of piss hit him first, then the metallic tang of bloodshed. He burst into the Great Hall and skidded to a messy stop, his boots slipping and sliding through a pool of mixed fluids.

He howled at the sight of two of his Youngbloods dead, three reivers disposed of and not a captive to be seen. Somebody had rescued them while he'd been down below, hunting ghosts. As old Briar had taught him, he set about studying the corpses, wounds, boot prints and blood spatter to try to come up with a mental image of how the attack had played out. The attacker must have come from the rear of the throne and taken Kendhal down unawares. They had then most likely attacked the reiver with a broken arm, and possibly Cardew too, judging from the mess of different-sized bloody boot prints there. The two axemen had driven the attacker over to the far wall, but the tides had swiftly turned, and the two men had been expertly dispatched.

Cardew had then made a run for the main entrance, probably hoping to reach the stairwell and call for reinforcements. The man's eyes had been boiled away, and his ankle was a charred and weeping mess, the fingermarks obvious. Sorcery. Surely that Exalted bitch of an ambassador from the Holy Wrendal Empire. He cursed, wishing Imperatrix had cut off the woman's other hand, and her feet too for good measure.

The captives had then fled through the main door, but any tracks had been washed away with the piss-bucket, and he could find no other obvious trace of their passing. They had certainly not gone down to the lower floor. "Ruith!" he screamed. "Check nobody has passed our guards on the upper floor."

As Ruith ran to investigate, Hardgrim's gaze returned to the scene to try to glean further details. It had been a fast-and-furious assault using the element of surprise and superior skill to slaughter the guards. He would have carried out the assault against greater numbers in exactly the same way. The way Briar had taught him. He scowled and went back to the very beginning of the fight, trying to pick out the attacker's footprints and study their movements. The to and fro of battle grew into a vividly detailed scene inside his mind, and he could not help but note the lack of movement in the attacker's left foot – almost as if they could not entirely rely upon it to bear the weight of combat. He scowled and spat on the floor of the Great Hall.

Briar.

It had to be.

Ruith pounded back down the stairs with three men at his back. "The guards on the upper floors are all alive and have not seen a soul pass by."

"These Wildwood Reivers are all incompetent," Hardgrim snarled. "You cannot trust them to do anything well, save scratching their hairy arses and getting themselves killed. We must search this floor ourselves."

They raced from room to room, kicking open doors and storming in, weapons raised, hoping to kill. In that they were sorely disappointed. All they found was shuttered and locked windows and the corpse of their ally Jund with his throat cut. Of the captives there was – impossibly – no sign at all. "Where have they gone?" he asked Ruith, bewildered. They had not gone up, and they had not gone down. They had seemingly vanished into thin air. "This is impossible!"

Ruith shrugged, not having any answer to give.

"Briar!" he screamed. "I don't know how you did it, but I will find you, and I will kill you." Hardgrim raged, kicking Jund's corpse until his toes throbbed. He went in search of more men to form into search parties to scour every corner of the palace for how he had been fooled. Then he would have the joyous task of explaining his failures to the accursed sorcerer.

In the supposedly safe refuge of the third-floor guest rooms in the derelict East Wing, Selma held her breath and listened. Sounds of movement filtered through the cracks in the old wall. The shuffling and scuffling were coming closer: more than one person, trying to be stealthy. Hairs raised on the back of her arms. She shuddered, biting her lip to stifle sounds of panic.

Selma swallowed her fears – she had already killed four blackhearted brigands, had she not? – and hefted a stone in her trembling hands. The cook prepared herself to bash in the skull of whatever vermin came crawling out of the wall – if it wasn't Briar back to take her out of the palace, of course. She prayed to see the Shield's stern expression, and only that.

The sounds ceased right outside the secret entrance. The stone slid out of place, and a man's hands lowered it to the floor carefully, to minimise noise. Bram's bald head emerged from the darkness, and his watery eyes stared up at her and the stone about to shatter his skull. "Ah, Selma," he said, nonplussed, "do help us out. I fear my poor back is not up to crawling about these tunnels. Many of us have broken bones and suchlike."

She sagged with relief, set the stone down and began helping the other survivors into the room. The hearth mistress was a sight for sore eyes, and the brief hug they shared did much to calm her nerves. She took great care with the once-pretty-and-pristine Wrendal ambassador – one look at the woman told a tale of the harrowing ordeal she'd suffered. There were more survivors than she had thought, given her own experiences with the reivers, but fewer than she could contemplate.

Once all the people were through, Selma peered into the darkness of the tunnels. "You didn't see Brutus in there, did you?"

"The regent's dog?" Bram asked. "Not a sign. Why?"

Selma swallowed. "Briar asked me to keep him safe in here, but I turned my back for a few moments and he'd stolen his bone and was back down the tunnel before I could close it up behind me."

Bram shook his head. "That greedy old dog can take care of himself. Now, help me get the wounded comfortable."

She glanced one last time into the tunnel and then slid the stone back into place. The survivors were in a sorry state, but they were all lucky to be alive. All they could do now was wait and pray to the gods and spirits of the ancestors that Briar would get them out.

After resting and eating a lavish meal while her hungry captives looked on, Imperatrix had led the way down into the tunnels beneath the palace, laden with a satchel of tools and supplies for her task. Her favoured assassin, Maddox, followed, carrying a pair of lanterns to light the way for her two guards. The former Shields Phelan and Owyn had their hands full escorting the gagged, bound and stripped-naked regent of Sunweald.

The sorcerer strode confidently into the darkness in the sure knowledge that she was the most terrifying creature there. Over her years masquerading as a simple maid, she had found her way past the myriad arcane protections put in place to prevent her sort from entering the catacombs, and her magic was now well masked from the ancient spirits set to ward off evil creatures and dark magic. Others might fear the dark, dank depths of the catacombs, but to Imperatrix they felt more like home than painted walls, cosy halls or wild forests.

She had spent days beyond counting down there, digging in forgotten tombs and caves, searching out ancient secrets and arcane artefacts, and the dead of this place no longer held any terror for her. The silence and solitude agreed with her, and she found it preferable to the inane chatterings of the servants and so-called nobles of Sunweald. Once she was done with this last great task, she would have enough wealth and power to do whatever she liked and no longer have any need to suffer the presence of self-important idiots like Hardgrim. Sunweald would fall, and Imperatrix would rise to heights of power beyond anything their feeble minds could dream of.

The foot-thick bronze door protecting the Heart of Sunweald stood wide open, its elaborate system of chains and counterweights jammed. Two loyal Shields set to guard it lay sprawled where they had fallen, their throats cut from behind by Iden. Her ally had been in a hurry and had left a right mess behind for others to pick up. Hardgrim was an odious man, she thought as she picked her way past the corpses, but his treachery had been well planned. Over the years, she had learnt to tolerate much that was repellent, so long as it worked to further her goals.

The regent of Sunweald tripped over one of the corpses of his beloved guardians. He snarled through his gag and struggled against his escorts, but his efforts only served to amuse Imperatrix. She was about to say something to twist the knife in his distress, but the sight of the cavern did that job for her. She had let her uncouth allies run amok in there for just such a moment.

Elaborate carved and painted wooden shrines had once lined one wall of the Heart, containing the dark and leathery preserved bodies of the Summerson ancestors, those mighty high queens and kings of old. Alaric stared in sickened horror at the sight of the hacked-open shrines and the revered bodies of his ancestors, torn from their housings and left sprawled on the floor like refuse. Reivers had snapped the arms and fingers off some of them to steal gold armbands and rings, and then trashed any remaining historical relics for good measure. Hundreds of ancient pots, clay tablets, and brittle, storied weapons lay in bits, and delicate stone and wood effigies of mortal and god alike had been crudely smashed with axes. Of the gold crown of Sunweald, there was no trace – stolen, and hacked up into pieces to be found in many belt pouches.

The Heart boasted few other intact contents save for a common table and benches for weary guards to rest upon, but the cavern itself was a treasure of the realm. The place was ancient, predating the palace above by... well, Imperatrix was thoroughly educated in the architectures of past peoples, but even she had no comprehension of just how long ago it had been built. The stone walls were rough, natural outcrops chipped smoother by antler picks and stone hammers before being painted all over with ochre symbols. The most ancient caves Imperatrix had previously ventured into had boasted charcoal-drawn hunting scenes of humans stalking stags and boars and long-extinct tusked beasts with their bows and spears. The Heart was different: in this place, it was beasts of legend who mercilessly hunted humans and trampled their stick-figure prey beneath their feet. Beside them were taller figures differently drawn in yellow ochre, sometimes fighting beside cruder charcoal human figures, and at others falling in a heap with them under the claws of large and fearsome beasts.

Certain areas of the floor, wall and ceiling had been polished smooth with sand and pumice and painstaking effort over generations to expose the skeletal remains of long-dead beasts sunken into the stone, every one wicked in fang and claw and barbed tail. One enormous serpentine beast occupied the entirety of the far wall, a truly mighty wyrm that even Imperatrix feared to imagine in life. The great skull was the size of a horse and carriage, and the vicious fangs were the length of her forearm. There were no other obvious doors and nothing else in the cavern, but the sorcerer knew from her divinations that the remains of this mighty beast guarded the Wyrm Vault. Somehow, the door protecting the Vault's fabled treasures had been hidden with a combination of artifice and sorcery. Hardgrim's Youngbloods had been the only Shields on duty some nights, allowing her access to study its arcane protections. Now she had it all to herself for the days of gruelling work that would be required to open it.

The assassin, Maddox, whistled in appreciation, craning his head to take it all in. He set one of his lanterns down on the table and then prowled the cavern, holding the other aloft to gaze at the shapes on and in the walls.

Imperatrix managed to tear her gaze away from the cavern. "Finally," she said to Alaric, ripping the gag from his mouth. "Here we are, together in the one place in this crumbling palace that is of true importance. I am sure little Kester will be joining us soon. All that now remains is to see if you will cooperate with me in order to save his baby-soft skin from suffering my knives. I need royal blood, but it remains to be seen how much it will take to force the Vault open. Maybe, if you behave, I'll let him live."

Alaric remained stoic and silent, his eyes dark and full of deadly threat.

She patted him on the shoulder. "Aw, how precious to think you could possibly hurt me." She slapped him, hard enough to split his lip. Then, again from the other side, reddening his cheek. "Do not forget that you live or die at my whim. As does your nephew."

She paced around the cavern, studying the skeletons embedded in the stone. "Now, Alaric, you will speak – or you and yours will suffer unimaginable pain. Where is the secret door leading to your riches? Where have you hidden the arcane weapons that your vile ancestors used to scour noble Hisparren from the land?"

Alaric worked his jaw and spat blood on the floor. "My 'vile ancestors', is it…?" He chuckled. "Is this some misguided revenge for events five centuries gone, when all involved are dust and bones? You cannot blame me for your own impoverished line when it was they who attacked Sunweald first with their sorcery and enslaved monsters."

She slapped him again. "I can, and I do. All the ills that have befallen my family over the years can be traced directly back to Sunweald. Your tales of sorcery and monsters are lies and a blatant excuse for the fact that your kin did unspeakable things to towns and cities full of innocent people."

"On that last point we can both agree," Alaric replied. "Which is exactly why I will never allow any to get their hands on such power within my realm, and most especially, wicked creatures like you. That is why I had every last one of those weapons destroyed. This Vault is empty and guarded only for tradition, nothing more."

"Wicked, am I?" Imperatrix replied, a sneer growing. "You are not a good enough liar, Alaric. Not even close. You have no idea the lengths I will go to in order to get what I want. Restrain him." Phelan and Owyn held Alaric tight as she drew a long bone needle from its calfskin sheath inside her satchel.

"This needle is made of wyrm-bone, the rarest and most valuable material in the world. Even the crumbled remnants of old and broken artefacts are worth more than carts of gold and fields of cattle. The preserved bones of ancient wyrms are the most potent conductors available to sorcerers such as I, and with this sliver of ancient power in my hand, I will break open your Vault and seize the artefacts stored within."

Alaric threw his body this way and that, but there was no escaping his captors' grip. She grabbed his hair in one hand and held the tip of the needle to his eye. He stilled, swallowed and forced his eyes to remain open and fixed on her.

"Get on with it, then," he said, his voice bearing only a slight tremble. "You are boring me."

She snorted and slowly shook her head. "You are no fun at all, Lord Regent Alaric Summerson. But this is just the beginning, and I assure you, you will not become bored. You think yourself so very brave, but you have never been tortured. All men break, sooner or later." The needle trailed down his cheek to his chin, then jabbed in until it grated against the bone.

Alaric stiffened as she pierced him but did not cry out. She withdrew the needle and studied the blood beading its tip. "I have done my research on this place and its protections. Summerson blood is the key."

She turned her back on him and approached the great wyrm skeleton at the back wall, studying the fanged maw that could have swallowed her up with one bite and barely notice doing so. "Maddox, bring your lantern closer." The assassin did as he was told, and the atmosphere deepened as the flame of his lantern flickered and flared in an unseen, unfelt breeze.

She held the wyrm-bone needle out before her, a fingertip's breadth from the wall, and traced the petrified bones of the great beast, her eyes fixed on the swollen red droplet hanging from the tip. She started at the top of the skull, barely within her reach. The needle passed back and forth, back and forth, dropping by a finger span each time.

"Ahh," she sighed as the drop of blood trembled while traversing the hollow of the left eye socket. "A knot of power." She touched the needle against the skull, and blood seeped into it, staining the stone dark in the shape of an arcane rune. She smiled at the regent. "The protections your ancient druids have put in place will prove inadequate. I don't suppose you would care to save yourself the torment and open it up for me? No?"

He said nothing.

She stabbed the regent in the chin to draw another bead of blood, and then resumed her search of the wall. She identified a total of thirteen focal points, each one at the price of a drop of Summerson blood.

Imperatrix stepped back and examined the patterns of magic woven into the wall. "Complex," she muttered. "A true work of art. It will be a shame to ruin it." She turned and stared at Alaric, his face a mess of bloody pinpricks. "Do you know what opens a door quickly?" she asked. "An axe."

He snorted. "By all means, try brute force."

"But this is no ordinary door," she added, wagging a finger at him. "In this case, you will be my axe and your blood the cutting edge. You or your brat of a nephew are all I need to force it open. If you run dry, I will need to cut him open – unless you agree to open this Vault for us? I assume there is some secret method far easier than draining a king or queen of their blood."

Alaric snorted. "You will learn nothing from me, witch. And you have not laid hands on Kester," he added, a forced smile flickering. "Otherwise, you would have him bound and bleeding on the floor before you in a futile attempt to force my hand by using my kin against me. A shame that he still eludes you."

Imperatrix's eyes narrowed. "Let us see how long you keep up this pathetic defiance." She pulled a rock-crystal bowl and a flint knife from her satchel. "If I am honest, I was hoping you would refuse to cooperate. As easy as it would make things, I don't want it and I don't need it. All I require is your blood and a little time. The torture is just a pleasing extra."

The guards held Alaric in place as she sliced open the back of his arm and drained the blood into her bowl until it was half full. She tied a bandage over the wound, none too gently. "Little by little, I will bleed you dry. Thank you for your aid."

She dipped her finger into the bowl and muttered ancient arcane words as she began writing runes across the wall of the Wyrm Vault. The stone skull trembled at her touch, and the entire cavern shook with it.

CHAPTER 19

Kester ran for his life through the forest gloom, his footsteps crumping through ice and snow. It was grey and dingy overhead, the light poor – but sadly not enough for him to lose his pursuers.

An angry shout from somewhere behind startled him – they had spotted him again. Twigs lashed his face and tore at his cloak as he ran blindly into the undergrowth in what he hoped was the right direction. His clothing was in tatters, and he'd lost his sword in a bad fall; it was probably lying in a muddy ditch a ways back, but he'd had no time to spare searching for it. The reivers had been chasing him for several stones, and the more he tired, the more any chance of losing them drained away. An arrow soared over his head and plunged into the bushes ahead of him, dislodging snow and startling a fox sheltering inside. The animal was a blurred streak through the undergrowth, fleeing the hunters with enviable ease while Kester lumbered through snow drifts like a clumsy ox.

"Stop running, boy!" a man shouted. "Don't make us put an arrow in your back."

Kester veered right and kept his head down as he ploughed through a bank of holly bushes, the prickly leaves tearing through his woollen cloak and the skin beneath. Better that than an arrow in the back, he thought as he plunged out the other side and broke into a sprint across the clearing beyond. He glanced back to see two of the Wildwood Reivers who dogged his heels tangled up in the holly, cursing and vowing to make him pay.

He'd bought himself a little more time and distance. His breathing became laboured as he pushed himself faster, cresting a rise and then running along the hollow behind it, leaving tracks in the snow all the while. He tried to throw them off by scrambling down a slope of scree and picking his way through a maze of boulders. He hopped from stone to stone across a frozen steam, then landed awkwardly on the other side. His foot gave a twinge of warning, but the gods had granted him luck enough to avoid a sprained joint and certain death. Only a moment of rest, he promised himself as he leant against a tree to catch his breath and let the sharp pain in his ankle fade to a dull ache.

Sweat cooled rapidly on his brow, and his eyes were stinging from a mix of that and the grease that had helped him squeeze from the palace latrines. He scrubbed them with the back of his hand and only succeeded in smearing it around. The stink on him was eyewatering, but he couldn't afford the time to wash until he reached Shield Gwilherm and the warband at Blaen Mhòr.

He'd thought himself so lucky to escape the palace and be given a chance to become a hero. Those hopes had lasted for less time than it usually took him to eat a hot meal. His pursuers must have come across his tracks in the snow and given chase. He chastised himself for not moving faster, somehow.

Imperatrix might have entered the palace with thirty-five warriors and traitors, but it seemed she had also left men patrolling outside to keep watch for anybody escaping. Two of them had caught up to him before he'd been able to reach the nearest village that might be rich enough to have a horse worth riding. He had been forced to give the nearest humble farmsteads and hamlets a wide berth – to go to those goodly folks for aid would only have invited their murder.

A shout and the scrape of scree tumbling down a slope set nearby crows flapping and cawing in anger. Kester launched himself deeper into the woods, blood thudding in his ears. He forced himself onwards, legs burning with exhaustion – staying alive was a powerful motivator.

He prayed for a blizzard to blow in or an afternoon mist to rise and hide him from his pursuers, but as if to mock him, patches of blue peeked through the grey clouds. The gods, it seemed, had cursed him with fine weather. Something splashed down into the stream he had been resting beside. His feet were sodden, and he could barely feel his toes, but he forced himself to go even faster, the exertion making him feel nauseous. These hunters were relentless, and he had no idea what he could do but keep going. He refused to give up.

The ground underfoot became stony and uneven, and his eyes were red and weeping, blurring his vision. He missed an exposed tree root, and it hooked his foot. He crashed to his hands and knees. The snow cushioned the impact some, but his knee was still bruised and bleeding. He scrambled upright and forced himself onwards. He was young and quick, but the sky was lightening, and these reivers made a living from hunting the forests – both game and human prey – and they were far fitter and more adept at navigating the terrain. They also had proper winter clothing and footwear, while he wore a light tunic, kilt, torn cloak and boots that let water in. Kester knew as soon as he stopped running the cold would become just as much of an adversary. He'd seen Shields with missing fingers and toes and didn't want his own turning black and falling off.

Another arrow whooshed past his ear to thud into the trunk of a silver birch. The reivers were closing in on him as he grew exhausted. It was just a matter of time before they had him. He asked himself: what would Briar do? She'd find somewhere to stand and fight. He almost laughed at the idea of him fighting them off, but he couldn't come up with any better option.

His breathing was laboured, and his ribs ached from the strain. He stumbled again, his wet feet almost entirely numb from the cold. It was now or never. On a slight rise up ahead stood an old man of the forest: a gnarled oak, thick of trunk and broad of bough, that must have stood there for generations. It was the sort of place a spirit might dwell – hopefully a friendly one. He angled left and circled it. There, on the other side, was a shadowy hollow in the trunk of the wizened tree. He took a few steps further on in the snow, then a few backwards, stepping into his own footprints to disguise his location. He backed into the hollow and tried to quieten his rasping breath. "Spirit of this great tree, aid me now," he whispered, then fell silent. His heart pounded as he drew his knife and strained to hear any hint of the men approaching.

Boots crumped their way towards his hiding place. A man in white-grey furs that blended into the snow stopped right in front of the hollow, blocking out the light. He had a bow in his hands and an arrow nocked to the string. Kester glared his malice – this was the rat that had been shooting at him. His fear spiked as the hunter crouched to study the ground where the trail of footprints stopped in mid-stride. It was all the distraction Kester needed. He leapt from the hollow and plunged his knife hilt-deep into the man's back. The reiver screeched and fell forward into the snow, the Royal Heir on top of him.

The man kept screaming. Kester kept stabbing. His little knife rose and fell, spattering the snow with drops of red. After a dozen or so wounds, the man shuddered and lay still in the snow. Kester sat there on the dead man's back for a few moments, shocked into stillness and staring at the knife jutting from the corpse. His panting misted the air, slow curls rising and dissipating.

The crack of a branch drew his attention. A grizzled reiver with an axe and half a left hand roared and broke into a charge through the trees, closing the distance with horrific speed.

Kester rolled off the corpse and scrambled for the hunter's bow. He fumbled the arrow to the string and bent the bow back, staring directly into the charging man's eyes as the shaft slipped from his fingers. He couldn't miss. It took the man in the chest, piercing furs to lodge in the lung. His attacker stumbled, but still came on, confused and wheezing for air that hissed right back out of the hole in him.

Kester dropped the bow and scrambled backwards through the snow. He didn't know where his knife was. He didn't have any weapon.

The reiver came on, face twisted in hatred. "Supposed to bring you back to Herself," he wheezed. "I'll take you back in bits, so I will." He lifted the axe overhead.

Kester's flailing hands found no weapon but snow. He grabbed a handful and squeezed it solid, then flung it at his attacker's eyes. It caught the man square in the face, but his bronze axe was already falling. Kester rolled, and the axe seared a path down the back of his arm instead of splitting his skull. The reiver overbalanced and fell atop Kester's legs, preventing an easy escape.

They rolled in the snow, the axe abandoned, punching and tearing at each other. His attacker was heavier and stronger, but he also had an arrow jutting from his torso. Kester seized it and pushed hard, twisting. The point grated against bone and then crunched deeper into his torso. The man screamed, and blood sprayed from his mouth.

Kester let go and went for the axe. He grabbed it, rose to his feet, then swung it up and over with all his might. The head bit through the reiver's ribs. Even then, the man still struggled to survive: gasping for air, pawing at Kester's leg with his half hand, pleading. The axe rose and fell thrice more until Kester was sure the filth was gone into the darkest pit of the otherworld.

He staggered back, staring at the butchered man's insides steaming in the sunshine. He had just killed two men. A wave of nausea welled up inside, an unstoppable eruption. The axe dropped to the snow, and he doubled over, vomiting as tears of relief streamed down his cheeks. It took him some time to register the pain radiating from his left arm, where the axe had scraped him. He swallowed and gingerly peeled back the ripped cloth to reveal a dangling flap of skin. He felt like throwing up all over again.

His breathing came in short, sharp pants. It took all he had to stop from panicking. What would Briar do? he asked himself again. What would Briar do? She certainly wouldn't panic. She'd survived much worse. His heartbeat slowed, and his breathing calmed. He could almost hear her stern voice chastising one of her warriors, accompanied by a slap on the back of their head: "Fool! Clean and bind that wound before you bleed to death." So he did just that. He avoided looking at the bodies and peeled the scraps of bloodied fabric from his wound, then cleaned it with a handful of snow before wrapping a makeshift bandage around it. There would have been no time to sew it up even if he'd known how, or had a needle and thread, come to that. The heat of fast-and-furious battle was swiftly fading, and he had to get going before the cold overtook him.

He stared at the forest ahead and thought of how far he still had to go. The lack of sleep, and exhaustion from the chase and fight, had caught up with him all of a sudden, and his body felt like a lump of stone dragging his willing spirit down. He groaned and turned his attention back to the dead men. Sweat chilled his body, and he started to shiver. These men had proper winter clothing, weapons and a waxed deerskin satchel of supplies. The Royal Heir shuddered and then resigned himself to looting their mangled corpses. He stripped a pair of coarse but thick breeches off one of the corpses and pulled them on, finding them much warmer in this weather than his foot wrappings and kilt. From the other he acquired a thick cloak of expensive beaver fur that certainly hadn't originally belonged to any reiver. He eyed their pine-resin-sealed winter boots and tried on the smaller of the pair, finding them only slightly too large for his feet. Now he had winter clothing, an axe, and a bow and arrows. The reivers also had a waterskin on them, as well as flint and tinder, dried meat and oat cakes.

Kester wasted no time in wolfing down a dry cake and washing the crumbs down with water.

"What's all this, then?" a gruff woman's voice said from behind, startling him.

Kester choked and spun, reaching for the axe. Another reiver!

A grey beast that was more wolf than dog darted for his arm, growling and snapping. He snatched his hand back and held it up in the air before the thing ripped it right off.

"Back, girl!" its master said. The wolf snarled and slunk off to one side, but its unblinking amber eyes never left him. The old woman was well wrapped in worn leathers and old furs and wielded a flint-tipped spear. A scowl twisted her weather-beaten face, with its cold, hard eyes. Eyes that dispassionately took in the two corpses and their killer looting the bodies.

She thrust the butt of her spear into the snow and grinned. "Looks like I've caught me a whole heap of trouble," she said, rubbing calloused hands together. Hands caked in dried blood...

The wolf growled, and Kester's stomach sank into a pit. After all he had been through, the panic and pain and fleeing for his life, he had failed. He wanted to curl up into a ball and cry. But he didn't do that, not this time. He was not the foppish boy he had been this time last year. Now he had to be a man. He had to be a king. His people were relying on him.

He marshalled all his remaining strength and readied himself to fight, probably for the last time. His heart was hammering, but, strangely, most of the fear melted away before his resolve. The fear was still there, bubbling below the surface, but he had faced it down and defeated it before, and he would do it again. He took a deep, shuddering breath and slowly stood to face these new foes.

"You won't take me alive," he roared. "Better to go down fighting than betray my people." The boy launched himself towards the wolf, fists raised...

CHAPTER 20

Hardgrim paced to and fro in the tunnel outside the cavern of the Heart, chewing on his moustache. He was not one to waste his time worrying over words, but this was Imperatrix, and he did not have good news for her.

Even he had been taken aback by her depravity in the Great Hall. Eating a woman's fucking hand? What sort of person would even consider such a disgusting act? Until today, he had entertained thoughts of seducing the woman to use her power for his own gain – she was just a woman, after all: a slave to her emotions, like all the rest – but, in light of that recent act of cannibalism, he had swiftly re-evaluated the sorcerer. Now the mere thought of ploughing that nest of vipers gave him goose bumps. He'd imagined her mouth around his cock a fair bit, but now all he could think of were those white teeth biting into Carmanilla's charred fingers, and it made his manhood shrivel right up. She was not a woman to be taken lightly, and never, ever to be angered. Maybe that had been the point of such a disgusting display. Or perhaps she really had tried to devour the priestess' magic. He shuddered and concluded that a wise man had best leave those questions unasked and unanswered if he wanted to sleep well at night.

Hardgrim turned and peered into the darkness as a light bobbed around at the far end of the tunnel. Ruith approached, lowered his lantern and shook his head. "Nothing. I checked the Hall of Broken Shields and a short distance down each of the other tunnels he might have accessed. No sign of Newlyn and Nealon, or any sighting of the boy since the attack. They must have chased him into the deep tunnels, where I dare not venture unprepared. The only thing of note was a scorch mark on the floor of the hall, where somebody had recently set fire to something. Smelled like burnt pork to me."

Hardgrim lifted a shaking fist, staring hard at the wall he wanted to pound a hole through. "That odious brat..." He mastered his anger before pointlessly bloodying his knuckles. "I can't trust any of those bastards to do their jobs right."

"What do you want me to do now?" Ruith asked.

Hardgrim stared at him, mind awhirl. As if he had any idea... But then, sometimes you just had to look like you knew what you were doing. Doing anything was often better than to look weak by being seen doing nothing. "Take two men and search the tombs, then the drains and latrine pits. Search every accursed place no right-minded man would ever think of. Then search them all again."

Ruith glanced back the way he had come, and his hand crept to the protective amulet around his neck: an eye carved from rowan, bound with red thread. "Uh, the tombs of the Shields?"

"Am I speaking Ves?" Hardgrim said. "You will crack the lids of the tombs and check inside."

Ruith swallowed and shifted his feet. "I – Well... But what about the unquiet dead? That eerie howling from earlier..."

Hardgrim guffawed in his face. "You fear angry spirits will curse you for a little desecration? Come now, my loyal friend, after what we have done here all manner of spirits will already be cursing our existence. As if a few more feeble mutterings make any difference to men like us. We are strong of mind and arm, and you have that amulet of yours to ward off the evil eye and dark magic, yes? We will take what we want from this place and leave their forlorn spirits to forever wail in the ruins while we joyously drown ourselves in wealth, women and wine. If needs be, we will have wealth enough to acquire the services of priests and magicians to protect us from any evil spirits."

After a moment's thought, Ruith lifted his chin, and his hesitancy vanished. "You can rely on me to get it done."

"Trust me," Hardgrim replied, "as unpleasant as your task is, I have a far worse one. You do not want to be stuck in here with me and that sorcerer."

Ruith's eyes darted to the thick bronze door leading to the Heart and then back to his commander. His cheeks paled. "I think you might have the right of it there, Commander. Good luck." He straightened his sword belt and then moved off towards the stairs to gather a pair of men to do all the heavy lifting.

Hardgrim marshalled his bravery, raked a hand through his hair and strode into the Heart like he owned the place. He arguably did, he mused, due to the right of conquest. The stench of blood assailed his nostrils.

Phelan and Owyn gave him nods of greeting, and he thought those two hard-as-stone men appeared peaky and skittish. One look at the bloodied mess of a regent hanging in their arms told him why. Alaric's bruised hands and face were beaded with blood like he'd been thrust face-first into a holly bush several times. The man groaned, barely conscious. Hardgrim didn't even want to know what manner of torture she'd put him through.

The smirking assassin, Maddox, yawned and rose from the bench. He sidled over and pressed a dirty finger to his mouth. "Shh. Herself is concentrating. Don't disturb her unless you want to doom us all. She's not having the best of days. It is day now, is it not?"

Hardgrim nodded. "Several stones after noon." He swallowed and watched Imperatrix work.

The sorcerer had her back to the huge wyrm skeleton on the far wall, both hands outstretched, holding up a highly polished obsidian scrying mirror that she turned this way and that, examining the reflection of the wall behind her, a wall now covered with spiralling patterns of faintly glowing arcane runes that hurt the eye to look at. Blood trailed down her arms, dripping from the black mirror clutched in her hands. It had been anointed with Summerson blood, Hardgrim assumed. Her lips moved, saying nothing that he could hear. All the same, he sensed some kind of... vibration emanating from her, which filled up the chamber with a potent but unseen presence, like the air before a thunderstorm.

Sorcery. A shiver rippled up his spine, and the hairs on his arms stood on-end. Give any man or woman in the world a weapon and Hardgrim would not be afraid to face them, but this was unnatural, more in the realm of gods and spirits than of men. How was any warrior supposed to fight what they could not comprehend? He could only just bring himself to accept the weird ways of druids working with nature, but Imperatrix practised some unspeakably dark perversion of life and death.

Imperatrix slowly backed towards the wall and, without taking her eyes from the scrying mirror, awkwardly stretched a bloodstained finger out behind her to trace an arcane symbol on one of the great wyrm's fangs. The blood steamed on stone that was unnaturally warm to the touch. The symbol lit up, and the room shivered, dust drifting down from the ceiling. A breath of hot air escaped from the dead beast's stone maw. "The seal has been broken," she said, setting the mirror down on the table. "The first of the Vault's seven protections has been undone."

She sighed with relief and turned to face Hardgrim. "You have brought me the boy, yes? I need more blood."

Hardgrim swallowed. "He evades us still. I sent two of my Youngbloods after him, but they are still missing. They must have chased him into the deepest tunnels."

Imperatrix stared at him, unblinking for entirely too long. Long enough to make him sweat. She turned back to her bloody captive. "They gave chase before the dawn," she said, "and this day is nearing its end. If they are not back by now, they are probably dead." She exhaled, slow and heavy. "It seems that I must give our dear regent here a little time to recover his strength." She looked to Maddox. "Get him meat and water, and stuff it down his throat. He needs to replace some of that lost blood. The more we have, the better."

The assassin scowled and went to say something sarcastic, but the shadows in the room deepened and swarmed around the light. Imperatrix's knife eased from its sheath without any hand touching it, spitting orange sparks. He clamped his jaw shut, nodded and did as he was told.

The sorcerer fixed her raptor gaze on Hardgrim again. "We need to find the boy," she said. "Alaric alone may not be enough for my needs, and I had hoped to use him all up today to speed my progress. With the impotence of your men in the face of a mere youth, it seems I must now waste more of my precious power to lend you aid." She put the little finger of her left hand between her teeth and tore off the fingernail, letting blood drip into the well of the nearest lantern, causing it to hiss and spit. Her face paled as black veins spiderwebbed up her neck and crowded around reddening eyes. "Come, rekhcorryn, you are summoned to honour your oath. What is mine is yours, and what is yours is mine. A service for a service, the bargain upheld."

Three fat, spidery man-sized shadows, each with eight smouldering eyes, split from the doorway and crawled across the ceiling of the cavern, then down to the blood-spattered floor in front of the stone wyrm. The things curled up atop the regent's blood and began sucking it up. "Find the kin of this blood," she said, her skin turned grey as a corpse. "Disable the boy and bring him to me." The shadows screeched and scuttled off, swallowed up by the dark tunnel beyond.

"No matter where he has hidden himself," she said to Hardgrim, "or how far he has travelled from here, they will find him."

Imperatrix's gaze faltered and fogged over. Her breathing became ragged, and she stumbled forward. Reflexively, Hardgrim caught her hands to steady her. His skin sizzled. Searing pain shot up his hands. He hissed and snatched his scorched hands back, smoke trailing from blackened fingertips.

Imperatrix shook her head and steadied herself. "I need to rest," she said, struggling for breath. "Just for a while..." She stumbled over to the bench and slumped down, eyes closed and forehead resting on the table. The wood charred and smoked where it touched her naked flesh, and the black veins took a disturbingly long time to begin their retreat towards her heart.

After some time, colour returned to her face, and her breathing slowed and steadied. She cracked open an eye to see Hardgrim still there, nervously hovering as he tried to figure out how to broach the next bit of bad news.

"Spit it out," she demanded.

"The captives," he said, "er, they are gone. The guards you left have been slain. Somehow, they vanished into thin air, travelling neither up nor down the stairs past the guards set there."

She cursed and sat up. "How?"

"Briar," he replied. "I'm sure of it. One person assaulted two former Shields and three reivers. They didn't stand a chance. As to where they went..." He shrugged.

Imperatrix grimaced and clenched her hands until they shook. "She is not a spirit, able to disappear at will. Find the woman and kill her. That's your bloody role in this, Hardgrim. Mine is to open this accursed Vault before the warband discovers our ruse and returns to hack off all our heads."

He stiffened, about to snap back when Ruith appeared in the doorway. "Commander, I've found something."

"The boy?" Hardgrim asked. "Please tell me you've found him."

Ruith shook his head. "It's the twins, Newlyn and Nealon. I found their corpses. I reckon they've been dead quite some time, and" – he swallowed nervously and clutched the amulet at his throat – "Nealon was burned to death. Looks like from the inside out."

Imperatrix stood. "Take me to him. Bring the regent with us. I am not about to lose another Summerson to the ineptitude of others. There will be no rescue for him."

They made their way to the Hall of Broken Shields.

Hardgrim's sword was in his hand. He muttered curses upon Kester and Briar. "They burned Nealon alive," he growled. "I will kill them for that."

Imperatrix stared down into the opened tomb, examining the corpses of Hardgrim's Youngbloods. "No, those righteous bores don't have that in them," she said, prodding the charred corpse with a fingernail. "This was my curse. Nealon here was interrogated and tried to tell the enemy what he should not have." She looked into Hardgrim's eyes, unblinking. "I have put contingencies in place. It is never wise to betray a sorcerer."

Hardgrim swallowed and abandoned every thought he'd ever had of killing her at the end of their mutual endeavour, or of taking the artefacts in addition to the treasure contained in the palace strongroom. Better to keep his word and make off with a fortune than to wager his life against her dark powers. Some things were just not worth gambling on. He nodded in grim acceptance of her warning. "This interrogation might explain how Briar rescued the captives. It is likely she also saved Kester from his pursuers, and she possibly knows how many we are and what our plans are."

"I care nothing for the others," Imperatrix said, "but I urgently need the boy's blood to speed up access to the Wyrm Vault. If I keep the regent alive and drain him more slowly, then our timetable slides towards the warband's return, and none of us want that."

"Does it have to be Summerson blood?" Hardgrim asked. "We have plenty of other bodies to spare."

"I wish that were an option," she replied. "Their ancestry is vital. There is a touch of fae blood in their accursed line that the protective seals on the Vault recognise."

Hardgrim sucked on his teeth in annoyance.

"How can you be so sure that Briar has the boy?" she asked.

He paused. "It's a Shield for certain, but based on the slaughter left in the Great Hall and the attacker favouring the right leg I am convinced it is her. She must have spirited Kester and the others right through the palace walls, but I have no idea where they are or how she managed it."

"Do you have an item that once belonged to her?" Imperatrix asked. "Or perhaps something she once touched?"

Hardgrim glanced down at his chest and the golden brooch denoting his position as Commander of Shields. He grimaced, reluctantly unpinned it and handed it over. "What are you going to do with it?"

"I am going to find her," Imperatrix replied. "Something that your Youngbloods and my reivers have proved themselves equally incapable of." She laid the brooch flat on the palm of her hand and studied it for a few moments. Her little finger still bled from the summoning of shadows, and she smeared some more blood over the gold face of the commander's shield, drawing a geometric rune across its front. "Unfortunately, this enchantment can be cast only once a lunar cycle, and it will only last a stone at best."

Imperatrix whispered half-audible words that sent a shiver up Hardgrim's spine. The brooch shivered, and the rune flickered and flared into life. The brooch floated into the air above her palm and slowly revolved several times before slewing round to have the pinpointing to a dusty old tomb near the back of the hall.

"Well, that is surprising," she said. "You wanted to know where Briar is?" She pointed to the tomb of Quinn the Eel.

"Why, she is right there. Briar is currently lurking in a secret compartment and listening to our every word." She slapped the groggy regent to wakefulness. "Say hello to your little pet, Alaric, for it will be the last time you have the chance."

"Flee!" he shouted. "Four treacherous Shields and–"

The guards twisted his arms, and he screamed as his shoulder dislocated with a sickening pop.

Hardgrim and his men ran to the tomb and heaved off the stone lid. Nothing. He picked up a chunk of stone and battered it into the side panels. "Break it open."

CHAPTER 21

Briar stifled a curse as any chance of surprising the scum vanished. She awkwardly turned around inside the cramped tomb and began crawling for her life. Fucking sorcery! She squirmed up through the narrow tunnel and, in her haste, cracked an elbow off the wall, but a few scrapes and bruises were the least of her concerns. Alaric had been right there in the Hall and she'd been powerless to save him. Charging in like an enraged bull would have helped nobody – right here and now, she would be lucky to save herself.

Behind her, people had picked up rocks and had begun smashing the tomb apart to get to her. After repeated blows, something gave way. The secret panel cracked and let in shards of lantern light. They jammed the haft of an axe through the gap and used it to lever the rest of the door open. Stone crumbled and fell outwards, letting more light into the tunnel behind her. Somebody forced their way in through Quinn the Eel's tomb. She glanced back to see a familiar face sneering up at her.

"I see you, Briar," Hardgrim yelled, his tone gleeful. "Running away like a dirty little rat, eh? You won't escape us this time." He pulled back. "In there, men. After the coward!"

Imperatrix chuckled. "And waste more of our dwindling forces? We are in a tomb, Hardgrim. Let us raise the old bones of her own brethren to do the deed for us – I just require a little blood from you big strong men. Goodbye, Briar – I hated your righteous arrogance, but unlike most of the dirty-blooded

243

buffoons running this accursed realm, you were worthy of respect."

This time Briar didn't bother to stifle her cursing as harsh chanting echoed up the tunnel. Imperatrix's laboured words grated on her soul like nails down a slate. "That proved more difficult than I had expected," Imperatrix said between pants. "Shields are stubborn, even in death. Rise!"

A moment of silence, pregnant with dread.

The stone lids of the tombs scraped open and thudded to the ground. Briar broke out in a cold sweat at the creak and clatter of old bones rising from their graves, and desperately crawled for her life as the dead surged into the pitch-black tunnel behind her. Dry bone and sinew creaked and groaned, scraping against stone as they dragged themselves towards her. Hardgrim's harsh laughter echoed up through the tunnel as Briar turned a bend and angled up towards the first floor.

Her pulse was loud in her ears and the tunnel seemed to be stifling hot and squeezing in on her, making it difficult to breathe. She was blind and confined, and the way behind her was choked with animated corpses. The macabre scuff and clatter of the dead was closing in on her, and her thoughts filled with unseen horrors. Her only faint hope was that the bones of the honoured dead would resist the command to slay one of their own.

Briar gritted her teeth and kept crawling, her hands and knees scraped raw in desperate flight. She knew if they caught her in these narrow tunnels she wouldn't stand a chance. They would take her apart like a bear brought down by a pack of hunting dogs. Or, more aptly, like a rabbit caught in its burrow. Her only chance was to head for the nearest exit. The tunnel branched, and she crawled left towards the temple in the hopes that a sacred place dedicated to the gods might serve to ward off the abominations behind her.

Something tugged at her boot. She kicked back and felt grim satisfaction as bone smashed. They had the numbers, but she wasn't yet so old and brittle. The tunnel became damp due to the closeness of the sacred spring that fed into the temple, and as she continued onwards the dusty stone beneath her hands turned to sticky mud. There – a square crack of light in the stonework ahead. She shoved at the block, but it didn't budge. Her fingers scrabbled at the crack, trying to find some kind of lever or mechanism to open the bloody thing. She prayed some bastard druid hadn't inadvertently stuck a heavy table on the other side.

Two skeletal hands grabbed hold of her leg, and a skull sank its teeth into her boot. Most of its ancient teeth shattered, but it still bloody hurt. She kicked out, and its head broke like an eggshell. Splinters of bone dug into her calf, but she ignored them and explored the exit as more of the dead tried to squeeze past to get to her.

Her fingers brushed a small wheel recessed into the block. She twisted it, and a hidden counterweight freed the block. Briar shoved with the might of desperation. The stone block slid free and thunked down onto the floor of the temple. Two narrow, horn-slatted windows high up in the wall showed her the sun was setting, staining the room red.

In Wrendal, the temples were filled with exquisite statues of their gods, worked in white marble and purple amethyst, whereas the Ves princedoms preferred to worship in gaudy martial edifices draped in silver and gold and just as much steel and blood from too-frequent sacrifices. In Sunweald, the greatest temples were circles of ancient stones out in the forests and hills, and all indoor temples were filled with all the trappings of nature: wooden decorative panels, fragrant plants in pots, abundant water in silver basins and simple carved and unpainted standing stones of much smaller stature. Most also boasted niches where the leathery bog-preserved bodies of grand druids and great heroes were interred for all to see and commune with. The temple was a quiet place for self-reflection and personal contemplation, a peaceful atmosphere now brutally ruined by Briar's cursing and the chattering of the dead things behind her.

Briar praised the gods that the room was empty as she squirmed on her belly through the narrow opening. She drew her sword and hacked off skeletal limbs that reached for her while she attempted to shove the block back into place. The dead pushed from the other side, limbs flailing, yellowed teeth clicking and gnashing as they tried to bite her fingers off. She had weight on her side, though. She put her feet up against the nearest altar and shoved, her left leg crying out from the strain. Old bones shattered, and the block slammed back into its rightful place. The stone mechanism clicked, and it became part of the wall once more. From this side, there was no hidden wheel or any sign at all that it had ever been anything else.

The dead scraped and scratched at the wall like trapped rats, but they couldn't dig their way through solid stone to get to her any time soon. She was safe, for now, and the swiftly approaching nightfall could only benefit her: most of the palace was gloomy at the best of times, but she knew the layout and the enemy didn't. Finding her in the darkness would be a far more difficult task without sorcerous aid.

Sweat stung her eyes as she flopped to the floor and gasped for breath, waiting for her heartbeat to slow. The hurt from her scrapes and bruises and bitten ankle clamoured for attention as the imminent danger of being torn apart ebbed.

She wiped her eyes, then groaned and sat up to examine her wounds. Her questing fingers found her boot ripped open, and she felt faintly nauseous as she pulled shards of tooth and bone from it. The skeleton had strength enough to bite right through the leather, and given a few more moments it would have chewed right through her too. It hurt but would not hinder her in a fight. Just another annoying guest invited to the party of pain that was her body.

She heaved herself up, gingerly testing the ankle and finding it sore but serviceable. Her left leg was a throbbing mass of pain, telling her she'd pushed it too far too fast. She had been on the move all day, fighting, crawling through tunnels, and she was hungry and fatigued and yearned to sit down with a hot meal. As if she could possibly afford the time to rest. She did take the time to cleanse her wounds before the corpse dust caused them to fester, dipping the hem of her tunic into the sacred spring that trickled out into a stone basin and using it to clean the worst of the muck from her scrapes.

She quickly finished tending to her wounds, taking less time over them than she would have liked. Hardgrim was no fool. He would know the tunnel came out somewhere and would already be on his way up to see if she'd managed to escape Imperatrix's puppets. Wherever she went, Hardgrim would follow, but he had just shy of a stone before that accursed enchantment faded. Assuming Imperatrix had not been lying.

Nineteen men and one sorcerer left. She could still do this if she was quick about it, she thought, readying her sword and buckler for battle. And then there were the dead to consider, but they would find her tougher prey when she wasn't confined in a narrow stone passage.

Briar limped to the doorway and cautiously peered out into the hallway. She flinched back at the sight of a reiver turning a corner: a red-bearded man, laden down with a coil of rope, a bundle of wood and a basket of hammers meant for throwing up barricades and blocking off exits. He wore a felted cap, along with a studded leather kilt and a shirt of shining bronze scales, stripped from a dead Shield. He scratched and pulled at the armour, wincing. The fool had no idea how to even wear it properly: he wore all that winter-chilled metal without a padded tunic underneath, and tufts of sweaty ginger body hair peeked through the scales, catching and pulling with every movement. All the metal hung loose from his shoulders instead of being cinched at the waist with a thick belt to help redistribute the weight.

She waited by the doorway, listening to the clink, clink, clink of his stolen armour – that noise was exactly why she had done without armour. Until now. Now it would be a brutal bastard of a running battle with an enemy who could track her, and this scum would have to donate his shirt to serve the Sunweald cause and aid her survival.

As the murderous brigand passed the doorway, her sword swung round to meet his throat. It jarred against his spine but cut most of the way through. Surprise erupted across his face as his head tilted back in a spray of blood until it dangled from a strip of skin and muscle. She grabbed the twitching corpse before it fell. "Eighteen," she murmured as she stripped the dripping scale shirt off him. She had to push the man's head back into place to do it, a messy endeavour.

Briar buckled on the studded leather kilt and then shrugged the gory armour over her padded tunic, tightening the leather straps so half the shirt's weight rested on her hips. She felt like half a warrior again now she was properly dressed for battle. With Kester well out of Imperatrix's reach, the woman would have to keep Alaric alive for a while longer. All Briar had to do was cut the enemy's numbers down to size, and then there would be a reckoning. She couldn't face them head-on, so she would have to get more creative now the secret of the tunnels was out. But first she had to lead Hardgrim on a merry chase through the maze of the palace until his tracking enchantment wore off – only then could she attempt to strike back.

She ignored the very real risk of parasites to slip the reiver's felted cap atop her head, hoping that in the poor light it would be enough of a disguise. It took an effort of willpower to disarm herself and return the buckler and sword to her belt. She picked up the reiver's long coil of rope and estimated its length, a rough plan forming in her mind, one that her leg was not going to like at all. The rope seemed long enough, just. She slipped one arm through the coil and then held the bundle of wood and basket of construction supplies up high in front of her face so only the top of the cap could be glimpsed. A poor disguise, but the hallways were empty for the moment, and with no servants left alive to refill the lanterns, most had burned dry. She hoped the darkness would be enough of a cover to see her to the central stairwell unopposed. Everything hinged on getting enough of a lead up the steps before the enemy gave chase. Somewhere nearby, men were ripping a room apart, still searching for the missing poisoner. She stepped quickly past those doorways and hoped not to meet any patrols before reaching the steps. Her luck held steady, and she got closer than she'd expected before being noticed.

The stairway guard, a short and stocky man with black eyes and a broken nose, stepped out from his post and peered into the gloom, half blinded by his own lantern. He wore a vest of wooden slats and wielded a crude half-spear almost as long as he was tall. The man had a cocky sneer that she yearned to wipe off his battered face.

She kept walking and said nothing, but simply lowered her rope and basket to expose a little more of the felted cap the dead reiver had worn.

"Ho there, Leith," the guard said, relaxing. "Was you not supposed to take that to the main gate? Need to board up everywhere to stop any... Wait, you're not–"

She heaved the basket of hammers and wood at the man's head. He went down hard, but there was no time to kill him – she spotted a second guard and readied her weapons.

The second man got up from the step he'd been sat on and drew a stolen sword. He was a big brute of a man in bloodstained leathers, who clearly knew his way about a murder. In his right hand he held the sword and in his left a crude wicker shield bound with cow hide. She went in hard and fast before he could bring his greater strength to bear. Swords were versatile and deadly weapons if you knew how to use them. He didn't. Her buckler forced his shield down, and he didn't know how to block the sword that thrust over his guard and into his flesh.

She missed his heart, and the blade slid into the softer flesh below his collarbone.

The big reiver squealed like a stuck pig and flung himself backwards. He didn't realise the stairs down were right behind him. His eyes bulged, and his hands flailed comically as his feet found only thin air. He tumbled down the stone steps, shrieking each time he slammed into the wall on the way down.

"Well, that's the whole damned palace alerted," she hissed, glaring at the man on the floor, moaning under a pile of hammers.

"My facesh," he slurred, drooling blood and tears. His nose had been flattened and his jaw broken. She stabbed at him, aiming for the spaces between the wooden slats in his vest, but he thrashed in panic, and her sword deflected and bit a shallow wound into his arm instead of through his heart.

Shouts erupted from below, and she didn't have time to waste trying to finish him off. Instead, she settled the coil of rope over her shoulder and started the long ascent of the stairs, leaving him bleeding and broken. With her leg, she would need all the time she could get. Hardgrim would soon be after her like a hound on a hare, once he realised where she'd gone.

Her left leg quickly tired, the repetitive strain of climbing so many steps depleting whatever reserves of strength it had left. She gritted her teeth against the pain and pushed on, trying to keep most of her weight balanced on her right – no easy task on spiralling stairs. The shouts quickly faded as she ascended, letting her hope that anybody on the higher floors might not have heard the din she'd created.

Maybe they did and maybe they didn't, but either way, the reiver she met on his way down the stairs was surprised to see her. Even less happy when her sword lashed out and cut though the tendon of his left foot. He flailed and fell into her. She shoved him off and sent him bouncing down the stone steps, then resumed her climb.

The angry clamour from below erupted sooner than she'd hoped, and then the thunder of boots pounding the steps gave her cause to doubt she'd make it to the regent's tower. She climbed as fast as she could, closer to hopping by the time she reached the third-floor landing, lathered in sweat. How she yearned for a few of those herbal pellets in her pouch to dull the pain.

There was only one guard there waiting for her at the top of the stairs, an older man with a long felling axe, wearing a patchwork coat of studded leather and tarnished bronze plates. He was a canny one and didn't risk his life attacking. He just stood there, blocking her path and waiting for his reinforcements to arrive, swinging his long axe to ward her off.

Briar heaved a sigh and slowly limped towards him, shield up. He swung the axe at her skull, but she deflected it and tried to stab him in the belly. He stepped back out of her reach and twirled his axe, grinning to show off his three remaining teeth.

"Ain't getting past me, what with that leg," he said. "Least not afore my friends arrive to butcher you like a hog."

"I doubt you have any friends," she said. "Not ones that wouldn't stab you in the back for a bite of mutton." She limped to the attack again, and again he stepped back. Angry shouts echoed up the stairwell, getting louder with every passing moment.

The third time, she dashed forward, catching him by surprise. Her leg screamed at her, but what choice did she have? She had shown him a fatal weakness, and he hadn't thought she had it in her. He didn't have time to swing his axe, so he thrust it out at her face. She snarled and knocked the blow aside with her buckler, earning it a new dent. Her sword struck at his belly. It hit a bronze plate sewn into his coat and skidded sideways, then punctured his side.

He gasped in shock as Briar ripped her sword free. She grabbed his axe and used his own grip to haul him face-first into her headbutt. His nose broke on her forehead. Before he could recover his wits, she hauled him round and sent him tumbling down the stairs. "Looks like I did get past you," she said as he bounced into the wall and then down the steps, out of sight.

That headbutt had seemed like such a good idea, she thought, but she'd forgotten the headaches they gave her. She hooked the buckler back onto her belt and used the haft of his long axe as a makeshift walking stick. Behind her came the clatter of impacts and another man tumbling down the stairs – practically a new sport of her own invention, she mused. Hopefully it would knock over a few more of the bastards to make up for lost time.

She turned right and dragged her cramping leg down the twisting corridors leading to the regent's tower. Doors crashed open somewhere behind her as reivers searched the nearby rooms. She gritted her teeth and forced her feet onwards, every arduous step taking her a little closer to Alaric's study.

She reached the stairs and ascended the tower. Step. Step. Step. Each one a unique spike of agony. She heaved a sigh of relief when she reached the top, and began hobbling towards the open and unguarded door to the study.

"I see you, Briar," cried a familiar voice from behind: Iden. For a moment, she wondered if by some miracle of the gods the man had also escaped the slaughter, but no, he was pointing his sword at her. He was just another oath-broken Shield nurtured beneath Hardgrim's dark wing. Every revelation of treachery was a fresh wound in her soul, but this one truly hurt. She'd thought Iden better than this.

She didn't spare him a single moment, and instead kept limping towards the study.

"Surrender," Iden shouted. "Don't throw your life away. If you put down your sword and shield, you'll be ransomed." She could hear men running as his allies charged up the stairs behind him.

Briar tried to decide if he was deluded, deranged or just a damned good liar. "Like the servants were all ransomed?" she countered as she reached the doorway. "Or do you honestly believe that Hardgrim will let me live? Do you even know what grotesque magic your leader is up to in the catacombs?"

Men boiled up the stairwell, and Iden charged her. She slammed the heavy door and dropped an oak bar into the slot just in time. Iden crashed into the door, but it barely moved. It was bronze-bound black oak and one of the strongest interior doors in the palace. It would take their axes a long time to hack through it, but she shoved broken tables and chairs behind it just to be doubly sure she was wasting enough of their time here for the tracking enchantment to fail.

She took the opportunity to sag into the comfiest-looking intact chair, groaning in relief as she took the weight off her throbbing leg. It wouldn't have stood for much more abuse before buckling beneath her.

Moonlight streamed through the open window. The fire was cold and dead, and a chill wind set torn scrolls and ragged tapestries fluttering. Alaric's study was in ruins: cabinets and shelves looted, baskets upturned and scrolls scattered everywhere. What loot they couldn't carry off they had ruined out of spite. The reivers had tried and failed to upturn his monstrous desk of heavy black oak, instead settling for taking a shit on it. The bedchamber reeked of piss and spilt mead. His priceless amethyst clock lay in pieces on the floor – somebody had ripped the gold cogs and gemstone innards out. Alaric's beloved cherry-wood lyre and flutes had been senselessly smashed to splinters and scattered around like garbage.

Briar gazed at the devastation with deep sadness. It was so much easier to destroy than create. She'd never had the skill with hands or voice to make her own art, but she did appreciate it. A little piece of an artist's soul went into everything they crafted, and that was a beautiful magic all of its own.

The door rumbled with repeated impacts, and then came the *thwock, thwock, thwock* of axes biting into stone-hard oak. She suspected the door would outlast the edges of their crude axes. She rested, and she listened to all their cursing and impotent promises of brutality. They offered nothing to excite the warrior in her. She'd heard it all before, from friends and foes alike.

The axes ceased their work. "Hello, Hardgrim," she yelled. He'd surely had more than enough time to race up the stairs from the catacombs and catch up to her. "Managed to slip your master's leash, have you?"

After a moment's pause, the pompous prick shouted through the door and barricade. "You are nothing but a shit stain, Briar. I'm not the daughter of a pig, trapped and cowering behind a door. There is no escape for you now. Soon your skull will adorn a spear – but here's what I'll do for you: if you surrender quickly, I'll stick it up right next to Alaric's so your spirits can keep each other company."

Briar laughed at him, loud and mocking. "A feeble attempt, you rat-cocked little toad."

She thought she could hear him ranting and raving to his men in response. Something about savage dogs, hammers and sharp knives, if she were to venture a guess. Then he quietened down, and the axes started on the door again, this time with more muscle behind each swing. The din did not help her headbutt-induced skull ache at all. She waited a good stone to see if she could waste any more of Hardgrim's night, but the wretch remained stubbornly silent to anything she shouted at him.

When she finally glimpsed bronze cutting through the splintering oak, she knew it was time to make her move. "Well, this is no time to be lazing about," she said, heaving her battered body up from the comfy chair. Agony spiked up through her thigh to her hip, forcing her to bite her lip to stop a scream erupting – oh, how the scum outside the door would love that. "Rancid pig-fucker of an archer," she snarled, pounding her fist into the wall. The leg she'd been resting was stiff as a board.

She worked her thumbs into her thigh muscle, did some gentle stretching exercises. Eventually the pain ebbed back to manageable levels. She uncoiled the rope from her torso and secured one end to the regent's ridiculously heavy desk before she tossed the other out of the window.

She would descend from the tower and then swing to the roof of the East Wing, and with most of the reivers and Hardgrim distracted trying to get into the study, she would make her way down to the Heart of Sunweald, rescue Alaric and get him to safety before they could open the Wyrm Vault. From what she'd overheard earlier, he didn't have much time left. It was do or die, but she much preferred the doing bit.

Briar moved to the window, took a firm grip on the rope and then eased herself backwards out and over the edge. The frigid wind bit at her ears and nose, but it was a mere annoyance compared to all her other problems. She walked herself down the stonework, her palms rubbed red-raw by the time she reached the bottom of the rope. The end dangled with only an easy drop to the roof below, once she was ready to swing herself over.

She shoved off the tower and set her weight swinging. Back and forward, back and forward, until finally the swing took her over far enough to make the leap. At the height of the swing, she let go. The air took her for a few terrifying moments before she crunched down onto mossy slate and heaped crow crap. She hissed in pain as the roof cracked beneath her, making a worrying groaning sound. It sagged beneath her weight, but held. The many crows that made their nests in the crevices of the roofs croaked and complained, but they knew who she was and repaid her gifts of food with silence.

It proved a struggle to get back onto her feet, but she gritted her teeth and managed it. She limped across the narrow stone walkway hidden between uneven roofing. The footing was treacherous, but the moonlight proved just enough for her to pick her way towards the trapdoor at the far end of the West Wing, furthest away from the concentration of reivers currently trying to break into the tower behind her. They had one sorcerer left and probably fourteen healthy men and four wounded, though she couldn't be certain how much more of a fight the wounded could put up. Her kill count was increasingly unreliable, and she reminded herself not to fall into the trap of thinking she knew their numbers for a certainty. Maybe she'd killed more than she had counted – but they might also have called in reinforcements from outside. She had no way to know the truth, and her own strength and stamina were dwindling. Whatever their number left, she had killed more than a few and had no doubt the rest would be frothing at the mouth to pay her back with rape and murder.

Just before she reached the trapdoor, it burst open, and an armoured form clambered up to join her on the roof of the palace. She cursed at the sight of Hardgrim dressed for battle, with bronze armguards, studded kilt, helmet and scale shirt.

He smirked as he fastened the gold Commander of Shields brooch to a cord around his neck and readied his weapons. "In the end, I didn't even need her magic to track you down."

Briar's eyes were drawn to the sword in his hands. It was Alaric's exquisite bronze blade decorated with gold and amber. Hardgrim noted her simmering rage and seemed to glow with smugness. "What a joy it will be to take your head with the regent's own blade."

He casually swung his sword and buckler before him to stretch his arms, then cracked his neck and fell into an easy fighting stance, left foot forward and back foot braced. "What a glorious night this is," he said. "I have seen through your plan and thwarted this doomed attempt to rescue the regent. These plans were years in the making, and you were so absorbed in your pain you never suspected the final death stroke was coming. How does it feel to be such a failure, and know that I have surpassed you in every way?"

Briar took a deep and calming breath and raised her own weapons. She spat at his feet and said, "Less talk. Come at me, little boy, if you think yourself so very grand."

He snickered. "What a sorry state you are in. Do you really think you can beat me?"

She rolled her eyes. "Obviously, you oath-broken bastard. You are so dim-witted I'm surprised you can put your own boots on. Your uncle wanted rid of you so much that he called in a blood debt to force Alaric to take you in."

Hardgrim snarled, and they came together in a furious clash of bronze.

CHAPTER 22

"You won't take me alive," Kester roared. "Better to go down fighting than betray my people." The boy launched himself towards the wolf, fists raised.

He should have gone for the old woman instead of the wolf. As it turned out, she was the more dangerous of the two. The moment he charged, she whipped the butt of her spear up and slammed it into his belly, knocking the wind right out of him. He had a vague recollection of something hitting him in the chin before he passed out... and the swollen jaw when he woke seemed to confirm that.

He found himself in a ramshackle shepherd's bothy, naked and cocooned in a dry blanket. The wolf was licking his face, its breath moist and meaty. Kester yelped and struggled to free himself, but stilled when the old woman pointed a knife at him and shook her head. The wolf padded over to her and settled down, its amber eyes never leaving their captive.

He hadn't been carried back to the palace. Yet. That was... good? He was also still alive, with all his body parts. Even better. He studied his surroundings: the dry-stone and mud walls and turf roof of the cramped hut looked none too sturdy, but the old woman had a fire going, and feeling had returned to his toes. His clothes were hanging from rafters near the fire, steaming as they dried.

He freed his arms of the blanket's comforting warmth and wiped the trail of wolf drool from his cheek, puzzled as to why he wasn't tied up. "I'm alive," he said.

"Aye," she said, frowning at him like he'd been knocked on the head one too many times.

"Are you taking me back?" he asked.

She squinted at his face so hard her leathery face seemed to crack. "Nah."

The silence deepened. He cleared his throat and sat up slowly so as to not alarm the woman or her wolf. "How long have I been out?" he asked.

She sucked at her teeth. "Couple of stones," she said.

He waited for more, but she wasn't forthcoming. "You're not a Wildwood Reiver, are you?"

"Nah," she said again. "Just an old woman and her wolf out hunting. Got assaulted by a boy thick as pig shit."

He flushed. "I'm sorry, but I—"

"Need to get to the warband at Blaen Mhòr," she supplied. "What with the palace being invaded an' all."

He stared at her open-mouthed, and then looked at the wolf. "Are you a druid?"

"Nah, nah, not me," she said, chuckling. "You kept on tossing and turning and muttering all that. Coblaith – who be me, by the way – has no magic but what her own two hands can make, and this one's keen nose." She stuck a thumb out in the direction of the wolf, who yawned and somehow looked smug.

"Borrowed a cart horse from a friend," she said. "Right outside, she is. A small but tough old mare, like me." A gap-toothed grin spread across her face as the information sunk into Kester's head. "Take the path outside, and it'll lead you on to the trade road to Blaen Mhòr."

"I need to go," he said. "All I can offer for now is my thanks. When we come back, I will see you richly rewarded. Wealth like you have never dreamed of!"

Coblaith dismissively waved a liver-spotted hand. "Just bring the horse back. What need have I for all that gold and silver and jewellery?"

He extricated himself from the blanket and donned his clothes and boots, luxuriating in the warmth. They were not yet fully dry, but near enough to get going. "If you don't want wealth then I insist on treating you to fine feasts at the palace whenever you wish. As much as you can eat and drink, as often as you like." He slung the reiver's satchel of supplies over his shoulder and kept an eye on the wolf as he very slowly and calmly hooked his axe onto a hanging loop on his belt and inserted a knife into a wooden sheath on the other side.

The wolf's hackles rose. Its throat rumbled, and its teeth were bare. It spun and darted from the bothy they sheltered in.

Coblaith grabbed her spear and ducked outside. "Ride, boy. Hurry! Be on with your quest."

Kester followed her, the reiver's axe in his hand, fearing more men had tracked him down, but he scanned the nearby trees and didn't see anybody. A stocky horse with woollen blankets belted to its back was tied to a stake outside, seeming skittish. "I–"

She clapped a hand over his mouth. "Hsst." She watched the wolf as its ears flicked and its nose bobbed in the air. Then it looked up at the trees and growled.

Kester looked beneath the unnaturally shadowed boughs and saw something monstrous there, looking right back at him. Eight smouldering eyes fixated on him, and only him. More hairy limbs than he'd care to count unfurled, eager to grab hold and take him back to its nest.

"Run," Coblaith ordered, smacking his arse with her spear.

He ran for the horse as something big thumped to the snow behind him. The wolf spun and snapped. As he vaulted onto the horse's back he heard the old woman grunt with effort, and her spear crunched into something. An inhuman squeal sent shudders rippling up his spine.

The terrified horse took off down the twisting, narrow forest path, and it was all he could do to hold on to the reins as it tossed him to and fro. Of all the noble arts, riding a horse was the one thing he failed miserably at. Queens, kings and clan chiefs were meant to ride in all their splendour so their power could be witnessed by those of lesser station trudging through the mud. There was an art in being one with a horse, but Kester had always felt like a precariously perched sack of grain.

He glanced back to see Coblaith and her wolf fending off some sort of monstrous spider-thing cloaked in shifting shadows. She thrust her stone-tipped spear into its bulbous abdomen again and yanked it out in a welter of black and smoking blood. The wolf buried its fangs into one of the thing's hairy legs and ripped it free. Kester gritted his teeth and held on to the horse's mane for dear life as it shied away from the bank of pine trees to his left. Another of those unnatural things crawled down a trunk and came after him, scuttling across the ground.

The horse had its ears back as it fled down the trail at full gallop, hooves thudding and an ungainly boy bouncing up and down on its back. "Run like the wind, you bloody magnificent beast!" he urged.

Another of the monsters came from the trees on his right. Mandibles snapped shut just shy of the horse's tail. He glanced back to see the things giving determined chase. They were not spiders, not exactly. They had too many limbs that boasted too many joints and he shuddered at the sight of delicate-fingered human hands at the tip of each 'leg'. Their bulbous bodies and swollen faces displayed shudder-inducing hints of humanity: nipples, a flattened nose, shaggy eyebrows above eight nauseatingly human-shaped eyes and a seemingly normal chin that split in two to reveal a nightmare maw of fangs and a pale, glistening tongue more like a feeding tube. They had been summoned from the darkest pits of the otherworld by twisted sorcery; of that he had no doubt. Imperatrix wanted him badly enough to bargain with the darkest powers of the otherworld, and even Kester knew those debts were always paid in blood and pain.

The boy and his horse raced ahead of the monsters and eventually came to a fork in the trail. He tugged the reins and steered the horse right, along the trade road. With a wider, open path ahead, his mount needed no encouragement to flee for its life, and they soon left the nauseating things behind. He couldn't hope to stop its gallop without tumbling to the ground, so he held on tight. Eventually it tired itself out and slowed to a more manageable walk, its flanks heaving. He gently patted its sweaty neck and murmured soothing words. He knew exactly how it felt to flee terrified for one's life.

As they crested a rise, he looked back along the road and shivered. There, in the distance, two patches of darker shadow scuttled along, following their tracks.

"Come on, girl," he said, swallowing. "You and I are in this together now. A little faster now, and onwards to Blaen Mhòr and the warband. I promise you will be safe there."

For the first time in his life, a horse obeyed him. It sped up to a gentle trot, and they made great progress, alternating between walking and trotting. It wasn't a fine mount, bred for clan chiefs or royals and fed on rich grain, so he made sure to give it frequent short stops for rest, feed and water. It devoured the rest of the reiver's oatcakes like a starved beast, but all the food and encouragement in the realm could not keep the hardy little horse moving at any sort of pace with a rider on its back. It had been walking for stones and was just about done.

He came to a hamlet of three thatched roundhouses just as the sun began to sink over the dark sea of forest. The tumbled remains of a circular stone tower hinted at the site's martial past, when the land was more lawless and packs of brigands roamed the woods. Fenced-off pens contained a few goats and chickens, and even a shaggy longhorn cow and its calf, but no horses.

He rode in hard, and a woman took one look at him and hurriedly ushered her three curious children indoors. Two burly, black-bearded men came out to meet him. One held an axe and the other a wooden mattock, but they didn't brandish them threateningly.

"Ho, stranger," the elder of the two called out. "What brings you here in such a hurry?" He looked at Kester's mount, eyes narrowing. "And where did you get that horse?"

Kester heaved a leg over and slid to the ground, groaning as muscles he didn't know he had complained. "A woman called Coblaith loaned it to me."

"Coblaith, you say?" the man said, scratching at his beard. "A fair-haired comely maiden, is she not?"

Kester snorted. "She is not. That woman is tough as old boots. Comely before I was born, perhaps." The man nodded and relaxed. "Can you look after this exhausted horse? I said I'd get it back to her, but now I need to continue on foot. Many people's lives depend on me." He looked back at the road as the moon rose and the shadows beneath the trees deepened. He didn't have much daylight left. "You had best arm yourselves and take refuge in that stone tower tonight. There are monstrous dark fae tracking me in an attempt to thwart my quest."

The man's brow furrowed as he followed Kester's gaze down the road. "You are serious? Monsters?"

Kester looked him in the eye and made sure he still had his axe and knife ready to use if they caught up to him. "Very. I swear on my noble name, Kester Summerson."

They knew his name, of course. The men's eyes widened. "The Royal Heir!" They hesitated, unsure if they were meant to nod their respects, and how to speak to him.

"I need to get moving now," Kester said. "Keep your families safe."

The woman screamed. She was staring into the distance with an expression of horror. "What... What are those things?"

He was too late, and they too swift. The rising moon illuminated two scuttling shadows approaching the hamlet, heading straight for him. He had a tenth of a stone, maybe less, before they caught up to him. They were more tenacious than he'd feared, and he couldn't possibly outrun them.

"A wicked sorcerer and her men have attacked the Sunweald Palace," he explained. "They aim to stop me reaching the warband at Blaen Mhòr to call them back."

Families with young children began emerging from their roundhouses to see what the scream was about, blanching in horror at the sight of the twisted monsters.

Kester turned to face the creatures and took hold of his axe and his knife. "If we fight together, we can slay these twisted creatures," he said to the two burly men before him. "But if they somehow bring me down, you must run to the warband as fast as your legs can carry you and tell them what I said. I would ask for the bravest among your people to stand with me and defeat these foul beasts summoned by sorcery. Will you fight for me, you brave heroes of Sunweald?"

He had visions of the farmers and hunters roaring in agreement and taking up weapons to fight at his side. Together they would slaughter their foes and bring word to the warband, then ride home draped in glory to rescue the others. That was how it worked in all the stories.

No.

Instead, the cowards immediately turned tail and fled into their roundhouses, barricading the doors behind them. "You brought them here!" one woman shouted as her husband slammed their door. "And you can fight them off yourself. We want none of your troubles."

They left a young boy to fight the monsters alone. He stared in disbelief for a few moments, then scowled and sprinted for the ruins of the old tower. If they were not using it, then he bloody well would. The stones were slick and mossy underfoot as he clambered up heaped rubble to reach a section of fallen wall. The farmers had set up a couple of planks as a ramp to the top of it, and those he kicked aside to make any assault more difficult. The length of wall higher up was in ruins and inaccessible.

The old fortress was entirely hollow inside, with wooden ramps leading down to a space where the locals penned their pigs. The animals looked up and grunted at the intruder in their midst, but quickly lost interest when they noticed he didn't have any baskets of kitchen scraps with him.

He looked around for anywhere better to make his stand, but this was as good as it was going to get. He set his axe down close to hand and gathered a pile of good-sized rocks to fend off their assault.

Two dark and bulbous bodies darted across the hamlet, heading straight towards the stone tower. Kester shuddered as the movement of too many hairy legs set off some instinctive fear in him. He swallowed and readied his rocks. As they reached the foot of the rubble, he heaved the first rock into the air. It missed, clattering down beneath their raised legs. He cursed and tossed the next rock, not even waiting to see if he hit his targets before the next was airborne.

A rock thudded home into a bloated nightmare face, crushing several eyes. The creature wept black fluid and flailed oddly jointed legs, its screech of pain setting his teeth on edge. Below him the pigs took up the cry, grunting and squealing in fear. They could sense something unnatural was out there.

The things climbed the rubble faster than any human and began the climb right up the vertical remnant of the wall. He managed to land another rock on the head of the already wounded monster, and it lost grip and slid down onto its back. The second one's legs hooked the top of the wall, and it hauled its bulk up and over the lip.

Kester roared and swung his axe down to sever one of the human-like hands at the tip of its limb. The thing screeched but came on, flopping its swollen abdomen onto the walkway in front of him. He backed away, but to his puzzlement it turned away from him and lifted its rear.

He yelped as something squirted from an orifice in its body, splattering the left side of his face. He hurriedly wiped the sticky fluid away, fighting the urge to retch at the rotting stench. The spider-thing spun back round to face him and... did nothing but watch. He knew why a moment later, as his eye began to water and burn, and all sight fled from it. The whole side of his face went numb.

He stumbled backwards and set his back to a section of higher wall as the monster came at him. It reared up, the hands on the end of its legs grasping for him. He screamed and swung. The bronze head of his axe crunched into the thing, and hot fluids gushed out of the wicked wound. He attacked it in a frenzy, madly, blindly, feeling the weapon hit home each time, until by some miracle of the gods the thing collapsed to the stonework in a stinking puddle of what passed for blood.

His chest heaved as he looked around frantically for the one he'd hit in the face with rocks. He peered over the side of the wall, but there was no sign of it among the rubble below. His left arm hung limp now as the numbness spread further: he feared it would leave him paralyzed but horribly aware of everything. These things, it seemed, liked to eat their prey alive.

A pebble bounced off his shoulder. He looked up, eyes widening in horror as the second monster leapt from the wall above him, legs spread wide. He swung his axe upwards to meet it. The bronze head buried itself in the bulbous abdomen, but its bulk slammed him to the stone. Hairy legs curled underneath him in a sickening hug, and the grasping hands at the tips held him tight. Numbing fluids spread all over his body, and he lay helpless in its grip, unable to move a muscle.

CHAPTER 23

Hardgrim's sword went for her throat.

Briar deflected the stroke upwards with her buckler and countered with a cut at his exposed wrist.

He blocked with his own shield and slid back out of range, a smirk on his face. He was testing her with darting attacks, feints and fancy footwork, all designed to drain her mobility and stamina – two attributes currently in very short supply. Good footwork was half of a fight, and, given a more open terrain where he could freely sidestep and circle, that advantage would have destroyed her – but on the narrow stone walkways atop a palace with treacherous roofing, the benefits of his greater mobility and reach were merely significant instead of overwhelming. Briar had once struck like a viper and dodged like a cat, and while her hands and sword strokes were as swift as ever, her leg hampered every movement.

"You have become slow and weak," he said, stroking the gold brooch of Commander of Shields that hung on a cord around his neck. "Such a shame to witness my once-proud commander reduced to this pathetic wretch I see before me."

Briar's blood boiled and urged her to fling herself at the bastard and cut him apart. She swallowed her fury, gritted her teeth and somehow held her tongue. Instead, she limped backwards across the walkway, going carefully, since she couldn't take her eyes off him. A single trip or misstep and she was done for. Her leg made her slower than him, and

THE LAST SHIELD

that meant she had to pick and choose where they fought, to squeeze out every last drop of advantage.

He wore a bronze helmet and armguards in addition to the scale shirt and studded kilt she also had on, leaving him with fewer vulnerabilities than her. Hardgrim was younger and fitter, and he was – loosely – a man, with all that additional muscle mass in his favour. He was also an arrogant piece of shit with an ego the size of the palace and an inferiority complex the size of a mountain – all of which was in her favour. She could use that temper of his to lead him around by the nose. He should have launched an all-out attack, but he didn't just want to kill her quickly; he wanted to defeat his old commander and utterly humiliate her. Every attack was preceded by more mockery she paid little attention to.

A crash from the tower told her that reivers had broken through the door to the regent's study. Shouts of rage carried down from the tower as they discovered she had already fled. Three reivers found the rope she'd used, and they began descending in ungainly stops and starts.

Hardgrim looked unspeakably smug as he came in fast, swiftly changing his direction of attack, striking from the right, rebounding and coming in at her face from the left while blocking her sword with his buckler. She sidestepped clumsily but still managed to ward him off, backing away again, moving round ever so slightly each time to put the worst part of the East Wing's roofing directly between her and the tower.

The palace crows flapped and cawed, angered by the noisy humans intruding on their lofty realm. Black feathers rained down in the moonlight as swords and shields clashed.

Hardgrim's anger flared higher the longer his jibes and goading failed to get any response from her. She batted his blade aside and slipped away again, hiding the pain in her leg behind a false, mocking smile. When he again failed to get past her guard, he snarled and began cursing under his breath.

Briar reached a suitable spot to begin her counterattack. She batted aside a thrust and countered with a blistering slash that almost took his face off.

He lurched back, sweating. "Hah! Missed your target. You won't get another chance."

She sneered and pointed her sword at the gold commander's brooch she'd just cut off him, now laying on the ground. "Feeble," she said, breaking her silence. "No wonder your men mock you behind your back. You don't deserve that brooch: Hardgrim, oath-breaker and murderer of children."

Frustration overwhelmed him, and he abandoned his toying with her for a full-force attack. He roared and charged like an enraged bull. She sidestepped and deflected his blows rather than taking the brunt of his fury head-on. His sword screeched off her buckler, shaving off a curl of bronze. She countered with a slash that missed taking off his hand by a whisker to instead dent his armguard and bruise the flesh beneath it.

He snarled and scored a strike on her belly, but not hard enough to penetrate the bronze scales. She landed a glancing blow to the shoulder, to the same effect. His buckler glanced off the elbow of her shield arm, taking skin with it, but she gritted her teeth and held on despite the tears it brought to her eyes.

She smiled grimly as a section of the East Wing's roof gave way in a splintering crash and two men screamed behind her. They thudded into the rotten floor beneath, and crashed right through that, before a solid stone floor somewhere far below cut off their cries with wet impacts. The third, a younger man, had just dropped from the rope to the roof and stood frozen with indecision, fearing that his next step might very well be his last. "Down to twelve and four wounded left to kill," Briar said, updating her count.

Hardgrim couldn't help but look. With his attention broken, she counterattacked: a feint, a block and a thrust to the thigh that he couldn't quite avoid. Blood trickled into his boot from the shallow cut, but it only seemed to enrage him.

"Enough playing with you," he snarled. "You die here." He slammed his shield into hers and they came together, their weapons locked as they shoved against each other. His boot cracked into her bad leg, which buckled, and she fell to one knee, hissing in pain. She lashed out, sword cutting up at his groin. He jumped back out of range and rushed straight back in with a flurry of blows. She took a stinging superficial cut to the forearm, marring part of her tattoo, and a shield-bash to the elbow that threatened to disable her left arm entirely, and probably would once the joint swelled.

She rolled across a section of bad roofing, the slate and wood groaning in protest. Crows erupted from their nests in a cacophony, momentarily driving the intruder back. Hardgrim pushed through, savagely cutting birds from the air as they flapped and pecked at him. The crows considered Briar one of their flock, and they bothered her not at all.

The birds bought her much-needed time. With heroic effort, she rose back on to two feet, and faced him there on the shifting, sagging roof. "Why?" she asked. "Before we end this, at least tell me why you broke your oath."

Hardgrim paused his assault, and a little of his fury dissipated. "I was raised to be a clan chief," he said. "Before I grew to manhood my parents died, and my aunt usurped the power and positions that by right should have been mine. Instead, I was sent here without anything but my weapons, to bow and scrape to those who thought themselves my betters. Well, no more. Imperatrix made me a deal far better than anything Sunweald could offer, and now I will have the bright future that was denied me."

Briar snorted in derision. "Cry me a river, child. Do you honestly believe you are the only one living a life that doesn't measure up to your lofty dreams? The real world doesn't work that way. Do you think Alaric wanted a life without wife and family? He sacrificed his own happiness to maintain the security of the realm. Do you think *I* wanted to just fucking stand there by the side of the man I've loved for all these years and not kiss him even once? We do it because that is our oath-given duty to this land and its people."

He stared at her blankly, his armour spattered with crow's blood and feathers. "How does any of that help me?"

Briar trembled, every battered bone in her body demanding she rip the selfish little shit limb from limb. Instead, she glanced at the uneven roofing, chose her ground and waited for him to come to her. "Because of me, seventeen of your men are dead and four badly wounded," she said. "Your so-called Youngbloods were pathetic and unworthy of the title of Shield: I cut open Newlyn and Nealon, Cardew and Kendhal like sacks of rotten grain. You should have trained them better – but then you never were half as good as me. You are running out of men to hide behind, Hardgrim. Or perhaps you intend to scurry off and hide behind Aisling's skirts?"

His fury returned tenfold. "Stupid pig!" he screamed, charging her. "I'll gut you and fly your skin as a flag from the regent's tower."

She roared and swung her sword straight down at his helmet, all the might she could muster behind the blow.

He sneered and lifted his shield to block. It was a bone-jarring impact. Hardgrim was already heavier, and with the extra weight of bronze on him, and with such a heavy blow, his left foot shattered the old slates beneath and broke through the rotten roof.

Briar felt vicious satisfaction from Hardgrim's shocked expression.

He realised the roof was crumbling like sand, the rotten wood giving way in a widening hole beneath him. The traitor shrieked and abandoned sword and buckler to grab onto the nearest solid object – Briar herself. His fingers latched onto her boot, and she went down, holding the edge of the walkway to stop herself from sliding in with him.

His legs dangled into the void, flailing uselessly. One hand clawed for purchase at rotten woodwork, while the other remained clamped to Briar's boot, trying to haul himself back up. "That gods-damned assassin, Maddox, should have ended you at the solstice."

She kicked at his hand, trying and failing to break his grip. "That archer – he is here with you?"

"Oh, yes," Hardgrim hissed, clawing at the roof with his free hand. Crumbling stonework slid free and fell into the void below his dangling legs. It shattered far, far below. "When I kill you, I will go down to the Vault and toss your head into that failure's lap."

"Wonderful!" she snarled, savouring the snap of a finger as her heel relentlessly battered at his hand. "Good to hear I will have the opportunity for revenge."

Hardgrim shrieked in fright as his fingers slowly slid down her boot. His other hand gave up on its quest for purchase and went for her leg instead.

Angry night-black birds swarmed from their nests to peck at him and batter him with their wings. He was still coated in the blood and feathers of their fellows, and crows were clever and sadistic creatures that bore grudges as deep as the sea. Much like they did to weakened ewes and their newborns in lambing season, they went for the eyes and tongue. Beaks and claws tinged off Hardgrim's helmet, but he yelped as others found the soft flesh of his lips and nose and came away bloody.

In a panic to protect his eyes, he instinctively let go of Briar's boot. Hardgrim's eyes bulged in a moment of horrified realisation. He howled and plummeted into the depths of the derelict East Wing, condemned by his own idiocy.

A crunch and crack of bone cut off his screaming. Then came a series of descending thuds as he bounced off splintered beams and broken stone, the impacts progressively wetter. Then, blessed silence as he hit the floor.

"Eleven left," Briar said. The crows settled down but still

cawed in irritation. "I owe you all a feast," she promised them. "Once this is all over you will have so much meat and bread that the lot of you will have to waddle everywhere you go."

She groaned as she rose on unsteady feet, a task proving almost impossible with one leg that wouldn't bear most of her weight. It was barely holding up, and the rest of her wasn't much better. She was battered and bloody and badly in need of sleep. Across an expanse of treacherous roofing, she looked the remaining reiver in the eye and sighed.

The young man barely had a beard worth the name: a mere murderer-in-training. He didn't show any sign of attacking, and didn't seem to know which way to run either, so she sheathed her sword, untied the shepherd's sling around her wrist, picked up a stone and began swinging it round and round. He tried to back away – to where, he had no idea. He froze as part of the roof sagged beneath his foot.

Briar let slip the cord, and the stone flew. The light was bad, and so was her aim. It struck him in the side of the neck instead of the face she'd aimed for. He choked and stumbled back, hand outstretched to lean on a wall that wasn't there. He teetered on the edge of plummeting to the gardens far below, arms flailing. He caught his balance and fell forward on to his knees, facing her, gasping for breath.

She could kill him here and now. Send him plummeting to his doom and leave his broken corpse sprawled on the flowerbeds. That would leave her only ten men to kill. She had disposed of many of the enemy, but it was a hollow victory with so many still left alive, including several traitor Shields and an accursed sorcerer who could return the dead to a vile mockery of life. There just wasn't enough strength left in Briar to fight them all, and that was assuming she had their numbers correct.

Instead of finishing the boy off, she laughed at him, her voice harsh and mocking in the moonlight. "The Royal Heir escaped during your initial attack," she said. "By now the warband has been alerted, and they will run through the night to get here tomorrow. Maybe we'll skin you all alive, or perhaps I'll poison more of you and watch you puke up black and rotting guts."

The stone beneath the boy wettened: a spreading pool of piss.

"You are still young," she growled. "I gift you this one chance to save your life and change your ways. Now, climb back up that rope and flee this place while you still can. If I see you again, I will cut off your hands and feet and let the crows feast on your flesh."

His reply was a strangled sob, but he fled back towards the regent's tower and began scrambling up the rope. Maybe some of the reivers would believe her bluff and desert Imperatrix to run for their lives, leaving Briar with fewer men to cut her way through. Or maybe she'd just need to slaughter a terrified boy later. With her dwindling strength, it was worth grabbing any kind of advantage she could get.

She turned her back on the boy. The commander's brooch called to her like a lost child crying for its mother. Once she retrieved it and wiped off the vile sorcerer's blood, the golden shield was back home where it belonged. She bitterly regretted ever letting her own misery and self-doubt talk her into taking it off. Now, light duties and a comfy seat seemed to her tired body like they would be gifts from the gods. She pinned the brooch to the tunic beneath her scale shirt and drew strength from its presence, strength enough to keep her on her feet until she found somewhere to treat her wounds and rest. The constant running, crawling and fighting had taken their toll: she wasn't a god or one of the great heroes from legend, and even if her mind was still willing, her merely human body had hit its limit. All veteran warriors knew, when their hands and feet grew clumsy and their weapons heavy, to heed their body's message – those who didn't would die when they might otherwise have survived to fight again. She dragged herself over to the trapdoor and began the arduous process of climbing down the ladder into a storage space above the third floor. Her left leg was useless, and descending a ladder with only one weight-bearing leg proved to be a thoroughly unpleasant experience.

She landed in a long, low-ceilinged room with arrow-slit windows along one wall that let in only a little moonlight. It was a long-disused barracks thick with dust. A warrior's shrine occupied one corner, little more than a flat-topped block of shaped stone that had been blessed by druids. It wasn't dedicated to any one god but served as a gateway for many. Warriors often didn't have much time to pray before they pitted their arms and lives against the enemy, and to Briar's mind, any god that objected to sharing an altar wasn't worth her time. Empty wooden weapon racks and barrels meant to hold arrows lined the interior wall next to ranks of narrow bed frames now devoid of straw mattresses. In the event of an attack, archers and slingers would once have rushed up the ladder and taken up positions to rain death down on the enemy. Over the centuries, there had only been a few skirmishes beyond the outer walls, never mind the inner palace, and nothing like a full-blown assault. As the warring Ves princedoms and myriad Wrendal sects coalesced into stable realms more interested in trade, the danger of such a large attack had dwindled. New and more formidable hillforts had been built nearer the borders, and most of the important warrior-chiefs previously dwelling in the palace had moved out.

Briar was able to slide a wooden rod into place so the trapdoor could not easily be opened from outside, but the door leading into the inner palace was warped and refused to fully close. She jammed it into the frame as hard as she could, but its hinges were weak and wouldn't hold up to any kind of determined assault. What the door would do was make a right racket and wake her up if it were forced open.

Old beef bones stolen from the kitchen were piled up in the corner next to a flattened heap of empty sacks, where

Brutus had built a comfy nest. That smelly dog bed seemed immensely inviting to Briar right then, but she feared to sleep where the reivers might come upon her, and she didn't have the strength for another fight. There was an entrance to the secret tunnels here that might make for a better place to hide. She limped over to the far wall and searched for cracks that might indicate which of the stone blocks could be removed. Her fingers found a series of chisel marks at the very bottom that indicated the right area for a switch. She set her ear to the stone and listened, just in case the reanimated corpses of past Shields still crawled through the walls of the palace.

Hardgrim's tracking enchantment had certainly reached its time limit, and from Briar's knowledge of arcane matters, it would take an enormous mental effort for any sorcerer to keep such a powerful spell in place. It was a toss of the knucklebones: take a chance and perhaps encounter the dead, or almost certainly face the living, assuming they didn't just murder her while she slept.

She couldn't hear much of anything behind the wall, so she dug her fingers into the switch and heard the counterweight behind the wall groan into motion. The withered forearm of something long dead immediately shot through the gap.

She hissed and lurched back, reaching for her sword. It was halfway out of its sheath before she discovered the severed arm was clutched in a dog's mouth. Brutus trotted out of the tunnel, trailing dust and debris right over to his bed. His belly was round and fat with beef, and he looked immensely smug as he padded round in a circle and then settled down to gnaw on his bone, oblivious to everything.

She chuckled in sheer disbelief and relief. It seemed like the bloody creature had run away from Selma. Briar wasn't entirely surprised. Perhaps the eerie howling that had spooked her earlier had just been this dusty little rascal moaning that he couldn't get to his second-favourite bed.

Briar grimaced as she dropped to her knees and crawled into the tunnel. "Come on in, boy," she said. "You'll be safer in here with me."

Brutus thought about it just long enough to be annoying, then yawned and padded over to join her. She heaved the door closed, plunging them into total darkness. Brutus and she curled up together. The dog's warmth and welcome company were a balm to her battered body and mind. She couldn't go on without rest, and she prayed that Alaric would still be alive when she woke. Sleep came hard and fast, like a club to the face.

CHAPTER 24

Imperatrix slept like a baby, curled up atop a straw pallet in a corner of the Heart, resting to recover her energy before pushing through the next few arcane seals protecting the Wyrm Vault. Even powerful sorcerers needed to sleep, and the assassin, Maddox, considered how easy it would be to kill her right then and there. He regretted taking her commission, but the deal she'd offered had been too good to turn down, or so it had seemed at the time. Now he regretted ever associating with her – it was all so messy. All of this waiting about felt unnatural; he much preferred to do a job and get out unseen.

He sighed and returned to his work, chiselling and hammering rough holes into marked areas on the back wall. Each one had to take his finger up to its second joint, and as laborious and menial a task as it was, he didn't dare risk his leader's wrath with shoddy work. She had exhausted herself breaking through the second and third seals of the Vault's sorcerous protections and would be in no mood for excuses if she woke to find his work incomplete.

The two former Shields Phelan and Owyn took turns keeping watch over the ragged regent of Sunweald, who lay prone on the floor. They hadn't bothered to bind him – the man was not going anywhere under his own power anytime soon. Maddox was a hardened killer who enjoyed his work, but even he balked at the tortures Imperatrix handed out. Still, he was not paid to ask questions or voice scruples.

The heavy bronze door to the Heart was locked, leaving only a small spy and air hole open. While he felt secure in this place, he harboured a deep dislike of relying on others to tie up any loose ends, and the tedious work left him plenty of time to consider their failings. Who knew what was happening in the rest of the palace? Hardgrim and Ruith had proved less than impressive after the initial success of the attack. All that fine and sneaky plotting they'd done – and then they'd just fallen to bits at the first hint of something unexpected. He loathed putting his life on the line with so many uncertainties. The payoff would be immense, but only if he survived to collect it. He was getting a bad feeling about all of this, and it wasn't just the bloody sorcery and dark magic. Many reivers had already been slaughtered or poisoned, and that accursed Briar was, so far as he knew, still roaming free and impaling heads on sticks. Anybody who could survive red-scale viper venom and come out of the experience sane was not to be underestimated, and nobody even knew for certain if she was working alone. If they had missed her, why not others?

Time seemed to stretch as he toiled deep below the ground, the only light provided by lanterns whose flames danced to unfelt air currents. He spent what felt like an entire day chiselling and hammering, though it was probably only a handful of stones. Eventually, he stepped back and studied all eleven of the areas Imperatrix had marked with crosses of the regent's blood. The holes he'd made did not burrow into the wyrm skeleton itself but were placed into the softer stone around its skull and spine. He used his finger to double-check the depth of every one and found, to his relief, he had successfully completed the work.

The huge stone skeleton in the wall had been daubed with countless arcane runes written in royal blood, following some unseen pattern he couldn't quite grasp. Some seemed to flicker and move as if possessing an eerie life of their own, though he could only ever catch it out of the corner of his eye. Imperatrix hadn't thought to mention that the stone bones were oddly warm to the touch compared to the darker rock around them. Then there were the eyes... From time to time, he felt as if the black pits of the great wyrm's eye sockets were watching him, like a cat following a tasty little morsel of a mouse. He shuddered and reckoned that being locked inside this macabre place was starting to get to him.

Once he triple-checked he'd completed every last thing Imperatrix had ordered, he asked Owyn to wake their leader: he'd found it wise never to touch a druid or sorcerer without their permission, not unless it was with a knife slitting their throat open.

The former Shield knelt beside the sorcerer and shook her by the shoulder. Her eyes flew open, and the knife artefact leapt into her hand of its own volition. The knife was at the warrior's throat before he could blink, the glowing metal spitting and hissing.

Owyn didn't move a muscle; only his eyes swivelled towards Maddox, and it didn't take a genius to read the thought burning behind them: *This is your fault, you absolute cunt.*

Maddox shrugged.

Imperatrix blinked away the fog of sleep and stared at Owyn for a long moment before the knife was returned to its sheath. He swallowed and rubbed his throat as he gratefully backed away. "I'm awake," she said, rubbing her eyes. "Maddox, I take it you have finished the task I set you?"

"That I have," the assassin said, indicating the new holes he'd made in the back wall. "Your turn... unless you'd care to nap some more?"

She scowled at him and swung her legs off the pallet, groaning as she rose laboriously. Then she staggered and clutched her forehead, cursing something about "rekhcorryn", then several words he didn't understand but assumed to be expletives.

"Your hideous spider monsters?" Maddox asked. "Have they found the missing boy heir?"

She shook her head. "Somehow, that brat is still far from here," she snarled, flinging a priceless bowl at the wall. It smashed into a hundred shards but did little to improve her mood. "It seems I must make do with the regent. We will use him up. Blood and bone and mind and soul. Picked apart... ground down... burnt out..."

The assassin studied his employer as she ranted and raved. He noted the sallow skin, the bags under her eyes and the tremors that set her fingers twitching and clawing the air. It seemed to take her a long time to regain her full mental and physical faculties. Sorcery, it seemed, took a terrible toll upon the minds and bodies of those who used it. Well worth it, though, he reckoned, so long as you didn't bargain away your body and soul to inhuman powers that had roamed the land for uncounted generations before human feet ever trod the dirt.

The sorcerer grabbed her satchel of tools, muttering and cursing the vexing gods and spirits of this land as she rummaged through it. She finally found what she was looking for and shuffled over to the back wall with a small black sack in hand. She took several deep breaths to calm herself and steady her hands, then she scrutinised his handiwork and measured the depth of each hole with her finger. She didn't offer any words of praise for his all his effort, and he didn't expect any. They were all vipers here. She finally grunted her acceptance and got to work on breaking the next arcane seal protecting the Vault.

Into ten of the holes she inserted small rods of lodestone, a magical black rock that either attracted or repelled its own kind depending which way it was held. A small wooden hammer tapped them into a snug fit, and then she took three steps back. Nothing happened. She frowned and lifted her hands into the air, palms facing the wall.

BEGONE, a voice thundered inside their skulls. I WILL NOT OPEN FOR YOU.

Imperatrix gritted her teeth, dug her nails into the air and pulled. Veins of sorcerous darkness crept up her throat and hands.

The earth moaned and shifted against its will. Stone bones ground against the imprisoning earth. The great wyrm in the wall began to move, stone bones pulled through softer rock like it were butter. Maddox beat a hasty retreat as the horned head with a fanged maw huge enough to swallow an entire cow emerged an arm's length from the wall, and then turned to face Imperatrix. Eldritch green fires kindled inside the empty eye sockets, and a sudden heat flooded the room.

Imperatrix staggered back, chest heaving and sweat beading her brow. The black veins clustered around her throat began a slow and reluctant retreat. "The fourth seal has been broken. Only three more stand between us and unimaginable power and riches."

"What was that voice?" Maddox said, shivering.

She shook her head. "Just a warning."

The assassin swallowed and edged forward again once he was sure the huge stone skeleton wasn't about to come alive and devour them all. He eyed the last of the holes he'd made, right inside the beast's maw, where the throat would have been. "You had me make eleven holes. What of the last one?"

She didn't reply, and instead slipped her knife from its sheath, smiling at him in a way that had him itching to run for his bow and bury an arrow in her skull. He'd have aimed for her heart if she'd ever shown any hint of having one.

She walked right past the assassin and over to Alaric Summerson. She squatted next to the prone regent and cocked her head, her gaze running up and down his naked, brutalised body. He was covered in small scabs from her bloodletting, with no body part spared her tender mercies. A massive black and blue bruise bloomed across the side with broken ribs. Crumbs of meat and bread were still stuck to his beard from the force-feeding to keep up his strength and help replace some of the lost blood.

"How the mighty are fallen," Imperatrix said. "All that peace and prosperity you were so fond of made you weak. A goodly dose of fear and paranoia would have served you well." She glanced up at Maddox and the two former Shields, who all swallowed as one and began sweating.

"Phelan, Owyn," she said, "be ready to stop this man doing himself any further injury."

Imperatrix spread the regent's left hand on the cold stone floor and examined his fingers, sizing them up one by one before settling on the little finger. She drew her sizzling, sparking knife from its sheath and smiled as she sliced the finger off like it was a length of sausage. The stump charred and smoked, her weapon cauterising the wound.

Alaric woke screaming. Phelan and Owyn pinned the flailing man down, their faces twisting at the nauseating stench of burnt human meat, while Imperatrix stood and smiled at the macabre prize cradled in her hands. They stuffed a dirty rag into Alaric's mouth to stifle the din as he bucked and twisted in throes of agony, exacerbating the pain from his ribs.

Maddox stood back and watched, wondering if this was some sort of twisted revenge after years of feigned subservience, or if Imperatrix had been quite literal about using the man up.

She tore her gaze away from the finger and fixed on Maddox. "Take it," she commanded, hands outstretched.

He picked up the regent's finger between his thumb and forefinger, finding it still unpleasantly warm.

"Insert it into the last hole," she commanded. Her reddened eyes were wide and feverish and riddled with black threads of sorcery that showed no signs of dissipating.

He looked to the last hole, right inside the wyrm's fanged mouth. The whole skull – eerie burning eye sockets and all – now jutted from the rock wall, but the throat was still submerged in darker stone. "There is no way I'm sticking my arm into that thing's mouth," he said, eyeing the needle-sharp stone teeth.

Imperatrix didn't reply, but her maddened gaze was heavy and pregnant with expectation. She made no move to do it herself.

Maddox grunted. "Fine, but I'll do it my way." He retrieved an arrow from the quiver he'd left on the far side of the cavern, beside his bow and other equipment. He impaled the stump of the severed finger on the bronze tip and then gingerly approached the skull with the arrow and finger extended before him. He slid them between the abundant teeth of the skull and carefully manoeuvred the regent's fingertip into the hole he'd made, then shoved it in hard. Something gave way, and his hand went in further than he'd wanted. He snatched it back a moment before the skull's jaw snapped shut. If he hadn't used the arrow, it would have bitten his arm off at the shoulder.

Owyn flashed him a wide and gratified smile, as if the gods had indulged his vengeful prayers in answer to Maddox's previous prank.

The assassin turned an accusing glare on his employer.

"You are a wise man," Imperatrix said, without a shred of guilt in her voice or expression. "It is why you have survived this long in your particular line of work." Her attention was drawn to the stone throat of the wyrm, where he had just inserted the finger. The dark stone around those bones slumped and began oozing out, dripping to the floor in greasy piles, like warm butter. Of the man's finger, there was no sign.

"The third seal has been broken by Summerson blood and Summerson bone," she muttered.

Everyone in the chamber jumped as something struck the outside of the bronze door. "It's me!" Ruith shouted, hammering. "Open up."

Imperatrix nodded to Owyn, who rose from the floor, where Phelan was still pinning the sobbing nine-fingered regent face down on the stone. Owyn pulled a lever and triggered the druid-lock door mechanism to free the counterweight. The thick slab of bronze ground open and Ruith hurried in, dark circles under his eyes and his hair in disarray.

"We have a huge problem," he said, throat clenching like he was fighting the urge to retch. "Hardgrim and another cartload of our men are dead. Briar is still alive and free."

Imperatrix hissed and ground her teeth. "How? I sent him off with an enchantment to track the crusty old cow. How many men does it take to kill one maimed woman?"

Ruith swallowed and glanced back at the door. "More than we sent, apparently." He glanced at Maddox accusingly. "She trained all of us, and before her wound she could have taken any one of us – maybe all of us in this room, even if we came at her all together. She really was that fast. Now?" He shook his head. "Hardgrim and three of your men caught up with her atop the palace, but he fell into her trap – she sent Hardgrim and two others plummeting to their doom through the rotten roof of the East Wing, and left the youngest alive to come back with a message from her: she claims that Kester escaped right after the attack and is already on his way back from Blaen Mhòr with the entire warband."

A rough voice came from the open doorway: "Did that woman speak the truth, Imperatrix?" Two black-bearded and scar-faced reivers entered the Heart, shoving a sweaty-faced youngling with downcast eyes ahead of them.

"Ah, Uradech, a pleasure as always," she said, eyeing the man who styled himself chief of the Wildwood Reivers.

"I told you to wait up there," Ruith said, sighing heavily.

"Is this the little wretch who spread Briar's falsehoods?" the sorcerer demanded. The youth wilted under her fiery gaze.

"Aye," Uradech admitted. "But does that canny woman speak falsehood or the truth? Where is that bloody boy heir of yours, then? We've worked for you for years now, and I reckon we have a right to know."

All eyes turned to Imperatrix. "A right to know..." she whispered, eyes wide and maddened. She snarled, and the shadows deepened. "Do I look like I have the time to deal with your nonsense?"

Uradech took a step back, then steadied his nerves and met her gaze. "Nonsense? My men are being slaughtered out there like trussed goats. I won't be having it."

On the floor, the Lord Regent of Sunweald managed to spit out his gag. "That boy has always been trouble. He's away and free of your claws, Aisling. Whatever happens to me, the warband will soon be sticking all of your heads on spikes."

"Silence that fool!" she ordered. His guards pushed him face-down to the floor and fought to stuff the rag back between his clenched teeth as he bucked and twisted. "The boy cannot escape me. I set my rekhcorryn allies to hunt him down. And those twisted creatures are deadly hunters."

"Where are your bloody monsters now, then?" Alaric shouted before Phelan punched him in the side with broken ribs. The former Shield managed to stuff the dirty rag back into the regent's mouth as he gasped in pain, and his words were reduced to muffled groans.

The reivers didn't look convinced by her words. She ground her teeth and laid a hand on the hilt of her knife. "Ruith, get back out there and ensure all the exits and stairways are under proper guard. Maddox, be a dear and close the door behind him. It seems we need to discuss this further with our reiver friends."

Ruith slunk off, and Maddox walked past the reivers to work the mechanism that set the heavy bronze door booming shut.

Imperatrix sat the two older reivers down on the bench opposite her and began a seemingly earnest discussion with Uradech of his concerns about her leadership and the way the plan was going, throwing in some disarming platitudes for good measure. The young man sat gloomily in the corner, keeping himself well out of his elder's way.

Maddox got into position behind the two older reivers and waited for his employer to give him the nod. He drew two knives and plunged them into the men's throats, sawing outwards in a gory spray. Imperatrix didn't move out of the way as the self-styled chief of the reivers died. Instead, she closed her eyes and opened her mouth as their lifeblood gushed over her, soaking her hair.

The reiver youth trembled in the corner as his kin flopped to the floor.

Imperatrix rose from the table, grinning and glistening red. "What good timing you had," she said. "In Kester's absence, some extra blood to fuel my sorcery is most welcome." She drew her own knife. "Owyn, drag this boy to the wall. His beating human heart will grant me power enough to rouse the dead one more time. They will do a better job of guarding us while I break the last two seals."

She eyed her favourite assassin. "If Ruith doesn't come back with Briar's head in the next few stones, I want you to go up there and do what you do best."

Maddox nodded, figuring that he'd spent quite enough time in the damp and dreary bowels of the earth. He didn't feel that Ruith had the bronze balls on him to successfully take down his old commander. Maddox would see the job done right.

CHAPTER 25

Briar awoke in cramped darkness, head pounding, throat parched and every nook and cranny of her body aching like she'd been blind drunk and in a fistfight with a bear. A cold, wet nose nudged her cheek, and moist, meaty breath washed over her. Despite the dog's pungent stickiness, she found his friendly presence immensely reassuring. As she endured Brutus' affections, she mused that, as days began, it was not the worst she'd ever had; that honour went to the campaign in the marshes with all its biting flies, leeches, lost boots, bad water and fungal foot rot. Still, what she wouldn't give to go to sleep on a bed of roots and stones and wake up fresh as an autumn morning, like she used to back then... Not that she'd ever appreciated the joys of youth. Nobody did until they were gone. Getting old, she told herself.

Recent memory oozed back into her skull in an avalanche of panic. The moment she tried to move she deeply regretted it. Her whole body was seized solid, and her muscles howled in complaint. She bit her lip to avoid crying out and alerting the enemy. Brutus whined and scratched urgently at the secret entrance.

She gritted her teeth and fumbled for Brutus' muzzle, clamping her hands around it to silence him as she set her ear to the wall. Not a hint of a noise. They couldn't stay in the tunnel forever, so she took a deep breath and eased the entrance open. Brutus squeezed past her and darted into the room beyond. She forced her stiff muscles into action and crawled out after him, every ungainly movement sending spikes of pain through her body as she sprawled out across the floor of the old armoury. They were alone, praise the gods. She lay there breathing heavily as Brutus ran over to the corner of the room, where he cocked his leg and unleashed a mighty torrent of steaming piss that would shame a horse. The stench was eyewatering, and she thought it a small mercy he'd not just gone all over her right there in the tunnel. Drowning in dog piss was no way to die.

It took her an age to slowly stretch sore muscles and work herself up into a sitting position. She took stock of her injuries: every bit of her was covered in minor cuts and bruises that could be ignored. Her battered elbow was more of a concern. She flexed it, and bones clicked, feeling like quern stones grinding together, but despite the pain and limited range of movement it was still usable. As expected, her left leg was an angry, swollen mess, with Hardgrim's added boot print a vivid outline in black and blue. She wouldn't be running or climbing many more steps, that was for sure. But her injuries were a small price to pay to witness that rat-bastard's face as he plummeted to his doom. Because of his greed and treachery, her home had been invaded, and dozens of innocent, goodly people had been slaughtered in their beds – but that vermin had died far, far too quickly for her tastes. For now, the best she could do for her leg was to scavenge some rods of wood from old weapon racks and use her knife to cut strips of sacking, and fashion a crude knee brace.

Once she was done inspecting her wounds, she moved on to her equipment. The bronze scales of her armour were dented and scored by battle and crawling through tunnels, and one of her boots bore bite marks she could see hints of skin through. The padded tunic beneath her armour was sodden with sweat and torn in places, and the leather kilt was missing a few strips of leather and studs. Her sword was a little notched, but it was still sharp, and her buckler was as rock-solid as ever. It was all in better condition than she was herself, and would serve well enough. It would have to: there wasn't anything in the old armoury she could use beyond mouldy sacks and an old war horn still hanging from a peg on the wall. She tightened a few straps, made sure her sling was safely wrapped around her wrist and a few stones were in her pouch, and was then as ready as she would ever be.

The need to curl up and sleep weighed her down, but Alaric was relying on her, and weariness didn't matter – she could sleep when she was dead. Briar marshalled her reserves of strength and summoned her will to fight. She grimaced and attempted to get back on to her feet, a logistical nightmare when one knee could barely bend. She ended up on her front, palms on the floor and braced bad leg extended out behind her, then walked her hands back until she was able to stand up on her good leg, shaking with the effort.

A few deep breaths later, the pain had subsided enough for Briar to begin a series of stretches to loosen cramped and complaining muscles. As she worked out the tension, she ran through possible plans of attack. As far as she knew, she would face eleven healthy men and perhaps four badly wounded, if they hadn't died already. She prayed her count was correct and no more waited in the shadows. Then there was the accursed sorcerer to deal with after them. They knew Briar was at large and fighting back, and they knew exactly where she was going. They also knew the two ways to get there: through the tunnels or down the stairs. As much as she might have preferred to avoid the stairs and go through the tunnels, she judged it too risky: all it would take to thwart her would be a few of those corpses animated by dark magic to block the way forward and, in case she managed to squeeze past them, a man or two guarding the tomb with a hammer or axe readied to bash her brains in the moment she crawled out, utterly defenceless.

She finished her exercises and limped over to ruffle Brutus's ears. "A frontal assault is more my style anyway," she said to the dusty, disinterested dog. He padded round in a circle and then flopped to the floor.

Briar readied her sword and shield for more killing. The fear of what she would find even if she cut her way through every single one of the remaining reivers and traitors was upon her. Visions of Alaric's cold corpse seared through her mind before she ruthlessly quashed that line of thought: surely the sorcerer needed Alaric to open the Wyrm Vault, and she had to hold on to the hope his unique utility had kept the man she loved alive. The light of a new day shone through the arrow-slit windows of the barracks, and a scrap of blue sky hinted at it being a good day to die. She took a deep cleansing breath, wrenched open the warped door in a shower of splinters and stepped out into the hallway.

Gloom and silence in the hallway beyond: a good start. She moved out, slow and steady, sword and shield up, eyes darting to the next doorway along. She approached and passed it by. The storeroom had been ransacked in the search for loot, its sacks torn and baskets hacked open, but all the bastards had found were blankets, servants' clothing, pottery, rope, antler picks and wooden mallets, drop spindles, wool and bone needles and pots of coloured powders for dying yarn – none of which was the sort of portable wealth the reivers had been searching for. They wanted gold, silver and bronze jewellery, amber beads and polished gemstones that could easily fit in a bag, the sort of thing highly mobile brigands could flee with and trade for a fortune in livestock. Whatever lamps and oil that had been stored had already been taken for their use – a shame, as Briar could have used that oil as a weapon.

A few of the more important servants and master crafters had their bedchambers up here, and those rooms had been similarly defiled, their belongings scattered across the floor. The balding master of herds lay face-down across the threshold of his room, his back a bloody ruin. Approaching the royal weaver's chamber, she noted the buzz of flies and the stench of death and moved right on past without even looking in. All that skill built up over a lifetime... What a waste. Brutality made the scum of the land feel like big men and granted the weak an illusion of strength and power – but any lackwit could destroy something beautiful. Alaric and she had spent years struggling to bring peace to the realm and to improve the lot of all its people, and she'd rather die before seeing these greedy murderers tear down all that hard work.

She made her way right up to the central stairwell without incident. This entire floor of the palace was empty of life. Many of the enemy were now dead, and they didn't have nearly enough men to guard every area. Hardgrim was a wet smear across the floor, and their ability to plan had taken a serious blow, but there were still traitorous Shields left alive, with enough training hammered into their thick skulls to have pulled the rest of their forces back to fortify the central stairwell that was the only way down to the ground floor and the catacombs beneath the palace. Iden and Ruith certainly had enough sense to have already done that, curse their bones.

She held her breath and listened, straining to make out the muffled voices coming from below. She couldn't make out the words, but from the harsh tones it sounded like several men arguing. At least two bore rough accents of folk from the deep forest, where the reivers dwelled, while another voice sounded – if her ears were not mistaken – like the softer tones of the people up near Drew Nemeton. Reivers were arguing with one of Hardgrim's Youngbloods. Ruith, perhaps. If she hazarded a guess, she might face five men guarding the way down into the catacombs.

She sheathed her sword and hooked her buckler onto her belt. They had the numbers, but she had all the skill in warcraft. They expected her to take the stairs, and the last thing she wanted to do was march right into their trap without a plan.

She pondered heading back up to the roof to tie off a rope, descend to the garden and gain entrance through the main gate... but surely they had already closed and barred all the outer doors. She wasn't convinced she had it in her to make the descent only to have to heave herself right back up. She could go down and then run for help from the nearby farmers... A few extra hands would make all the difference now, but if it were her, she'd have stationed their best archers outside all the exits of the palace to feather the backs of any escapees or overly inquisitive locals who wandered out into the open, and with Briar's bad leg, she would be a fat pigeon ready for their pie. Even if she made it past their arrows and roused a warband of farmers, could she spare those stones when Alaric was in mortal danger every moment that she delayed? His life was only of use to the sorcerer while the Wyrm Vault remained secure. The moment it was breached she would surely kill him. No, Briar could spare no time at all.

She sighed and made the grudging decision to take the stairs. But that didn't mean she had to be a lamb led to the slaughter. She backtracked to the storeroom, rummaged through the stores of dyes and removed clay jars containing red madder and blue woad. Most things could be made into a weapon if used correctly, and these fine powders made from boiled roots and leaves would choke the throat and lungs of an enemy and stain and sear their eyes. Good luck seeing much with your vision painted blue! She prepared a cloth to wrap around her nose and mouth, which would spare her the worst of the effects, offering her a sorely needed edge in the coming battle. She left it knotted around her neck, ready to pull up when it was needed.

Weapon acquired, she returned to the old armoury, nodded to Brutus and grabbed the war horn from the wall. As any good commander knew, poor morale had lost many a winnable battle. Her father had taught her that, routing greater numbers of brigands simply by having a couple of warriors approach the flanks of the enemy, blowing their horns and making as much noise as they could, while he charged in from the front.

Briar could remember with exacting detail the look of terror in the brigands' eyes as she charged their camp at his side, spears thrusting. The enemy thought the battle lost before it even began, and in their panicked flight they lost everything.

She'd spared that one young reiver and told him the warband was returning, and there was no possibility the boy had kept his mouth shut. There was no proof her words were true, but the fear must have wormed its way into all others of his ilk. Some might have already fled into the safety of the forest during the night. With any luck, what she was about to do would frighten the rest away. Any brigand who had survived years of Sunweald patrols would recognise her call to attack.

She thrust the end of the war horn through a narrow window, took a deep breath and blew it. The urgent wail of the horn tore away the cold peace of the winter's morning: a double blast that would tell her warriors, had there been any, to advance upon the foe. Brutus whined and hunched down on his makeshift bed.

She put the horn down, much to the dog's relief. Another blow on it might have allowed listeners to determine that the horn was calling from the palace and not the surrounding woods. "Stay out of trouble, you daft creature," she said to Brutus. He gave her a doubtful look. "Soon your master will be back in his bed waiting for you to clamber all over him." That last bit set his tail to wagging.

She tightened the knot in the cloth around her neck then pulled it up to cover her nose and mouth, and with pots of powder in hand and her sword and buckler at her hip, Briar marched to battle.

CHAPTER 26

Briar was of the fervent opinion that whoever decided to build spiral stairs without any natural source of light as the only way up and down the palace should have been promptly beaten and then flung face-first into the nearest fire. There was only one lantern, sat empty in a niche on the wall, and there were no drudges left to refill and relight it. She gritted her teeth and resisted the urge to swear loudly as she fought on, taking it slowly and carefully, pressing herself to the outer wall and manoeuvring her bound and braced leg down each narrow step with the greatest of care. One slip and it was all over.

The argument below was heating up, the men snarling and snapping at each other like starving hounds fighting over the last bit of meat. Fortunately, it proved a grand distraction from her pain, and the enemy were too preoccupied with their bickering to hear the clinks of her armour that seemed so accursedly loud to her ears. She made her way down step by gruelling step, and gradually their voices became louder and distinct enough for her to eavesdrop on their argument. She carefully pulled up the knotted cloth to protect her nose and mouth from the powders she carried.

Three coarse voices raised in clamorous complaint.

"There is no warband coming," Ruith shouted over them. "I told you this already – they are days away, utterly fooled and impotent. All we need to do is stay here and stay strong. Trust me."

"D'you take us for fools?" a reiver replied, incredulous. "An' that war horn was a fucking fox's mating call, was it? You rich pricks from the big towns think you are so much better than us deep forest folk, with all your fancy scroll scratchings and pointless learnings. Trust you? I wouldn't piss on you if you were on fire."

"Look here–" Ruith began.

"That bloody-handed woman claimed they was coming," another butted in. "It's just as young Art said."

"And where is our boy, anyway?" the first Reiver added.

"Art is missing, along with a handful of others, dead or fled," a new voice added. "Ain't seen Uradech for a whiles either. Maybes they've more sense than us and have all done a runner with whatever riches they could carry off. Something about this stinks. The whole haunted tomb of a palace reeks like a rotten carcass. Nah. Nah, this ain't for me no more – I'm getting out before they take my head."

"Your men are assisting Imperatrix with her work," Ruith snarled. "Don't you boil-brained lackwits dare even think of running."

A new voice – the former Shield Iden: "Calm down, all of you. I'll go down into the catacombs and see how things are going."

"You do that, dog," a reiver snarled.

Briar paused on the steps, silent and alert, ears straining. The dim glow of a lantern showed from somewhere below her. Footsteps began descending, and the light dwindled with them. Iden was muttering something unpleasant to himself as he went, unaware his old commander was only two dozen steps above him.

Ruith and a reiver started screaming at each other. Briar grinned through her pain at the scuffle of feet and sudden smack of fists. Yelps of pain and clangs of metal echoed up the stairwell as she made her way down the last few steps unopposed and unnoticed. They were not even guarding the landing or the stairs down to the catacombs but were arguing out in the hallway beyond it. Never rely on brigands to do a Shield's job, she thought. With any luck, the fools would end up slaughtering each other and save her the effort. There was even a good chance she could sneak down into the depths without them noticing, but it was folly to leave enemies at your back, especially when you also had them in front of you.

A reiver roared and called Ruith's mother the spawn of a sow, but his cursing was cut off in an *oof* and a gasp. Another squealed like a stuck pig, briefly, and fell with a heavy thump. She edged down the last step and risked a quick look through the archway. Ruith stood with his back to her, resplendent in his shirt of immaculately polished bronze scales. One reiver was sprawled at his feet, bleeding out from a chest wound, and another man clutched his bruised belly, wheezing in pain. Three others stood facing him, their weapons wavering.

"Enough!" Ruith yelled. Silence reigned for five heartbeats. "That was just some drunken buffoon of a deer hunter's horn, not a warband hunting us. None of you big and brave Wildwood Reivers are going anywhere, unless you fancy your chances against me. Imperatrix knows what she is doing, and you will all be drowning in riches and wanton bitches soon. All we have to do is kill one wounded old woman. How hard can it… be…" His words faded as three reivers' eyes bulged at the sight of Briar stepping out behind him. Ruith turned, and his jaw dropped, recognising her despite the cloth over her face.

Briar tossed the clay jars of dye at the ceiling and shouted, "Suck on poison, you pigs." The jars shattered, and clouds of fine blue and red powders billowed out into the hallway, snuffing out the lanterns and plunging the space into gloom, with only slivers of daylight shining through narrow slit windows and the main gate, at the furthest end of the hallway. Briar drew her sword and buckler and advanced into the cloud of colour. The men in front of her breathed it in, screaming in fear as it clogged their throats and noses and stained their eyes red and blue. After losing four of their fellows to dreadful poison, they wholeheartedly believed her, clutching at their throats and rubbing at their eyes with the conviction their faces were about to melt off.

Ruith breathed in only a little before his jaw snapped shut. He held his breath, turned and ran coughing towards the sliver of daylight that marked the main entrance to the palace, all while weeping coloured tears from burning eyes. Briar squinted against the powders and limped through the clouds of red and blue, cutting down two panicked reivers before they rallied. The third had been at the back of the cloud, and he staggered towards the main gate and the promise of escape, coughing and scrubbing the dye coating his broken and bruised face – she reckoned he was the unlucky bastard she'd tossed a basket of hammers at when ascending the stairs the previous day.

Ruith furiously blinked through blue tears, and in his haste to get outdoors he stumbled into the wall, then spun and fell into the hallway of the servants' quarters. He yelped and blindly crawled down that side passage, wheezing and wiping at his eyes, not realising he was headed into a dead end. There would be no escape for him, so Briar first targeted the reiver closer to freedom.

She stalked the man with the broken face, his jaw black and swollen. He heard her closing in and forced his stinging eyes open as he raised a short spear and readied to thrust it into her. "Come onsh, yoush scwhore," he mumbled. "Lesh dwo thish."

"Coming as fast as I can," she complained. "You seem strangely eager to die."

He had better reach, and it allowed him to strike first. Notched bronze plunged towards her chest, but his aim was terrible, thanks to his watery eyes. She leant to one side, and it passed by her, allowing her to push forward before he could draw it back for another thrust. The reinforced centre of her buckler rammed into his face. His head snapped back, exposing his throat to a precise, oft-practised cut. Briar backed away before the blood started spurting. He stared at her for a disbelieving moment before the air and blood pushed its way out of the new red hole she'd given him. He collapsed, hands clamped to his throat, gurgling and groaning and drowning in his own blood as it bubbled between his fingers. She sheathed her sword, grabbed his spear and left the man to his demise. She made her way down to the servants' quarters, where Ruith was only now realising that his throat and eyes were not melting from some wicked concoction.

He squinted up as she rounded the corner and came towards him. His eyes were bright blue and weeping, but he had his sword and shield at the ready. His back straightened, and his legs spread out into a low fighting stance.

Briar didn't give him any opportunity to talk. She wasn't remotely interested in last words or pointless boasts. She flung the spear with all her might. It pierced through his shirt of bronze scales just below the heart. Blood gushed from his mouth as he looked down.

"Oh," he said, and toppled backwards.

She removed the cloth protecting her face and wiped a little powder from her eyes and forehead as she stood over Ruith, looking down on his ruin and shaking her head sadly. The man blinked up at her in confusion. "Hardgrim was irredeemable scum," she said, "but it was your fault for slavishly following an honourless rat of a man without any shred of morals. Still, even I did not realise how far he had fallen, so I will give you that to take with you on your journey into the otherworld to face the scorn of your ancestors." She put all her weight onto the spear. He jerked as it plunged deeper into his chest. She twisted the haft of the weapon for good measure. He shuddered once and stopped moving as all life fled his vivid blue eyes. Blood began pooling around her feet, hot, dark and sticky.

She spat on his face and wrenched the spear free, inspecting its head. The notched bronze point was folded over from hitting bone. She immediately discarded it, relying on the sharp edge of her own sword to carry her through the coming conflict. She asked herself how many were now left. Eight, at a guess she could only hope was correct. She had wounded three more, though how badly she couldn't tell. One certainly wouldn't be walking again any time soon.

Another oath-sworn traitor slain, she mused. Righteous wrath warred with the grief of their betrayal, and the chagrin that she hadn't seen it coming. She'd had her own problems, but that was no excuse for such blindness and dereliction of duty.

Before she reached the main hallway, the sound of footsteps caused her to flatten herself against the wall of the servants' quarters.

"The shit is this blue stuff everywhere?" a man said in the stairwell. He didn't have the harsh accent of the reivers, but he didn't sound like any Shield she knew. A hint of the Ves on his tongue, perhaps. He paused, likely studying the corpses and the red and blue powder everywhere.

Briar backed into the nearest doorway, ignoring the buzzing, fat flies and the sickly stench of blood. She peered through a crack in the door and listened as the newcomer scuffed his feet and gasped. A few moments passed before he resumed walking, his careful footfalls picking past the gory mess. She quietly eased her sword from its sheath as he approached the intersection of the hallways. The weapon was lifted, ready for her to burst out into the hallway and strike him down the moment she sighted him. The man must have been thoroughly confused as to why he'd found three men dead and the place stained red and blue like an angry bull had been let loose in a dyer's workshop.

The reiver who had tried to escape the palace was still stubbornly gurgling away, somehow clinging to his odious little life. The newcomer made straight for him through the shadows, passing into the intersection. He turned and squinted into the gloom, looking right past Briar for a moment. He noticed no looming threat and turned back to the dying man, his back exposed.

Briar froze as she noted braided hair, a shaved chin, that crooked smile and the fine bow in his hand. That moment of indecision let the man pass through to approach the gurgling reiver beyond her hiding place. Her forehead beaded with cold sweat. Her stomach lurched and her heartbeat thudded fast and heavy. Her wounded leg trembled with remembered pain.

It was the assassin.

The archer from the summer solstice.

Here.

Now.

CHAPTER 27

A septic pus of disgust and anger welled up from the wound in Briar's soul at the sight of the assassin who had buried a poisoned arrow in her leg and changed her life forever. An unexpected taint of fear seeped out to join that heady mix of emotion. It wasn't that she was afraid of the man himself; it was entirely due to the memories of sickness and panic and pain his face evoked. She had almost died by his poison, and at the time, she'd wished she had. Briar knew she should have immediately charged the loathsome creature and cut him to pieces before he could defend himself, but instead the shock of his appearance and the surge of emotion had stayed her shaking hand.

She swallowed, shook her head and silently snarled. She was Briar, the last Shield standing between Alaric and harm, and she would end this accursed creature's life. She emerged from her hiding place and limped back into the main hallway, slow and steady. She turned to face the assassin, full of purpose and dire portent.

The archer spun at the sound of armour clinking, and his eyes widened at the sight of her: a battered figure leaving bloody footprints down the hallway. In the sudden silence, they could both hear the drip of traitor's blood from the tip of her sword, keeping time with her laboured steps. Ahhh, she thought, as the man took a step back and swallowed. He fears me as much as I do his poison. Hardgrim's death had been far quicker than the traitor deserved, and Briar realised she might also have hesitated because she needed to see this man suffer instead of taking his head there and then.

"Praise the ancestors," Briar rasped. "They have delivered the wretched creature I was so yearning to meet right into my hands." She flashed a reaper's grin at the startled killer. "Come, assassin, let me return the gift you gave me on the summer solstice."

The archer replied with that crooked smile that had plagued her fever-ridden nightmares for so long, though this time it oozed uncertainty. He bowed mockingly. "Maddox, at your service." He frowned at her battered and bloodied armour and made a show of scratching his chin with the upper limb of his bow. "And who are you meant to be?" he asked. "Am I supposed to remember every dirty little guard living in this shithole of a palace?"

Briar levelled her sword at him, tired hands trembling with barely repressed fury. She ground her teeth but didn't rise to the bait – only an idiot wouldn't know who she was after she'd butchered so many of their men.

"Don't take me for a fool," she replied. "You failed to kill me once. This time I will beat you to a bloody paste."

The archer sighed. "No, perhaps not a fool," he admitted. He shifted his stance, readied his bow and nocked an arrow to the gut string. The bronze tip of it glistened with poison, the sight of which made Briar's heart strain against her ribs and a cold sweat slick her back and armpits, but she crushed the urge to turn and run. A Shield did not flee.

"Anybody who can survive red-scale viper venom has my utmost respect," Maddox added. "I don't suppose you'd care to let me go? I could make it worth your while: I am, as it happens, fairly wealthy. Bronze bars? Silver rings or amber beads? A gold arm ring or a herd of cattle? Name your price, and it will be done."

She snorted in disbelief. "You murder and maim so many and think you can simply buy your way out of this? You and your pack of vermin crept into our home at night and slaughtered our people in their beds. Their lives cannot be bought, and your blood debt can only be repaid in kind."

He blinked in surprise, and that crooked smirk crept back onto his face. "No need to get all emotional about it, woman. We are both practical, hardworking people just doing our jobs. Surely we can come to another sort of bargain? There must be something I can offer that could persuade you to look the other way while I escape this accursed place. A man you want murdered? Or, I could have–"

Briar had heard more than enough of his prattle. She was so enraged that she didn't even notice her bad leg as she broke into a sprint, buckler up to protect her chest. Every bit of her lusted to return two seasons of pain and indignity to him threefold, but she had survived when many had not, and this fight was also for them. She would fight instead of the slain and would hack him open, snap his bones and dance in his fountaining blood. It was the only way to slake the dead's thirst for vengeance, a dark lust that matched her own.

Maddox's annoying smirk crumbled like an old wall in a gale. His eyes were dead, the soul behind them as hollow as his heart. The assassin drew his bowstring back and loosed his arrow in a single smooth movement, aiming for her face.

She jerked to one side and felt the wind of it passing her cheek, even as he hastily drew and loosed the next at her belly with all the speed and accuracy granted by decades of practice. He'd expected her to instinctively lift her shield to protect her face, losing sight of the next arrow's target. She was wise to that tactic, and her buckler was already in position to block the second shot. She batted the arrow aside with a shuddering screech of bronze.

He backed away and reached for another arrow as she charged like an enraged bull, the distance between them swiftly disappearing. The pain in her leg fuelled her fury. Both of them knew he wouldn't get another chance. He bent the bow and loosed his last arrow.

She spun, shield rising to deflect it into the wall, grimacing and lurching sideways as her leg almost buckled under the strain. The arrow clattered down at her feet, and she noted the milky sheen of poison on its bent bronze tip. The assassin tossed his fine bow at her face, turned and ran for the gatehouse, intending to escape into the courtyard. He laughed, harsh and mocking. "Good luck catching me with that bad leg," he yelled. "I promise you I will return to put a shaft in your back when you least expect it."

Briar dropped her sword and buckler. She swept up his bow and arrow, putting shaft to string and bending it back as her eye settled on his exposed back. She preferred the down-and-dirty close combat of sword and buckler, or the thrust and spinning strikes of the spear, but that didn't mean she hadn't spent stones beyond count practicing archery. A good warrior used every weapon at their disposal.

She exhaled and loosed. The shaft wobbled in the air, its bent tip and her tired arms throwing off her aim. Her stomach lurched as the arrow dipped from the centre of his back towards the floor right between his legs. Cloth ripped, but it missed its mark by a whisker and deflected off the stone wall. Maddox sped out into open space and daylight and disappeared from her sight.

Briar snarled, dropped the bow and snatched up her sword and shield again before giving lumbering chase. Rage gifted her strength enough to ignore the pain of her wounds – the bastard that had crippled her life was there, within reach, and she'd be damned to the deepest, darkest pit of the otherworld before she let him escape! She gritted her teeth and sped up, bursting from the gatehouse to see the assassin just standing there in the courtyard, staring right back at her with wide, disbelieving eyes. She slowed to a careful yet relentless advance, suspecting some manner of trickery.

He pointed to the small tear in his clothing, and the glistening beads of blood oozing from a shallow wound on his leg. He tossed his head back and laughed, but only for a moment before he stumbled, clutching at the wound and hissing in pain. "Stinking red-scale viper venom," he snarled. "It was a complete pain to milk those accursed snakes, and this is what I get: grazed by my own poisoned arrow." He looked her in the eye, and all his fatalistic mirth vanished like mist on a sunny morning. "This was nothing personal, Briar, but now I will cut your throat and drag your stinking soul down to the otherworld with me." He pulled twin daggers from his belt and waited for her attack.

Instead, she stopped and waited, watching him carefully. "Nothing personal?" she said, shaking her head. "You honestly believe that I wouldn't take it personally after spending a whole season in my sickbed thanks to your poisoned arrow? I will have to deal with this wounded leg for the rest of my life, and you will pay for that with your joyless life. You are a deluded piece of shit I will scrape off my shoe."

"Come at me, then, you ugly old bitch," he spat. "I know you want to."

"Of course I do," she replied, smiling at the new beads of sweat oozing from his brow. "But first I want to see you suffer from your own wicked poison. I remember that agony only too well, and now it's your turn to burn up from the inside."

His breathing came fast and shallow. His face was already flushed, and slick with sweat that started to drip from the tip of his nose. He cursed and ran at her, twin blades weaving and slashing for her throat. Despite the poison, he was fast and precise, but he wasn't used to a fair fight. Especially not one against an experienced armoured warrior wielding a sword and buckler.

Briar blocked his leading fist with her buckler and parried the other knife with her sword, pushing his strike out wide. She shoved inside his guard, getting all close and personal, and rammed her forehead into his nose. It crunched sideways, and he reeled back, blood gushing down his chin.

The assassin was a canny one, jerking back out of reach before she could finish him off. The blades in his hands flashed in a defensive blur of sharp bronze, momentarily warding her off.

She snarled and redoubled her assault. They traded blows for a few more heartbeats before her shield slammed into his hand. Small bones snapped, and the knife went flying from his grasp. Her sword hacked at his other wrist, but he managed to jerk back out of reach, chest heaving for breath as he fought the growing inevitability of his approaching doom.

He used his arm to scrub stinging sweat from his eyes, then howled something indecipherable and flung himself directly at her without a care for defence. If he'd been in his right mind, he would have used his mobility to dance rings around her, darting and lunging until his shorter blade found a home in her flesh. The pain of his own poison was driving him mad. He seemed uncaring if she ran him through, so long as his knife shed her blood – as if she would allow him to be that lucky!

She sidestepped and brought her sword down on his hand. Three fingers flew into the air as she turned and broke his face with the central boss of her buckler. He collapsed on to his back, dazed and drenched in blood and sweat.

"Stay," she ordered as she brought her boot down on his right knee, then his left. The crunch under her heel and his screams were the very songs of the gods to her ears. "You won't be getting away this time."

She whistled jauntily as she rummaged through his half-empty quiver, pulling out two more arrows with tips coated in milky poison. She stepped on his arms to restrain him. "I return your gift threefold," she said, pushing the points into the palms of his hands. Then she hammered the points through and into the earth, pinning him in place. He howled and writhed, eyes bulging and gasping for breath as poison pain flooded through his extremities. She could have stayed and spent the time to skin him alive, peeling him like a ripe fruit. She wanted to, but she had a sorcerer to slaughter and a regent to save, and this callous bastard wasn't worth wasting any more time over. She could have cut his throat or plunged the arrows into vital organs to make a quicker end of it, but she wasn't exactly known for her mercy – this way it would take a long and agonising time for the poison to finally end his life. It was a compromise she could accept.

She stamped on his belly for good measure. Steaming vomit streaked with blood erupted from his mouth, and he wheezed for breath through the froth. "Much as I would love to stay and watch your own poison eat away your flesh," she said, "I have more important places to be. You are a nothing. You die with no great deeds to your name, unmourned, unloved and unremembered. Your corpse will be dumped into a midden with the other refuse."

She turned away.

"Your stinking regent is already dead," he gasped. "Imperatrix gutted him like a fish and cut out his heart." The ghost of a sneer appeared on his face, but it twisted into a snarl of agony before he could laugh.

She ignored his lie – it had to be a lie – and limped back into the palace, leaving the assassin's own poison to burn through his veins. His tortured howls were exquisite music to her ears, more viscerally satisfying than the otherworldly tunes of the Sleaghan Mhath. She hoped dreams of his torment would replace her fevered nightmares of an arrow in her leg and druids' knives scraping red and rotting flesh from the wound. Many good people said that to rise above revenge was a noble thing, but forgiveness had its limits, and Briar felt it best to cut grotesque tumours such as him out of the world whenever possible. It would be a far better place without that vile man in it. Far better to end him and then try to forget he ever lived. She shoved the assassin's entire twisted existence to the back of her mind and focused on the only thing that mattered: saving Alaric.

She took a deep breath and then began her final descent into the depths of the earth.

CHAPTER 28

Briar's slow progress down the stairs afforded her the unwelcome gift of time to think. She couldn't shake the assassin's last words, and they rampaged through her mind leaving a burning trail of fear and regret in their wake.

"Lies! Nothing but the lies of a desperate and defeated man," she muttered to herself between laboured breaths, as if the act of speaking and hearing a rebuttal might make it true. The viper had been beaten and broken by her own two hands, and his barbed tongue had been the only way left for him to hurt her. She knew his self-involved sort only too well, having dealt with politicians for many years; of course the scum had spat one last parting shot at her, knowing he had failed and was dying by his own terrible poison.

Alaric was alive and waiting for her to save his life, as she had done many times before. He had to be. He was almost within reach, but the fear hastened her steps.

Impatience almost ruined everything.

She took the steps too quickly, and her weakened leg spasmed as she put too much weight on it. The knee partially gave way. If she hadn't had the foresight to wear a wooden brace on it, she would have pitched head-first down the worn stone steps. Instead, she flailed for the wall and managed to slap a hand to the stonework. Fingernails dug into cracks: they tore free, but she managed to transform a deadly plunge into an ungainly tumble into the wall. Her shoulder slammed into the stone hard enough to bruise but not break.

She clung to the reassuring solidity of the wall, her breath harsh and rasping. Blood oozed down her hand from the jagged shards of her nails, each rapid heartbeat a hot spike of pain spurting from her fingertips crying out that she was still alive.

Briar groaned and used the steps and wall to push herself upright. She tested the leg and felt it might hold up if she was careful to keep most of her weight off it. She didn't linger, but kept moving while she still could, taking one small step at a time. Sweat slicked her trembling body by the time she made it to the bottom, and despite the urgency, she was forced to rest and recover for a short time, or risk being of no use in a fight. She leant her back on the wall, chest heaving, as she spent precious moments mopping her brow and trying to regain her breath.

In the chamber at the bottom of the stairs, a single lantern flickered and flared, burning the last dregs of fat in its reservoir. The door leading down to the Wyrm Vault had been left open by the assassin, inviting her onwards to victory or death. Either way, there would be an end to this sad and sordid story. The gods and ancestors knew she'd tried her best. What more could any woman give, other than her life? She'd give that too if needs be, albeit grudgingly.

She was almost done.

Her body was a ruin. Every muscle ached.

Bone-tired and bleeding.

How many more traitors did she have to kill? Three? Four? More? She wasn't sure how many were left, or if she could overcome them in her current state.

A twinge of pain caused her to shift, and the sword and buckler at her hip clicked in complaint. She drew the blade and studied the golden metal by the flickering light. She was the sword and shield that protected Sunweald. Her pain mattered not at all. It was far better to be the candle standing against the storm, burning bright for one glorious moment before being snuffed out, than to never try at all. She would not succumb to the sucking swamp of despair.

She was a warrior, and battle was in her blood.

The golden brooch of the Commander of Shields pressed cold and hard against her chest, where it hung from a leather cord beneath her tunic. She fished it out and held it tight in her bleeding hands. The weight of centuries of determined duty and history gave her its blessing of courage. She kissed the brooch for good luck and let it hang outside her armour for all to see. For all to fear.

She took a deep, shuddering breath and then let it out slowly. "I'm coming, my love." The sword and shield were in her hands and thirsting for the fight. If the gods were unkind and Alaric was dead, she vowed to wreak bloody vengeance before her soul followed him into the otherworld, dragging his killers down with her.

Briar advanced into the darkness, dragging her bad leg across the slick stone, splashing through unseen puddles and crunching over gravel. The scales of her armour clinked, and leather straps creaked. Her breath rasped loudly in and out, and she couldn't quite hold in every groan of pain. She channelled all her fear and pain into a simmering rage that strengthened her resolve. She was looking forward to getting her hands on those surviving oath-broken Shields, and then it would be the turn of that worm-hearted sorcerer they served.

Her assault was not going to be stealthy, but it would be exceedingly brutal.

Iden gingerly approached the Heart, doing his best to ignore the armed corpses standing in orderly ranks as he passed between them. Most of them were old, anonymous bones held together by the darkest of magic, but the rotting forms of Sleen, Barik and Cathbad were just recognisable as the warriors they had been. Worse still, Shields Etain and Keir had been guarding the place when they'd been slain, and he'd known them well enough to call them friends. Their slack grey faces, drooping lips and dull, staring eyes made his stomach churn with bilious regret. But they could not have been bought or swayed to join Hardgrim's plot.

Iden's betrayal in exchange for a lifetime of riches and all his debts paid off was not a bad deal, but that wasn't why he'd joined their side. Hardgrim had uncovered enough tales of Iden's misspent youth to forever tarnish his reputation, as well as the truth about the murder of a clan chief's eldest son. It had begun as a drunken fistfight around the campfire, a squabble about some harm done to a woman whose name Iden couldn't even remember now. A moment of fury and, before he knew it, his knife was in the other boy's chest. One act of madness and his life was forever ruined. And somehow Hardgrim knew all about it: a few words in the right ears and his commander could have him outcast from Sunweald, with an entire outraged clan hunting for Iden's head. Hardgrim had promised that all prior transgressions would be forever forgotten if Iden saw this through. He had wrestled with the decision – still did – but what was done could not be undone. He had to put himself first.

He kept his eyes down and brushed through the ranks of walking dead set to guard the tunnel outside the thick bronze door, currently open to let out the stench of blood and vomit wafting from the cavern. "Aisli... Ah, sorry. Imperatrix, your reivers are getting out of control. I know you already sent Maddox up there as reinforcement, but the brigands claim their leader has fled the..." He spotted Uradech's corpse, discarded on the floor. "Oh. That explains why they have not seen him lately. Ruith is–"

"Ruith and Maddox are already dead, or close to it," the sorcerer stated. She didn't bother looking up from her work on the wall as she finished the last of a spiralling circle of angular glyphs in human blood. "I felt their souls fade a short time ago, and the heat of Briar's rage burns like I stand too close to a bone fire. Sadly, I seem to have surrounded myself with incompetent men. I must fix that flaw in my judgement once I have what I came here for."

The bloody mess of Sunweald's regent lay slumped on the floor, unconscious but still breathing. For now. Phelan and Owyn stood over him, though they no longer needed to restrain him. They glanced at each other, then cast a worrying look at Iden. Owyn offered a terse shake of his head as the younger man opened his mouth to question the sorcerer further. His jaw shut with a click of teeth.

Imperatrix sighed and stretched, her shoulders and elbows cracking. The woman stepped back and cast her gaze over two stones' worth of intricate, meticulous effort at the back wall. She nodded in appreciation before slapping a palm to her arcane working, grunting with the effort of pushing her magic deep into the rock. A slow ripple of stone emanated from her palm, washing across the room at glacial pace. Here and there, it hit areas she had already worked her magic on, and new ripples burst outwards from those points of sorcerous importance to form an ever-shifting pattern of arcane confluence.

The sorcerer gritted her teeth and snarled, wrenching open the penultimate seal. She stepped back as the glyphs written in Summerson blood blackened and burst into flame. Stone ground and clunked all around as something in the walls shifted in its slumber. Dust drifted down from the ceiling as the rumbling intensified into a thrumming vibration that set armour rattling and teeth chattering. A smell like burnt bread spread across the cavern, followed by a sickly taste of honey clumping at the back of Imperatrix's throat.

Iden's nose twitched, and he spat to one side to cleanse the cloying taste from his mouth. The attempt proved futile, but at least it warded off the mouldering stench of old bones and decaying meat he'd had to pass through to get here.

An ear-splitting screech erupted from the wall, as if a hundred inhuman voices shouted their torment to the world beyond the Vault, abruptly silenced as arcane energies snapped and crackled back into place across the back wall.

"What was that vile din?" Iden asked.

"I don't much care," Imperatrix said. "One last seal to go, and all those potent treasures will be ours. Then we will be gone from this wretched place." She gasped and doubled over, clutching at her chest as her heart began to race. None of her guards moved to aid her. Eventually she straightened and spun to face Phelan and Owyn, her face sheened with sweat. "You two, get out there and take command of my army of corpses. Iden will stay here to look after this... creature." She waved in the regent's general direction as she took deep, calming breaths.

Owyn cleared his throat. "Can those dead things even fight? How do we... uh... command them? Won't they resent our control and resist? I don't want to end up cursed by angry spirits."

She smiled, a mirthless crack in her blood-spattered face. "Oh, these things are little more than puppets. It would take much more power than I can spare to breach the veil to the otherworld and rip out unwilling human souls. These corpses are inhabited by minor fae spirits that owe me service. They are stupid but obedient beings when fed on a little blood and magic. The human bones that temporarily house them still remember some of what they were and how they acted in life, and while their martial skill will be a shade half glimpsed through the fog of death, it should prove enough. Once, these bodies were accustomed to obeying their commander, and in the skeletons of their minds you now inhabit that role. They will obey you well enough, I think, while I break the last seal protecting the Vault."

Phelan's hand wrapped around the hilt of his sword. "I mislike that word, 'think'," he said. "What I seek from you are sureties."

Imperatrix narrowed her eyes, and the shadows deepened around her. "In life, only death is certain. Just do your fucking job, and we will soon be driving off a cartload of arcane artefacts on the way to fame and fortune."

Phelan's jaw muscles clenched and a vein pulsed in his forehead, but he held his tongue and marched out into the hallway. Owyn shot Iden a commiserating look and then followed after.

"Just you and I, then," Imperatrix said to Iden. "How wonderful. If you value your life, keep your mouth shut and let me work." She crouched next to the prone regent and dipped a bone needle into one of his many small wounds, breaking the scab and coating the tip in fresh blood. The regent gasped and stirred, turning his head. "Be a good boy and keep an eye on him until my well has run dry."

Iden nodded, grateful that she ignored him and got on with her sorcery instead of trying to fill the silence with small talk. Alaric's bloodshot eyes stared up at him accusingly until his former guardian swallowed and looked away, shamefaced.

He heard the clink and scrape of metal from outside. "Somebody is coming," Owyn shouted from outside.

Iden shivered and made sure his own sword and buckler were ready.

Briar was here to kill them all.

CHAPTER 29

Briar shuddered in the darkness as an ear-piercing screech echoed up through the ancient tunnels. She was certain it boded more ill for her, but whatever dark sorcery awaited her, she was not about to turn tail and run.

It felt like an age trudging through the darkness before she picked up the first hint of the enemy: the scuffling of walking corpses and the muffled curses of living men waiting in ambush. As the curving tunnel began to straighten, she could make out the flickering orange-and-yellow glow of several lanterns. She took a deep breath, wiped the sweat off her palms, took a firm grip on her weapons and stepped into the light to bring battle.

Two skeletons of long-dead Shields guarded the path ahead, their old bones clothed in cobwebs and caked dirt. Corroded green swords rattled loosely in their grips, the wooden hilts long since rotted away. Their skulls snapped to face her, and yellow teeth chattered in mockery of human speech. She paused her advance and grimly waited for the things to come to her, lips twisted in disgust at this desecration of such honoured dead.

The dead things attacked faster than she'd imagined, creaking and clattering, teeth chattering and swords swinging.

Briar marshalled her courage and moved to meet them. She blocked a slash with her buckler, faintly surprised at the feebleness of the blow that bounced off it. Her return attack severed the arm like a dry twig and then caved the thing's skull in on the backstroke. The abomination fell, arms still flailing, and her boot crushed its ribcage to dust.

The second skeleton launched a series of cuts in a classic pattern once trained into Shields who were old when she was young. They were the most basic of moves and full of openings, thanks to the decrepit sword wielded in its bony grip. She casually warded off the blows with sword and buckler, studying her foe. Her fear drained away as it rained weak and wobbly attacks upon her.

No, as it turned out, she wasn't afraid of these atrocities one bit. In the cramped confines of the secret tunnels, they had been terrifying, but now all she felt was pity. Out in the open, where she could fight back, the things were just brittle bone and shreds of sinew animated by a sorcerer's malice. She battered the skeleton's sword aside and smashed its head in with the reinforced boss of her buckler. It possessed the ghost of a Shield's skill but lacked the weight, the power and the ability to properly hold its weapon.

She growled as she limped past the debris of her ancient brethren and brought the door to the Heart into sight – and, blessed be the gods, it was open!

Two familiar faces were there, waiting for her, ready but not keen for a fight. "Owyn," she said. "Phelan. Leave this place while you still can." She felt a wave of relief that no more living warriors stood with them – two she reckoned she could manage. She had to.

The oath-broken Shields shot sickened looks at each other at the sight of their old commander advancing on them with a face like thunder, but they swallowed their fears and raised their weapons. "We have come too far to do as you ask," Owyn stated.

She hocked a glob of spit at them. "Then here you die."

They were armoured up and surrounded by the walking dead, and seemed to take some reassurance from their advantage in numbers. "Look at the sorry state of you," Phelan said. "You have walked to your own death at our hands, old woman."

She snorted in derision as she closed in on them. "My vengeance will not be thwarted by the likes of you limp-dicked little whelps. Imagine consorting with dark spirits and dragging the honoured dead up from their tombs. You disgust me, and your ancestors must be ashamed you share their blood."

"Shields up!" Owyn screamed. "Hurry up and kill her."

The ranks of honoured dead turned to face her and formed a battle line blocking the entire tunnel. They lifted their shield arms as one, some with remnants of bronze discs still strapped to them, but most without. Briar's eyes narrowed at the sight of the newer corpses at the back of their ranks, taking a defensive posture: Barik, Sleen and Cathbad were eyeless, wet and mouldering. Etain and Keir were freshly slain but milky-eyed and waxy-skinned. Her people had been so cruelly defiled.

The walking corpses advanced on her. Fortunately, the tunnel was too narrow for them to swarm her. She went on the attack, cutting through the first lot like she was cutting reeds at the riverbank. The skeletons crumbled before her sword and shield. Shards of bone pattered off her armour as she battered her way through them, inexorable and relentless and really shitting angry.

Weak as the skeletons were, even after so many years their corroded bronze swords and daggers were still sharp. She advanced carefully, destroying the foul things one by one with meticulous precision. Her foes were clumsy, and she could see her victory was dawning in the eyes of her living former brethren as well.

"Charge," Owyn screamed. "Kill her!" The grotesque mass of dead flung themselves forward, the sheer number of their attacks driving Briar back.

A heavy blow thumped into her buckler, hard enough to bruise the hand behind it. It was Etain's fresh corpse, with more muscle behind her blow than any feeble skeleton could muster.

"Ah, my loyal Etain," Briar said sadly, shoving the corpse back with her shield to tumble into the mass of magically animated bones behind it. The other corpses instantly covered the gap in their battle line like they remembered the Shields they had once been. Had they been entirely mindless things, it would have been simple to destroy them all.

She blinked. Could it be possible? Could the bodies of the dead recall a little of what they once were in life?

A stain of horror flowed across her emotions. But, if so, there was a slim chance she might be able to use that.

Briar stepped back and jutted her chest out, so the brooch of Commander of Shields showed proud for all to see. "Loyal Shields," she cried, "I am Briar, the eighty-eighth Commander of the Shields of Sunweald. Throw off your sorcerous bonds, rally to me and fight off these invaders in the palace."

The battle paused, and the air crackled with a sudden tension she felt deep in her belly. A strain in her bones and blood. The weight of their regard lay heavy upon her breast. The brooch of Commander was centuries old but contained no magic at all other than the mountain of duty and honour it represented. The dead shuddered and rattled where they stood, as if the dark magic forcing them into a mockery of life warred against the remaining fragments of a sacred oath and a duty that had been battered into their bodies over a lifetime of service to their realm and its people. The air reeked of burning hair and spilt blood. Briar's head pounded with mounting pressure, and her chest constricted like it was seized in a giant fist. She couldn't move. Couldn't breathe.

Some unseen web of power snapped, and the crushing pressure vanished from her body. She gratefully sucked in fresh air. The dead shook off their confusion and clattered back into motion. Before she could recover, two slimy, browned skeletons flung themselves right back at her, swords swinging.

She managed to block a cut with her buckler and fend off another with her sword, but the attacks forced her off to one side, too close to the wall to fight effectively. She stepped back for a better position, and her heel came down on a human thigh bone. It rolled beneath her, and her left leg strained under the sudden weight. Her arms flailed in an attempt to regain her balance, breaking her guard and leaving her front wide open to attack.

And attack they did. One sword scored a line across her scale shirt, but the other swung for her throat. Before she could react and try to counter, a fist crashed through the slimy skull and put it down for good.

She looked up into the milk-filmed, dull eyes of Etain and saw no emotion or recognition in the woman's face. Her soul was gone to the otherworld, but her duty remained behind in her body. The crash of battle echoed down the tunnel as the more recently deceased turned their weapons upon the long-dead still under sorcerous compulsion. The shrunken, eyeless forms of Barik and Sleen traded blows with a knot of skeletal foes dead long before they had been born.

Briar recovered herself and locked gazes with the oath-broken Shields at the back. She grinned and began her assault anew, the corpses of Etain, Keir and Cathbad marching ahead of the woman they recognised as their commander even in death. She hoped their souls were watching and cheering from the otherworld as their mortal remains smashed their way towards the wretched traitors hiding behind the bones of men and women better than themselves.

Barik and Sleen fell beneath the volume of attacks, hacked to pieces. Briar and her dead friends advanced into the horde, weapons lashing out with deadly precision. Bones snapped and crumbled with every step forward, but Cathbad faltered and fell to a lucky sword strike to the neck. Etain and Keir closed ranks and marched relentlessly on, blocking numerous blows with their bucklers. They were freshly slain and far stronger, with all that meat and muscle still on their bones. Their flesh was being shredded, but having no need for blood, they easily weathered the storm, and their every blow sent one of the long-dead back into the grave.

Owyn and Phelan saw the battle turning. If they kept back and did nothing, they would be facing Briar's fury with both of her dead Shields at her side. Instead, they waited until there were only a handful of their weaker skeletal forces left before they joined the battle.

The traitors were full of the fires of life, making them swifter and stronger than any dead thing. The fight against the remains of Etain and Keir was brutal and brief. They hacked the dead Shields down, at the cost of more skeletons crushed.

Phelan's sword was stuck in Keir's corpse, and he had to wrench the blade free of his torso. That moment of distraction was all Briar needed to stab him in the side. He squealed and lurched back, shocked by the blood gushing from a rent in his armour, where two scales had been torn loose in the fracas.

Briar drew her bloodied sword back for another thrust. "Stuck like the pig you are." She beheaded another skeleton and finished the last of the reanimated dead by slamming it against the wall hard enough to shatter its breastbone and ribs.

Phelan staggered back towards the Heart, trying to stem the hot flow of blood drenching his legs and pooling in his boots.

"Just you and me now, Owyn," Briar said. "I don't think you are up to the challenge, you sad little man."

He swallowed, then glanced down at her maimed leg and seemed to gather courage from the sight of it wrapped in sacking bandages and wooden braces. "I'll take a shit in your mouth when you are dead," he snarled.

She snorted in derision and limped forward, her sword probing his defences. He blocked with his buckler and replied in kind. They traded feints and cautious cuts for a few moments before he seized on the idea of exploiting her weakness. He attacked with more ferocity, cutting at her leg, forcing her to move it or lose it. After the third concerted attack on it, she lurched sideways, the knee buckling.

He lunged at her, intent on finishing her off.

Briar grimaced as he took the bait, the effort of regaining her balance aggravating her wounds. She spun, her sword cutting at his overextended, exposed arm. Bronze bit to the bone, half severing the limb. He didn't seem to realise he was already a dead man, roaring and attacking with shield instead of sword. Bronze clanged, and they fell to the floor, a tangled mass of arms, legs and weaponry. Fresh blood gushed over them both.

Owyn tried for a headbutt, missed and bruised her collarbone instead. His elbow cracked into her mouth, splitting her upper lip.

Her sword slid up between the bronze scales of his armour and stabbed deep into his side. He rolled them both, and she lost hold of her weapon, punching him in the face instead. His struggles weakened as the blood loss took its tool. Face to face, she glimpsed the realisation of his doom birthing panic. He shoved her aside with the last surge of strength granted him by terror. He tried to rise, collapsed back onto one knee and clumsily yanked her sword from his side. More blood flowed, and he turned his confused, angry eyes on her.

She drove her shield into his face, pulping his nose and lips and sending him sprawling on his back in a growing pool of blood.

Briar retrieved her sword and leant on the dying man's chest to help her regain her feet. She immediately wobbled and flailed for balance. Some of the wooden rods bracing her knee had been broken in the melee. She gritted her teeth and limped onwards.

"Close the damned door!" a woman screeched. It took Briar a moment to recognise the voice as Aisling's. The maid who had once looked after her in her sickbed now bore a hard and vicious tone that Briar could never have imagined.

The mechanism inside clanked free, and the massive bronze door groaned and began to swing closed. Briar hissed in pain as she sped up. She wasn't going to make it. Her entire plan had been based on getting in there quickly to rescue the regent.

But Phelan was still crawling through the doorway, leaving a slug trail of bright blood across the floor behind him – and he was in the way. He screamed as the heavy door slammed him against the wall. Bones snapped like twigs. The man shuddered and gurgled for breath that couldn't come, his face purpling as the weight of all that metal pinned him to the stone with crushing force.

The door was blocked from closing and locking. Briar flashed a bloody smile at the gap just wide enough for a person to pass through, and made for it as fast as she could manage.

"Shit!" Iden said from inside. Phelan's body jerked as Iden grabbed the dying man's hands and yanked, to no avail.

Briar squeezed through sideways, sword and good leg forward, using the dying bastard as a steppingstone. Had she been as fit and muscular as she was the year before, she would have struggled to get through, but her long illness had granted her a sole benefit: a slimmer frame more suited to this task.

She swung her sword and nearly took Iden's ear off. He yelped and backed away, clutching his weapons as Briar limped into cavern.

Iden and Aisling – Imperatrix – awaited her inside, along with Alaric, who now exposed the assassin as a miserable little liar by still being very much alive.

CHAPTER 30

At the sight of Alaric alive and breathing and curled up on the floor, Briar's heart offered joyous thanks to the gods, even as it broke at the sorry state of the man she loved. Her mind and soul and blood and bones kindled a raging inferno inside her at the tortured mess they had made of him.

Imperatrix was a sallow, haggard figure spattered with blood and filth. Her hair was a greasy, tangled mess stained red with clotting blood, and her eyes swivelled, mad as a goat. She hissed at the sight of Briar and pointed a gore-caked finger at her.

The Shield spared a glance to take in the rest of the scene. The stone wyrm bones were covered in arcane symbols and eerie spiralling and geometric designs daubed in blood. The air sparked with all the dark magic being used to break into the Vault, and the relics and leathery preserved remains of Sunweald's revered ancestors had been desecrated and tossed into a pile with the fresh corpses of several of the sorcerer's own brigands atop them. The woman was irredeemably insane and had to be disposed of like a diseased beast.

Alaric looked up at Briar's entrance, and his reddened eyes widened. His naked fear hit her like a punch to the gut. "Run," he mouthed. "Leave, and live." Then, when she made no move to flee, "Please!"

She didn't have time for such foolishness. Hard as it was, she ignored him and limped further into the cavern. "I've slaughtered all your men," she said to the sorcerer, trying to keep the woman's attention fixed on her and away from the regent.

Iden backed away towards Imperatrix, his sweat glistening in the lantern light.

"Surrender while you still can," Briar continued.

Iden shook his head. "We will–"

"Shut your mouth," Imperatrix snarled. "The adults are talking, and you have nothing of worth to contribute."

Iden's cheeks reddened, but he closed his mouth, as he was bidden.

"The Vault is almost open," Imperatrix added. "I will not leave without the treasures I came here for, and you are a fool to think I will give up when I am this close to achieving everything I have worked so hard for. You are a broken woman, Briar, and you cannot win against us."

"Us?" Briar said. "Hardgrim. Ruith. Phelan. Owyn. Newlyn. Nealon. Kendhal. Cardew. Apart from the filth standing beside you, every oath-broken Shield is dead, as are all your Wildwood Reivers, save a few who must have fled my wrath. As for your assassin, Maddox, I took enormous pleasure in stabbing him with his own poisoned arrows. He is screaming even now as it melts through his veins. There is no 'us' for you, Aisling."

"Imperatrix," the sorcerer snapped. "I have returned to my noble Hisparren roots. That Sunweald slave name was a false cloak I am glad to have cast off. I should have murdered you in your sickbed while I had the chance, instead of thinking you would succumb to your wounds."

Briar nodded. "That was your second mistake."

The woman's brow creased in confusion. "Second?"

Briar increased her speed as much as she could, her muscles burning. "The first was daring to target Sunweald under my watch."

"I dare much," Imperatrix said. She drew her knife, grabbed Alaric's hair in her other hand and yanked his head up to face Briar. Her knife was held at his throat, and beard bristles smoked where they met the angry, flickering edge of the deadly artefact. "I dare because it is I who holds all the power."

Briar stopped dead.

A sickening smile slid across twisted Imperatrix's face. "I would love to see your expression when I cut his throat in front of you. You will be forced to watch your beloved Lord Regent kick his last before pissing himself when he finally dies."

"If he dies, you die," Briar stated. Her grip tightened on her sword and buckler as she gathered her strength for one last desperate assault. Alaric mouthed, "Do it. Kill her," and then he closed his eyes, expecting to feel the knife go in.

Imperatrix snickered. "There is no way you can possibly win this. Was this the great Commander Briar's plan? To storm in here and demand my surrender? The knucklebones have been weighted, and the game will come up showing my victory every time."

The truth was that Briar hadn't possessed much of a plan beyond getting in here. There had been too many possibilities to account for until she could scout the lay of the land. "It seems we are at an impasse," Briar said.

"Not at all," Imperatrix replied. "If you take one step from that spot, I will kill him. Until you drop your weapons, I will slice parts of this pompous prick off." The edge of her blade seared a shallow, smoking trench in Alaric's neck. "How long can you afford to wait? What parts can he afford to lose?"

Briar had no choice. She dropped the sword and buckler to the stone. "May the gods curse you!" The clang of her weapons echoed weirdly in the chamber. Alaric sagged, his eyes welling up as all hope drained from him.

Iden exhaled with relief. "Put your hands together and hold them out," he ordered. He found a length of twisted rope and expertly bound her wrists. "On your knees," he demanded. When she declined to obey, he booted her bad knee.

Briar fell to the floor. She hissed in pain but did not give him the satisfaction of crying out.

Imperatrix looked down on her and nodded in satisfaction. "Hardgrim and Maddox were of less use than I imagined. Never send a man to do a woman's job." She drew the knife back from Alaric's throat and pointed it at the last loyal Shield in the palace. "For what it is worth, you have my admiration for overcoming all obstacles to reach this far despite your injured leg. You have made my work far more difficult than it should have been."

The sorcerer looked to Iden. "Kill her."

"Hold!" Alaric gasped. "I will open the last seal for you."

Imperatrix lifted a hand, and Iden stayed his sword.

"Don't do it," Briar cried. "Kester escaped, and he will be coming with the whole warband behind him."

Iden booted her in the leg again, hard enough to bring tears to her eyes. She shuddered and sucked in air through gritted teeth.

"Let her live, and I swear I will open it," Alaric said. "You have my oath as Lord Regent of Sunweald."

Imperatrix pursed her lips. "I can open this seal with my own power," she said. "Hmm. Time, it seems, may become an issue. Very well, open the last seal and you will save her life."

Iden stood behind Briar with his sword ready to swing for her neck at the first sign of trouble. Imperatrix stepped back and played with her knife while watching Alaric struggle to his feet.

He rose on shaking legs and shuffled over to the back wall, every breath laboured. He laid a hand on the forehead of the largest skull. Then he chuckled weakly. "All that toil and exhaustion," he said, "and all I had to do was ask it to open."

Briar watched, bound and seething, as the wyrm skeleton hissed steam and writhed in the clutches of its stone prison like it had returned to the land of the living. The sweltering air tasted of dry bone, hot bronze and burnt blood, scorching her nostrils and the back of her throat with every breath. Dark stone rippled and transformed into a black liquid that devoured all light. The wyrm skeleton shifted round to face the ragged form of Alaric. The enormous skull emerged from the wall, while its body sank right back into the wall and out of sight. It bowed before him, and its great jaw yawned wide. The eye sockets flared into verdant torches illuminating the narrow tunnel that led right down into the dark depths of its gullet. The stone solidified, once more appearing like normal rock.

As impressive as it was, Briar had seen this once before, and much of the shock washed over her. Iden stared, slack-jawed and utterly awestruck. Imperatrix looked, for want of better words, greedy as a pig at feeding time.

Imperatrix kept her knife at Alaric's throat as she eyed the nightmare doorway of needle-sharp stone teeth that had appeared before her. "You first," she ordered Briar. The sorcerer's gaze dipped to double-check that the rope binding the Shield's hands was still in place. "Make no sudden moves if you want your beloved regent to live, because it is most likely I no longer have any need to keep him intact."

Iden hauled Briar to her feet and shoved her forward.

She locked gazes with Alaric for a burning moment, and he mouthed "I love you" and "Run", but Briar ignored the overprotective fool and limped towards the skull. As if she would ever abandon him to save her own life: he was her life, standing right beside her duty to the realm and all its people. If there was any chance at all she could save his life along with securing Sunweald, she would take it. She pressed the edge of a finger to one of the dead wyrm's fangs, and at only the slightest pressure it beaded with blood. She very carefully ducked her head and reluctantly entered through the jaws, every muscle tense. She relaxed when nothing untoward happened to her, and turned back to face the sorcerer. "Well? Are you coming into the belly of this dread beast with me?"

Imperatrix's eye twitched. "Iden, hand her your lantern and let her be our vanguard." She clutched Alaric tightly, her knife stroking his throat as her last living minion did as he was told and gingerly handed his old commander the oil lantern, like he was feeding meat to a ravenous wild beast.

Briar awkwardly took it with her bound hands, holding it outstretched before her.

"Listen well, *Lord Regent*," the sorcerer added. "If there are any traps or hidden guardians you have neglected to mention, it will cost Briar her life."

Alaric resisted the urge to swallow lest the movement cut him open. "There is nothing now between you and the contents of the Wyrm Vault. I swear it upon the honour of my ancestors. However, as I told you, it will avail you nothing. I maintain that the artefacts were destroyed long ago, and this has been nothing but a murderous fool's mistake. Let us go, and flee while you still can."

Imperatrix snorted. "I did not believe you then, and I do not believe you now. Power awaits me, and you will not dissuade me here, on the knife-edge of victory. Off you go, Briar, slow and steady, and keep yourself in sight at all times."

Briar held aloft the smoky lantern and shuffled down the dark tunnel. Iden was at her back, using the tip of his sword to prod her onwards whenever her leg trembled on the verge of collapse. The metal scales of their armour clinked, disturbingly loud in the narrow passage. "You don't have to do this," Briar murmured, quietly enough that only the former Shield could hear. "Hardgrim is dead, and so is whatever hold he had over you. Loosen my bonds, and aid me cutting down the sorcerer. I'll help you escape to a new life somewhere. Hopefully a more righteous one." She didn't mean any of it, of course, but it was, she hoped, a tempting illusion of freedom.

Iden sighed, weighed down by regret. After a moment's further thought, he replied, "It's much too late for me. I wish..." He never finished his words, because at that moment the tunnel ended, and they walked into the depths of the Vault, shards of brittle bone crunching underfoot. Briar lifted her lantern high to illuminate the room.

The inner chamber of the Wyrm Vault was not something to take your breath away. Quite the opposite: there were no elaborately carved and painted stone panels; no bronze, gold or silver in sight; and no decoration of any kind. It was a modest domed chamber crudely carved out of the bedrock below the palace, little different in form to any of the ancient tombs and barrows found the length and breadth of Sunweald. Niches filled every available space on the walls, most of them packed with bones. Thousands of yellowed skulls leered down at them in the flickering lantern light, not all of them human. The largest were the horned wyrms of legend in a variety of sizes ranging from beasts the size of a cow to those larger than an entire horse and carriage; others resembled those of humans but boasted larger eye sockets and protruding cheekbones that had to belong to the Sleaghan Mhath who had stood with Alaric's harried ancestors in the darkest days of Sunweald legend.

Other than those dusty old bones, the mystically protected Vault of the Sunweald Palace was entirely empty. No treasures. No arcane artefacts. The only evidence they might have ever existed were a series of narrow stone shelves that lined one wall, the empty spaces too small to hold the skulls of the larger wyrms.

Imperatrix loosed a strangled choke at the sight of... nothing. "What... What is this?" she demanded, her gaze scouring the ossuary chamber for any trace of the mighty treasures she had spent so many years of planning, plotting and murdering to obtain. "Where are the shitting artefacts your bastard ancestors used to destroy Hisparren? Why can't I sense any trace of their magic? This is impossible."

The regent sagged in her grip, so weak he could barely stand, but he could still chuckle. "I told you there was nothing here for you. This place is just a tomb, kept safe in remembrance of the sacrifice of our ancestors."

Imperatrix's nostrils flared, and her eyes bulged madly. "Where are they?" she screeched. "They must be here!" She snarled and lifted a hand. Light flashed in her palm, and the air before her shimmered in heat haze. Sparks of glittering magic drifted down like snowflakes and melted just as quickly. "No magical protections or illusions," she rasped, disbelieving her own words. "No hidden mechanisms..."

Briar slipped back into the shadows, momentarily forgotten by Imperatrix and Iden as all their dreams of power and wealth crumbled down around their ears. They gawped at the rude absence of their entire reason for being there, and Iden ran to the empty shelves, his eyes searching for any trace of something left behind from an earlier age of mighty magics.

Briar readied herself to act. If there was going to be any opportunity to stop Imperatrix from slitting Alaric's throat, it would have to be soon. Alaric caught her movement from the corner of his eye and nodded his acknowledgement.

Imperatrix, in that moment of horrified astonishment, let the edge of her knife drift away from the regent's throat. In his ragged, debilitated state, Alaric posed as much threat to her as a child, so it was understandable she'd become a little sloppy. He seized that moment to strike, and sank his teeth into the wrist of her knife hand, preventing her using the weapon on him. She hissed, and punched him with her other hand, but he held on grimly.

Iden turned. Briar threw her lantern. His mouth gaped as it shattered over his face. Flames engulfed his head. He screamed and dropped his sword and buckler to paw at the burning fat that filled his ears, eyes, nose and mouth. His beard and hair went up like a bone fire as he flailed in agony.

Imperatrix pulled and punched to free herself from Alaric's bite, but he closed his eyes and devoted every fibre of his being to clenching his teeth tighter. He chewed, hot blood gushing down his chin. She reached for his eyes, her fingers clawed and black veins of sorcery spiderwebbing up her arms and neck.

Briar's hands might have been bound, but her entire body was a weapon. Rage gifted her strength enough to break into an ungainly charge, using the very last dregs of strength in her bad leg to tackle the sorcerer before the blackhearted bitch dared use her magic on him. Imperatrix was torn from the regent, leaving a chunk of her meat behind in his mouth. The knife fell from her spasming fingers and slid guard-deep into the solid stone floor, spitting and hissing as its master was slammed to the ground beside it, Briar atop her. Alaric crumpled where he'd stood.

Black veins wormed up Imperatrix's cheeks to stain her bloodshot eyes. She lifted her head and clamped a hand around Briar's forearm. Briar's skin sizzled at her touch. "You dare–"

Too little, and much too fucking slow.

Briar's forehead crunched into the sorcerer's nose, ramming her skull back on to the stone floor. The woman's eyes fogged over, and Briar gave her no time to recover. She roared in victory as her bound fists hammered down in savage delight, beating the sorcerer's face like it was a filthy rug. Her fists burned and smoked from the dark magic in the harlot's blood. Every blow sent spikes of pain through her body like she'd touched lightning, but her fury shrugged it off. Fresh blood spattered her armour, some of it hers, from skint knuckles, but more of it from Imperatrix.

She clambered off the barely conscious bloodied woman and crawled towards the smoking, trembling body of Iden. The hungry flames that had covered his body had dwindled, and only the fat-soaked edges of his tunic around his neck still flickered with any fervour. His head was a mass of charred and weeping flesh and a lipless, eyeless ruin of a face. He stubbornly clung to life, a bubbling wheeze escaping holes burned right through his cheeks and throat. She grabbed his bronze buckler and didn't waste energy putting him out of his torment. Instead, she rose up on to her knees despite the pain, gripped the shield in two hands and hammered the rim down on Imperatrix's head. Once, twice, and the third time did the trick: a sickening crack and a squelch as it buried itself deep in the bitch's brain. All that plotting and all that magic, and it ended like a crude alehouse brawl. Briar spat on the corpse. "May all the dark creatures you bargained with rip your soul to shreds in the otherworld."

Briar abandoned the buckler and desperately crawled towards Alaric. Her wounds were a distant concern, any pain submerged beneath a gushing torrent of fear.

He lay sprawled face-down on the floor, motionless. Some of his cuts had reopened, and fresh blood stained the bone-shard gravel he lay upon.

Briar oozed panic as she fumbled at his throat, questing for a pulse. Her stomach fell away into a black pit of dread as her fingers failed to find any sign of life. "Please..." she prayed. "Not after everything we have endured. Not this..." Still nothing. She snarled and looked around the darkened chamber. "Listen up, all you gods and ancestors of Sunweald – you cannot betray this fine man, who served the land so honestly and well! If you let him die, I give you my oath that I will enter the otherworld right after him to hunt every last one of you spineless wretches down and gut you like rotten pigs."

His artery pulsed under her fingers, slow and faint but still desperately fighting to live. She wasn't sure if she'd just missed it in her frantic search or if some otherworldly force had intervened, but either way, she offered up her silent prayers, but no apology.

He cracked an eyelid that seemed to weigh a mountain. "Could you... stop poking me?"

Briar shuddered with relief as it poured out of her like a waterfall. She removed her fingers from his neck and pressed her lips against his. They met in rough and glorious affection. He grinned weakly and then slid back into unconsciousness.

"Don't you dare die on me now, Alaric," she whispered as the last of Iden's flames sputtered out, plunging the chamber into oppressive darkness. She tried to stand, but her legs buckled and pitched her onto her arse. There would be no carrying the regent off to safety, and no way she could summon assistance.

She grabbed Iden's sword, clamped it between her thighs and sawed through the rope binding her hands. The rough strands parted, and hot blood pulsed back into her hands, accompanied by pinpricks of pain. She gritted her teeth and forced her battered body to crawl back up the tunnel, where the burning green light in the giant skull's eye sockets gave her light enough to work by. She shrugged off her scale shirt and laid it over the stone teeth that guarded the entrance, and then heaved her body up and over, relying on the bronze scales to guard her life. They held, and she crawled over to the sorcerer's stash of supplies. She rummaged through her goods and tipped anything esoteric or impractical into a pile. A blanket, a waterskin with barely two mouthfuls left, some dry bannock breads and a handful of salted beef strips were stuffed into a satchel secured around her torso, and then she began the arduous journey back the way she had come.

She clambered into the maw of the beast, with only a mildly lacerated forearm to show for it, and then crawled back down its gullet. By the time she made it back to Alaric her hands, elbows and knees were in tatters, their pain joining the searing burns and everything else that didn't matter – because he lived! She found him by touch and shook him half-awake in order to tip the remaining water down his throat. Alaric was too weak to chew hard salted beef himself, so she did that for him and passed mouthfuls of food to him like he was a baby bird. He managed to swallow three times before passing out, and she couldn't wake him again. She listened for a while to his breathing, coming shallow but steady.

Her hands shook from fear and trauma, and her sweat-drenched skin quickly cooled in the chill air, but they both still lived, and she would take this as a hard-fought victory. She carefully wrapped Alaric in the blanket and claimed an edge of it to lie down beside him and provide the warmth of her own body. What a way to finally sleep together, she mused, on the verge of tears from relief and exhaustion.

There was nothing more she could do. They were safe for now, and help would come or it wouldn't. Perhaps tomorrow she might have strength enough to escape the catacombs... All she could do now was blindly wait and see if the man she loved lived or died. She closed her eyes, and exhaustion brutally crushed her down into a deeper darkness.

CHAPTER 31

The sound of heavy footsteps echoing down the tunnels outside the Wyrm Vault woke Briar, a warrior's survival instinct kicking her to full wakefulness. She licked dry, cracked lips and ignored the throbbing headache as her rough fingers stroked Alaric's soft, whiskered cheek. She took a measure of reassurance from the warm rhythmic breath that escaped his lips as she listened intently to the sounds from above. Her throat was parched, her belly a gnawing pit, so she must have been asleep for most of a day, but in utter darkness deep below the earth there was no way to know. The Shield in her had to assume the worst: that some of Imperatrix's reivers had returned seeking loot.

Whatever sleep she'd managed was woefully inadequate. Groggy, exhausted and hurting, she tried and failed to get to her feet. She'd misplaced Iden's sword and shield. She needed a weapon, any weapon, and could only think of one thing whose location she knew. She crawled over to where Imperatrix had dropped her knife, and swept the ground for the hilt. As her fingers brushed the cracked leather-and-bone pommel, the edge of the blade emitted a dim orange glow. She drew the artefact from its stone sheath and squinted against its steady light. In the inept hands of the sorcerer the blade had flickered, sparked and spat angrily, but now it felt solid and purposeful, content to be used. She had a strange feeling that it had once been a warrior's weapon instead of a murderer's tool.

With a weapon in her hand, Briar crawled back to Alaric

and shuffled round to face the entrance. It would most likely be her last battle. If the reivers had come back seeking her and Alaric's heads she'd gut at least one of them, and would hopefully send even more to the otherworld, before they cut her down.

The footsteps entered the outer chamber and then abruptly stopped, the intruders confronted by the corpses she'd left behind and the imposing fanged entrance leading farther into the depths of the earth. A man whistled at the gory sight and spoke in loud astonishment. "Told you she was a stubborn old nag."

Briar sagged in relief at the sound of that grumpy old goat's voice: Shield Gwilherm. She carefully set the knife down out of reach and laughed, a dry and pathetic wheeze. "Kester brought the warband home," she croaked to Alaric. "You're safe now." She lay her head down beside him as their rescuers rushed down the passage, and she let herself go. She slid back towards sleep, knowing their lives were in safe hands.

She felt those rough hands pick her up and carry her, half conscious, up into the light...

Briar jerked upright, and before she was even awake her hand instinctively reached for a sword that wasn't there. She immediately hissed in pain as every muscle seized up, and her vision swam. She blinked clear the tears and noted she was in a comfy bed located in the centre of a stone room that didn't look like it belonged to the otherworld. A fire crackled in the fire pit, and the window was cracked open to let in fresh air. The decoration was basic and unmistakably belonged to her own room. She was naked, washed clean, bandaged and covered by a fine blanket.

"How are you feeling, you wicked old she-wolf?"

It took her a moment to locate the grizzled warrior in stained armour, sat watching her from a stool in the corner of the room. She squinted in his direction. "Gwilherm?" she croaked. "Alaric..."

"That overworked git is every bit as stubborn as you," the Shield replied. "Don't you worry. He lives, but he's in a right sorry state in the room right next to this one. He's been drifting in and out of sleep."

Briar sighed and settled back into yet another sickbed. "Kester reached you?"

Gwilherm yawned. "Almost. That brat of a boy had a frightful time of it, harried by men and monsters all through the forest. Seems he made a heroic last stand in an old watch tower but was paralysed by some kind of spider monster." Noting her spike of concern, Gwilherm held his hands up. "He's hale and healthy now, so no need to look so concerned. While mostly incapacitated, he still managed to harangue one of the shamefaced locals into taking to his heels to deliver a message in Kester's place. The lad caught up with us as we sat about scratching our arses at Blaen Mhòr, trying to figure out what was going on. Then we ran day and night to get back here, only to find you'd already slaughtered most of the scum."

"I reckon you need to stop calling him a brat now," Briar said. "He acquitted himself well as a warrior under my command."

"You're right enough," Gwilherm admitted. "At his age I'd likely have pissed myself in fear. The boy killed two reivers on his mission to find us, as well as vile monsters of the otherworld." He scratched his chin sheepishly. "Never thought I'd see the day that foppish, self-centred boy was viewed as a bloody hero by the warband."

"I had hoped the boy had it in him," Briar said. "He began changing after the attack on the sacred mound, when his Shields died to protect him, but you never know if a person changes for good or slips back to their old ways. The man Kester is today has done his realm and his ancestors proud." She struggled up in her bed, grimacing at every slight movement. "I will see Alaric now."

Her old friend didn't object; he knew there would be no point. She'd crawled home once, and she would do it again if she had to. "Come on, then." He wrapped her in her blanket and helped her up out of bed, but her leg buckled instantly. He caught her before she fell, and moved to sweep her up into his arms like she was a helpless maiden.

"Don't you bloody dare," she said. "I'm no spoiled daughter of chieftains." She slipped an arm around his neck to take the weight off her left leg and then tested her right, finding it stiff and aching but holding. "I'll be walking in to see him."

Gwilherm feigned she weighed far too much for him, groaning and bowing under her great bulk. "Aye, Commander, though it'll break my back."

Briar spotted a walking stick in the corner of the room, and they hobbled over to it so that Briar could use it with her free hand to take some of the strain. "I'm not too proud to admit when I need help," she said.

He eyed her askance. "Mmmhmm. I believe you. That commander of mine is always asking for my help. I certainly don't remember a certain stubborn woman – not so long ago – choosing to crawl home rather than ride in a carriage."

She grimaced and took his friendly mockery on the chin. "Well, that won't be happening again. It was a hard lesson to learn, but I'm far more interested in the regent's health than in my prickly pride."

Gwilherm helped her out into the hallway, past grim-faced veteran Shields who offered respectful nods, and into the next room, where Alaric slept beneath blankets and sheepskins. A white-haired druid draped with bone beads, bangles and charms eyed Briar critically. "Can we have some privacy?" the Shield asked.

The old druid nodded and made for the door. "He's in no immediate danger."

The room was well lit, and Alaric had been placed in a large bed moved in from one of the ambassador's chambers, the smaller original in this room probably having been soiled or torn apart for firewood by the reivers. The regent's scab-dotted face was pale and drawn, but his chest rose and fell with ease, and his many wounds had been cleaned and smeared with healing salves and poultices. Dozens of talismans and healing charms dangled from the ceiling and bed frame, and the air reeked of rare oils and unguents in an attempt to mask the copper scent of an animal sacrificed to the gods – the wise and powerful of Sunweald were sparing no effort to aid Alaric's recovery. Were Briar to look beneath the bed, she would likely find a bowl with a great ox's heart, dedicated to granting him the mighty beast's strength and stamina.

Brutus snored on the bed, beside his master, and in a cot on the floor by his uncle's bedside, the Royal Heir lifted his head with some effort. Kester waved a hand at her, but the rest of him merely twitched. "I would rise to greet you," he said. "Unfortunately, that hideous monster's venom is taking an age to leave my body. At least I can feel my toes again; that was most reassuring. Now I glimpse an understanding of your many joys while being bed-bound."

"Good work, warrior," Briar said, her eyes drifting from the boy's haggard face to his sleeping uncle.

Kester blinked slowly in grave acceptance of the title she'd bestowed upon him. "It was past time I started behaving like a man. In fact, I have decided to take the throne earlier than Uncle had scheduled. It's more of a custom, anyway, rather than an outright ban." He looked to Gwilherm. "Tuck her into the bed, right next to him."

She gaped at the Royal Heir. "That's not–"

"Proper?" Kester said. "Decent? As if either of you are in any condition to do anything to anybody. Besides, now that I have decided to ascend to the Oaken Throne, his position of Lord Regent is no longer required. Uncle has been dismissed from his duty."

She was powerless to prevent Gwilherm manoeuvring her into the bed beside Alaric, her skin touching his. Gwilherm shooed the dog away and tucked her under the blankets and furs, making it all nice and cosy for her, smirking all the while.

She blushed furiously. "What do you expect me to do in here?"

"Rest and recover," Kester said. "Together. Knowing you, you'd not be leaving his side anyway, and at least this way you will both be warm and comfy."

"Then, for the love of the gods," Gwilherm added, "you will wed that poor bastard and fuck his brains out."

Briar glared murder at him. The regent slept on, blissfully unaware.

"What?" Gwilherm exclaimed, hands lifted in protest. "Kester and I'd just been talking about it a stone ago. Why pretend like you don't want to?"

Kester winced. "Quick, Gwilherm, carry me out of here before she gets back up and spanks the both of us until we're red-raw."

The grizzled Shield, ever-blameless, simply shrugged and hefted the Royal Heir over his shoulder like a sack of grain, before beating a hasty retreat, leaving Briar alone with the Lord Re... no, just Alaric, she corrected in her thoughts.

She shuffled round until she lay on her side, looking at him. It felt deeply unnatural to be under the blankets with the man she had spent ten years protecting and – due to circumstances beyond both of their control – keeping a certain professional distance from. That grim fortress of endless duty had now been demolished.

She told herself that if this was all that ever came of it, she could be satisfied she had saved his life... But then, she asked herself, was that really all she wanted?

She dreaded the long-delayed awkwardness of telling Alaric exactly how she felt. In her younger days she had, of course, dallied with smouldering young men once or twice, but this was a mountainous beast born of friendship and bone-deep respect, and it made her uncharacteristically skittish. In matters of the heart she was an inexperienced warrior, but a warrior she remained, and she mustered her resolve to face the situation head-on. Her pulse quickened as her fingers found his beneath the blankets and intertwined.

Once he woke, she would tell him everything.

Briar had entirely forgotten about his severed finger until she squeezed his hand and felt the bandaged stump twitch.

He hissed and jerked awake, flailing in panic until his bloodshot eyes met hers, beside him in bed. He immediately slumped back into his blankets, and the terror drained out of him. "That's not the best way to awaken a man," he rasped. "Still, good to know we are not dead." He paused for moment's thought. "Briar, why are you in bed with me?"

She choked and reddened and tried to extract her fingers from his, but he ignored the pain and held on tight with his wounded hand. He groaned and turned his head, just a little, and a bloodshot eye peered at her.

"No," he said. "Stay with me: I am cold, I am hurting, and I am lonely." His words were interrupted by a brief coughing fit that had her concerned. "Kester has proven himself strong and wise enough to be high king of Sunweald and all its clans," he continued, "and from now on I will merely be his advisor. I have waited long enough. You have kept me safe and sane all these years, and that is an unsurmountable debt I will nonetheless endeavour to repay for the rest of my life. If you... if you have any desire to stay by my side?"

She cleared her throat. "I would like that very much."

He suddenly looked sweaty and unsure, biting his lip and taking a series of deep breaths. She planted a hand on his forehead to check his temperature.

"Not as a warrior," he added. "As my wife, if you will have me."

"I knew what you meant, you big idiot," she said. "One way or the other, only the prospect of marriage could so perturb a man." She stroked his cheek and planted a sizzling-hot kiss on his lips. "I will take you as my husband. This time, I'll be the one in charge."

He snorted. "In private you always were, as I seem to recall."

She turned slightly and winced as muscles complained.

Concern flooded his eyes. "Are you badly wounded? Tell me the truth."

She smiled at him and edged dangerously close to his warmth. "Nothing a few weeks of bed rest won't resolve. You, on the other hand, lost a lot of blood."

He sighed in relief. "At least you will not be clawing at the walls from boredom. This time I don't intend on letting you out of my sight."

Briar grimaced as she lifted an arm to tempt him into her embrace.

Alaric reddened but accepted the invite. He rested his head on her chest and sighed in comfort as she stroked his hair. His eyes drifted closed. "I find the beat of your heart comforting," he mumbled, then fell fast asleep.

After some time, she noticed Alaric's dog, sat on the floor, looking up at her with pathetic big brown eyes. She sighed and gave in – he had defended Selma from that reiver, and such bravery should be rewarded with more than a hunk of beef. "Come on, then, you stinky beast." Brutus leapt up on to the foot of the bed, padded round in a circle and then settled down.

She struggled to stay awake, stroking Alaric's hair and savouring his warm presence. She was relieved to discover that it did not feel awkward in the slightest, and soon she joined him in his rest.

CHAPTER 32

The last of the winter snows melted as the Queen of Summer began waking from her deathly slumber. Blizzards and ice were giving way to the warmer winds and softer rains of springtime, and her earthen body would soon bud with new life, the renewing of nature's cycle returning to the people of Sunweald a small measure of joy after their many sorrows.

The pyres of the slain had burned down to ash, and the remains had been placed into pots interred beside their ancient kin in the catacombs beneath the palace. A few clans still held to wilder traditions, laying their dead to rest on flat stones in the forest for all its many creatures to pick clean the bones, the flesh of the departed gifted back to the land that had given them birth, and the creatures they had fed upon in turn. The wounds in the people's hearts were only just starting to scab over. That slow recovery would begin with a royal wedding feast celebrating life over death.

Briar had only been more terrified once, and recently at that. She was unused to being the centre of attention, especially where women and weddings and all their secret rituals were concerned. So far, she had managed to resist concerted and constant efforts to foist elaborate jewellery and fanciful dresses upon her, focusing all her energy on her work instead.

Briar walked – well, limped – with a stick down the halls of the palace, with the brooch of Commander of Shields standing proudly on her chest once more.

Gwilherm walked beside her. "I'm glad you decided not to retire," he said. "All that scrollwork and organising, pah. Not for me. How does it feel to be back where you belong?"

"I think I more than proved to myself that I can still do the job," she said. "With you as my Second, I have a trusted minion who can run about doing all the messy jobs I can't, while I ensure everything else runs smoothly."

Gwilherm scowled at her. "Minion, is it? I see, I see. Going to be that way from now on, is it?

"Oh, yes," she said, smiling.

"Well, just so long as we're clear on it," he growled. "How's Kester's training going?"

She rolled her eyes. "He wants to run before he can walk, but I'll make a proper warrior of him yet. At least now he won't embarrass himself tripping over his own sword."

"That only happened the once," Gwilherm reminded her. "He'll improve."

"He'd better," she muttered darkly. "Or I'll have to train him harder."

Gwilherm winced. "Poor bastard didn't know what he was in for when he asked you to train him."

"You know, I think he did," she replied. "He wants to put the work in on improving himself, and that makes me proud."

"Aw, listen his proud Auntie Briar," Gwilherm said. "Or you will be after you wed Alaric tonight."

She whacked his shin with her walking stick. "Be off on your rounds, checking the guards. Our new Shields still have a long way to go before they earn my approval."

Gwilherm stalked off, grumbling.

She limped towards the kitchens, leaning heavily on her walking stick. Her leg was now in a permanent brace of wooden rods after the abuse she'd heaped upon it, but she thought it a small price to pay. There were many new residents of the palace, as warriors, scribes and craftsmen had arrived with the turn of the season, but she met a familiar face in the hallway outside and was not entirely sure how to feel about it. Exalted Carmanilla stopped, and the woman's smile dazzled like the sun, immediately putting Briar on guard. The Wrendal priestess' scalp still had only a short fuzz of hair after the scum hacked it off, but somehow after tidying up the mess and adding hooped gold earrings, the annoying woman had managed to make it look elegant. There was already talk from the men and women of the palace about copying her bold new style.

"Commander Briar," she said. "Good morning to you." Carmanilla moved to clasp arms but remembered too late she was missing a hand. She stared blankly at the silk-capped stump for a moment before a twitch of anger appeared on her lips. "That is taking me a while to become accustomed to." She scowled and instead offered a bow of respect that her kind normally only afforded high priests and rulers. "I hope you have been well."

"Getting by," Briar replied. "It will get easier – the hand, I mean. Sometimes I still wake up and try to jump out of my blankets, but... well..." she waggled her walking stick. "We have what we have."

Carmanilla grimaced. "I had no conception of how difficult things would prove with only one hand. It was a small mercy that madwoman didn't take both off." Her gaze dipped to the new knife belted at Briar's waist, and she shuddered at the sight of the artefact Briar had claimed as spoils of war, the very one that had taken Carmanilla's hand off.

"If you want this artefact, I will give it to you," Briar said. "You deserve some kind of reward for killing two of that vile sorcerer's lackeys."

The Wrendal priestess shuddered. "It might have been touched by my gods," she said grudgingly, her faith struggling with her hatred, "but I do not have it in me to ever lay a hand on that thing."

Briar could understand that feeling all too well. "Then I shall cede it to your temple upon my death," she said. "Perhaps putting this weapon to good, honest use will cleanse the taint of evil from it."

"That would be a most generous gift indeed," the priestess said. "The Holy Wrendal Empire thanks you for it, and I thank you for it. I shall let you get on with your day. You must have a hundred things to see to."

That was a massive understatement. "Fortunately, I have learnt to delegate," Briar replied with a smile. "Gwilherm has ascended to the position of my Second Shield, and I have left many matters in his capable hands."

A shrewd look entered the Wrendal ambassador's eyes. "Has he now? Most interesting..."

Gwilherm had no idea of the seductive whirlwind that was about to hit him. Both could do far worse, Briar admitted, though she did not dare imagine what sort of a tempestuous relationship that might prove. She wished the priestess a good day, good luck, and followed her nose into the kitchens.

She was heartened by the sight of Hearth Mistress Morna's drudges carrying copious jugs of ale into the cool room, ready for the celebrations in the afternoon. The older woman still bore the last remnants of deep bruising all across her face as she barked orders at a dozen people, but if anything, it only made her appear even more imposing.

Selma was taking a fresh batch of bread out of the oven with her wide wooden paddle. The scent of fresh baking and the thought of devouring it with lashings of butter made Briar's mouth water. The cook glanced up and grinned. "Good morning, Commander," she said. "Are you excited for your big day?"

Briar cleared her throat and changed the subject. "Have you had bread and fresh meat taken to the roof? I intend to pay all my debts."

Selma nodded. "Oh, yes, those carrion birds will be well fed for coming to your aid. Some of the new drudges taken into our service are trying to befriend them as we speak. I think your story put the fear of the gods into those young'uns." She noticed Briar eyeing the fresh and fragrant loaves she'd just taken from the oven, and she reached for one.

Somebody dropped a knife, and Selma jumped at the clang, her eyes wild and fearful for a moment. She clutched at her chest as she took a deep, shuddering breath. Briar exchanged a grim nod with the cook, knowing fine well that some wounds of the mind healed slower than the flesh.

The hearth mistress came over and gave Selma a reassuring hug, then turned towards Briar and pointed a spoon at her like it was a spear. "There'll be no snacking before midday," she said. "You had porridge at dawn, and that'll do you until the feast."

"Just one little slice?" Briar urged. "With butter? I did save all of you, if you recall. I'm sure I'll manage the wedding just fine."

The hearth mistress frowned down her nose, unimpressed by Briar milking the situation. Then she smirked. "Not a chance, my dear. It's your wedding night, after all, and I am doing you a favour: a lady doesn't want an overfull belly come nightfall. Lend me an ear and I'll give you some tips and tricks passed down in my family from mother to daughter. Why, there is a thing you can do with your tongue that will make any man–"

Briar beat a hasty retreat, her cheeks aflame and that beastly old woman's malicious laughter echoing in her ears. She should have known better than to try to cross swords with Morna, and the hearth mistress knew Briar was ill-equipped to fight on that field of battle. However much gratitude Morna bore Briar, the hearth mistress would never play games when it came to matters of food and drink.

Briar took a while to compose herself before meeting Alaric at the top of the stairs down to the catacombs. Two Shields guarded the stairwell and offered her respectful nods before doing their best impression of statues. The master of spies was deep in discussion with Alaric. Bram had one arm bandaged and held himself stiffly, his ribs bound tight. He clutched a slate of reports and was running through a long list containing the names of people needing put to the question, and what looked like an even longer list of urgent palace repairs needing carried out.

Bram inclined his head respectfully. "My every good wish for you on this auspicious day, Commander. I shall take no more time from your husband-to-be and shall let you get on with your task." He shuffled off, muttering curses at every twinge of his broken ribs.

One look at Alaric set her cheeks burning again. For many years, she'd rolled her eyes at the folly of lovestruck young women, and now she'd discovered that for the right man she wasn't much different. Even the crude grey shawl of Briar's making that he wore around his neck didn't detract. It didn't help that all the older women of the palace wanted to offer her words of advice for bedding him on their wedding night. "Let's get on with this," she said gruffly.

He raised an eyebrow. "Anything you wish to talk about?"

Briar twitched and chewed on her lower lip. "Absolutely bloody not."

"Very well," he said. He glanced at the knife on her belt, then tore his gaze from it. "Must you keep that thing?"

"It's just a weapon, my love," she said. "And a bloody good one. All good and evil is contained in the hand and heart that wields it."

He frowned but let it go. "Let us head for the Wyrm Vault, then." He took a lantern from the wall and led the way down the narrow spiralling staircase.

Briar sucked in a deep breath and let it out slowly to steady her nerves. She set the tip of her walking stick on that first step down and went with her strong leg first, carefully planting her walking stick on the next while holding on to the wall with her free hand.

Both of them moved slowly and steadily – the last thing

they needed was a fall and a new set of bruises and broken bones. Eventually, Briar made it to the bottom, with only a burning ache in her leg. She didn't relish the thought of climbing back up.

Alaric leant against the wall, breathing heavily, a sheen of sweat sparkling on him in the lantern light. "Let's not make a habit of this," he wheezed, favouring the side that had suffered repeated kicks.

She took his arm and, despite his protestations, insisted on helping him walk. "You must eat more red meat," she chided. "A plate of fresh liver every day is what you need to help build muscle and replace all that lost blood."

His nose wrinkled in disgust. "I will take all those disgusting potions the druids give me, but I draw the line at liver." They made small talk as they walked, both avoiding all mention of the ceremony and grand feast later on. If it were left up to them, they would have had only a small ceremony with immediate kin and friends, but Alaric was, officially, still Lord Regent of Sunweald, and Briar was the shining hero whose deeds currently graced the tales of every bard in the entire realm. A small ceremony would be seen as a grievous insult to too many rich and powerful clan chiefs.

The tunnel ahead was well lit by dozens of fresh lanterns, and six fully armoured Shields led by Gwilherm had been stationed outside the Heart to ward off anybody who dared intrude. "The Royal Heir awaits you inside," Gwilherm said.

Alaric nodded his thanks. "Do not be alarmed when the door closes behind us." They stepped over the threshold, and Briar pulled a lever to trigger the counterweights. The massive bronze door slammed shut, and its elaborate druid locks clanked into position. Kester, Alaric and Briar were alone, staring at stone walls that had been washed of Alaric's blood and scoured clean of every last trace of Imperatrix's sorcerous taint. The damaged shrines of the Summerson ancestors had been repaired, or replaced with simple wicker baskets, and the leathery bodies were back at rest inside, with fingers and arms sewn back on. Alaric gave his distant kin a nod of greeting as he entered, passing through whatever relics of the past had been repairable after the deprivations of the reivers.

The stone bones of ancient wyrms once more guarded the passage ahead, the arcane protections having restored themselves. There was no sign Imperatrix had ever defiled the place, and even the holes Maddox had bored into the solid stone had healed over.

On a small plinth, atop a vibrant green cloth, sat the pieces of the golden crown of Sunweald. Alaric stopped before it and urged Kester to approach. "Most of the stolen fragments have been recovered, ready to be re-cast when you come of age."

"It won't be the same," the boy said, sadly.

Alaric shrugged. "Sunweald is not a crown, it is a people. This is just a symbol."

Kester nodded his understanding. "May I examine the cavern walls now?"

At his uncle's nod, the soon-to-be-king ran to and fro in excitement, squatting and stretching to poke his fingers against the petrified claws and legs of great beasts, patting skulls and teeth the size of his arm. Briar and Alaric exchanged gloomy looks when faced with the callous resilience of youth – despite his ordeal, the boy was as energetic as if it'd never happened.

"There is no sign of any doorway," he said, amazed. "I would not even know where to begin."

Alaric smiled thinly. "This is the most secure vault ever built. It was intended to be so by the ancient druids and the elders of the Sleaghan Mhath, who joined their powers to build it. Briar, if you would try to open the way?"

Her walking stick clacked across the floor as she limped to the back wall. She placed a calloused hand on the skull of the largest wyrm and pricked her forefinger on the tip of one of its fangs. Using her blood, she drew a spiralling sun symbol in the middle of the skull. Then her hand moved down to the great beast's fanged maw and pushed hard against solid stone.

Nothing.

She pulled a rag from her belt, wiped away her blood and shrugged.

"Now, Kester, you do the exact same," Alaric said. "I would show you myself, but my darling wife-to-be would kill me if I shed any more blood right now." Briar glowered at him in response, but her cheeks still coloured at the word "wife".

Kester copied her exactly, but when he pushed his hand into the stony maw, the rock gave way like greasy fat. He yelped as his hand sank deep, the wall sucking him in up to the elbow.

"Remain calm," Alaric said. "Let the Vault do its work."

Kester swallowed and remained still as something soft, rough and hot licked across his hand. "Is that a tongue?" he hissed.

The dead wyrm's eyes flared into life, twisting green flames gushing from its empty eye sockets. Its jaw opened, and Kester's hand slurped back out of the sagging stone.

A cavernous voice thundered inside Kester's mind and set his teeth rattling in his skull: WILLING BLOOD OF SUMMERSON, SPEAK YOUR COMMAND.

Briar and Alaric looked on expectantly, unhearing and unaffected. This was the Vault, with all its arcane protections in place.

Kester fell back on to his arse, staring up at the eldritch wyrm skeleton as a measure of life returned to it. "Open?" he ventured. "Please, and thank you."

The skeleton shifted in its stone prison, and its great jaw opened. The tunnel to the tomb beyond reformed itself.

Kester scrambled to his feet, his eyes wide and wondering. "Is it still alive?" he whispered.

"We don't really know," Alaric replied. "Even the druids can only guess. Personally, for several very good reasons, I hope not."

"That was far easier than I had expected," Kester said.

Briar chuckled. "What's the point of a vault if its owners can't open it whenever they want? The trick of it is you have to open it of your own free will, or the magic won't work. However much Aisling tried to force your uncle, it wouldn't open just because she used his blood. Coercion or torture cannot work. She had to expend an enormous amount of effort to break into it."

Alaric winced. "Let us not mention that filth again for a goodly while. Come, nephew, I have a family secret to show you now that you are to become high king of Sunweald."

"Why have you brought me here?" Kester asked. "I've already been in the empty tomb that lies beyond it. It is an interesting part of our history, but poking through all those old bones could have waited until you were fitter. You said yourself that you had all the artefacts destroyed."

"Is that so?" Briar said, leading the way with a lantern held aloft.

Kester looked from Briar's back to his uncle's eyes. "What does that mean?"

Alaric clambered over the stone teeth and followed after Briar. "Do you really think I would have let that vile creature know the truth of things? I lied through my teeth, my boy. Honest speaking is a noble thing, but never bare all your secrets to your enemies – and you will have many of those in the coming years."

The air was still and silent in the tomb. In places, the bone shards that littered the floor had been stained brown by dried blood spatter, and in others charred where Iden had died. Briar couldn't help but look at where she and Alaric had lain, where she'd thought they both might die.

Alaric took four paces right from the entrance, his feet crunching through shards of bone, then three forward. He dragged his foot across the surface to clear away the corpse-gravel and bent over with the lantern to inspect his work. He blew hard, getting rid of layers of dust and dirt. "Ah, there is the edge of it," he said, brushing more debris away to reveal a pace-wide circle on the dusty floor.

Kester squinted at the barely perceptible line. "What is this?"

"Imperatrix expended so much time and magical might breaching the Wyrm Vault," Alaric explained. "She never could have imagined that the last protection was a simple trapdoor beneath her feet. She never stopped to think that the power contained within all of this powdered wyrm bone would befuddle her own magic. And why would she? Nobody has ever encountered so much of it in one place. This stuff is rarer than flying pigs."

"I've seen one of those," Briar said.

Kester gaped at her.

"Still gullible, I see," she noted, causing him to huff and glower.

Alaric chuckled and set his lantern to one side. He worked the point of his belt knife into the line in the floor, then used the blade as a lever to lift the round slab. He grunted with effort as the others helped him drag it aside.

Briar grabbed the edge and slid it back to reveal a pit leading into darker depths. She eyed the stone ladder carved into the bedrock and shook her head. "This is as far as I've ever gone, and I'm thinking you two had best go on alone from here."

"It's only a few steps down to the next tunnel," Alaric said, shaking his head. "I'll help you down: this is something that my wife needs to see to truly understand why I do what I do, and why I restrained myself for so many years."

She snorted. "I already know you well enough, and likely better than you know yourself. Fool of a man, I didn't fight to protect whatever crusty old relics you have squirreled here. I fought to rescue you."

He smiled sadly. "You say that now, but only because you don't know the full weight of my duty. My life has always been spent in service to the realm, and soon you will know why.

Come, Wife, you deserve to see this as much as Kester after you fought to keep it out of that vile sorcerer's hands."

She grumbled but did as he asked. Kester and Alaric helped her down the narrow steps. She winced in pain as she found her feet again. "If you think I will be living in that tall tower with you, and climbing all those damned steps every day, you are hunting a stag with only a short stick."

He looked aghast at the very thought. "I've already had most of my personal items moved to a chamber on the ground floor. I would never dream of making you climb all those stairs every day with your leg the way it is."

She blinked at him. "Damn you and your considerate ways. How am I ever meant to seize the high ground in this relationship?"

"I'm sure I will make a mess of things somewhere else," he replied. "This is just gold in the pouch wagered against a day yet to come."

"Is it too late for me to run away?" she said.

He flashed a dazzling grin. "Entirely. With that leg, I can run faster than you now."

She just rolled her eyes and took his arm. "Come on, you daft old man. Show us these dusty old treasures you value more than your life."

The three of them traipsed down a narrow tunnel carved out of the bedrock by years of work with antler picks. The tunnel's high, arched ceiling was clearly meant for far taller beings than mankind, judging by the parallel lines of shallow scrapes down the centre, as if its creators had worn horned headdresses, much like Sunweald's druids.

"Once," Alaric said, "in a time beyond memory that lives on only in the oldest legends of the druids, humanity was a thriving civilisation spread across all lands. As our numbers grew, and our knowledge of natural law and magic increased our might, so too did our hearts grow swollen with pride. Our ancestors encroached upon the forests of the fae, the mountains of the delvinkin, and even dared to trespass upon the graveyards of the ancient wyrms to mine their bones. They carelessly took whatever they wished from those sacred places without thought of the cost. In their greed, it is said, they awoke a still-living wyrm from its ages of slumber and brought about their own doom."

Briar grunted. "Sounds about right. Kester, you would do well never to underestimate people's greed, or overestimate their morals."

"To think I'd thought that all a myth," Kester said, wide-eyed. "I'd thought it more likely the ancients warred among themselves and blamed a magical disaster upon some dreadful monster. But if they had possessed such power, then surely they would have feared no wyrm?"

Alaric shrugged. "We'll never know for certain. The Sleaghan Mhath might recall, but on the occasion one of our kind manages to resist their glamour long enough to ask, they refuse to talk and immediately retreat to their hollow hills. In any case," he continued, "what we do know is that all the ancients' power and their mighty artefacts proved inadequate. Their inhuman enemies harrowed the survivors without mercy. Our own ancestors were forced to flee into the sacred forest of the Havenswood. Even then, the fae folk were a dwindling people, ancient and few in number, but for some reason known only to themselves they took pity on our ragged clan of humans. It is only with their aid that some of us survived to found the realm that would become Sunweald."

Battle-scarred human skulls looked down on them from niches in the walls, dozens of them, all weighing the intruders' worth with empty eyes. "The greatest warriors of elder days," Alaric explained. "Their spirits still guard this place against our ancient foes."

The three of them emerged from the tunnel into a cavern so vast, the light from their lantern didn't touch the sides. Wooden posts had been hammered into holes in the stone on either side of the doorway, and all matter of protective charms and talismans dangled from pegs. Verdigris-hued waist-high copper and bronze idols of over three dozen gods had been placed on the floor by past rulers, entreating the great powers of the otherworld to ward this place against all evil.

Beyond the idols lay rank upon rank of exquisite crystal tombs with faerie knights armoured in gold placed inside, their bodies inviolate to decay and the ravages of time.

Alaric rested a hand on his nephew's shoulder. "Our family owes the Sleaghan Mhath an eternal blood debt. Without them, the remnants of humanity would have been reduced to grunting savages eating dirt and berries. They fought beside our ancestors, and for that we will forever honour their sacrifice by protecting the graves of their fallen kin. They also entrusted our bloodline with keeping this place and its treasures safe from greedy mortal hands."

Something vast and heavy stirred in the cavernous darkness, more of an oppressive, hateful feeling than a physical presence. A sudden wind set the sole lantern flame into a mad dance and then extinguished it.

Pairs of smokeless torches burst into silent green flame ten paces ahead, then another pair and another... until they formed a corridor of light sloping down into the depths of the earth and out of sight. On either side of that corridor of light waited a trove of ancient treasures more valuable than mortal gold, silver, bronze and beasts: arcane artefacts laid with reverence upon scorched granite pedestals.

Kester squeaked and shook; his hair lifting and tiny bolts of lightning crackling and snapping from his fingertips as ancient magics stirred in the cavern. The air was sweet and pungent, clean, like a thunderstorm had swept through to scour away the sweat and woodsmoke of palace life.

Briar swallowed her shock. "Sweet mother..." Then she turned her gaze on Alaric. "*This* is what that bitch wanted?" Her covetous eyes drank in the sight of all those spears, swords and hammers crafted from glistening white wyrm bone harder than bronze. Every one of the artefacts sat atop its own slab of stone, as if the ancients feared to put too many together in one place. Some of those weapons were etched with frost, others surrounded with a wavering haze of heat or sparks of purple lightning. Gem-studded headbands and helmets glowed with an eerie inner light, along with cups and bracelets, chairs and simple blocks of bone. Other bizarre and geometric items were beyond her ken, and she didn't even hazard a guess as to their original use.

"Aisling – Imperatrix – had no real idea what this place stored," Alaric said. "I image she thought to drive off with a cartload full of arcane artefacts at most."

Briar's eye was caught by a particularly handsome spear with a blade of smoky crystal embedded in a wyrm-bone haft. The crazed facets of the crystal drew her gaze in and held it, inviting her to wield its might. Her hand instinctively reached for it.

Alaric grabbed her wrist. "Feel free to look, but for all our sakes, please do not touch *anything* unless I confirm it is safe." He walked over to a pedestal and stared at the tiny cube of black stone atop it. He grimaced and, with exacting care, picked it up and cradled it in his palm to show them. It was no more than the size of his thumbnail, but darker than black, a void in the world that seemed to suck in the light around it. "This," he said, "was the artefact used by our ancestors to destroy Hisparren. Sunweald's queen was most skilled in druidic magic and communed with its power to save the realm from an invading army of men and enslaved beasts." He carefully placed it back on its pedestal and stepped back. "It was far more potent and hungry than her grove of druids could hope to control. Their grievous mistake devoured all life from that land instead of simply slaying an army. They made a desert of a fertile plain, and even now, centuries later, nothing can survive in that waste for long. This artefact is still alive, and it slowly eats away the life of anything that ventures into that accursed place. That atrocity was caused by a single artefact. One among so many."

Briar and Kester exchanged looks of horrified understanding. Briar glanced down at the knife sheathed at her hip and swallowed nervously.

The Royal Heir shuddered. "Can we not destroy the worst of them?"

Alaric winced. "In my younger days, I asked that very question of our wisest druids. I was strongly advised to not be a dribbling idiot and to leave them well alone. Who knows what manner of disaster might occur were we to somehow succeed? We have no idea what most of them even do. And then there is… Well, it is best that you come and see for yourself." He moved on, motioning for them to follow him into a vast cavern beyond.

After the tombs and the artefacts, there awaited a third surprise for Briar and Kester. They stared, struck silent with dread.

Eggs: a hundred bulbous stone eggs laid in silent ranks, each the size of a man.

Briar was struck with a horrid sensation that those stone eggs were somehow aware of her presence, and that the creatures within hungered. "Are those wyrm eggs?"

Alaric nodded. "Yes. The last remnants of their race."

"They can't still be alive," Kester said. "Can they?"

They all looked at each other. Alaric shrugged. "Who knows? I certainly don't intend to meddle with them to find out."

"When Aisling broke open the penultimate seal of the Vault," Briar said, "I heard a scream, as if countless voices cried out in torment. You don't think…?"

"I would rather not think about any of that day," Alaric said. "I pray that it was just a response from the protective magics, but we cannot know."

Briar grimaced. "Well, I guess we will be living in the palace the rest of our days. It's probably a wise move to ensure this place is kept safe and secure, just in case."

Alaric's eyes were downcast, as if he'd once again shackled her future to his own sense of duty. The fool seemed to forget she'd chosen that very same duty for herself the first day she gave her oath as a Shield. "Well, the East Wing is being rebuilt as we speak," he said. "We can live on the ground floor, closer to the gardens, instead of traipsing up and down the stairs to my tower every day, and I shall have the place reworked to accommodate your leg. No steps and suchlike."

She nodded in agreement. "After all of this," she added, "you'd better be damned good in bed, husband." She bathed in bright glee as the man flushed scarlet. Poor Kester didn't know where to look. She mused that perhaps the hearth mistress had taught her more than she'd thought.

Whatever the gods have in mind for us, Briar thought, her hand finding Alaric's, we shall face it together. At least our life together will never be boring.

ACKNOWLEDGEMENTS

As always, family comes first. Natasha, who puts up with me battering away at my keyboard for hours beyond count (mind you, that does let her rewatch Bridgerton...again...), and for their ongoing support: Mum and Dad, Billy and Lisa, Paula and Michael, Craig, Mary and Isla.

My friends, many of whom are exceptional authors, deserve an incredible amount of appreciation for their awesome mix of wisdom and silliness. They really do keep me going when the writing gets tough, self-doubt creeps in, or the day job saps away my energy and creative drive.

Thanks go to Creative Scotland for their support. Scotland's ancient castles, caves, standing stones and sacred circles are places that will forever influence my fiction (you might have noticed...).

Special thanks go to my agent, Ed Wilson, to Paul Simpson and Jo Stimfield for their editing prowess, and to the Angry Robot Books crew of Eleanor Teasdale, Caroline Lambe, Gemma Creffield, Desola Coker and Amy Portsmouth. You are all fab.

The Last Shield pays homage to those excellent 80s action movies, creaky old swords and sorcery flicks, TV shows, and historical epics that captured my imagination growing up, mixed with my enduring love of all things archaeological, mythological, folkloric and historical. Not to mention the books...so many books...

ABOUT THE AUTHOR

Cameron Johnston is the British Fantasy Award and Dragon Awards nominated author of dark fantasy novels The Traitor God and God of Broken Things. He is a swordsman, a gamer, and an enthusiast of archaeology, history and mythology. He loves exploring ancient sites and camping out under the stars by a roaring fire.

We are Angry Robot, your favourite independent, genre-fluid publisher, bringing you the very best in sci-fi, fantasy, horror and everything in between!

Check out our website at www.angryrobotbooks. com to see our entire catalogue.

Follow us on social media:
Twitter @angryrobotbooks
Instagram @angryrobotbooks
TikTok @angryrobotbooks

Sign up to our mailing list now: